ARIADNE

DANIEL AGNEW

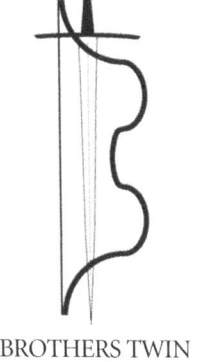

BROTHERS TWIN

Brothers Twin

www.brotherstwin.com

First published in Australia
by Brothers Twin 2018

Copyright © Daniel Agnew 2018

Daniel Agnew asserts the moral right to
be identified as the author of this work

ISBN: 978-0-6483164-0-4

Typeset in Minion

Cover illustration by Larry Rostant

Map artwork by Jennifer S. Lange

This novel is entirely a work of fiction. The names, characters and incidents portrayed in it are the work of the author's imagination. Any resemblance to actual persons, living or dead, events or localities is entirely coincidental.

All rights reserved. No part of this publication may be reproduced, stored in a retrieval system, or transmitted, in any form or by any means, electronic, mechanical, photocopying, recording or otherwise, without the prior permission of the publishers.

To Kylie Hetherington,

*Who showed me there was more
to history than Rome and Sparta*

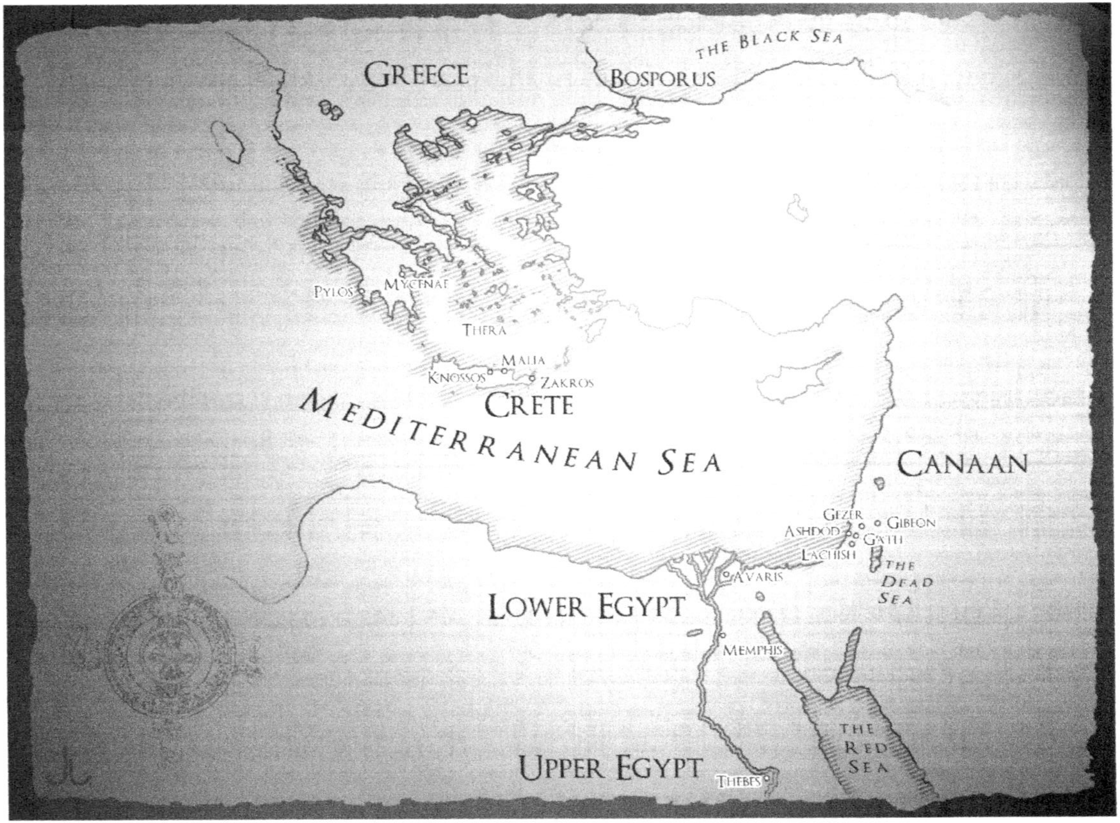
GREECE
THE BLACK SEA
BOSPORUS
PYLOS
MYCENAE
THERA
MALIA
KNOSSOS
ZAKROS
CRETE
MEDITERRANEAN SEA
CANAAN
GEZER
GIBEON
ASHDOD
GATH
LACHISH
THE DEAD SEA
AVARIS
LOWER EGYPT
MEMPHIS
THE RED SEA
UPPER EGYPT
THEBES

PART ONE

One

Hooves. Met dust. Met the stone beneath and didn't crack it. Horns. Tossed about. Tossed the air from side to side. Eyes. Locked onto a young priestess. Eyes driven to madness, a chance to reverse the roles of sacrifice. Muscles. Gleamed and roared. Grew larger with every stampeding step.

Ariadne stared at the bull charging towards her. Her arms wouldn't move, her legs wouldn't budge, not even her mouth would open and let her cry out for help. The only thing to respond was her mind. As it raced faster than the charging bull, all it could do was think on a single question—*how did I get here?*

***

Ariadne took another step in the darkness. It was like falling but you knew something was there to catch you. She was almost at the bottom of the staircase, almost there. As she took the last few steps, she smiled to herself. Soon, soon she would see the bull-leap.

Her dress seemed almost pale in the all-but-darkness of the underground workshop. Only a little while ago, the full radiance of the morning sun had brought out its greens and oranges, its hints of red and purple. For the moment, though, a dull garb was a benefit. There was always a chance someone else might be down here.

Ariadne peered over her shoulder as she stepped out into the room before her. Footsteps above, near the top of the stairs. She froze. If he caught her now, she'd miss it entirely. She wouldn't get to see the yearly bull-leap. He knew how much she loved somersaulting onto her bed every night. She couldn't believe he wouldn't let her see it for real. Who cares about going to Malia to see the ship festival anyway? How could it be anywhere near as exciting as this?

The footsteps had passed. No-one was coming down after her. Maybe she'd get to do it after all. As Ariadne stepped out into the empty workshop she thought to herself, *What's the one thing Papa wouldn't leave Knossos without? What's the one thing he'd spend a day, a week even, searching for?* Her fingers brushed lightly against the edges of the stone workbenches as she passed by. And then, finally, she was there. The bench. The one she had spent hours playing around, while voices chattered and wax sticks brought a glimpse of day into an otherwise eternal night. She picked up a chisel and ran her fingers along the handle, almost reverently. Then, suddenly, she grabbed the rest of his tools and started running, as if the whole palace were at her heels.

As she ran, Ariadne folded the edge of her dress over the tools to keep them from falling out. *Finally, this dress is good for something.* Holding her bundle with one hand, she felt the walls with her spare one whenever she came to a crossroads. *This way, it's got to be this way.*

A few moments later and she was sure of it. There was no mistaking that smell of wheat, of oats and barley. She must be at the grain stores. Only a few more rooms and she would be out in the open, free to dump her father's tools in some scraggly bush and run off to see the bull-leap. With any luck it would have barely started.

She turned into another room. Light was seeping through the door in the distance. This was it, the exit. She had made it. Ariadne grinned widely as she raced towards the door. *Did you really think I was going to leave without seeing it, Papa? Did you really think I was going to leave?*

Ariadne pulled the door open and ran outside into the blinding morning sun, slamming the door behind her as she went. She heard *a snort and people cheering. Her eyes adjusted. She wasn't at the grain stores. Not by a long shot.*

Now that the sun shone once more upon her dress, its rich array of colours drew the gaze of all around. Unfortunately, that included a rather angry bull staring at her from across the open courtyard...

***

Ariadne just stood there, staring back at the bull charging towards her. People began to scream, most as frozen in place as she was. Some of the young men nearby started racing onto the courtyard but all were too far away, and the bull had eyes for one and one only.

Ariadne heard some kind of scraping and scuttling sound on the roof above her. The bull didn't move its head so neither did she. She felt so stupid but she still couldn't even blink.

The bull lurched forwards in a final, victorious lunge. Ariadne could smell its breath as it—as it passed by underneath. The hand which had somehow grabbed the top of her dress lifted her high into the air.

Chisels and adzes, hammers and knives, all fell out of her now unfurling dress, her arms flailing in the air. The fierce grip which held her lifted her further upwards and back onto the roof behind. As it placed her down safely, all of her father's tools clattered and clanged as they crashed onto the ground beneath them.

The snorting bull, now even more furious than before, spun around searching for its lost victim, while the men who had jumped into the courtyard quickly began climbing back out of it. Ariadne turned around slowly, finally able to move again. What she saw did not please her, and, for a mere second, she thought about jumping back down to take her chances with the bull.

Hunched over behind her, his clenched and sweaty hand beginning to soak her dress, was her father, Spirysidos.

In the minutes that followed, as both of them recovered their breaths and their hearts started slowing down slightly, the scene below them began to return to normal once more. Trained acrobats drew the attention of the crowds around and the bulls beside them. Everything was as it should be. Or so Spirysidos thought.

"Come on," he said, breaking the silence between them, "we're leaving."

"We can't." Ariadne said, caught halfway between a smile of laughter and of fear. "They were your tools..." She pointed over the rooftop.

Spirysidos peered over the edge, understanding at once, then slumped backwards, a defeated man. Ariadne, however, shuffled her feet around and sat as comfortably as she could. The bull-leap had only just started. It was going to be a long day.

***

"A *day*! A day wasted!" Mariaten knew that voice, and that particular tone. Anger mixed with resignation that their twelve-year-old daughter had managed to out-smart him yet again. Ariadne always did find a way to get what she wanted.

Mariaten glanced back at the children sitting around her, listening eagerly. The sight itself was a tale as old as any she could have told them, a wise old woman imparting the wisdom of the ages under the shade of an ancient tree. Mariaten couldn't help but smile to herself at the thought; she wasn't that old. She opened her mouth in readiness to continue, staring each of them in their eyes and ensnaring them once more.

"And the men of Phaistos and Gortyn stood opposite the men of Knossos and Lyktos, together covering the Lasithi plain. The numbers of each side were beyond counting. The risen sun shone off their spears with such ferocity that it looked like they had set the plain on fire." Mariaten paused again, as two warring silhouettes made their way to the back of the crowd.

Mariaten was about to continue, she'd waited all day for them, they could wait for her now. But then she saw the looks on their faces. Two very tired faces. Two mouths still arguing despite the disruption they caused. Two people who, unfortunately, deserved her attention more than the others around her. She sighed.

"But the rest of that story will have to wait for another time..." Mariaten shook her head firmly in response to the protests that followed. Bribes and threats were offered, as usual; anything to keep her talking and postpone breaking the trance. It never worked, and they knew it. One by one, the children sitting around her started to walk off and she turned to listen to the squabble that still continued.

"—you never learn. Only three months ago you got up and walked out half-way through the monthly prayers. A hundred people all sitting silently and watching the High Priestess, and the only one who dares to leave is a priestess herself! We didn't send you to the priestesses to make a mockery of everything we hold dear. We sent you—"

"To make a better life for myself than you had." Ariadne interrupted Spirysidos, rolling her eyes. "So I wouldn't spend my life going blind in a candle-lit workshop or break my back picking saffron from the fields. *I'm so grateful.*"

"And yet you somehow find a way to profane every ceremony you go to, how do you manage that?"

In the silence that followed, Mariaten finally got a word in, "What happened this time?"

"Your daughter," Spirysidos began, turning to Mariaten.

"She's your daughter too." Mariaten replied, then looked up. Sure enough, Ariadne was off once more. At least this time she was running back home instead of away from it. Mariaten held back a smile as she saw her husband look down to where Ariadne had been moments ago then up to her running off in the distance.

"What are we going to do with her?" he asked as if she might actually have the answer.

Mariaten shrugged, she doubted the gods themselves could solve that one.

***

Spirysidos' hands and feet were already numb from the icy morning breeze but it would all be worth it. He walked towards the well, gripping the stone bowl tighter, his fingers almost white. Leave at dawn, he had said. And they would. He would make sure of it.

Water splashed onto his hands as he filled the bowl, the wind picking up and, together, cutting into his fingers. He couldn't feel his feet anymore but it didn't matter. He had the perfect punishment, and a guaranteed way to leave on time. As he made his way back home, Spirysidos couldn't help but smile, thinking of his most cherished memories of his daughter. Hearing her first scream and gasp for breath, guiding her first attempt to sculpt stone, taking her to her first day into the order of priestesses—he knew he was about to add one more to the list.

He entered through the front door to see Mariaten look up from her last-minute packing and shake her head firmly at him.

He ignored her and started walking up the stairs to their rooms on the second floor. As he entered his daughter's room, Spirysidos raised his arms and tenderly cradled the bowl in his palms. He walked forward and, as he stood over her, he paused, just watching her doze peacefully for a moment. Then, as perfect as any libation his daughter had poured, he slowly upturned the bowl over her tranquil face, not wasting a drop.

Calm and serene in the warmth of her bed, Ariadne awoke to the hard, frozen slap of the falling water. Spirysidos stayed just long enough for her to survive the torrent and stare up at him, realising what had just happened. But then he bolted, running out of her room and racing down the stairs only a few steps ahead of his soaking yet raging daughter. As he raced past Mariaten and out the front door, she called out after him,

"See where she gets it from?!"

Spirysidos couldn't help but grin to himself even so. Warmth was returning to his hands and feet and the sun was finally beginning to rise. The day had begun.

***

Ariadne shivered under her blanket despite the morning sun. She felt every jolt and bump of the cart as it meandered along the road. They hadn't even left Knossos yet and she already was sick of this stupid trip.

Every so often she would pull the blanket around her tighter and glare at her father menacingly. After one such time, Mariaten happened to be watching. She frowned with mild worry.

"If she gets sick and dies, I'm going to testify against you."

"Too right." Ariadne chirped though Spirysidos just shook his head and laughed.

"You're not going to die. Why not look around? You might actually enjoy it." And with that he flicked the reins putting the horse into a light trot.

Despite trying not to, Ariadne couldn't help but gaze at the sun shining onto the nearby walls. It was so beautiful the way it lit up the giant blocks of stone. They looked like they were on fire. As the cart bopped around a corner she saw the twin stone horns marking the boundary of Knossos. The sun was shining directly between them and straight towards her. It felt like the gods themselves were saying goodbye.

Maybe Papa was right after all. Not that she was going to tell him that.

Two

"Stop the cart!"

Spirysidos turned to Mariaten and smiled. Their daughter had already jumped off the still moving cart and started running off the track.

"Go on..." Mariaten said drowsily and Spirysidos obliged. He pulled the reins to slow the horse down just slightly. It wasn't long before Ariadne came running back with a fresh bundle of sticks and dead branches. They bounced and scattered as she dropped them into the already cluttered cart.

"How much further?" Ariadne asked absentmindedly as she rummaged through her father's belongings.

"Two and a half, three days?" Spirysidos said uncertainly then flicked the reins, stirring the horse onward.

"Gotcha!" Ariadne exclaimed, taking no notice. She pulled out a chisel and a small knife and grabbed one of the branches. She started making very precise cuts into it, bobbing along with the cart without once taking her eyes off the branch.

"Do you have to do that now?" Mariaten asked, slightly concerned.

"Heaira says I should practice my writing." Ariadne said without looking up. "She says it's really important."

"Bah. Grain tallies and sheep records. That's all it's good for." Spirysidos said dismissively. "You're not going to become High Priestess if all you can do is write."

"Heaira says..." Ariadne began but at that moment the cart dipped sideways going over a bump. "Gods of a whim!" she exclaimed as her hands finally slipped, carving a big, long line across the branch.

"I'm sure she does." Mariaten said and both she and Spirysidos laughed. "If you slip again," Mariaten continued, now stern, "I'm taking that knife off you. I don't want you getting cut. Is that clear?"

And, like every child, ever, Ariadne replied with a patronising, "Yes, Mama."

***

Flames crackled and their light flickered on the faces of those sitting around the fire. Ariadne lay sleepily on her father's lap while her mother put the last few herbs in the stew. Ariadne looked up at Spirysidos and mouthed, "I'm hungry..." though she could have heard his stomach rumbling too if she'd bothered to listen.

Instead, she turned to her mother and asked, "How much longer?"

"A little while dear."

"A big little while or a little little while?"

Mariaten had fallen for that trap more than once. Who knew children had such strict definitions of time? If she said one time then ending up taking the other she was apparently breaking a solemn promise, and would ruin her daughter's evening. Children.

"A big little while." That was always the safer bet.

Ariadne nodded, satisfied, then suddenly pushed herself up off her father's lap. He copped elbows and feet in places he least expected them, groaning as Ariadne rose to her feet. Oblivious, she walked off a little way from them both and, with a face tight in concentration, started stepping deliberately in what almost looked like some kind of pattern.

"What are you doing, Ariadne?" Mariaten asked, both she and Spirysidos staring at her in confusion.

"Heaira says we're going to perform the Tree Dance in a few weeks. She says whoever dances the best will get a special role." Ariadne stepped more confidently, following the same pattern again and again. Her arms, usually swinging freely suddenly raised high on either side. She stood there in perfect stillness, staring straight out.

"And what's this role?" Mariaten asked, already knowing and dreading the answer.

"You get to hold two snakes! One in either hand." Ariadne said, still motionless, barely moving her lips.

Mariaten looked over in concern to Spirysidos and Ariadne began stepping once more. Spirysidos kept his gaze on his daughter who kept spinning faster and faster. She didn't see the rock behind her and, as she raised her arms, spinning backwards, she tripped over the rock and fell.

As Ariadne rose and patted herself down, Spirysidos looked to Mariaten and gave her a small smile. They had nothing to worry about.

To her parent's dismay Ariadne started stepping once more. She might be terrible now but there was a small chance she might actually get better. "Do you know why we have the Tree Dance, Ariadne?" Mariaten asked, anything to distract her.

Ariadne frowned, thinking hard, then eventually shook her head. "No-one knows." She looked up at her mother, as if she needed to explain her ignorance. "Nobody ever says why we do these things. Maybe it's so long ago everyone has forgotten."

"Not everyone has forgotten…" Mariaten replied. "Those who spend all day in the palaces, so busy with their rituals, they forget. But those of us who work the fields have plenty of time to keep the old stories alive."

"So you know?" Much to Mariaten's relief, her daughter had completely forgotten about her dancing and had come back to the camp. Ariadne sat down next to her father, staring patiently at her mother; she knew she didn't have to ask.

"There's not much your mother doesn't know, Ariadne." Mariaten said and smiled. And, with an entranced child staring back at her, she began.

In the times when men were few while gods freely roamed the land and the seas lay as silent as a babe. When gods wove their own destinies in a world still fresh from creation, there lived a beauty greater than any goddess before or mortal since.

Rinatair was fairer than the ocean mists or sights from hilltop heights. Her breath was later woven into the earth, a hint of its beauty remains in the fragrance of saffron. Her eyes looked up to the sky which tried in vain to match her, creating the starry array. Her lips, never once touched by those of another, spoke with a sound only heard in the silence of a storm. They enchanted all whom she spoke with.

So began the test between Glanaron, Master of Animals, and Birchidar the Master Builder. Rinatair had not spoken for a thousand and score years, a third of the time of the celebration of creation where all gods gathered on the great plain, feasting and merry making. Her first words were uttered after a mournful ballad sung by one with time sight, who sung of the lives of mortals to come. No words of empathy were sadder said, no words more gladly heard. The gods immediately forgot whatever warning was being foretold, they had seen her beauty for eons, but those few words captured the hearts of all near.

It was quickly decided that only the two greatest gods had a chance to wed fair Rinatair: Glanaron of the world, as it was and always would be, and Birchidar of creation and change. They asked Rinatair what challenge to set so that she could decide between them.

Rinatair spoke confidently yet softly, her words capturing the hearts of her suitors who agreed immediately. She told them that each would have a day and a night to impress her and then she would decide. Birchidar tried first.

Birchidar took her to the rockiest plain and sat her down to watch. With soft footsteps he levelled a field flatter than a hair's width. With one sweeping arm he took a mountain from its base. From the rock he formed walls, roofs and floors—the first house. From a nearby forest he made tables to eat at and chairs to sit on. All this was done by midday so Birchidar rested and started again. He added rooms to room and floor to floor, filling the space with more wood crafted handiwork, calling his masterpiece a palace. By night he invited the rest of the gods in and they feasted. All the while Rinatair said nothing, merely watched thoughtfully.

The next morning was Glanaron's turn. While the rest were sleeping from the night before he woke Rinatair and led her silently out of the palace. They walked lazily for some time until coming upon a forest. He took her to the centre and made her into the likeness of a tree. Deer came by to drink from a nearby stream and birds began nesting in her branches. When they had left, he turned her back and led her out of the forest. They climbed the highest mountain and he held her there upon his shoulders as eagles and hawks flew by, encircling her. Finally, he took her to the depths of the sea where he caused the fish to follow her every turn, surrounding her from all sides. At night, he took her to the softest field of the lushest grass, laid her down and slept beside her.

Rinatair stood the next morning before the assembly of gods, her two suitors waiting patiently in their respective abodes. She declared she loved the world as it was with all that it had, and loved the one who showed it to her. She ran off to the woods and found Glanaron, she became the Mistress of the Animals. It is said Birchidar is waiting for her still, ever adding to his palace hoping she will come and claim it as her home and that he aids all who follow him in his endeavour.

As Mariaten finished those last few words she couldn't help but smile at what she saw. Spirysidos stared out into the darkness, entranced, while Ariadne lay under a blanket, her eyelids flittering. They had all eaten the stew she made; time seemed to have sped up under the spell of her words so hours went by in what felt like minutes. Or was it the other way around? Mariaten wasn't fully sure.

"That doesn't explain anything." Ariadne whined sleepily, interrupting her thoughts. Mariaten sighed.

"The Tree Dance reminds us to remember Rinatair's choice and her decision." She paused and then laughed quietly to herself. "Ironic those living in a palace have forgotten that."

"You're ironic..." Ariadne mumbled as she drifted off to sleep. Mariaten looked out at the fire, the stars and her peacefully sleeping daughter. She looked over to her husband entranced with her still, though perhaps for a different reason. She'd take the beauty of nature any day.

***

Ariadne felt the warmth of the morning sun on her face. It was nice. All the more reason to keep sleeping. A head bent down to lovingly nuzzle the base of her neck. As it withdrew, big, sloppy lips seemed to clumsily kiss her ear and a chunk of hair beside it. Ariadne rolled over, eyes still closed.

"I don't want to go to rituals today…" Ariadne whined as she did every morning.

Mariaten smiled and loosened her grip on the reins once more. Ariadne opened her eyes as the horse licked the side of her cheek.

"AIIIGH! Shoo! Shoo!" Ariadne sat up in an instant and started thumping her small fists against the horse's jaw. Mariaten tugged the reins to turn the horse's head before it could bite her now raging daughter.

Ariadne was on her feet in seconds. Her head scanned left and right. The cart had all been packed for the day ahead and her father was leaning against it with a tired grin. Meanwhile, her mother looked down at her with an odd mix off sternness and frivolity.

"You are the worst parents *ever*!" Ariadne shouted suddenly before stifling a yawn and turning back to her bed. As Ariadne started folding the blankets, Mariaten looked to Spirysidos who shrugged and yawned himself. Mariaten smiled and patted the horse's neck fondly.

It wasn't long before they were off again and following the track once more. Once again Ariadne pulled out her father's tools and once again Mariaten warned her to be careful. She watched her daughter as the minutes rode by and couldn't help but feel proud. Ariadne didn't slip once. She might not know everything about Crete, and she might be the most mischievous child in Knossos, but she did her best.

"Ariadne! Look!" Spirysidos shouted hastily, disrupting Mariaten's thoughts.

Ariadne looked up immediately and peered out to where her father was pointing. It seemed as if trees had huddled together and decided to swim as one atop the sea in the distance. Ariadne saw canvas sheets rippling in the wind and could just make out long wooden poles with a flat bit at the end. They were drawn into the side, resting beside what looked like men just sitting there.

"Is that a ship?" Spirysidos turned around and saw the search for knowledge in her eyes. He couldn't resist. Why not give her wisdom too?

"Yes, Ariadne. That's a ship. It's what makes Crete great. It is what keeps us from the rest of the world when we wish it and what opens the rest of the world to us whether they wish it or not."

Ariadne gaped at the crafted wood, able to move so many people across the sea. A thought occurred to her, a dark thought but one she couldn't deny, *surely Rinatair made the wrong choice. How could we be so great without the things we make?* She frowned as one thought led to another, *maybe we survive because we change things. We get the best of both gods and that's why we're here and they're not.*

That night Ariadne tossed and turned to her mother's tale. The magic had been lost. *Why does it matter how we got our bull-leap if the gods don't make wise decisions?*

Before she finished the end Mariaten looked longingly at her daughter and softly asked,

"What's wrong dear?"

Ariadne looked at her and saw the magic gleaming in her eyes, saw that she didn't see. She glanced at her father, his eyes curious and hidden. She tried anyway.

"Mama, you said Rinatair chose the trees and the cliffs and the animals, the way things always were. But we choose to make things and use them instead. What's the point of the story then?"

"It shows us that while that is how we live our lives. Maybe it isn't for the best."

"But it is." Ariadne protested. "Papa said that we are strong because of our ships. We have palaces and," she paused trying to find the right words, "and we don't all have to work all the time sowing seeds and hunting."

"There's nothing wrong with a country life, Ariadne." Mariaten replied with a sure confidence, unsure of her daughter's distress.

"You can go picking saffron all day, Papa's got the right idea making things with his hands." Seeing confused eyes stare back at her Ariadne came out with it, "The story shows the gods can be stupid and that they don't understand real life."

"What would you know of real life, little one? Gods! The things they teach you hidden away in Knossos. No-one knows why we do things anymore, no wonder—"

"So why do we trust them if they make stupid decisions?" Ariadne retorted, her voice rising louder with every word. She continued as if in a trance, almost ecstatic as she held the answers to her questions on the tip of her tongue. "Where are they even?"

"Ariadne!"

"Where is Rinatair and Glanaron or even Birchidar? They're gone Mama, because they can't keep up with us."

Mariaten and Spirysidos both looked at their daughter, horrified. Mariaten turned away speechless while Spirysidos broke his patient silence.

"Listen to your mother, girl, and stop asking things that should never be said."

"But—"

"We make our future, yes, but we came from the past. Do you know what the cost of life is now? It is not an easy road we tread and maybe that is our doing as much as anyone else's."

Ariadne turned in her blankets with all the full fury a shouted down child could muster. Staring at the dirt, she brooded herself to sleep.

And she awoke. After dreams unknown and forgotten still. After father and mother had joined her in slumber. She awoke, to the sound of stampeding horses but none could be seen. She awoke, to trees swaying to a greater force than the strongest wind. She awoke, to the very earth beneath her rumbling in anger.

Crash! A nearby tree lost its footing, as if it were a drunk man stumbling home who trips on an unseen step. Its tumble to the ground woke her parents who peered out around them in terror. More and more trees began falling and the thundering hooves grew quicker and the growling earth grew louder. And it seemed as if it would never stop. Ariadne ducked beneath the enveloping safety of the blankets and her parents followed her shortly after; mother and father holding her in their arms, cowering alongside.

***

Sunlight came eventually. The shakes had stopped hours beforehand but the frightened little family still shivered and huddled together. A slow, ominous rumble still continued beneath their feet as they began packing for the day ahead. No-one had thought to check on the horse while the trees flew all around them. Spirysidos found him some way from the cart, as jittery as a foal on its first day of being broken in and as sour as an old craftsman blind from years of poor light. It took a good deal of hay and the gentle patting of all of them to calm him once more.

And so they continued, hoof following hoof and wheel edging forward creating a new track among the faded old ones. Ariadne rose excitedly as they passed a mountain, or what was left of it. It seemed the trees weren't the only ones to dance to the rhythm of the earth. The mountain itself seemed to have tripped and fallen.

After some time they emerged into a small valley. While the horse bravely navigated the perilous, rubble-strewn ground, Ariadne gazed up toward the encircling mountains. Crags called out to her, somehow menacingly, whispering of the beating they too had taken. She brushed the thought aside, and turned back to her carvings.

The valley narrowed further and further leaving Spirysidos with a choice. He could try and find some way up and around the mountains, or continue straight, through a narrow pass. It wasn't much of a choice. Spirysidos coaxed the horse forward with a reassuring nudge and they continued straight ahead.

It wasn't long before walls of sheer cliff enveloped them from both sides. The horse seemed jittery once more but Spirysidos ignored it, flicking the reins and urging it ever onward. Then, all of a sudden, a little pebble struck the cart from above. It was swiftly followed by small rocks which missed Ariadne and her parents, mostly. The horse was not so lucky. He received more than one across his back, bouncing off into the ragged walls around. Suddenly the rain stopped as soon as it began and Ariadne peered upward. She saw figures crouching, still, wedged between available cracks. A voice boomed down,

"Leave the cart and everything in it. Keep moving forward on foot and you won't be harmed."

Three

An uneasy silence spread over the numerous pairs of eyes. Spirysidos glared at the speaker some way up the rocky slope in front of him. His nostrils panted louder than the bruised horse. His fists clenched tighter than the focused pupils of the raiding party. Suddenly his breathing stopped to less than a whisper and rock-filled hands were raised overhead in anticipation.

"Ha ha ha ha ha. Go on boys, go home." Ariadne didn't know how he could see from that distance. "Nice try, you've had your fun now clear off." She didn't know how he could dare stare them down, let alone laugh at them while doing so.

This time it was the aerial phantoms who held their breath. Mariaten and Ariadne winced as Spirysidos whipped the reins once more, not for the pain it caused the battered horse but for calling the bluff of the clouds above. Each clip and clop of the horse's hooves reminded them of the crashing stones, each pant, of the agony they might feel at any moment.

"Rotten old man!" boomed from wall to wall. "How did you know?"

As Mariaten and Ariadne released sighs of relief, a chorus of nervous laughter began above them and, more confidently, from the seemingly carefree Spirysidos. While they slowly trotted through the narrow pass, four boys bordering on the verge of manhood carefully climbed down.

Once they reached the relative safety of the ground, they began walking along to the pace of the cart. None of the boys seemed willing to break the awkward silence that was emerging so Spirysidos piped up, cheerful as ever.

"So, you boys are from Malia, eh? Didn't realise we were that close."

"How'd you know?" The oldest looking boy replied, the only one who dared meet his face, "Most of you travellers don't seem to know if you're heading to Gortyn or Zakros."

"Not me, boy." Spirysidos smiled as the boy looked at him, genuinely lost. "I came from here not so long ago. Besides, I recognised your voice—from the first few words I knew I was among my countrymen."

"Sorry about your horse, sir. We didn't mean to hit it, or any of you for that matter."

"So you should b—"

"I was wondering, well me and the lads, if we could push your cart for you? It was just meant to be a bit of fun and we feel kind of a bit bad for hurting your horse." Spirysidos agreed. With years of practice calculating punishments for Ariadne's unique crimes, he was quick to see the fairness in the deal. Besides, though he looked calm, he knew well enough how different things might have gone.

The horse, for its part, was grateful for the stop and relieved at being unharnessed. Two boys headed to the front and two to the back while Spirysidos walked ahead, leading the horse. Not a single boy grumbled as they began pushing and pulling the cart, with Ariadne and Mariaten still on it.

"Right lads, now heave away." Spirysidos called back to them. And so they did. It didn't stop them reverting back to the idle chatter they had while waiting for someone to come through their pass. The older looking one took the corner near Mariaten and smiled. After getting into the rhythm of his work he began chatting shamelessly at the cart dwellers.

"So, heading to Malia are we?"

"Yes." Replied a curt Mariaten, wary of unduly angering her newfound workforce.

"Going to see the ship festival I suppose?"

"Yes."

"Have you been to the ship festival before?" Ariadne leaned over her mother, close to the now sweating face of the pack mule oblivious to the knowledge that a general lack of words usually went with the job.

"You were the one who spoke on the mountain, weren't you?" she asked.

It was his turn, "Yes…" He said in a way that implied, "oh that, nothing to worry about. You'll soon get used to the customs around here, don't feel bad."

She brought the force of her hidden arm out towards him, her hand flicking liked a coiled snake, the stick it held striking with vengeance.

"Ow." His head, obviously his greatest asset, received the first blow. She seemed angry that he didn't just vanish there and then.

"Argh." Not the knuckles, no that wouldn't hurt enough. She caught the part of his fingers which curved over the corner of the cart, gripping it. The cart seemed to instinctively jerk forward as he stumbled, though how his smirking friends managed to time that was a mystery.

Dirt stuck to his face and sweaty clothes. Although bruises had already begun to form on his fingers he lurched forward and grabbed the corner again. Ariadne looked down at him with a warning in her eyes that didn't need to be spoken. His grim calm stare ahead convinced her to lower the stick. She turned around satisfied with the silent heaving mass that was her creation. Once she had turned however, he grabbed her dress at the base of her neck and yanked backward.

They had come out of the pass a while back. As Ariadne hit the ground the unnamed rascal whistled a signal and the boys dropped the cart as one and bolted in all directions. Again unfazed, he stopped in the distance ahead and said,

"Sorry sir, but we have to renege. Your daughter's too much trouble." With a slight bow, as one might give to a priest or a governor passing by, he followed his friends in their flight.

Ariadne had already gotten up and started off after them before he finished speaking. While she saw them on the hills ahead, confident of catching her prey, she was cut off before she could properly begin,

"Ariadne, stop. Leave the cowards and come back at once." Grumbling, at the boys, at her father; at life, she stumbled back.

***

Sometimes the sight of half-collapsed ruins in the distance was a welcomed one. While all of Malia had been struck by the tremors it seemed to Ariadne that only a few houses suffered serious damage. Most had little more than a few cracks, serious, sure, but bearable all the same. Every now and then though, they passed nothing but crumbled remains. Still, the odd pile of rubble aside, overall it was a comforting sight.

It had taken a long while to get there. Once they boys ran off Spirysidos was obliged to harness their horse and force him to trudge the final day, agony or no. While it dragged their cart, each step bringing fresh pain and misery, the rest of them were not much cheerier. Ariadne was the worst of them. Seething in silence and snappy when spoken to, she sat there oblivious to the rolling hills and luscious trees around her.

"What are you making this time dear?" Mariaten tried to wrestle her from her mood.

"An arrow."

"That's nice."

"It's to shoot those boys if they come back."

"Now, now dear, you haven't got a bow? How can you shoot those boys without a bow, hmm?"

"Fine, then a spear. I'll stab them."

"You can't do that. It's not long enough, they'll see you coming."

"I'll hide it like I did before. It's long enough for me."

Mariaten turned away in a mix of amusement and mild worry. She looked over to her husband who didn't seem at all concerned with their daughter's mood.

"When does the festival actually start, Spiry?"

"It should be two days from tomorrow. We'll have time to explore Malia." He leaned back, looking over his shoulder at Ariadne. "You could go swimming on the beach, Ariadne, would you like that?"

"I'd rather hide somewhere so I can sneak up on those boys."

"Ah girls, it's never too early to start thinking about boys…"

"Papa! I am not. Well I am. But only thinking about hurting them so it doesn't count."

Their journey continued to Malia in a similar fashion, light-hearted questions and mocking of Ariadne's determination while she made "arrow" after "arrow". All were grateful to see the village when it finally came into view.

"Where are we staying, Papa?" Ariadne asked after sharpening the point of her eighth arrow.

"We're renting a room from a local Malian." He replied tiredly. Satisfied with his answer and too bored for any further questions, they made it through the city in silence. Even Ariadne had cooled down to watch the sunset. Her temper, unyielding all day, had all but dropped once the light faded and she could no longer make her tools of revenge.

As they finally stopped outside a well-worn but still standing house Ariadne was convinced she knew where her skill at navigating mazes came from. Not stopping to unpack, Spirysidos knocked on the door and entered as soon as it opened. Ariadne followed to see him hugging a woman. And kissing her on her cheek. An old woman at that! Before she could race back to the cart to test her new tools Spirysidos turned to her and said,

"Ariadne, allow me to present your Nana to you. Now I'm sure you'll have lots to talk about while I unpack." Her gobsmacked jaw didn't do justice to the confusion inside her.

Mariaten ushered her forward and broke the silence, "It's good to see you again, Garnia." The wrinkled woman being addressed couldn't speak for the tears in her eyes. She bent down, ignoring her creaking joints as she did so, arms outstretched for her unknown granddaughter.

Under normal circumstances Ariadne would be revolted to touch let alone embrace the husky creature before her. She felt the longing though, felt the painful loss in the woman's eyes. She saw, in every twitch of the outstretched fingers, a long-withheld cry now being bared plainly in hope. She felt it for herself, the chance to know someone who loved her before she was born. She felt all this in a single twitch of her grandmother's fingers, a single flitter of her eye and came running forward into her raw embrace.

Words were not needed or used in those first few minutes. As careful and tender hands stroked her hair Ariadne nuzzled into the arms of her grandmother. After what seemed at once like a long while and an instant, her grandmother spoke,

"You'll have to tell me all your adventures, little one. You must have had so many! You'll have to tell me of the great life up in Knossos that all my boarders speak of. Yes, and what you're doing with yourself, what you're making of your life—that most of all."

As Garnia began to show Ariadne around her home she was told all the rawness and truth of life as children see it. Ariadne told her of bull-leaping and tree-dancing. She told Garnia of guiding herself through dark mazes and finding her way. Knossan life in all its glory was retold in that moonlit evening and every word was revelled in, as if Garnia was a child hearing all the legends for the first time.

Once Garnia began preparing dinner she started telling Ariadne of Malia and tried as a faithful grandparent to answer all questions that burst from Ariadne, whether related or not. By her age it seemed she knew how to drag the conversation back to its main points even after half an hour of tangents.

Have you ever been to a bull-leap?
What is it like swimming in the sea?
Did you feel the ground and its anger?
Do you think you could beat me in a race?
Do you want to see the things I made on the trip?
And the dreaded, So Nana, how old are you?

Ariadne's questions only slowed once food was placed in front of her. With every bite, not only was she filled with warmth but also a tiredness she hadn't know was there. By the time she had finished the bowl, her head lolled almost onto the table itself and her eyelids fluttered constantly. Garnia couldn't help but smile the whole way as she led Ariadne upstairs and to a waiting bed. Her granddaughter collapses on it straight away, asleep before Garnia could drape the blankets over her.

Four

A peaceful, oblivious face slept that morning, ignorant of the tangle of hair that had covered it. As footsteps softly and slowly approached, the serene face continued, closed off from the world. It was unaware even when the shade who had entered launched itself into the air above.

Crash! The bed creaked as the shade fell from the sky. It was Ariadne's favourite way to wake her parents, other kids might laugh at her failed attempts at bull-leaping but she always landed so they weren't in a position to be laughing. She tossed her head from side to side waiting for the judgement call on her accurate flip. No-one looked up.

"Wake up, Papa!" Spirysidos rolled over in a futile act of defiance. "Me and Nana are going to the markets!"

"Bye." Spirysidos said with utter indifference.

"Don't you want to come?" Ariadne continued unfazed.

"Bye." Ariadne started climbing over her father, her eyes fixed on her still sleeping mother. "Your mother doesn't want to come either."

Ariadne frowned. All she had needed was a good night's sleep in a proper bed and she was as good as ever. *Parents, not in touch with the seasons, with the rising and falling of the sun.* She shrugged and jumped off the bed as quickly as she had come. As Ariadne ran downstairs, Spirysidos heard her calling out in the distance.

"You were right, Nana. Let's go."

Spirysidos rolled over again to face Mariaten. "Do you think we could get my mother to sell her?" He asked.

Mariaten smiled, keeping her eyes closed the whole time.

Garnia was waiting near the bottom of the stairs, chuckling as her granddaughter came down.

"Ready, Nana?" Ariadne asked excitedly, content with her parents answer and ready herself to start the day.

"Yes, trickster, now come along."

"So, Nana," Ariadne began, intent on learning everything there was to know about the world in that one morning stroll, "why did you stay here? Why didn't you live with us in Knossos?"

Garnia looked at her granddaughter, wondering for much of the night the same question. "Well, when you grow up in a place, Ariadne, when you get to know each corner and bend, the salt breezes and the lives of those around you, you get stuck there. Year by year you put roots down and it gets harder to leave. Your father wanted to try a chance at a different life even though he had spent his whole life here. I was angry with him. No-one should leave their home if they can help it, well that's at least what I thought. But leave he did. Thinking he could make a fortune for your mother and any kids he had, he packed up and moved off to Knossos."

"Couldn't he work here in Malia?"

"Of course. But that wasn't the same, dear. Everyone knows, if you want to get ahead, you have to go to Knossos."

Ariadne was on the point of saying something polite but heartfelt, in the ways of adults, like "that must have been hard for you" or something similar when they walked into the market. She wasn't distracted by the stalls of men waving plucked chickens in both arms, pointing to intricately carved furniture or wearing layers of their merchandise to catch people's eye. No something far more important had caught her eye.

"Bye, Nana, tell Mama and Papa I'll see them back home." Garnia followed her granddaughter's gaze and cheerfully shook her head. She had been told of the stoning incident while the rest of them sat up later the previous night, where the events of the years were unravelled and again relived.

"Be nice dear. Don't do anything I wouldn't have done at your age." She continued to the stalls as Ariadne raced off down a side alley. While Ariadne had not actually been there before, she found she could feel her way through the village as naturally as any underground tunnel. After weaving her way back and forth through the alleys and houses, she came out behind the youthful mob, hiding herself behind some bushes.

With the sun shining and the group's easy-going banter, one could easily mistake the world for a kind and enjoyable place. Slowly, she crept forward. Something about the boats, that was what she could hear them discussing, the size of their masts or something... She rose cautiously, no higher than need be. Her arm was poised and aligned itself with her eye. In an instant she threw the stone she had picked up along the way. It travelled perfectly, striking with a satisfying thud. Ariadne had already crouched down in the bushes by the time it struck, was already creeping quietly away as the outspoken leader of the day before got his retribution.

Ariadne skipped her way through the back alleys, chuckling the whole way. *I'll be able to find Nana before she goes home. That was easy.* As she replayed the fresh memory over in her mind, savouring every detail, time seemed to reverse itself. Blocking the start of the alley were three angry boys who'd suddenly found a reason to grin.

"Well, well, well. Hello again," came a voice from behind. The three in front started closing in as she turned to face her former target.

"Oh, hi! Fancy seeing you again. Malia mustn't be that big after all." He walked up to her slowly and deliberately, his face an unreadable, faint grin. He stopped, an inch from her face. He looked down, into her eyes, tossing the stone absently up and down in his hand.

"What's your name anyway?" Ariadne interrupted his menacing vibe. He stopped tossing the stone, turned his hand and held it outstretched before her.

"Adro," he said as he looked into her eyes, searching for any sign of weakness. Satisfied, he gestured forward with his hands and said, "truce?"

She picked up the stone slowly, staring at it the whole time. She looked up to stare into his face. At once she raised her hand and brought the stone down onto his head in three rhythmic taps,

"Ari-ad-ne." As he staggered backwards slightly she answered him, "Ok, Adro, truce."

Emeko, Macanra and Zedeck quickly rushed forward to seal the agreement now written in blood. Emeko and Zedeck lightly punched her on her shoulder and she turned and did likewise as Macanra steadied a still wavering Adro. Ariadne turned and started walking away and, after a moment, Emeko and Zedeck started following her. She looked back to Macanra and the still-dazed Adro, calling out to them both,

"You coming or what?" Adro shook his head to steady himself and, together, he and Macanra raced after them.

It didn't take long for the boys to start competing with stories of their great exploits. All wanted the attention and approval of their new friend, such as it was.

"You see that tree over there, eh?" Zedeck proudly asked.
"I see it."

"I climbed it before my head could touch the lowest branches."

"Well when I go back to Knossos, I'm going to dance with trees, spinning around and around to the hidden pattern of the wind." Ariadne shared in response, ignorant of the slight he felt at being undone.

"Once, once we spun poor old Chidek around in the back streets and left him. Took him hours to find his way out." Emeko's admission was met with a chorus of, "poor old Chidek."

"I've cracked the maze of Knossos." Ariadne said proudly, "I have walked in constant night with a vain hope of escaping. I was starving and weary, I was alone but I survived." They couldn't help but look on her in wonder.

"Oi, Oi you ain't seen nothing yet." Macanra began, eager to impress their new strange and outspoken friend. "Once when me Pa's ox was pulling our cart down the main road, well, so it took fright and broke from the harness. It bolted down the middle of the street and Pa only barely got out of the way."

"I have seen the bull-leap at the court in Knossos. I have seen men jump at the last possible instant, some spinning gracefully through the air and others paying the price for imperfection." Ariadne smiled at them, beaming. Who would have thought these Malians had never experienced anything? Adro, who had walked silently until then, gave her another challenge.

"Hey, Knossos is kind of inland isn't it?"
"Yeah, so what?"

"Well, I bet you've never been to a beach then. I bet you've never swum in the sea." He looked sideways at her, across the line of failed friends between them and after seeing her proud smile waver slightly, he burst into a cheer. "Not so fancy now, eh?"

"I've swum in a river…" One by one the outdone gang gathered the falling remains of the smile she had worn and clothed themselves in the single fragment of beating her at one of life's experiences.

"To the beach!"

Ariadne looked at them crossly and tried to save her superiority,

"Well, I'll be going to see the ship festival soon, I'll see the beach all I want then."

"*Well*," Adro mimicked, "we've seen the festival every year of our lives. Haven't we boys? I hardly think you can do it justice in just one year."

"Hear, hear!" As the boys began running off her towards the beach, Ariadne gave up trying to outdo her new friends and started running off after them.

***

Ariadne could smell the salt-ridden breeze as they twisted their way through the beginning of the dockyard. The others could feel her excitement now, all thoughts of far-away palaces forgotten. They raced to the dock so fast they seemed to be guided by mere memory alone. No time for thought or even instinct to decide. Ariadne still had no idea how to get there but followed them, feeling every sudden jerk before they were about to turn and often racing down corners at the head of the pack. Eventually they were hit with a fresh gust of the chilling salt air. They stood bent over for a time, panting, feeling the victory of knowing you had arrived.

While the others were still recovering their breath, Ariadne took the time to savour her ignorance a moment longer. She closed her eyes and imagined, seeing herself swimming in a rich, dark blue ocean. And then she opened her eyes and saw nothing but a horrible mass of grey and black and red.

"What have you done?" she looked at the locals, convinced they were in on the job.

Zedeck pointed upwards and, as one, the confused group looked up at the sky to see a greater mystery. The sea had done nothing more than reflect the chaos of the heavens. Clouds were woven in bright red fire and the darkest enveloping black. The sky seemed to burn and more, to writhe in pain. They heard it now, what they had been hearing since they raced off to the beach but hadn't listened. They had all thought it was just the earth grumbling again and ignored it. Yet the sky was crying out and could be ignored no longer. It boomed louder than the harshest thunder, a tortured thing never before in such agony.

"What's happening?" Although she conceded to herself that this wasn't their doing, surely they must know something, surely somebody must.

They stared back at her. No longer brave adventurers and wild rogues, these brave men were mere boys. She saw the same look of dread in their eyes, fear, that the world had suddenly changed forever, that something was happening that not even the legends told of.

And so, as quickly as they had come, the group raced back the way they came. None spoke a word and each one flinched as the sky thundered around them. One by one the boys tailed off, going their separate ways. Only two boys were still there as Ariadne reached her grandmother's place. Emeko was already rushing past her, glancing behind in slight acknowledgement but Adro stayed for a moment and raised his hand in an awkward wave before he too raced away.

Five

Swirling, spreading, oozing its way across the sky, Ariadne stared down at the base of the table, her mind on the heavens. She kept picturing over and over, an unnatural, seething cloth being draped over them all.

"Ariadne! Ariadne are you even listening to me?!" Her father's volume didn't matter, she had gradually droned it down to a low buzz for the last half hour. Apparently her instinctive nodding and head shaking had failed her. She quickly looked up.

"Yes, Papa."

"Women," he began again, "women can't look after themselves. They aren't safe." Spirysidos paused as three pairs of eyes pierced him from all directions. He continued apparently unfazed, "Outside the home people will take advantage of you (*As opposed to inside, Papa?*). You saw firsthand with that rabble as we came here: the world is not a safe place, Ariadne (*Which world, Papa? The one we used to have or the one with fire in the sky?*). You can't just go off like that with complete strangers!"

"They were only boys, Papa."

"I'll have you know, dear," he lapsed back into his former playful self, "that I was once a boy. And I'm telling you, we can't be trusted." His tone changed back under the mocking gaze of Mariaten. "So, so Ariadne, no going off with unknown strangers; you can't just live life thinking the sky will never fall on your head just because it hasn't so far."

"Papa…"

"What dear?"

"You have seen the sky outside, haven't you?"

"What is it raining? I heard a bit of a rumble. We might be in for a bit of a storm but don't worry the fleet can handle it. It will still be an exciting day."

"You bet," she muttered to herself, "Papa, could you take a break from punishing me for just a second and go look outside?"

Spirysidos rose cautiously, as if he might forget his line of argument if he rushed it. He was muttering as he walked towards the door, "See the sky, who thinks I have time for watching the clouds go by when my daughter's gone and run off? What sort of a father would I be if I wasn't here the moment she got back, to make sure she would never do it again? Hey what's that? What...?" Spirysidos stared at the sky outside, the blood draining from his face.

"Is it something we all should see, love?" Mariaten asked.

Spirysidos' lack of answering brought her quickly to his side. Once she glanced towards the sky, she didn't so much as faint as collapse while still awake.

"Is it spitting, Papa? A slight breeze, Mama?" Ariadne asked almost innocently. As Spirysidos half-carried Mariaten back to the table, Ariadne saw a glint of the fear she had seen in the boys in his eyes.

"Ariadne, go up to your room now and get some rest." Suddenly being punished didn't seem so bad. Surely they would sort it out. Surely between them, her parents knew everything and could fix anything. She crept up the stairs without daring to look them in the eye, just in case they read the plea in her eyes, and couldn't answer it.

They began in soft whispers after Ariadne was out of earshot.

"So, what do you think it is?" Spirysidos looked from wife to mother.

"Maybe the gods are angry with us..." Mariaten responded with a hushed voice. "Or maybe some new gods are fighting them in the heavens."

"You think so?" Spirysidos asked.

"What else could it be?" Mariaten replied fearfully. "We've never had anything like this before, not even in the oldest tales. Whatever it is, it isn't good."

"It's some no good, rotten trick of these youngins if you ask me," Garnia said, breaking the silence that had emerged. Mariaten could never tell when she was joking. "Seriously though, whatever it is, we'll be fine," Garnia continued. "We always have and always will." She said and then started up the stairs herself. "I'm off to bed."

Mariaten and Spirysidos sat there a while longer, neither saying a word, just pondering. Eventually, Spirysidos spoke.

"Do you think Mama's right?"

"About it being nothing to worry about?" Mariaten asked.

"No," Spirysidos said and shrugged, "about heading off to bed." He said with a gleam in his eye. Mariaten paused and smiled to herself before replying.

"You know, Spiry," she went over and rapped her arms around him, "I think you might be right."

As they rested for a moment, senses heightening and tiredness fading with every breath, their peaceful embrace was disturbed by a friendly but audible knock on the door. Spirysidos paused, lingering for just a moment before rising to open it.

"What do you—" Spirysidos stopped and stood there gaping at the three men standing outside. "Fasilos! Charib!" he opened his arms wide as the men walked towards him. Each gave him a firm embrace before moving inward. "Pretan!" Spirysidos said with joy as he hugged the last man before closing the door behind them.

Each of the three men looked rough and hardened by sun and wind. They had the same appearance as Spirysidos of looking older than they really were. Only Fasilos stood out, being dressed in a colourful, almost regal robe.

"You remember Mariaten, don't you?" Spirysidos asked excitedly.

Fasilos took a step forward, smiling and, as he reached Mariaten, held her hand in his, bowing his head in faint reverence.

"Who could forget?" he said. His hand slipped from hers and he raised his head, still smiling, before standing off to the side. Mariaten smiled in turn though as one thoroughly unimpressed. Charib and Pretan simply nodded at her, both of them bearing the same look as the one across her face. Her smile changed to one of warmth as she nodded back at them.

Meanwhile Spirysidos continued on, oblivious. He moved further into the room, shuffling stools around the table and upturning a wooden box for a fifth seat. As the rest of them started to take their seats, he spoke excitedly, "So, what needs fixing?"

Charib chuckled though somehow his heart wasn't in it. Fasilos replied instead, with a hint of reproach, "Straight to the point, Spiry?"

"It's been—what, ten, twelve years? Can't we have just come to see an old friend?" Pretan butted in almost defensively.

Spirysidos laughed. "The last time you came here, Fasilos, you'd broken the table of your future bride's parents and needed me to fix it before they came home."

Fasilos frowned, though more than one tried hard not to smile.

"If I remember correctly," Spirysidos continued, "one of the legs had snapped. And her back was sore for days!" he turned to

Pretan almost in tears, who couldn't help himself either and burst out laughing.

Once they had calmed down, Charib spoke softly, almost tenderly. "We do actually need your help Spiry."

"What's so bad it's got all three of you out on a day like this?" Spirysidos asked, genuinely curious.

"You've answered your own question," Fasilos said with foreboding, "'a day like this.'" Spirysidos turned to look at Charib and Pretan but one by one they nodded, though with a great weariness.

"I'm not sure how I can help with that. The sky's no business of mine." Spirysidos said half in jest, trying to lighten the mood.

"I have become governor of Malia since you left, Spirysidos, and it is my role to look after and protect it, no matter what the cost." Fasilos began. "The ground trembles and shakes our houses so hard that some collapse on those inside. The sky darkens in every direction in the middle of the day, the only light coming from a dark and unnatural red cloud intermingled with the black ones around it. The seers tell me this is only the beginning and we have much worse to come if whatever is causing this is not appeased..."

"Go slaughter a goat then. If you need me to build you an altar, fine, but surely you've already got one?" Spirysidos interjected.

"I'm afraid that's not enough," Fasilos replied. "The seers say we have one chance to appease the gods... we need to return to the old ways..."

Mariaten, who had been listening intently but quietly up to this point suddenly spoke. "Tell them to leave, Spiry," she said softly but fiercely, "tell them to leave now."

"Are you going to let your woman tell you what to do?" Fasilos asked darkly, all hint of charm now gone.

"Another word like that and you're all out the door." Spirysidos said, looking each of his friends in the eye in turn. No-one spoke. "Tell me, and tell me plainly, what do you need from me?" he continued.

"We need a virgin, Spiry." Fasilos said simply, a direct answer to an old friend. "A pure unblemished calf ready for the knife. A saviour for Malia and, perhaps, the whole of Crete..." Spirysidos rose slowly, rage filling his eyes, but Fasilos continued quickly before he was ordered out. "I can't take a child from anyone who lives here or there'd be rioting in the streets. But the child of a wanderer, one who forsook Malia for a different life, well that child wouldn't be quite so missed..."

"How… dare… YOU!" as Spirysidos moved towards his former friend, he grabbed a knife from the table and flicked it through his fingers so that he held it blade upwards. He moved forwards ready to send it curving up into the neck of the man before him.

"You want a sacrifice?" Spirysidos bellowed. "I'll give you a sacrifice and one that won't be missed." Spirysidos lunged at that moment only to be anticipated by Pretan who punched the side of his wrist as it travelled towards Fasilos. Spirysidos groaned, clutching his now unnaturally curved hand.

"Now let's be calm and talk this one through." Fasilos said, his heart racing. He looked at Mariaten who glared at him with darker eyes than the sky outside. He turned back to Spirysidos. "I think, dear friend, we had better go outside and start from the beginning again. I don't think you fully appreciate the situation we're in."

At a nod from Fasilos, Pretan stayed behind while the others dragged Spirysidos towards the front door. Pretan spoke to Mariaten, no longer friendly but with a menacing confidence.

"Sit next to me, Mariaten. It's been so long. I won't hurt you. I won't even touch you unless you start to make a noise or try and climb those stairs." Mariaten glanced at the stairway and thought of her daughter sleeping peacefully above but, as she looked back at Pretan, something caught her eye. Slowly, she walked over towards the table, clenching her teeth in an effort not to scream. She walked over the fallen knife unseen by Pretan. She curled her toes over it and grabbed it, sitting down with less of a fake smile than Pretan assumed.

***

"Look out beyond the narrow view of your home, Spirysidos. Tell me what you see." When he didn't answer Fasilos, Charib encouraged him—one shoulder to another.

"I see fire Fasilos. Fire in the sky as far as my eyes can see."

"Good, Spirysidos, good." Fasilos led him around the street gesturing towards the houses they had grown up around and played between, now barred from within in fear. They climbed a hill not far from the cluster of houses and Fasilos pointed towards the ocean. "You can see much better from here. Tell me, can you see the island of Thera?"

"In the distance I see a mountain of fire rising from the sea." Spirysidos said as he peered at the lone light in the darkness below the heavens. "Our sky comes from there then? Thera…" He mused, "The gods are destroying our colony. They mean to destroy our empire; they have chosen a fitting warning." Fasilos nodded, satisfied.

"Now do you see?" he broke his calm demeanour, his illusion of control, "we have *no choice*. I didn't pick you out of hatred old friend. It… it just makes more sense, it is more fitting, more acceptable to take a child not of the city but one it can still claim as its own."

"She is a priestess!" Spirysidos groaned.

"They make sacrifices for us our whole lives," Fasilos murmured, "maybe it is time for such a one to pay the ultimate sacrifice…" Spirysidos turned back towards his house, tears streaming down his face as the heavens boomed around him in anger. He felt each tremendous clap of what could not be mere thunder, felt it pierce into his soul, an unquenchable anger demanding an unpayable crime.

Fasilos bent his head towards Spirysidos, seeing the turmoil inside him. "It must be done, there is no other way."

Spirysidos stood there long after he had made his decision. He eventually looked up at Fasilos, looked him in the eye and said with all the care a father could possess,

"Make it quick."

***

Mariaten couldn't just sit there in silence. Her mind conjured up possibility after possibility. They would murder Spirysidos and bury him in the forest, then come back and take her daughter, killing her if she tried to stop them. Spirysidos had fought them off singlehandedly but they were coming back with a mob. They knocked him unconscious and were now going to set the house on fire as a means of making the sacrifice. No! She had to stop.

"How is your wife Pretan?" he looked at her in grim apathy.

"She's dead. Been dead the past three years."

"I'm sorry, she was a nice girl."

"She was a slut! Still don't know if that bastard she left me with is mine." Mariaten paused thoughtfully, as if she cared about the child of this man and his own personal pain.

"What's the child's name?"

"What does it matter to you?" he shot back, suddenly angry.

"Well I was wondering if it was a girl?" she asked accusingly, her meaning obvious.

"The child is a boy. Now be silent." Mariaten went back to torturing her mind with possibilities and absentmindedly spinning the knife around with her toes.

"Mama." A sleepy voice broke the silence. "Mama, I heard voices. Is everything alright?"

Both seated enemies saw her at the same time but Mariaten reacted quicker. She needed less time to act and, besides, her instincts took over.

She drove the knife into his leg with one solid kick. Before he could reach out and strangle her, even before he realised what was happening, she brought her arms around his neck and sent his face crashing into the table. Not quite confident that she had succeeded in knocking him senseless, Mariaten brought him up and smashed him down again, onto the wooden table. Once more for good measure and she stopped, having heard his nose snap and felt his muscles go limp.

Ariadne looked on, horrified.

"Mama, what have you done?"

"There's no time to explain, Ariadne." She got up and raced over to her daughter. She stroked Ariadne softly on her head, tracing her hair with a finger down to her shoulder. Finger became hand which tightened uncontrollably.

"All you have to know is that I love you. We love you. Now run out that door and don't stop running until you are far away from here. Get back to Knossos. If you find those boys at the pass make them escort you back." Ariadne looked on in a mix of fear and confusion. "Do you understand?" She was wide awake however.

"Yes, Mama… will I see you again?"

"If we can, we will find you."

Ariadne ran to the door only to see it slam open in front of her. She gave her mother the final glance she had sacrificed for time; the quickest way to ask, what now? Mariaten looked joyfully at Spirysidos only to have joy turn into despair as two more entered the house. He saw his daughter, now shaking with uncertainty as she eyed the strangers before her, he bent down and wrapped his arms around her. He spoke softly to her.

"Ariadne, you are going to go with these men. Don't worry. Everything will be alright." Mariaten screamed then. She screamed as if the deed had already been done. She let the tear she now felt in her heart out with words.

"How… how can you? She is our *daughter*."

Spirysidos nodded to Fasilos and Charib. He wrapped his arms around Mariaten, stronger than the most comforting embrace yet more chilling than an empty bed.

"No… Noooo." She wailed. She didn't stop but grew louder and more piercing as they picked up Pretan and dragged out her daughter, who all the while stared in confusion back at her.

Six

An icy wind bit deep into the tired travellers, cutting through their furs like a knife through fish. Sleep had fought with them and lost; now only a grim climb would bring release from their dull agony. All would be well, once they reached the cave.

They had left Malia long behind, a patchwork blighting the otherwise serene landscape now a distant glimmer down below. An unsettling terror gradually rose in Ariadne. Once they had left, when the last signs of humanity vanished, she felt a loneliness rise from the invading wind and the constant half-darkness. Her mind kept replaying those final moments: her mother, desperately beating one of these men she was with now. Although the memory increased her fears, she drew courage from it as well. When they decided, after an hour or so up the mountain, to have a rest and eat, she tried to slip quietly away.

Ariadne took the bread they offered her and sat down on a log—just far enough to give her the chance but not too far to alert them. She was curious why they hadn't tied her hands, *maybe Papa was right and I should go with them?* This thought held long enough for her to finish the food, no longer. She bent over the log as if searching for something on the ground below. Her feet touched the edge of the ground and she flexed her legs ready to bolt. Ariadne sprang from the log like a new shoot reaching for the sun, and kept going.

Down the pass she flew, each step undoing whatever plan they had in mind.

Pretan, meanwhile, was nursing his aching head. The cold wind bothered him the most, constantly battering into his freshly cracked nose and split lip without mercy. His bound leg was also throbbing but no blood seeped through the bandage—he could continue, it would hold.

"Hey, where did she go?" Charib interrupted Pretan's dour thoughts.

Frightened more than the fugitive herself, they dropped food, blankets and logs, spread out and raced down after her. Ariadne turned in the darkness at the sound of pursuit. She jumped by instinct, narrowly missing a cluster of fallen branches, and kept running. Down the mountain raced hare in flight followed by determined hounds. And they ran.

Many an upward step was undone as Ariadne found her way back down. Slowly, though, they gained on her. Childhood fitness was no match for men who knew every stream, every patch of trees. It was no match for those who trained to fight all day long and row throughout the night. And so, with Malia no longer just a speck in the distance but alive before her, a panting Ariadne, close to collapse, was surrounded.

Fasilos took her arm in a mix of strength and tenderness. While they started walking the track all over again Pretan spoke,

"I still think we should have tied her."

"She is not to be harmed in any way," Fasilos replied, "not even chafing from a rope." *Maybe I misjudged them, he doesn't sound so bad.* "She is to be unblemished. Thank the gods they protected her on the way down, I do not even see a scratch." Ariadne stumbled back up the mountain shivering at the dark thoughts now creeping into her mind, *unblemished…*

***

After the sun had risen, seeped through the red tinge and lit the grumbling sky, they arrived at the cave. Ariadne peered forward to catch a glance at the roof as they stumbled into it. Every one of the countless grooves, fading into darkness, felt like still snakes surrounding her. The gaping hole they walked into scared her less than the everlasting darkness ahead. Knossos... Knossos was one thing. Knossos was walls and rooms, occasionally light and, on a good day, even people. Here, this cave, was emptiness; an eternal cavern forever dark—her only companions sinister and silent.

Ariadne witnessed the greatest futile gesture she had seen in her life. She saw one of her captors light a torch. O how the darkness flees on sight! O the great boon of humanity! Nope, not even close. For all their efforts, Ariadne could only see a step in front of her and, despite herself, she laughed. Laughed at the futility of trying to tame the cave, as if they could stop it swallowing them whole if it chose. Still, she continued further, into the abyss.

Endless steps and timeless minutes passed. She stepped on something. Something crude but not rock. Something loose; something made. Ariadne bent down to pick it up. She held the curious object in the light—the others, eager for a break as well, gladly stopped as she stared at the mystery. At long last she decided it must be a fat clay woman. A really dodgy one at that. Ariadne shrugged and tossed it—enjoying seeing the men jump as sound returned to the cave in a shatter. Fasilos raced after it. After staring at the broken pieces before him, he returned to the group.

"We're not far now. The votive offering she just destroyed means we have almost reached the sanctuary."

Offering? Ariadne remembered the priestesses telling her about the caves. Back in the old times when things were simpler, and darker. Back when they worshiped the gods of the ground rather that just giving them a token of respect. Caves, were their temples. And people came. Came from afar bringing all manner of gifts seeking the gods' favour. But then the dark times arrived. Evil seeping throughout the whole of Crete and no offering was given. "Now we honour the rest of the gods," they told her, "but everyone forgets the earth gods. No-one comes to the caves anymore, assured that dancing and leaping in the sun is enough. No-one wants to return to the darkness." Ariadne remembered the offerings she made at the pillars underground and thought that might be their attempt to placate the earth gods. *It is too easy, not the same as coming here, to a cave. The cave we have made under Knossos doesn't feel alive like this place.* Ariadne paused in thought then realised with horror, *No, the difference is that Knossos does feel alive…*

As they kept trudging along more and more objects littered their path. Every crunch under foot felt like an accusation, another offense to add to the gods whose power she now rested in. *How are we going to make up for disturbing them? How many offerings can they be carrying?* At last they stopped. Ariadne peered forward and saw the silhouette outline of what used to be a door, now just another empty hole to pass through. One by one they climbed through the hole. Moving from the widest vast expanse to this little room felt like the gods had become impatient and brought the cave on top of them. It took Ariadne a few moments to realise the walls were not actually moving. The very air seemed stifled and hard to breath. Fasilos moved to each corner of the little room and light the ancient torches still fastened to the walls. Ariadne peered at the bronze holding them there. It was decorated in fantastic patterns she had sometimes seen on the oldest of their ritual tools. Ariadne noticed that the light from the new torches converged on the centre of the small room. Fasilos put his torch in an empty socket there, on the side of a similarly decorated stone altar.

Ariadne stared at it, entranced. Dots and swirls seemed faded somehow, not by sunlight but they seemed covered with a reddish-brown layer, itself now faded. She peered around the room, her eyes adjusting quickly to the light. She noticed another object at the foot of the altar. At first, she thought it was another clay model, another gift to the gods. Curiosity got the better of her, even in this place, and she walked over to pick it up.

"Stop her! She will pollute it." Pretan's voice seemed like a shout in the echoing silence of before.

"No, it is fitting. Besides we picked her for her purity, remember?" Fasilos countered, unfazed. He went on to think to himself, *Why, she could handle the knife itself and it would not make a difference. Best not to give her the opportunity though.* He stopped then in thought and saw once more the deed he was about to perform. He saw the ignorance, remarkably, still on her face of what was about to happen. Saw every wrinkle that time had yet to form and the height to which she would never grow. *It is the only way. This is not for me, this is for Crete.* Casting all thoughts from his mind, he moved to the back of the room where it was said he would find the knife.

Ariadne looked down at the thing now in her hands. It seemed to be shaped like a bull, the head of a bull. Black eyes stared back at her—as if all the darkness of the cave could be captured in those two gems of emptiness. She turned it over and, seeing the hole and its hollow form, realised it was a rhyton, a libation vessel like back at Knossos. It was used to pour some kind of liquid. But what?

Her thoughts were interrupted by the sound of metal scraping on stone. It wasn't a harsh scrape, merely the sound of something being taken out of a recess and grazing the edge. It was the softest, most chilling sound Ariadne ever heard. Fasilos slowly returned and said,

"It is time."

Pretan and Charib sprang into motion, all the more frightening since once they had entered the sanctuary they had been little more than statues. Charib caught the falling bull's head as Pretan grabbed her arms. He dragged her onto the altar, pinning her arms behind her back in a way to cause immense pain if she tried to move them. Although she tried kicking wildly, Charib had put down the bull's head, and he simply held her feet together. Ariadne, to her horror, realised she hadn't even started screaming. She made up for lost time with a shriek to rival her mother's, a cry of desperation that not even the entombing cave could withhold. Pretan moved his hand to cover her mouth but Fasilos motioned for him to stop and said,

"Her cry will awaken the gods. It will beckon them, ready them for the offering they are about to receive." He looked to the shrieking girl and said, "Do not worry. Know that your loss will save all of Crete. You are fulfilling the destiny of your role in life. Instead of sacrificing on our behalf you have now become a sacrifice for us." Fasilos, content with his admission, walked slowly over to the bull's head rhyton and picked it up, all the while beginning a soft chant.

Ariadne felt the pain shooting through her arms and the strength of the men who restrained her. She felt the rough cold of the altar top despite the surrounding torches. It took all her effort to stop the shiver she felt forming from turning into a violent spasm. There was no will left to break free as the knife came forward, no strength with which to fight it.

She saw Fasilos walk over to her. In one hand he bore an ancient bronze knife, itself covered in the same symbols now long forgotten. In the other he held the bull's head, and she had no doubt now what would fill it. He motioned to Pretan who withdrew one of his hands from behind her back to grab the top of her head. She felt his greasy hands upon her still clean hair and shuddered. He pulled down softly but firmly and bared her neck to Fasilos.

Rhyton, was cupped dearly under her neck, ready to catch every drop.

Knife, was guided slowly towards her neck. The hilt rested against her throat, ready for the single sideways swipe to open all in one fluid movement.

Eyes, Ariadne's eyes, opened wide.

Yet it was not for the blade resting near, a heartbeat away from taking her life—for Pretan's eyes opened as well. Both of them could see the entrance to the sanctuary. Both of them saw the movement and the silhouette emerging from the shadows.

Fasilos noticed the startled look on both and held the knife still. Pretan formed words, maybe not in strict accordance with the ritual but appropriate all the same.

"A god has come, Fasilos, saviour of Crete—come to accept our offering."

Fasilos turned to see that which he hoped to appease. The hilt still rested against Ariadne's throat. Charib also turned to witness the shadow standing in the darkness. A figure could be made out slightly, enough to know that something was there.

While the rest stared at the god, Fasilos turned back to Ariadne once more. He would perform his deed with it watching, yes, it was fitting. He would not waver now. He drew a breath in and moved the knife right slightly, in anticipation of drawing it left in one perfect slicing action.

And a stone came from the darkness, travelled through the air and gave its judgement. It collided with his hand and the knife which it held. Hand burst open and knife clattered to the ground.

A horizontal torrent followed. Rocks and pebbles flew out of the darkness. Each one hit its target with perfect accuracy, as if the god of the cave had power over everything within. Every collision made a muffled thump, for every stone hit a body before returning to the ground below.

Ariadne saw blood began to flow from the splitting skin that was the aftermath of each airborne strike. Each strike hitting the men around her. Each stone missing her entirely.

Each man buckled under the judgement of the god before him. Bruises and cuts manifested themselves as a sign of the sacrifice about to be demanded of them. They just stood there under the continuing rain, bewildered, frozen; unable to understand the situation before them. The storm only eased after a significant number of head collisions. One by one Fasilos, Pretan and Charib dropped, like stones.

Ariadne let the convulsions take her then. She let the shiver she had long felt in her spine resonate through her body, let the sick, churning feeling in her stomach out, quite literally. She was bent over on her hands in this way as the god entered, twice convulsed by cold and fear alike.

As the shadows around it lifted, fled on contact with the light, the god stood bare, peering down over her. She couldn't raise her head to see it or hear its heavy panting over the ringing in her ears. More footsteps entered, and encircled her. Suddenly she felt a warm hand rest on her shoulder and she found the strength to look up,

To see Adro staring back down at her.

***

They continued in such a state for some time. Eventually, her shakes ended and the gang stopped panting. Ariadne voiced her first thought since terror had taken over.

"I want to leave this place, now." The boys were silent. Adro reached down and took the torch from the clasp on the alter and began to leave the room. Ariadne still sat there, however, so he stopped. He walked back to her, his face inches away, strange patterns flickering over it in the torchlight.

"Ariadne, what's the matter?" he said very softly. She looked at him and paused for a moment before speaking.

"Did… did you kill them?" Adro shrugged and moved over to the bodies lying on the ground. He bent over and felt the neck of each of them.

"Hmm, apparently not. No matter, come on then." Ariadne rose and was caught between the desire to run screaming out of there or walk calmly over to the knife and fill the rhyton with vengeance. Instead, she fumbled around on the floor until she found the bull's head rhyton, remarkably still intact after being dropped in the chaos. She walked over to the side of the altar and rested it in the centre with both hands. Ariadne then lifted the bull's head, all the while gleaming defiantly back at her, before bringing it crashing down onto the altar. After the shattered pieces had all landed, Ariadne quietly walked out into the darkness.

***

They walked on and on in the seemingly endless cavern. Trudging… was the right word; nothing else conveyed the slowly demoralising march. The torch made little difference, once again, but this time things were different. For the walls were closing in every so often, or so it seemed as, every now and then, one of the pack would walk into jagged edge of the cave. What felt like a straight path to the shrine somehow became a maze back to the world beyond.

"Gods!" Macanra exclaimed on having stumbled into another wall—one that just seemed to appear before them no matter which direction they took. "Gods," he spoke a bit softer, reverently, "of the cave. Do you think we've annoyed them Adro?"

Ariadne looked at him through the darkness and answered instead. She dredged her mind for the phrases her mother told her not to repeat, the ones she occasionally heard after Papa came home from a night out with his fellow carvers.

"Bastard, evil gods! Who cares? We'll find our way out of this cave."

There was a silence, no-one wanting to be the first to agree with her. Ariadne felt Adro's hand gently come out of the darkness and clasp hers. She breathed a sigh of relief a moment before Adro broke the silence.

"She's right. We don't need to honour these gods. We came here to stop that and if that made them angry with us then so be it. It was the right thing to do even if we never get out of this cave."

So they continued trudging. But not in submissive silence. Ariadne led the pack, not with the torch but by the light of her hands. They guided her through the cave, sometimes facing nothing but air and at other times prising the route from the walls that tried to block their path. All the while the boys broke the stillness by telling her of their lives back in the outside world.

Zedeck started first.

Well, the first thing I remember about Malia was feeling the sea breeze. Don't really know where or how old I was. Just the feeling, you know? Guess it's not all that surprising, see Papa's a fisherman so our house is near the sea. You felt the breeze seep through the walls on a good night—on a bad night, well, they did their best.

The first real memory I have is of being out in a boat with Papa. Wind wasn't up that much and it was kind of nice. I soon learned to stick more than just me feet in the water—he's had me hauling in the fish with him the past few years.

Reckon I'll be a fisherman one day. Papa's thinking of expanding though. Maybe even trading. See he likes navigatin' the waters more than gutting the critters all day long. Yeah, maybe we'll be trading off to Rhodes even. That'd be a good dream, eh?

Zedeck nudged Macanra who muffled in agreement. Not understanding, he nudged him again then said, "Your turn." Macanra shrugged and began.

Some say we stink but I can never tell, just smells like home that's all.

Have ya ever spun wool Ariadne? See that was my first memory: watching me Mama spinning the wool off our sheep. Papa's gotten me up with the sheep doing stuff since I could run about. Why I helped him shear them the other day. Pesky ones are sheep. You gotta watch out for 'em. They'll go you so they will.

I've had to get up before the dawn sometimes. It can be a rotten job. The worst is when he puts you on guard duty. Fending off those wolves all throughout the night, never knowing if they're coming or where they are. You can always tell though—the sheep smell them a mile off and get jittery.

"You've never had to fight a wolf Macanra!"

"Hmph. Well I've just gotten luck so far. Papa says they're out there."

"His papa sends him outside all night after he nicks off and spends the day with us. Seems to be an uncommon number of wolf sightings whenever his papa's annoyed with him…" Adro whispered to Ariadne who chuckled despite everything.

"Well if you're not listening, I'll say nothing then." Macanra grumbled into silence.

"Come on Emeko, your turn." Ariadne cheerfully said to the quiet member following behind. Emeko walked a few steps faster to get closer to the group then softened again to a steady rhythm. He began.

I grew up in the palace at Malia. Guess it's not as big as Knossos but we've got one all the same. You've just seen the outskirts of it, the town around it. Papa was a soldier. He's almost retired now. He's spending the last few years on formal duties inside the palace rather than having adventures abroad.

He used to tell me stories, of being away. He was the chief guard to the governor on Thera at one point. He even told me once how he went raiding. They sailed west for a while and found some people living on an ocean of sand. He says they wore furs instead of clothes and fought wildly but Papa and his men beat them and sailed back home.

Papa doesn't tell me those stories anymore. I never saw him that much, only at winter times when he was back in Crete. Mama was nice though. She cared about me. Sometimes when Papa would come back they would send me outside. I stayed back once and overheard them; they were shouting. They were yelling at each other. I heard Papa shout and then I heard tears. I realised though, they weren't Mama's tears, but his. That night she had some bruises on her face.

Anyway, Mama got a cough about three years back. She didn't last the winter. I woke up one morning and she was just there, lying in bed, not moving. Papa stopped going on adventures at that point, stayed home to look after me I reckon. He doesn't say much though, doesn't tell me stories anymore and he's grumpy often. I'd be happy to stay up all night in the dark as a punishment but he just beats me instead.

"Why do you guys sneak off together if you get punished for it?" Ariadne asked.

"Dunno. something to do. Everyone's gotta have a break sometimes. Kids more than others." Adro replied. "You ever nicked off Ariadne?"

"Oh, once or twice," he caught the glint in her eye, lit up by the dancing flames, "you know how it is. Adro, Adro your turn." As Adro cleared his throat, about to speak, a hint of light emerged as they passed a corner. They quickened their pace as it got closer.

"Looks like I'll have to tell you some other time. We made it!"

Adro passed the torch to the others as they raced past him to the entrance, still a while off. For Ariadne had tugged at his hand and slowed her pace. With the fleeing torch getting further away with every breath, they were once again in darkness.

Adro stood there, unsure of what to do. In the middle of a heartbeat, he felt Ariadne's cool, searching hand find his face. It rested there, on his cheek, for a moment. Guided by the sight it gave her, she saw all in the darkness and moved in. He felt her kiss before the still air between them had time to give way. Blind, yet seeing all he needed to, Adro returned her gift and wrapped his arm around her. When they eventually paused, she uttered into his ear a soft, but audible, "Thank you."

Seven

It was a faster journey down the mountain. Trees tried to stop their path, cluttering the way before them. But these they could see—they were nothing compared to the total darkness of the cave before. No-one turned as Adro and Ariadne finally left the cave, they had already started walking. Instead, the rest simply quickened their pace.

The first thing Adro noticed was the lack of noise. There was no trace of the constant rumbling of the night before, though the sky was still dark and seething. Really it seemed nothing more than a storm cloud… the size of the sky and lit with fire. A storm cloud without a storm, just sitting there, waiting. He mused to himself, *Have we reached the calm after the storm—or a lull within it?*

While Adro stepped along, lost in thought, the rest managed to lose themselves with talk of the trees and shrubs around them. Although some of the trees had taken part in the chance to dance for themselves, many remained still standing. The boys pointed out the survivors to Ariadne, asking her if she knew any of them.

At last she got sick of patiently answering them,

"I don't know! I think I saw it on the way here from Knossos. How am I supposed to know what it's called? As if it's important." They were not taken back, however, and moved to talking of the various shrubs they spotted along the way.

"Did you see that, Ariadne? It's a Frostbottle." Macanra proudly declared.

"Why is it called that?" she asked, actually interested.

"Because, if you eat it, you shiver then you die," Macanra said, just as proud.

"Charming."

"Oi Ariadne, check out this—" Zedeck was cut off by a less than cheerful Ariadne.

"I don't care! I will never need to know the names of Malian plants. It's useless." Ariadne almost ran into the back of Emeko who, along with the others, had stopped in shock because of her impatience. "I mean, sorry. Let's just talk about something else. I've been meaning to ask; how did you find me?"

They started walking once more and the rest of the boys looked to Adro who cleared his throat, almost nervously, and then began.

"My house isn't that far from yours. Everyone in the street heard a woman wailing. I was still up so I went to our window to see what was happening. I saw you being led off through the streets by those men. Even if your mother hadn't kept sobbing I would have known that something was up. Some of the neighbours had gone and knocked on your front door but your father appeared and told them everything was ok."

"I didn't believe it however. I went and got the lads. First, I went to Emeko's house because Macanra was staying with him overnight. Then we went down to the docks to find Zedeck. We were rushing so Macanra slipped and fell in."

"Oi!" Macanra interrupted then promptly blushed. While Ariadne chuckled, Adro continued.

"Once we got Zedeck, we ran off in the direction I saw them leave. Macanra is a pretty good tracker and he found their trail once we left the city. See, his papa is always sending him to find sheep that have run away all throughout the hills. Sometimes we make a game where he as to try and find us. Anyway, he found their trail and we tracked it to the cave. That's when we knew things were serious. No-one has gone in that cave for years, not even us. No-one that I know of anyway. We figured taking a girl for a ritual in an abandoned cave seemed pretty suss, even though your papa was fine with it."

"Each of us picked up a few rocks at the entrance then we walked into the cave. We were going along pretty comfortably even without a torch. Then we heard your scream. We ran and found the sanctuary and we figured they couldn't hurt us if they couldn't see us so we pelted them with rocks from the darkness, as you well know…"

There were tears in Ariadne's eyes as Adro finished speaking. As soon as he mentioned entering the cave, all the horror came back to her; enveloped her like the darkness when she entered. She was silent for some minutes but, hating the silence as much as anything else, and the thoughts it left rambling through her mind, she started another round of conversation.

"What do you think is happening with the sky? Why is it still so dark and angry?" Ariadne asked.

Zedeck glanced accusingly at Adro who turned his face away and kept walking. Zedeck frowned then faced Ariadne and began, "Last night, Ariadne, when Adro came banging on our doors he told us he'd overheard his papa talking to someone. He heard his father say Crete was going to end; that the sky is a sign and that's what it means."

"How can his papa know that?" Ariadne asked, irritated.

"He's the High Priest of Malia." Ariadne stared at Adro. He seemed so simple, so normal. She was a priestess, true, but that was one thing. Anyone could become a priest or priestess. The High Priests were almost royalty and the High Priestesses, well, some said they were almost goddesses.

"Papa said 'It will not be enough, we need to leave Crete.' I didn't know what he meant until we got there but I think, maybe, he was talking about you..." Adro quietly explained.

"Anyway," Zedeck continued before Ariadne had a chance to relive the chill down her spine, "when Adro came to our house he told Papa about the warning. He asked Papa if he could round up our families throughout the night and take them to the ships in his fishing boat. Adro thinks his father will know what to do, and that he'll organise the fleet to do something."

"So?" Ariadne inquired, confused. "What do we do?"

"Oh." Zedeck answered. "I was coming to that. We are planning to meet at my house and take Papa's boat to one of the ships. Before then, we plan to visit your house and find your family to bring them along too. See, Papa didn't know where it was."

Zedeck finished speaking just as they reached the edges of Malia. Upon entering the forest of crafted stone, Ariadne noticed the people around her. She saw the occasional hurried family buzzing towards the sea. Fathers carried children, not on their shoulders but cowering in their arms. Mothers dragged children by the hand, turning and scolding them if they made more than a whisper. The children, meanwhile, were silent for the most part. Those who cried out were dragged faster than they could comfortably walk, with a tighter grip than was reassuring.

Although there were such families edging towards the sea, they were not the most common sight. Mostly, Ariadne saw barred shutters over windows and doors, usually open by this hour but instead firmly shut. Often, they also saw plumes of smoke rising from the rooftops, signalling that most had just decided to forgo the day's festival. They continued winding their way through the streets amidst the stillness, occasionally punctured by the sound or sight of another scuttling family.

Eventually they emerged from the clustered stone forest into a clearing, and a familiar house. Ariadne stared at it. *Strange, how something can become familiar in such a short space of time.* She tried to imagine what they were doing inside. *Were they fighting constantly? Mama angry and Papa defending himself? Were they just sitting there in gloomy misery or in expectation? Was there a slight hope left in their hearts that I would come back, or had that too been taken away? Would they even be there?*

Ariadne stopped herself in thought. *Do I want them to be there? Even if Papa does hope I'll come back somehow, do I want to return?* She stopped then and thought for the first time about her father, his reassuring face as he sent her off, despite her mother's gasping tears. *He must have known. How could he?! He is my FATHER! How… how could he? How could he?* She trembled over that one thought, as lost as when she was stumbling around in the cave.

Eventually, Ariadne turned, with tears in her eyes, and walked down a side street. The rest followed her. They rushed up to her, confused, and Adro spoke.

"Why aren't we getting your family?"

"I HATE him. I will never see him again." Ariadne said more to herself than those listening horrified. "I have no father."

Adro paused then spoke softly.

"What about your mother?"

"And what about Nana too?" Ariadne turned and shouted, glaring at him. "They are with him. I… I can't risk it. What if he takes me and sends me back to the cave? Not even that. How *could* I stand to see him again?" Tears rolled down her cheeks then, in great heaving sobs. "*I can't* see them…" she said as if only just realising it, "I can't see them ever again."

"What if we knock on the door? Maybe he'll be sleeping or out or something?" Adro pleaded.

Ariadne stopped in mid-step. Froze. Her mind suddenly all too aware of the decision she was making. *Separated for life? What if this is the last chance, my last chance to see her? She promised to find me; surely I should try it. Surely? I can't not.* Ariadne took a breath.

And kept walking.

***

Meanwhile, in Garnia's run-down home, there sat two people. They sat there not talking nor making food nor carving stone. They didn't stare at each other, they were not staring at anything. Both merely had the blank look of someone who was beyond staring, save into their shattered heart.

Both Mariaten and Garnia had been sitting for some time. Hours had come and gone and thoughts occasionally drifted in and out of their minds. These were lost, vague thoughts— nothing relevant, nothing to be remembered; vague wisps. They had cooked at some point, well, they is stretching it. Garnia had been able to muster some energy that morning.

The fight had been the night before. It did not start until well into the night, when every last drop had drained from Mariaten's eyes. Spirysidos had not moved for the first hour, save to open the door and lie to unknown strangers asking him if everything was alright. *Of course everything is alright. Our world has just ended that yours might not.* He tried to touch her once, a loving arm around the shoulder. Surprisingly, he survived having it almost torn off. He almost cried then, *She won't forgive me, will she?* Almost cried for the loss of his daughter and, it seemed, his wife as well. He couldn't cry though, even a single tear would be to admit to Mariaten that he had made the wrong decision. And, even if he had, he couldn't change it now.

Eventually though, she spoke.

"Get out!"

"This is my mother's house," he replied, unsure of how to tactfully put the situation.

"Get OUT! Get out of my life, you monster!" *Monster? Don't you see? You who know more tales about the gods than anyone. Why can't you understand?*

"Mari—" he tried but failed.

"Don't *talk* to me. Don't *look* at me. Don't *touch* me."

As Spirysidos stared at the fire, dazed and shocked by her words, he heard footsteps creep down the stairs. Garnia walked off the last step with a soft thud, looked at both Mariaten and Spirysidos and sat down.

"Now dears, what is the matter? If you can survive starting your life again in Knossos I'm sure you'll get through whatever's troubling you. Stop anyway—you'll wake Ariadne."

While Mariaten found room for more tears, Spirysidos replied.

"Mother, there's something I have done…" Garnia looked eagerly at him despite the horror on both of their faces.

"We've all been tempted, Spiry. I know it hurts, Mariaten, but I'm sure he still loves you. In time every mistake is healed." Garnia butted in, convinced she had guessed correctly.

"Not this mistake." Mariaten muttered furiously.

"That's what they all say, dear."

"It's not about another woman," Spirysidos said with less joy than usually accompanies such a statement.

"What then?"

The argument lasted almost the whole night after they told Garnia. When Mariaten was lost for words, as happened more often than not that night, Garnia would pick up the slack and strangle her son with it. Although no-one gave in, they eventually ended it in the small hours of the morning. Garnia's last words as she stamped up the stairs cut Spirysidos deeper than he thought possible, as if there was any room left to wound.

"You are no son of mine."

Everyone awoke that day with a grimness only partly blameable on a lack of sleep. As Mariaten plodded down the stairs and sat at the cold stone table she felt, for the first time in many years, a lack of her daughter's presence. It was in the morning, when the day was still to come, when she always saw her daughter. She felt a growing ache; a space once filled, one she couldn't bear to lose, torn from her nonetheless. Garnia came down quietly and started up the fire, reheating a stew. Spirysidos emerged from his bedroom as they were eating. Mariaten had slept in Ariadne's room, not only because a hint of her daughter's smell was the only thing that could put her to sleep. As Spirysidos walked into the icy stillness of the room before him, he dared to speak.

"Any left?"

Mariaten didn't seem to hear him, she just kept sitting there, eating silently. Garnia had heard him though. She rose menacingly, walked over to her son and spat straight in his face. She then sat back down.

"I'm going to the beach. I'm going to see if the sky has cleared," he declared with the thinnest facade of composure.

"You mean you're going to see if it worked?" Mariaten hissed. "You're going to see if letting those men kill our daughter has done anything."

He looked at her for a moment, unable to speak, then he left. For the first time since he last saw Ariadne, Spirysidos wept. His tears didn't stop flowing even when he passed the dockyard, or when he reached the water at last.

Meanwhile, Mariaten and Garnia merely sat there, in silence.

***

Every footstep Ariadne took tightened her resolve. Her feet were chisels and every step she took chipped away at the life she had known. And she continued. Not even Adro dared to speak; the boys merely followed her silent lead ahead. After some time, they emerged at the markets. Stalls were deserted. everything was either covered over or had been taken away, leaving only a bare shop behind. As they walked through, Emeko lifted the occasional lid searching for anything left behind.

"They can't all know that it's all about to end. Why is it deserted?" Macanra inquired.

"I suppose the merchants think people will either be inside or at the festival," Zedeck replied. "Maybe they're right."

"You mean people will still go along to see it?" Ariadne asked.

"It's possible," Adro butted in, "I mean it's all a bit weird but who really knows if it's anything more than a bit of a storm? Maybe Papa got it wrong."

At the mention of the one who organised her sacrifice, Ariadne was once again stunned into an unforgiving silence. The rest of them quickly followed suit and walked on as before. Ariadne didn't so much as remember the path to the dock in her mind but in her feet. Hands by darkness and now feet by light, her body seemed to guide her through the world around. There was one thing she noticed though, the sea was nowhere in sight. If she peered out to the horizon Ariadne thought she could just make it out but all around the docks there was nothing but damp sand.

Zedeck led the way once they reached the dock. Although the rest of the group had lulled into a gloomy march, he all but skipped towards his father's house, cheerful despite everything.

Upon finally seeing it in the distance, Zedeck noticed a man sitting patiently outside, mending a net. Forgetting the rest of the group for a moment Zedeck rushed forward, sprinting at his father. That time he spent in the cave had changed him. Zedeck felt that he had witnessed a hint of just how fragile life could be. Ariadne hadn't helped matters either, seeing her just walk past her home, with not even a tear, had spooked him; frightened him and shaken his belief that things would always stay the same.

Zedeck collided with his father. It was a close call—he had only just risen from his seat, only just braced himself for the charging child a heartbeat away. Their embrace only ended as the others arrived. Zedeck's father looked down at the group, confused, then asked,

"Where's her parents?" Ariadne stared at him with a coldness she didn't know she possessed.

"It's just us." Adro replied quickly. Zedeck's father paused for a moment then shrugged.

"Eh, suit yourselves. We haven't got time to waste. We have to leave, now."

Zedeck looked pleadingly at his father and said what all the rest were thinking.

"We've been up all night and haven't eaten anything. Please, Papa, just give us enough time to get a bit of food."

Zedeck's father looked out at the wet sand and frowned deeply. He turned and pointed to the fishing net he was mending, "You have until I finish the row."

Zedeck nodded and raced past his father into the shack. The others followed him behind, Ariadne scrunching her face in curiosity as she tried to understand what was happening. Zedeck began rummaging through amphorae stacked against a wall, while Macanra, Emeko and Adro elbowed each other to be first in line when he found something.

"Zedeck," Ariadne began, "why are we rushing? What's wrong with the sea?"

Zedeck fumbled, dropping a lid though thankfully it didn't shatter; it simply bouncing along the wooden floorboards. He looked up at her.

"Papa used to tell me the sea was like a child. As soon as it got bored doing one thing it would do the opposite."

"Meaning?" Ariadne asked.

"Sooner or later the sea will come back," he said nervously. "And we won't want to be here when it does..."

***

"People don't know what we are doing. They don't seem to care. Don't look scared and, whatever you do, don't warn them. We don't have enough room in the boat to take many more, that's just how it is. Understand?" Those were the last words Zedeck's father had said before they left his house. They had all nodded solemnly and walked out in a sombre mood.

Now they were put to the test. Each pair of curious eyes that stared at them caused Ariadne to shudder and quicken her step. *They'll be ok. Maybe. Well it's like he said, if it isn't ok we don't have enough room anyway.* Ariadne marched to the water's edge more disciplined than a veteran in an honour guard. The sweat-stained muscles of the others had no rest as they put the boat down into the water and pushed it for a time through the shallows. Each of them jumped in after a moment's rest, ready to row out to the ships in the distance.

Although it was obvious that Zedeck was the only boy who knew which way to face when rowing, let alone how to do it, the others picked it up with an excited determination. Despite the seriousness of the past day, they were merely boys again, learning anther game. Ariadne enjoyed herself too. She stared back across the boat, past the eager rowers to the beach beyond. She looked back at them and, after witnessing their ingrained "ability" for rhythm, decided to help with the beat.

"And one, and one, and one and—" she stopped.

Ariadne was not out of breath, but she had noticed something on the beach:

A figure, a lone man, racing through the crowd into the shallows, racing towards the boat.

Her throat tightened as she saw his face. It clenched as if she was being strangled once he shouted.

"Ariadne! A-ri-ad-ne!" her name boomed over the waves.

Emeko, Zedeck, Macanra and Adro all stopped rowing after they finished their current stride. Zedeck's father stopped a stroke later, curiosity getting the better of him too. Spirysidos kept going however, encouraged by their stillness, and quickly closed the gap between them. The water was just below his shoulders when he finally stopped, quite a feat for a man who couldn't swim. He was still too far to reach out and touch the daughter he thought he'd never see again. He was close enough, however, for her to hear every word.

"Ariadne! Dear child! They've brought you back to me! They have accepted the offer but were merciful! Why it's more than I could have hoped for, dear little one."

"Look around you, Papa," Ariadne said quietly with only a hint of the menace she felt, "it wasn't those gods you sent me off to die for that saved me but these boys you see here now." He looked at the daughter who had not known where she was going. He saw understanding in her eyes of what he had done, *oh yes, she knew*.

"You are safe, dear one," he edged closer, "brought back to me," he said with outstretched arms.

"Do you know what you did?!" she screamed at him then. "You sent me to *die*. Gave your only child to the whim of a scent sniffing priest."

"Can't you understand, dear? Sometimes the gods require sacrifices…"

"*How could you?*" Her face was a frightening mix of tear-stained patterns glittering in the sun and contorted muscles in agony. "What right had you?"

"I am your father," he all but whispered. *This is our world. This is how it works. Girls honour their father's wishes and sometimes we need sacrifices we don't want to give. Why can't anyone understand me?* "I did what I thought was right."

"*You didn't think!* Any thinking father would have weighed up my life higher than the whims of some old gods we never see. How can you say your choice came from thinking? It was thoughtless! Mindless! Giving in to fear."

"But the gods, Ariadne—"

"Death to the gods, Father!" He stared at her, helplessly lost. "If these boys could save me from your gods then they aren't worth honouring. They are weak. Maybe that is why Crete is ending… maybe the world is sick of us and our gods."

Spirysidos looked at her, dumfounded.

"I am sick of them anyway, Father, whether the world is or not. I'm sick of Crete and, Father, I'm sick of you."

Spirysidos slumped back, arms slack at his side. He mustered a feeble,

"But—" only to be cut off by his daughter.

"I died to you in that cave!" Ariadne mustered all her pain, all the terror she had felt in those few seconds with that knife pressing against her throat. "Go! I have no father!"

Silence stemmed forth from father and daughter alike.

Stillness stayed in the arms of boys and man gripping damp oars.

"Row!" Ariadne whispered.

"Row!" Louder.

"ROW! Row! Row! Row! Come on, one and one and one and one."

Spooked into action by her words and haunted by the spectre behind them, the rowers jolted into a fast but synchronised rhythm. They started panting but didn't slow down, not even when the sweat started to flow. Ariadne, with no further role now that the boat was on its way, crawled into the corner of the prow. She sat there, hunched into a ball, feeling the sick, churning feeling in her gut rise at every cry of her father. For the boat holding his daughter, rowing further and further away, had spurred him from silence. He could not travel out any further so he channelled his helpless plea not into actions but words. As the fishing boat edged over the water towards the ships anchored in the distance, his shrill voice could be heard, even if it faded with every stroke. A short repetitive wail pierced all who sat aboard that boat. The constant cry of,

"Ariadne!"

Eight

Aching muscles and the boys that held them breathed a sigh of relief as their boat gently knocked against the ship. There had been excited shouts as passengers who had taken the trip the previous night saw what they had been waiting all day for, their children's return. Voices had grown hoarse long before their hands reached over the sides of the small decks to bring the eager rowers aboard. Ariadne's by now salt-stained hair whipped into her eyes as she was hauled onto the ship by an unknown arm. Before she could push it from her face Macanra and Zedeck were yelling at her impatiently.

"Ariadne! Ariadne! Come and meet my parents!"

"No, over here! Mine are closer."

"At least mine don't smell like goats!"

"Sheep! And besides, she's already met your papa."

Ariadne felt torn, quite literally; pulled in two directions and stretched thinner than her frazzled temper preferred.

"Stop! One at a time. Yes, Zedeck I've already met your papa so I'll see Macanra's first." Macanra beamed as if she were a prize ram to show off to all the shepherds of Malia. He walked towards his father with an air of confidence, almost swaggering. The hard slap his father gave, once within striking distance, shocked him back to reality.

"Son, don't go off without asking me. How many times do I have to tell you? I should be giving you another one for bringing a girl back before your time. What's your name, girl, anyway?"

"Ariadne, sir," she replied, "daughter of Spirysidos." She stopped. It was an old habit, one she had repeated countless times. She took a breath and started again, "Of Mariaten. It's good to meet you."

"She seems alright. Didn't see her doing any rowing though. What is she, a princess? She's way out of your league, boy." Macanra's gaping grin had sprung back to life a few seconds after he had been hit. It slowly faded though with every word his father spoke.

"She's not my girl anyway, just a friend," he mumbled quietly.

"Well, you seem lovely, dear," Macanra's mother declared. "It will be good to have another woman aboard. I'm sure we'll get on fine." Until she spoke, Ariadne had not noticed the woman standing in the shadow of the bulky farmer before her. She had not noticed any of the women aboard that boat. Now, seeing those mothers before her, Ariadne suddenly felt the pain in her gut return. She muttered something polite in reply and moved away.

Ariadne couldn't bear to stare back at the beach behind her nor could she stand to meet another obliviously friendly mother. She went and sat down at the edge of the deck next to the men hauling the fishing boat aboard. The rest simply ignored her, happy to be reunited and chatter away. She heard somebody quiet them after a few minutes and then speak,

"Now that we have those we promised to wait for, let's be off. We can still catch the rest of the ships if we cast off soon. It will take them longer to row in formation and, besides, I requested that they keep a slow pace until we rejoined them. So, men, to your seats."

While the loud man was busy giving orders, Ariadne noticed Zedeck's father talk to a woman. Another woman, presumably another mother. *Oh great, now you're coming over to me. Go away! No, don't come over here. Don't come—no just—please—*

"Hello there." *Perfect.*

"Hello." Ariadne replied. *Wonderful, lovely chat, can I go now? Would you believe there's somewhere I've got to be? Anywhere… but here.*

"Poor girl, you're not alright, are you? Not by a long shot." The woman had been staring into her eyes. *You can't know what I'm thinking. Go away!* She sat down next to Ariadne, carefully and close, too close.

"Get off me!" Ariadne had skipped the warning hand and gone straight for elbow to the face. The woman just sat there, took the blow without complaining then, after a moment, opened her slightly bleeding mouth.

"I heard about what happened. You must be feeling more horrible than I can imagine." Ariadne just stared forward at the ground. "Firstly, I heard about the man who ran out into the water. Your father, Ariadne…" She still stared defiantly, yet she didn't flinch as a warm, clean arm wrapped itself around her shoulder. "Zedeck then told me about the cave. You poor girl… come here." Ariadne dived into her arms then and rocked there as the ship started to cut through the water.

They sat there for hours, not moving, not thinking and, best of all, not even feeling. They were just a numb pair bobbing to the rhythm of the waves. Eventually, after what seemed like an eternity of peace, they were disturbed by another who came and sat down beside them. Adro sat on the other side of Ariadne and didn't speak, didn't even move. Ariadne turned her face slightly to see who had disturbed them. She didn't say anything but moved her arm towards him. She reached for his hand, and held it tightly.

The ship started to rock over the next few minutes. What had been a calm sea, bare and flat before them, was now churned up and foamy. The ship bobbed precariously to every wave that had emerged and surged beneath it. As the ship writhed under the fury of the waters, the sailors turned to get one final look at their homeland.

Turned, to see a wave forming from out of the storm.

Turned, to see the wave surging towards Malia. And, what's more, the fire in the sky seemed to stay there no longer. It too seemed to rain down on that poor village.

"The girl! It is the girl." Ariadne looked up.

Adro's hand tightened.

The loud man who had ordered everyone to start rowing had re-appeared. Instead of stamping around the ship, feeling important and yelling at the men around him, the frightening figure was towering over Ariadne and shouting more to himself than her.

"Father…" Adro interrupted the hypnotic stare of the man before them. Quick, intelligent eyes, now brought back to reality, bored down into him. He felt them pierce him long before that booming voice, which he knew only too well, began again. This time it thundered around, commanding the ears of all on the ship.

"This is the one the gods spoke of. They came to me, men of Crete. They warned me."

Adro shook his head in fear.

"This child was shown to me. They told me Crete would fall. They told me your families would die in agony, that all we knew would perish; that there would be utter destruction." All eyes stared at Adro's father, the high priest of Malia. The wind picked up to match the fury of the waves but his voice boomed over it. Indeed, it seemed to harness it, to carry every sound crisp and terrifyingly clear to everyone on board. "They said all this would happen, if we did not give them this girl."

Eyes stopped staring at the priest but darted to the quivering child.

"It is not too late. The wave is our final warning. If we do not send her into the sea it will continue and, in its anger, destroy Malia. And Malia will only be the first. The whole of Crete will be ravaged by the gods' fury if we do not stop it, now."

Soldiers stared at her. Many had not been home in six months, some for a year or longer. Despite the time though, it was not hard for them to picture the faces of those waiting behind. The closest few oarsmen pulled themselves up and started walking solemnly over towards Ariadne.

"You can't do this, Father! The gods don't care about her. When we saved her from the cave—"

"You did what?! You have put our people in jeopardy, my son. You are young so I will forgive you your folly, but now I must put things right." He stared at the other rowers and called out to them, "Today, right now, we save Crete, men. You save Crete."

The men were almost upon her and she stared up at them, defiantly calm.

"Look at me." She commanded. Her voice was as soft as the priest's was loud, yet it was even harder to resist. The closest soldier couldn't help but glance. "Right now, I am your daughter." She rose and stared at the others coming towards her. "I am your son, your wife. I am your parents and family and friends. I am the child you didn't know you had when you left your wife with a hopeful kiss."

They looked at her, confused.

"This man tried to have me killed by night, in the darkest depths of the earth. Now he commands you to do his deed when even the darkness recoiled from it." She stood taller and stared up into the priest's eyes. "I ask you, do not be darker than the darkness; when you reach for me think of the loved one you are trying to save and imagine them here in my place."

A heartbeat.

And another.

And then a hand reached for her. A soldier drew close and grabbed Ariadne's shoulder—only to have a hand clasp around the side of his neck. The fellow soldier it belonged to stared menacingly at him and spoke.

"Put her down. She's right. How do we know the gods would stop anyway? I wouldn't let my son take her place, I'd kill every last bastard here before I let you touch a hair on his head." The soldier being slowly strangled somehow managed to relax. The rest of them stopped edging towards her and just stood there, still. Adro's father, alone, seemed unfazed and full of fury.

"It must be done! Otherwise Crete will fall. We must sacrifice the girl." Adro rose then and stared at his father. He shouted at him with a voice close to breaking.

"If there's anyone who should be thrown over, Papa, it's you!" Ariadne saw, for the second time that day, a father slump in the face of his child's hatred. This second father stood there in the howling wind, unmoving like all the rest. Eventually he whispered an agonising,

"So be it."

***

The waves died down after another hour of tossing the ship around. Once the calm came, the quiet soldiers returned to their oars sombrely. Ariadne felt more exhausted than ever before, eyelids fluttering as she was led below deck. Adro placed her down into a hammock and whispered to her as her mind fled to emptiness,

"Don't worry. I'll watch over you."

Meanwhile, on deck a ship was spotted in the distance. It didn't take long before one ship became many as the Cretan fleet came into view. Men rowed harder seeing friends in the distance and the gap between the ships quickly narrowed. In no time at all, their ship was side by side with one of the ships of the fleet.

As Adro's father called out across the crashing of the waves, telling of the destruction of Crete, Ariadne awoke in the darkness of the hull. She awoke to a racing heart and freshly trickling sweat. She awoke, hearing the sound of her father calling across the waves,

"*Ariadne!*"

PART TWO

Nine

Sand. Swirling sand. Shapeless and shimmering then still and silent. Secretly deadly and always unforgiving. This is the land we have come to.

Ariadne turned from the harsh desert gaping through the window before her. She turned as if she could simply walk away from the path that led them through those sands. Turned as if she could sit in peace, forgetting the war they unleashed. She turned in vain as every grain of sand which blew through brought the past back with a gritty clarity.

The wind blew stronger and Ariadne rose, quickly tying her papyrus scrolls before hastily snatching the bundle. She would not relive it again. Ariadne steadied herself as she walked from her office and out into the corridor. With her head unwaveringly straight and her footsteps a slow rhythmic pace, Ariadne felt her composure return. As she passed room after room of busily working scribe, those within instinctively hunched over their tasks with a renewed vigour. Well, an attempt at vigour—in Egypt scribes weren't really known for that particular quality.

Having reached the edge of the corridor, Ariadne turned sharply and spoke even before she was seen.

"Habshut I will be leaving for the court earlier today. I can't stand sitting in here any longer." Ariadne's deputy fought not to roll her eyes at her master's constant restlessness. *Why a scribe? No amount of buzzing around the hive will be enough for this one.*

She needs to be free. "The reports Habshut, are they the same as the ones I have read?"

"Each province sends the same news: the Nile has barely flooded this year. It hasn't been this low for centuries." Ariadne paused then replied.

"Then it is time to tell the pharaoh. He will want to know."

"He has failed us then…" Habshut whispered.

"Quiet with your people's superstitions! All will be well. My pharaoh is your god," Ariadne said mockingly, "he will fix it. He won't let your people starve." This time Habshut did roll her eyes. She had gotten used to Ariadne's callous disregard for her gods a long time ago. Still, she didn't always enjoy her little quips.

"It's too late. He can distribute as much grain as he likes, if the Nile doesn't flood then the gods have deserted him. We all know this to be true."

Ariadne dropped her reports on Habshut's table silently. She slowly raised her head to look at her friend, this time the creases of worry were showing on her face. In a rare moment of openness she rarely showed to her deputy, Ariadne answered,

"Yes, maybe you are right, but we will see what can be done."

Once more resuming the confident demeanour of her corridor stroll, Ariadne turned and walked out into the courtyard. Seeing the passages across the courtyard never failed to remind her of Knossos. *Mazes, mazes are in my blood, they are a part of me.* As she strolled through the scent of blooming flowers, she tried to stop the memories flooding back. She breathed in deeply and exhaled slowly, savouring the rich aroma around her. As it was deserted Ariadne relaxed her strict walk; her professional facade. She let her hands free from staying by her side, let them wander to touch the plants as she strolled by. It would have worked if not for the wind which blew through the courtyard carrying grains of sand into her hair. Her calm, so painfully fought for, was shattered. *Can I never escape this infernal sand?* Ariadne felt each grain and was again reminded of the first day she set foot there. It seemed as if those early years were nothing but hardship and the desert and, of course, the unrelenting sand-strewn wind. Another gust came through and, with it, the torrent she sought to avoid.

Ten

(Thirteen years earlier)

Ariadne slowly climbed up from the hull, still shaking. It was the third time she had had that dream in as many nights. She wondered if she could ever rest again without being haunted by that face—the face of her father. It wasn't really his tortured expression that disturbed her, no; the dream was quite pleasant until she woke up. She was escaping from him every night—she could live with that. The sweat only broke as she awoke, every time to that soul piercing cry. It felt like a curse, as if in her efforts to be free he had somehow bound her to him by crying out her name. That is what scared her, the feeling that she might just see him again.

Shaking her head to clear her mind, Ariadne welcomed the fresh sea breeze as it quickly swept through her, at once ridding her of her sweat and dark thoughts. She turned around for a second or two before glimpsing the boys. They had been put to good use, each one doing his part to help row the ship. They were even cheerful about it. *How could you be cheerful about sailing away from home?* Ariadne didn't understand but they seemed either oblivious or resigned. She sighed, maybe she should be resigned to the future as well.

As she had nothing much to do, Ariadne sat at the prow of the ship and stared out watching the fleet travel across the ocean. She was entranced the first time she had watched their armada.

Now the mystery had faded. She felt the straining muscles of men she could barely see each time the oars plunged into the water. She sat there for a while watching the laborious pattern repeat itself, content that she was not a part of it. Eventually, one of the ships in front slowed down to row beside them. A message was hoarsely shouted over the now narrow gap between the two ships.

"The admiral wishes to board. Slow down. He wants to inspect the newcomers."

The rowers, glad for a break, duly complied and drew their oars in. A plank was placed between the ships and a tall, scarred man stepped over, creaking as he went. No sooner than he had boarded, his eyes darted briefly around and then he spoke.

"All Malian survivors I want to speak to you. The young first then the old, got it?" Adro, Macanra, Emeko and Zedeck all jumped up from their oars and stood proudly in front of him. They stood as if the three days' worth of rowing had already toughened their bodies to look like men. As usual, Adro spoke first.

"Sir, we are the surviving youths of Malia." The admiral looked at each of them briefly then replied.

"Four? I would have expected more but I guess there was never much in Malia to begin with, eh? Guess I had my hopes up. Now lads we're on hard times, I won't deny it. The question now for everyone is, how can I serve Crete? See lads right here, right now, we are Crete. So lads, what do you reckon? How can you serve Crete?"

"We've been rowing this ship for you, sir," Zedeck replied at once. "We're getting pretty good at it if I say so myself." The scars around the admiral's face tightened as what could pass for a smile emerged around his mouth.

"Sure lads, that's a good start. I've got the answer for you: you lads are going to learn to fight. I will need every able man I can get and if you keep the rowing up you'll be strong enough once we reach shore."

"Where are we going sir?"

"Wow fighting!"

"Soldiers!" The boys' excitement rose at the news and they weren't afraid to show it. The wizened smile on the admiral twitched again at their enthusiasm.

"Now lads, I can't say what is going to happen, merely that in uncertain times it pays to have brave men behind you. We may not even need to fight, and pray to whatever gods you believe in that it might be so."

"Gods!" Ariadne scoffed, sitting away from it all, still on the prow. The admiral nodded approvingly at the boys and turned to her.

"A young woman," he paused, "I'd be thinking that you are from Malia as well then?"

"In a manner of speaking." She casually turned around and replied.

"Now, since we have agreed that everyone must pull their weight, and I don't see you rowing along with the rest of us, I wonder what use you could be. We can't afford to carry slackers. We can't feed people who won't do us good in return."

"Yes, yes! Quite useless," a voice rose from the back of the ship in quick agreement, "we should throw the girl overboard straight away and lighten the load of our hard-working rowers."

"Quiet Euouk!" The admiral turned and walked towards Ariadne. "No, give her a year or two, and she'll be worth her weight in gold." As Adro's father slumped down, Ariadne's heart started beating quickly again. "If these young men can be *vigorous* for our survival, you can be *vigorous* in rewarding them, no?" he all but whispered to her. The soft tone frightened her all the more. Ariadne turned and slid back into the boat then stood facing the admiral.

"Admiral, I was a priestess back in Knossos." She started with the obvious, wondering where it would lead her. In an instant she realised and continued with confidence. "And I think that I have a skill even more valuable. I was taught how to write. I only know the basics but that should be enough to help with your records, shouldn't it? You will need people to keep accurate records of food supplies and such things. If things do go well then you might need someone to keep track of all your plunder as well."

The admiral looked at her again, from head to toe, and then replied.

"Yes, you do have the look of a priestess about you. I bet you have never known a day's hard work. No matter. You're in luck girl, I am in need of a few more scribes. You will have your chance. Come aboard my ship when I leave and I'll bury you in reports. You'll earn your keep, don't worry."

Ariadne raced to Adro and the boys as their families talked to the admiral, telling of their various skills and uses. She looked them in the eyes not daring to speak what was creeping into her mind. Adro broke the silence.

"Don't worry Ariadne, we'll see you again. There will be plenty of spare time once we land. It's a good job—take it." He looked into her eyes, pleading. The rest of them quickly nodded their agreement. The admiral was almost ready to leave by the time she had finished hugging each of them. As she started walking across the plank the admiral looked over at the boys and muttered cheerfully to her,

"Hmm, it's not too late. If you want to stay with those lads you can; you might be suited for the other profession. Can't know if you don't try…"

She kicked at his heel as he strode ahead. He didn't miss a step but kept going, seemingly oblivious. Once Ariadne crossed she turned around to wave a final goodbye only to see another figure walk across. He couldn't even manage to fake a smile, he merely grimaced as he met her eyes. Adro's father, Euouk, crossed the plank.

***

Ariadne felt the time creep by as achingly slowly as any heaving rower. The tallies seemed endless and the calculations were tedious at the best of times. Working side by side each day with the man who tried to have her killed didn't help. Euouk didn't even look at her for the most part, he would hand her records when required, always with a grim tone. The rest of the time he simply ignored her. There wasn't much actual record keeping for her to do as they fled Crete. Most of her time was spent going over old records and practicing the careful strokes. Once they landed and started gathering supplies, she would be ready.

When land was finally sighted it was with a great cheer. First from the foremost ship then quickly racing back through the fleet, stirring the rowers for one final push. Ariadne looked up curiously and was amazed as they drew closer. It seemed as if they were sailing to where the edges of two seas met; one of water and one of sand. Euouk didn't even look up, oblivious to her awe, he started speaking,

"The admiral wants us to go back through the records and make an accurate tally of our food and the number of mouths to feed. He wants to know how long we can survive living off

merchants." He dropped a large number of tablets at her feet. "This is your pile—report to me with the figures once you have sorted through."

"How does he know there are merchants here, let alone people?"

"Do you think an admiral of the Cretan navy would just sail off in a random direction?" Euouk paused for a moment, for once chuckling, "We're in Egypt, girl."

"What's that?" Ariadne asked, having only heard vague stories of other lands. Euouk turned to her and his sadistic chuckle became a sickly smile.

"It doesn't matter what it was, girl. What matters is what we make it to be." Ariadne turned away and shuddered.

Meanwhile while Ariadne began sorting through her tablets and the first of the fleet started landing, the admiral stared out intensely at the land they had come to. He thought to himself as he saw his people step foot on this new land, *now all we do is wait.*

The waiting did not last long, by the evening a hasty delegation had come to see who had dared to land so many ships on their coast. While they marched confidently down to the ships carrying blazing torches, the flames were nothing compared to the anger inside them, to the fear. The delegation did not have to walk far for the admiral had set up his tent at the edge of the camp. He had also set up torches all around it, a beacon beckoning them to him. He stood outside the tent, waiting for them as Ariadne, and the rest of the scribes working by lamplight, peered out from within.

The delegation stopped outside the tent and a man stepped forth, robed in arrogance and confidence. He opened his mouth and, to Ariadne's ears, nothing but gibberish came out. To her surprise the admiral replied in what seemed like gibberish as well.

The envoy paused for a few moments then began again, this time with real words.

"Shall we speak with this tongue then?"

"That would please me greatly," the admiral replied. "My Egyptian is not too good. I am Apepios, admiral of the Cretan navy. Our land has been ravaged by our gods and I have brought the survivors to your people. I was hoping your pharaoh could help us. Our peoples have been tied together by trade for many years; I hope our friendship will only grow in this hard time."

"What does the hyksos of the Keftiu expect of the Great King of Upper and Lower Egypt, the Mighty Bull, He who is strong of arm, the oppressor of the nine bows, Ra incarnate, son of Ra— Seqenenra? What do you wish of us Apepi, and what will you do for us in return?"

Apepios breathed deeply, knowing the importance of the request. He knew their fate may very well hang on convincing this man of their desire for peace.

"Tell your great king that I wish to submit my people as his servants. We will fight in his wars against his enemies; we will be loyal soldiers for him. We will give the lives of our men so that our women and children may live under his protection. He will have no subjects more loyal than us. This is what I ask of your great king."

Now it was the envoy's turn to pause and consider. It wasn't long before he spoke again.

"I thank you for your offer of service on behalf of the Great King. I will carry your message to him and shall give you his answer personally. Until that time though, since you are such a great number of people, I ask that you do not enter our cities— it may cause havoc. Rest assured, while you are waiting I will inform the merchants that they should meet you here."

"As you wish." Apepios replied coolly. "Send my greetings to your king." The messenger nodded then barked an order in gibberish to the men standing silently behind him. They turned and walked off in silence. Apepios waited to see them disappear over a sand dune then promptly entered his tent. He looked at the eyes staring back at him and remembered the task he had set his scribes.

"Alright, so how many weeks can we survive here on this beach, buying from merchants?"

Euouk was about to answer but the chief scribe of the navy cut him off and replied.

"Three weeks admiral, give or take depending on whether the grain is a normal price." Apepios nodded, satisfied.

"Alright scribes, we're done for the night. It's been an important day and the next will be even more so. I want you all up at dawn to get ready to barter with the local merchants once they arrive. Send word throughout the men—anyone who understands the Egyptian speech can have the day off to translate."

As the rest of the scribes left the tent, Ariadne stayed behind with a curious look in her eyes.

"What do you want, girl?" Apepios asked gruffly.

"What do 'hyksos' and 'Keftiu' mean?"

"Ah, quite the little learner aren't we?" Apepios started to put the lamps out and continued. "He didn't know some of our words so he said them in his own tongue. Hyksos means 'foreign ruler' and I guess in a sense I am now, no priests and governors to worry about. Keftiu is what they call Crete. If you are interested in their language you should try learning it. It will be useful in this land, I can promise you that. Now go and let me get some sleep."

Ariadne left Apepios' tent and found the one she had seen the Malian boys set up earlier. She carefully undid the entrance and cautiously popped her head in, scared that she might have the wrong one. To her relief, each figure bore a face she recognised, though each one was snoring away quietly. She coughed to try and wake them and softly called out to each of them in turn.

They slept on, obliviously.

Impatient now, Ariadne tried a different approach. Macanra was, by far, snoring the loudest. It was he whom she decided would wake the others. She carefully pulled herself through the tent and slowly exhaled, then kicked his feet as hard as she could.

"Goat thieves on a windy night!" Macanra exclaimed as he burst wide awake. The others awoke as he stumbled forward in an attempt to catch the phantom thief. They scrambled forward as one, knocking into each other as they all tried to catch the thief who waited patiently at the entrance, smiling in the shadows.

"Hi guys. Mind if I come in?"

Ariadne could see as the moment of realisation hit. It was half a second before they all slumped back on the ground and groaned. Well, not quite all of them. Adro stayed sitting up and didn't groan with the rest.

"Sure, how was your day?"

"Guess what, guess what?" Ariadne chirped as she climbed through the opening, over the sprawl of legs to squish herself beside Adro.

"I know, you left our tent open." Emeko moaned.

"Anyway, guess what I heard the admiral tell the locals?" Emeko groaned again and rose to fasten the tent flap. The rest of the boys stared at her eagerly, wanting her to keep going. "His plan is to make us work as soldiers for the Egyptian king."

"What's Egyptian?" Macanra asked.

"It's the name of the people here. This is their land, I think it's called Egypt."

"Sounds like a good plan," said Emeko as he laid back down, "at least that we all get to be warriors. That sounds exciting."

"But have you thought about it? Apepios told us that we might not have to fight. That sounds like a better deal doesn't it? Why can't we just make pots or something? Haven't enough people already died in Crete without us needing to go killing others?" She tilted her head back and looked at them, earnestly expecting them to agree.

In the silence that followed she thought they were weighing up her question. She was sorely disappointed.

"Who's Apepios?" Zedeck broke the silence.

"Urgh, that's the admiral's name. So, what do you think?"

"I think," Adro began with an air of wisdom, "that this tent is a no-thinking zone." Macanra burst out laughing. "It's not up to us to question the admiral. I'm sure he knows what he's doing."

"But what if they ordered you to kill a harmless, innocent young girl?" Suddenly she was deadly serious. Despite the flap having been secured again, it was as if an icy wind had swept its way into the tent. Adro turned his head so it was barely an inch away from hers and spoke each word very carefully,

"I would refuse and then take up pottery."

"Hmph, just as well." Ariadne rolled over and closed her eyes. The rest of them took it as a signal that they could start breathing again. Macanra was snoring in minutes. Shortly after, with Ariadne sound asleep, Adro placed his hand on her hair and stroked it softly. He rolled over as he heard Emeko and Zedeck holding their breath. He saw them staring at him and glared back for a second before taking his hand from Ariadne's hair and then rolling away from them.

***

It felt to those inside as if only the briefest of moments had passed in the cool darkness of their tent before the flap was wrenched open. This time sunlight beamed through and in popped a bristlier face than had during the night.

"Up with ya pups! You should have been awake hours ago." The soldier noticed Ariadne blinking tiredly back at him along with the rest then continued with a smirk. "Ah, well I'll give you another five minutes then eh…?" His companion was faintly heard as he lowered the flap and they started to walk off,

"Five minutes?! Never took me that long…"

While the others rolled over and savoured the reprieve, Ariadne sat up with a burst of energy. She started scrambling over them in an effort to leave the tent, mumbling as she went.

"Up at dawn he said. Important day he said. Merchants and tallies and food he said." She stumbled out of the tent, tripping in the dust, without a backwards glance or word of goodbye and raced towards Apepios' tent. As she ducked through tents and between similarly busy people she thought of excuses. All of them were forgotten as soon as she arrived since Apepios was occupied, talking to a richly dressed man who stood in the entrance of the tent. Ariadne didn't want to anger him further so stood outside in the already burning sun and waited. To her surprise the man spoke their language perfectly.

"—so yes, in short, I would be delighted to supply my fellow countrymen with grain. You won't get a better price from anyone else I assure you." *Fellow countrymen?* "It has been too long since I have returned home. It would be an honour to help you Apepios and serve our people in their time of need."

Apepios stared at him, satisfied. The merchant stood there, uncertain of whether to leave or keep speaking. Apepios broke the silence. "Thank you, Mepsiad. I will not forget your generosity. Now," he shifted his tone to barely more than a whisper and continued, "I have a delicate question for you. One which requires an understanding of where your true loyalties lie…"

Mepsiad replied immediately, "With Crete first, admiral. Don't doubt me on that."

"Good. Good. Well I want to sound you out on something then, in case things do not go as well with the Egyptians as I hope." Mepsiad nodded and Apepios continued. "I want you to tell me which towns are well guarded and which are not. I want to know if I can expect allies in this land besides the pharaoh. I want to know every scrap of information that might help our people survive. Do you understand?"

"Yes, of course admiral."

"Good. Be off then and get the grain ready for our soldiers. When you come back we will discuss the other matters."

Mepsiad bowed with a smile on his face and replied cheerfully before he turned and left, "May Birchidar favour you in your endeavour."

Ariadne scoffed as she entered and Apepios tilted his head to the side as he saw her.

"Well, well, well. You're late. Find Euouk out the back. He'll find a soldier who can translate for you. We still have a lot of grain to get and a lot of Egyptians to barter with." As she started walking to the back of his tent he continued, "Why do you mock our gods, girl?"

"Let's say they haven't always been good to me in the past."

"Ha, a priestess that has been forsaken by the gods. You're alright, girl. I suppose we have all been forsaken though, otherwise we wouldn't be here. No matter, men can do plenty without the gods. You'll do fine."

Ariadne kept going and turned into a side room where Euouk was patiently interviewing soldiers eager for a day free of hard work. A shrill voice announced the presence of another merchant entering Apepios' tent.

"Apepi, hyksos of the Keftiu, let me tell you of my wares!" Apepios groaned and thought to himself, *bloody Egyptians, can't even get my name right.* He smiled at the merchant and replied,

"Of course, dear friend. I would be delighted."

***

Throtar rose as the vizier entered the antechamber.

"Pharaoh will see you now." Sweat already dripped from Throtar's body. They all knew how important this was. Throtar breathed deeply as he entered Seqenenra's presence. The pharaoh looked and him and spoke immediately after his formal titles were recited.

"Speak then, subject. Tell me what the Keftiu desire."

"My king, they ask that you let them serve in your armies in return for land to settle in and safety for their wives and children."

"A very straightforward request." Seqenenra mused. "What say you vizier, what are your thoughts?"

"Well obviously sire we cannot give them any land in Lower Egypt. We need the fertile fields to feed ourselves; we can't just go giving them away."

Seqenenra paused then replied, "We could send them against Cush and let them settle on the lands they conquer. Who knows, we may either crush Cush once and for all or be rid of these friendly invaders…"

"O Great King, unsurpassed is your wisdom, boundless and infinite in its capacity." The vizier Natash began, "However, if I may make a suggestion?" Seqenenra nodded slightly. "To get to Cush the Keftiu would need to pass through the entire length of Egypt. How do we know they can be trusted? We would be putting you and the tombs of your ancestors in jeopardy if we let them through the heart of our land. It is too great a risk, O Wise and All-knowing King."

"Hmm, what about if we sent them against the nomads of the deserts?"

"If I may remind His Highness; the nomads are rightly scared of us after their last incursion under the reign of your father. They do not journey near our lands in great numbers. This is why we have not sent our own men against them. Even if we loaded all our camels with a year's supply of grain, it would not last before we caught them. You would not only be sending these men to their deaths but wasting a great deal of resources in doing so."

"Hmm, Natash, it seems we have no need of this 'Apepi' and his men. Their merchants have been good for us but it seems these armed soldiers are a hindrance and nothing more."

"Does the Great King wish to rid himself of this hindrance?"

"Yes, that sounds like a good idea, Natash."

"Praise be to the Great King, the Mighty Bull, He who is strong of arm, the oppressor of the nine bows—"

"That is enough, Natash. Ready my army. I will march against these foreigners who dare to invade our land. Spread the word to the troops that a hostile people from the sea has come to take our land from us. Tell them that we must fight for they are wild men who will give no quarter and utter profanities against our gods. That should fire the men for war."

"Indeed, sire. I shall do as you have commanded. Why it will not even be a war, Great King, a single battle should suffice to rid us of these pests."

Throtar followed Natash out of the king's hall. They talked in whispers as they hurried quickly though the many passages in Seqenenra's palace.

"Why did you tell Seqenenra to attack them? His glory will grow once more and we won't be able to touch him."

"You still don't understand, do you Throtar? The trap is tightening; we can't let any more pieces onto the board. What if these people join his army, what then? If they fight well their leader will soon be one of his advisors, someone he trusts. We will need to corrupt yet another unpredictable and powerful man. We have worked for years and now we are almost ready. Let him rid us of this final obstacle and then we will take his life. No-one will expect a victorious pharaoh to die."

"Why does he need to die? He is weak, you already rule in all but name…"

"It is the perfect time. He is weak so no-one will mind the change. Egypt needs a strong ruler again. I will restore it to its former glory. I cannot do that unless I am pharaoh. The people don't just need to be guided in the right direction; they need to believe in the one leading them."

Eleven

The javelin pierced its mark with the ease of a ship surging through the waves. Zedeck, panting from his efforts, smiled nonetheless. It was a good shot. Though, to Ariadne looking on, the bale of wheat seemed almost defiant in its posture. It barely flinched as it was struck, and it was still standing. It almost seemed to be goading him, *is that the best you can do?*

Ariadne turned to watch Adro and Emeko dancing to the age-old melody of strike or be struck. They looked silly, boys fighting with sticks rather than real spears but she knew they didn't see it that way. Each one had murder in his eyes as he circled the other.

Shields raised and sticks held back ready to strike, each boy waited for the smallest opening. Then Ariadne had an idea. Adro lowered his shield slightly, inviting an attack and Emeko stabbed, confident of victory. Adro parried the stab with his own spear—only to be struck from behind with a powerful blow.

Adro turned around, but not quickly enough, and he was struck again on the other side of his back. Wincing, he finally saw his attacker. Ariadne smiled as Emeko charged into Adro from behind. As Adro fell to the ground, Ariadne sidestepped Emeko and hit him on the head as he passed by. Dazed, he half-stumbled forward, his arms flailing. As he caught his balance, Ariadne grabbed the edge of his shield and knocked it up and into his face.

"Stop right there!" some grumpy man shouted as Emeko fell to the ground. The man came running over. "You can't fight!"

Well, evidently I can... Ariadne thought. "I've been watching them for days. I know all their moves!" she said excitedly.

"Go and make yourself useful! Go get us some water or something."

Ariadne stared at the man as he stared back at her. She still had the stick she had picked up but he carried a proper knife by his side and he looked almost ready to use it.

Time seemed to stop as they glared at each other. Neither backing down. Then, finally, Ariadne bared her teeth at him and stormed away, still carrying the stick.

***

"—so how on earth does this pharaoh expect us to live off merchants? I've offered to sell our very selves, surely that is enough? How much longer must I wait?" Sweat poured off Apepios even inside the cool of his tent.

"Dealing with the bureaucrats of Memphis always takes time. Those around the king seem to think that if they slow time long enough, the pharaoh will live forever." Mepsiad mockingly agreed. "Why it took me three years of waiting before I received a permit to sell in the market of the capital! I wouldn't be surprised if he waited until you sold your boats and arms…"

"But how are we meant to serve him without weapons? Surely he doesn't want us to kill his enemies with our bare hands?"

"Well you should consider your options before it is too late." Mepsiad murmured looking into Apepios' eyes. "As I have said, the governors around the delta are weak and owe their allegiance to the king only in name and in the grain that they send. They are ripe for a civil war amongst themselves. If you should stir the nest carefully I think you might come out having left all the wasps sting each other, with the nest as your prize…"

"You are too cynical, Mepsiad. Their pharaoh would be mad not to take the offer of loyal, willing soldiers."

"You do not know this land, admiral," Mepsiad said with resignation, "but you will. Nothing is ever as simple as we would think; their customs are strange and complicated. Even if he were to make you vizier, you might wake up one day with a knife in your back. Such is the guile of these people."

Apepios looked at the freshly tallied records before him and stifled the worry rising within him. "If they don't answer us in four days I will reconsider my position. So far I think the best decision is to trust the pharaoh." Mepsiad strategically downed his cup to avoid having to nod in agreement. He moved to leave from the tent as a soldier burst in. Before Apepios could ask him why he did so, the soldier started speaking in between heaving pants.

"Egyptians… here… in the distance…"

"See, Mepsiad, you worry too much. Tell me soldier how far away is the delegation?"

"Not… delegation…"

"Really? Do you mean we might have the pharaoh come to meet us himself? That would be worth the wait."

"Army… huge army, admiral…"

"Army?"

"The pharaoh may indeed have come to meet you personally, Apepios…" Mepsiad said with a look words would only cheapen to describe.

"Army?!" Apepios roared. He checked himself in a moment, his mind suddenly buzzing away. "How far away are they soldier?"

"They… are…"

"Yes, come on, out with it!"

"Five hours march, sir."

"Hmm, it seems we have no choice. That is enough time though. Soldier, get some rest, I will ready the men."

***

Adro stood silently, trying not to shiver in the burning heat. The stench of the men packed around him didn't even register, not when the host marching towards them kept coming, every heartbeat bringing death closer. He didn't need to peer around to see his friends either side of him; that was the design, the cruel design. They had enthusiastic men in the front few rows and them behind. At the back were the grumpy veterans, only too eager to push them along with their shields if need be.

And now he was here, standing in a line he didn't want to be in with bristly men behind him; all too willing to spear him if he didn't move forward when the time came. It was madness. And still, the pharaoh's army marched towards them.

***

Ariadne struck and parried and struck again. It seemed there was no end to her enemies despite none of them actually being there. Rocks and branches of unfortunate trees, unlucky enough to cross her path, they copped the brunt of her attacks.

Be a good dear and get some water. Wipe my arse and make my dinner—they can all rot. In the end, Ariadne decided to get water for that man after all. She couldn't wait to see his confused face as he gulped it down, unaware that she'd pissed in it. *I wonder if he'll be able to taste it?* She grinned, finally arriving at the spring.

As she began filling up the bladder she had brought with her, Ariadne looked absentmindedly out from the top of the hill. Then she dropped everything, and peered closer. In the distance she saw two armies opposite each other, one numberless like the grains of sand, swarming forwards like flies to meat. The other, a small thin line by comparison, even thinner at the centre than at the sides. It just stayed there, unmoving, like a rock about to be struck by a wave. With horror, she realised the Egyptians had finally arrived.

***

"Steady." Adro could see their faces now. The gap between them seemed pitifully small. It took all his strength merely to hold his spear upright and not give way to the shit that wanted to escape.

"Hold your ground!" He'd wanted to charge them. At least that way he'd get his blood up and maybe, just maybe, lose himself in the chaos. Anything was better than waiting, staring death in the face as it stared back at you.

Then, as the Egyptians were almost upon them, as Adro could see individual faces among his enemies, another cry was shouted through the ranks.

"Charge!" As Adro started forwards he realised he was wrong, the only thing worse than standing there waiting for death was running forwards to embrace it.

***

It looked to Ariadne as if the bigger army was about to crash onto the smaller when, at the last instant, it surged forwards as well. In a few heartbeats, the armies clashed together. She could just make out the detail of what was happening but the more she watched the more she wished she could look away. Bronze-rimmed shields crashed into men wearing nothing more than a loincloth. Some Egyptians were luckier; some had shields to push back with. Those wicker and leather defences cracked quickly under the force of the Cretan's charge. All along the line, where the Cretan's charged, it was like a bronze battering ram was being hurled against a wicker fence.

Adro saw spears reaching back towards them from the ranks of the Egyptians. They seemed to bounce off either the shields or, failing that, the armour they found behind. Adro saw the men in front of him fight like gods—enemies dying around them like flies. Each desperate attempt to stab them was pushed aside—each man who dared to try, quickly despatched. Seeing the ease at which they killed the enemy, Adro felt his fear drop and urged the others onward, eager for his turn at glory.

Ariadne frowned at what she saw, despite the strength of the Cretan charge. Most of the Egyptian force was concentrated on the centre, and the rest seemed to be skirting around the Cretan flanks to envelop them from behind. It wouldn't be long before they broke through the thin centre, made up as far as she could see of archers and men with javelins. It wouldn't be long before those who were left would be surrounded on all sides.

That didn't seem to dismay those men in the centre though. They kept firing and casting away, conjuring a storm of death from above. As their cruel points struck, men screamed and fell but still the wave surged onwards. Nothing was going to halt their advance, not even a hail of skin-piercing rain.

Within moments they were so close the archers wouldn't have time to reload their bows again, this was to be their final shot. Eager at the chance to cut down those who had killed the men beside them, the Egyptians raced forwards.

And the ground opened up beneath them.

Men fell into the sand, suddenly dissolving beneath the multitude.

As men fell and disappeared, their screams of agony conjured spikes from the ground. The more men fell in the unstoppable surge forward, the more the horror was revealed. Sharpened stakes gleamed back at the Egyptians, somewhat sated with their brothers, cousins and friends. Still, the gaping mouth smiled, and beckoned them forward.

***

Seqenenra stared into the distance watching his land swallow his army. He felt a chill despite the thousands of men standing between him and the pit. He breathed deeply then looked again at the battlefield. *The flanks, they might have bought some time but they will soon be surrounded.* Seqenenra looked at the edges of where his army and theirs clashed. He saw his men streaming along the sides, quickly surrounding the Cretans. They seemed to turn and face them, weakening their already thinned lines even further. It would not be long before the stretched Cretan position would break.

As Seqenenra felt calm returning he noticed the sand hills on either side of the Cretan army seem to dissolve. To his horror he saw ants emerge from their nest and come streaming down towards his men attempting to envelop the Cretan army. Seqenenra moaned to himself as he saw the horde of insects crash down like a plague on his soldiers. *That general must have hidden half his forces in the sand!*

Emeko had laid there under the boiling sand for hours. The one mercy was the kind reprieve of not having to wear any armour. They would really be boiled if they had to. He waited along with the rest, for that triple note to sound. Each time a signal was given he fought with himself not to brush the sand off and charge down. But he waited. He waited in almost silence, only occasionally hearing new trumpets calling orders or the cries of a man loud in his dying. Eventually though, the triple note came.

Emeko was one of the first to jump up, brush the sand from his face and chest and race down towards the Egyptians trying to encircle his friends. Maybe they're still down there. If we make it in time, surely we can save them? Surely they'll be alright. *Thoughts of fear buzzed through his mind as he charged towards the enemy. Fear became anger as he crashed into the first Egyptian staring back at him, terrified.*

A scout ran panting through the ranks of bodyguards to the king of the Egyptians. He collapsed at his feet as Seqenenra grimaced at the massacre quickly unfolding. Seqenenra turned to a servant holding a jar of water and pointed towards the scout.

"Drink," he commanded the scout. "Drink then speak."

The man gulped the water down gratefully then began.

"All is lost, o wise and mighty King—"

"Quiet! I know about the deceptions of the Keftiu. All is not lost. We shall still crush them yet."

"No, King," the scout replied as he moved inches away from Seqenenra's face. "All is lost for you."

Seqenenra flicked his arms at the man before him, intending to brush him aside.

"How dare y—" His anger at the intrusion of the mortal before him was cut short, literally. The scout raised his arm in a sweeping motion that avoided the feeble attempt of Seqenenra to push him away. The shard of sharpened stone he held grazed across Seqenenra's neck, splitting it in an instant. For a second there was a curved line running from just under Seqenenra's jawbone down to his collarbone on the other side, then the blood started to rush. He managed to utter a final word, "Guards!"

Meanwhile the guards stood motionless. Each one staring ahead as if nothing had happened. The scout stared back at Seqenenra, smiled, and whispered to him,

"Natash sends his greetings."

After the king's knees had buckled and then his collapse on the blood-soaked ground beneath him, the scout turned to the soldiers and spoke.

"You know your orders. Remember, your families will be rewarded for your loyalty." One by one the guards took knives from their belts and cut their own throats. The scout paused for a moment, then did the same.

***

Apepios sat busily in his tent that evening. It was crawling with Ariadne and the other scribes shouting out tallies in the background as soldiers queued up to tell him their account of the battle.

"—so once some of the Egyptians had managed to climb beyond the pit the javelin-men went to work. They cleaned up any who were fortunate enough to survive it. Most of the centre started to stream off to the sides once they saw the trap, but our lines held. These men are dead easy to kill."

"Hear, hear!" came a shout of agreement from men further back, waiting to give their reports to Apepios.

"And what of the flanks?" Apepios inquired.

"Well, once we charged into them the Egyptians fought for a short while then fled," another man replied. "That was the beginning of the rout. They had nowhere to flee to though besides their own army but those further back didn't want to flee. The cowards were caught between us and their own army, both of us massacring them. It seems these Egyptians are unforgiving..."

"Well if most of the army didn't flee from our trap then what caused it to?"

"We are hearing reports from some of their survivors. It seems their king died in the middle of his army and that sent panic through the rest of it. They seem to place a lot of weight on the life of one person... they all practically gave up or fled once they heard."

"A most fortunate day it would seem then." Apepios mused. "Thank you soldiers, I think I understand enough for the moment. Anyone who thinks he still has something significant to tell me, come to my tent tomorrow." The exhausted soldiers were only too eager to leave and many spent the rest of the night drinking the horrors away.

Mepsiad emerged from the shadows of the tent and spoke quietly to Apepios.

"What are you going to do now? We have our victory; your victory. Many paths lie before you."

"Whatever happens, I will need more men. I was thinking of sparing some of the captives to keep in our army."

"Admiral, you can't do that. Think on why the Egyptians fled so easily." Mepsiad paused for a moment then continued, "It was because their pharaoh died. All Egyptians have a belief that their pharaoh is one of the gods. Their loyalty is absolute. They may fall into despair if he dies but they will always be loyal to him. You cannot trust these men to fight for you."

"Hmm, are you sure?"

"That was the greatest army under Pharaoh's control. They have had no real enemies for a long time. They are weak; you do not need any more men."

"Very well, your advice seems sound. I will execute the captives tomorrow. If this is the case though—if we cannot trust them—then what makes you think we can turn the local governors against each other? None will side with us."

"So you want to continue with that plan then?"

"Yes, it seems like our best alternative."

"The peasants fear their pharaoh absolutely but men of power are prepared to risk a bit of heresy. Many are more concerned with controlling their own little kingdom than worrying about the king they never see. You cannot trust them but some will side with you so long as you are victorious and they can benefit from you."

"Ah I see. I have come to a desert full of leeches. I wonder how they survive at all…"

"This is the perfect time, admiral. They are harvesting their wheat as we speak. If you move quickly you could take not only enough for ourselves but enough that Upper Egypt starves. You would have power over your enemy… what better way to survive in this new land?"

Apepios paused and thought for a while. He turned to the scribes pretending not to be listening and asked, "How many of ours are dead?"

"Not many, sir." Ariadne replied. Euouk agreed as did the others. "The reports keep coming in but I doubt it'd even be a hundred." Apepios felt tears emerging but cut them off with a wizened and cheerful smile.

"Well then, girl, it seems that the gods favour us after all. Are your boys still alive?"

Ariadne nodded.

"Then go, be with them. They've earned it."

Ariadne dropped her tablet she was reading through and raced to the entrance. She turned and gave a quick look of gratitude then ran off into the night.

Twelve

Apepios smiled as he took the wine being offered to him. The governor of Avaris gave it to him with his own hand, despite the servants standing quietly around them. The man fidgeted nervously, waiting for Apepios to finish the cup. Enjoying himself, Apepios drank slowly, savouring every drop. Finally, when he was done, Apepios waved his had to signal the governor to begin.

"We were glad, mighty hyksos, to hear how you have spared the villages and towns you pass through." The governor began. "I shall not deny it; all of Lower Egypt trembled after the great battle…"

"Be at peace, dear friend," Apepios replied, "I have not come to kill or take what is not mine. I have not come to harm anyone save those who choose to be my enemy. I have been living off the generous gifts of grain your fellow governors were kind enough to donate to my weary troops—"

"Rest assured, you will have as much grain as you need to carry your army through my region." The governor eagerly butted in.

"Well, dear friend, that is not what I had in mind this time."

"No?"

"No. See my army is tired and in need of rest. I was wondering if we might be able to impinge on your generosity and spend a few days filling the inns in your grand city. I want to give my men a reward: each man shall spend a night sleeping in a proper bed in a proper house. It shouldn't take more than a week at the most to rotate the army through your inns. What do you say?" The governor looked back at him, speechless. "I would be *eternally* grateful."

The governor said nothing for a long while then broke the silence with a whisper.

"Your troops in my city?"

"Yes governor. One way or another I want my men to be able to rest in your city…"

"Well when you put it like that—"

"Hush, dear friend. I was not threatening you. As I said, I will be grateful, and I always reward my friends."

The governor hesitated even so. Apepios quickly continued. "And, as a sign of our mutual friendship I have two slaves to give you. They are brilliant boys trained in the arts of engulfing you in luxury. They are masseurs and musicians and willing catamites, should you so desire it." The governor lit up and stood to cover his rising. "They should make a nice change from the eunuchs you Egyptians usually keep."

"I would be most honoured by this gift of friendship. Thank you Apepios, great hyksos of the Keftiu. I guess, I guess I could allow such a thing for a friend."

"Here are your slaves—come Adro, come Emeko—they do not speak much Egyptian but they are all too willing to oblige you. I'm sure you can make your wishes known." The governor grinned as Adro and Emeko stepped forth from the shadows.

"Thank you again, Apepios. Marteth, go now and tell the soldiers to open all the gates. Once you have done that go to every pub and inn personally and let them know they will have many visitors."

Apepios bowed and walked out with Marteth following close behind. The governor pointed to Adro and Emeko then back to himself. He started walking to the hallway and motioned for them to follow with a flick of his hand. The two Malians followed him down the long hallway and then off through the winding passages, eventually emerging at an entrance draped in a curtain of silk. The governor didn't stop but brushed the curtain aside and kept going. Once Adro and Emeko had followed him into the room filled with soft luxuries the governor turned and draped the silk curtain back. He walked over to the bed and laid down on his back.

"You can play me music later. Adro, wasn't it? You're first."

The Malians looked at each other for a moment before speaking in their own tongue.

"I think he wants to fuck you." Emeko said calmly.

"I can't do this." Adro replied.

"Don't worry it's not what we're here for. Do you want to get started?"

"No that's what I mean—I don't think I can go through with it." The governor shouted something at them impatiently.

"Listen, we've got to keep him occupied long enough for the men to get into the city. I make that three hours." The governor rose and started walking over to them while Emeko kept speaking, "No-one will come looking for him. Let's just get it over with before he makes you do something Ariadne will regret…"

The governor was upon them and he started to stroke Adro's cheek with the back of his hand. Adro pushed him away and raised his arms in the air in defiance. While the governor's face turned from confusion to anger, Adro muttered quickly to Emeko,

"I can't do it."

"Oh, seriously!" Emeko shouted as the governor's hand came down once more, this time in a strike of fury. As the hand struck Adro's previously stroked cheek, Emeko unsheathed his hidden knife and stabbed it straight into the governor's throat. The man gurgled in surprise, unable to raise a voice as he slumped back onto the bed.

"And now," Emeko said as he wiped his blade on the sheets, "we wait."

***

Apepios walked cheerfully through the streets of Avaris as his soldiers marched around him. He began to speak to Mepsiad while men kept pouring through the still opened gate far behind him.

"Did he really think I would let him keep such a defensible place? Doesn't he realise how useful these walls are? I've been waiting months for a fortress such as this."

"We haven't taken it yet. The hardest part is still to come."

"I know that…" Apepios grumbled, leaving a bare silence but for the clopping of feet marching down the road.

Zedeck looked up from staring at the grimy feet of the man in front of him and peered at the city around him. All along the road doors were being slammed fiercely. He noticed a small child peering out of a window to his right and nudged Macanra. Macanra turned quickly and waved at the boy who grinned and waved back. Macanra strained his head to keep looking back at the boy as he walked onward. In his final moments he saw a fearful woman glance out for a second, grab the boy and disappear beyond the reach of the window.

Such scenes of dread continued as they wound their way through the streets. With every corner they passed, Zedeck felt a knot slowly tighten within him. He saw their eyes stare back and him, their faces blurred together until it seemed like the city itself was somehow alive and watching him from all around. By the time they reached the palace Zedeck's fingers had started to twitch around his spear every time he saw another Egyptian.

Guards stared down at the armed array walking confidently towards them. One started to race off inside the palace but was cut short by an arrow fired from somewhere in the ranks. As the rest of the guards hesitated, the Cretans charged. While Zedeck raced up the steps he saw Apepios bowl over one of the transfixed Egyptians bare-handed. Neither stopped but raced into the palace with the rest of the swarm. The seething mass of men ignored the side rooms and twisting passages before them and followed Apepios as he led the way to the main chamber he had been in before. It came without warning; in an instant, after a sharp left turn, they started gushing out into a large empty room.

Apepios walked to the centre, turned to the men still pouring in, and spoke.

"I want the first twenty men to stay here with me. The rest, search this place for the two Malian boys I left here earlier. Go!"

Zedeck walked through the room and, finding a comfortable wall to lean against, took his position. After a moment Macanra sifted through the crowd, which was still streaming through the antechamber, and, without a word, stood beside his friend. The minutes that followed were not filled with silence but the distant sounds of scuffling feet and the occasional shriek. Each time one of those short and piercing, or worse—long and wailing, cries reached Zedeck's ears, he felt nothing. The rising bile in his throat came after the sudden silence which inevitably followed each cry. He could still here them in the distance even after Emeko and Adro were escorted in.

Emeko led the entourage, his face beaming with a smile he was constantly fighting to control. Adro walked a few paces behind, head hanging low with a look Zedeck couldn't tell if it was fear or shame. As they stood before Apepios the soldiers escorting them placed a body caked in already dried blood at Apepios' feet. The two boys stared intently at Apepios who gazed down at the body before him. Satisfied, he raised his head and addressed them.

"Well done my brave, young soldiers. You walked into the den and came out with a fur cloak. You deserve to be honoured, for that is what awaits those who fulfil my wishes."

"Ach hmm." Emeko interjected, turning to glance at Adro. Apepios followed Emeko's eyes, his gaze resting on Adro. Adro raised his head and spoke,

"Admiral, Emeko was the one to kill the governor—"

"What does that matter? It doesn't take two to kill a man. I was just taking precautions."

"It matters, sir," Emeko replied, "because Adro disobeyed your order. The governor was moments away from alerting his guards; he knew something was wrong. Adro didn't kill the man when he should have and probably would have let us be found out and captured before he was prepared to do so."

Apepios gazed once more at the downtrodden boy before him. After a moment, he spoke.

"Listen well, soldiers, to what I have to say today. This is not a rock war in a back alley in Knossos, Phaistos or wherever you come from. At the end of the day we won't be joking together with the Egyptians about who struck a good blow and who was courageous. We won't smile and hold each other's bruised arms and race off home with only our parents to fear. This is our life now and I would have thought you had all already learnt this; we are at war. We kill these people who threaten us or whose death aids our cause. We are fighting for a home in this land and the Egyptians made it very clear that we must either rule them or die trying.

See now a sign of what to strive for. Emeko, since you have done as you were asked, you will be made a member of my personal bodyguard. Adro, since you have not yet learnt the seriousness of our task, you will stay in the ranks facing the death you are afraid to wield in our favour. See this sign: two boys tested. Today one has become a man, the other remains a mere child."

Two boys stared back at him: one with a look of triumph, the other of seething resentment.

"Take the head of this corpse and stick it on a spear." Apepios commanded the soldier nearest him. "When the Egyptians in this city get over their initial fear they will challenge us. You will follow me with it when the time comes—I want them to know they are too late."

***

Rich, sweaty men huddled together despite the heat in order to fit into the already cramped hall. There was no room left for servants to bring cool water and parch their rising thirst. The rest of the Memphis waited outside these private rooms without a hope of even entering the outer edges of the palace. Nevertheless, the irritated nobles slowly began to grumble.

Meanwhile, in the deeper rooms which fewer still had seen, Natash was leading a small and frightened child away from a mother trying her best to look brave. *She had seen; she had realised from the moment she heard the news that only I could protect Egypt now. Wise woman,* Natash thought. *Although, her boy cannot be allowed to live too long; a few years and the people will accept me. A victory over these invaders and they will see my fitness to rule.*

They emerged from the inner rooms of the palace to the grand hall filled with the sweating nobles. Natash smirked with his eyes to see such a sight but kept the rest of his face motionless as he had long trained himself to do. He motioned to the child to sit on the throne while he stood confidently beside it. Natash couldn't help but take a breath from excitement before he stepped forward and began.

"Great men of Upper Egypt, do you know how honoured you are today? You stand before the new king of Egypt: the mighty Kamose. This you already knew and, although it is an honour in itself, I tell you that you will speak of this day to your children with awe still in your heart. When they are old and blind they will still tell your descendants that you were here on this great day. For Kamose, in his divine wisdom has decreed that we will gather an enormous army, greater than any which has come since the first unification of our land. This will be the fist of his fury and with it he will drive the hateful invaders from us. Also, his divine wisdom plainly evident, he has decreed that, due to his unfortunate youth, he should not be the one to direct this undertaking. Rather, under his blessing, I shall be fortunate enough to serve as the instrument of his will. I ask you to stand with me, great men, and together we will aid Kamose to save Egypt and free her from this evil threat."

Kamose sat there cheerfully as Natash's followers started the first shouts of support. The other nobles were shocked to silence at first by this break of protocol but after seeing the enthusiasm on the young king's face, quickly joined in as well.

***

Zedeck ducked gracelessly as the stinking missile was hurled at him. As the crowd's numbers grew there was an ever increasing supply of the foul ammunition. They had their orders though—stand your ground and wait for the city to assemble before them. Only fight if they start to storm the palace. Sadly, the crowd was content with simply verbal and aerial abuse.

Beside an equally cheerless Macanra, a few paces down the line, stood Adro. He ducked along with the rest but there was a coldness in his eyes which hadn't crept into those of the other two. He stood there in silence as did they but his had an icy edge to it. The rest of the guards were just bored and sick of dodging shit but he gave the impression he had already been drenched in it. No-one for a moment though could say that he looked defeated by it, but rather that the stench had inflamed him. As Adro stood there his mind was at work. It wasn't racing from thought to fleeting though but kept repeating a single one over in a calming rhythm. *She will understand me. Ariadne will know I did what was right.*

The crowd kept swelling over the long minutes that followed. The once barren and frightened city awoke and seethed before them. Zedeck could see weapons being passed between them as the standing protest grew in confidence. The pelting stopped as they were arming themselves, which was a sort of relief. A greater one was the sight of Apepios walking down the stairs to confront the crowd. His grizzly banner was held by none other than Emeko who carried it behind him with pride. The crowd started murmuring and continued while he began to speak in their own tongue.

"Egyptians of Avaris, men of this great city, look before you. See this here. This is your governor. This is one who opposed me." The murmurs rose at that to a sinister rumble.

"I ask you to think for a moment, for I know you are intelligent men. What kind of a man can come into the city of a governor and take his life? We know the gods intervene in our lives—everything that happens is guided by their will. They would not allow an evil to rise in this great land of Egypt, for they love it dearly. In troubled times they show their favour by the simplest signs: victory. This is one of those times." Apepios had the gaze of every Egyptian and their attentive silence as well.

"I ask you again, what kind of a man can come into the city of a governor, one granted authority from the Great King himself, who can come into his city and kill him? Who has the right to take his power from him? Surely, it can only be one aided by the gods. The Great King's authority comes from being divine himself and that is why his word is always just and true. The great evil of this age, dear men, is that you have been tricked. The Great King you had was not divine but an imposter. The gods brought me here to your land to rescue it; to rescue Egypt from the evil it has fallen under. How else could I have come here and taken this man's life? I would have been struck down for challenging the will of Heaven." He paused and stared out into the crowd, letting it sink in.

"No, I have Heaven behind me and that is why I succeed. The real test came before now and many of you know of it. When the Great Imposter fought with me the gods would not allow him to succeed. Although I was greatly outnumbered, I triumphed and the imposter died. The gods took his life to show Egypt that he was not fit to rule and gave me victory as the age-old sign of their favour. Men of Avaris, I am your true king. I am the true king of Upper and Lower Egypt and I, Apepios, have decided to make Avaris the new capital. You are honoured above all to be the first and greatest city of a new Egypt. I, your true king, ask you, my true subjects, to serve me. As you would serve me, so you should serve these Cretans, for they are my spear. They are a holy army sent from heaven to rid Egypt of evil and to protect it from descending back into darkness. Great men of

Avaris; loyal subjects and first among all Egypt, I ask you, no, heaven commands you, to kneel before me now."

While Apepios stood there in silence gazing back at the crowd, and while the shit-strewn Cretans tried to rise to the look of holy warriors, the dumbfounded crowd, as one, kneeled.

Thirteen

Kathoth stared out over the palisade once again as he finished climbing the splintering stairs. Another cold morning, another barren and deserted desert. He shuffled along to the guard tower, his shoulders already aching from the cold. *Ra's icicles, bloody sentry duty,* he thought, *third bloody time this week.* He turned around and looked back at the barracks. *Won't even be any point getting them lot out for the drills at sunrise. What now with all the young whore-spawn sent up to Memphis, wouldn't have twenty men left; couldn't even practice flanking with so few. Rest of these bastards will get to sleep in and I'm stuck out here.* He stared out once more at the desert, still minding its business in complete silence but for the whispers of a wind howling far off.

The sun hinted that it might rise at some point that day but lazily delayed fulfilling its promise. Kathoth creaked his way around up and down his stretch of the wall before coming to rest at the tower once more. *Nothing. Still nothing. Always had been and always will. Cush is broken. That whipped dog knows its place. How long has this fort been here? They're used to it by now, probably brings them comfort. Yeah, our new king is probably pretty wise sending most of the lads away from this forsaken place. No use for them here.*

It seemed to Kathoth that his life was the constant flow of suffering one ache or another. As the sun finally began to rise he realised his bladder was giving him the latest one. *Captain's tent? Would have worked in the past but now there's too few people to blame. Looks like I'm stuck with over the wall then.* As he moved forward and started his relief he noticed a speck in the distance. Night was coming although the sun was rising. The golden hue lit up the dark storm surging towards him in the distance. Kathoth quickly turned and raced to a corner of the palisade. He stared out in a different direction and noticed the same cloud slowly marching in the distance as well. He took a breath and shouted.

"Nubians!" He started running down the stairs towards the captain's tent. "Nubians! Cush is attacking! Get up, men! Get up!" He ducked into the captain's tent without waiting for him to emerge. The man was already up and scrambling for his shield. The captain looked at Kathoth with a piercing glance. "Yes, captain," Kathoth replied to the unasked question, "a Cushite army will soon be here." The captain nodded and pushed passed him out of the tent. As he was walking out however, Kathoth continued, "We're all going to die captain, you know that, don't you?" The captain turned and spoke.

"Soldier, it's a good day to die."

To which Kathoth thought, *no sir, it's a bloody awful day to die. Every day's an awful day to die.* He looked up helplessly at the empty palisade and all but laughed at their chances to fill even one row. He raced off into the barracks and woke the still sleeping men by means of many a rough kick.

"Get up, dregs! No more point sleeping now, there'll be plenty of that soon enough."

The pitiful band of rejects still left behind grumbled their way to the stores gathering their weapons with a resigned drudgery. Most were either crippled or so old the young ones used to joke about skinning them for the superb pouches which could be made from them. No-one really knew what positions to get into. Most tried to fill the wall but there was still room enough for two or three Nubians between each of the waiting soldiers. A fortunate few were left down the bottom guarding the gates, not that they could stop those decayed and creaking barriers from giving way at the first charge.

Kathoth stared out beyond the palisade once more, this time with the entire fort to keep him company as he completed his sentry duty. The Nubians grinned as they came closer, each one savouring every step which brought their kingdom closer to freedom. It was a long while before they reached the fort itself, Kathoth's muscles had stopped aching for the sun had finally risen and warmed them. He stared back down at the first few Nubians as they reached the edge of the fort and dipped his spear down ready to strike them. Apparently there had been some bows still in the stores for every now and then he heard the dull thwack of an arrow fleeing the fort. The first few Nubians raced up to the palisade and started climbing it. He tried to stab one but it let go and grabbed his spear as he struck. While he was wrestling with the dangling Nubian he didn't notice the others who had reached the base of the fort. He didn't notice the spear one of them threw towards him. He didn't—

***

Haseth's eyes darted from man to man as the last of them sat down. He smiled slowly and began.

"We have to decide what to do about the hyksos at Avaris. For those of you who don't know, he has now laid claim to the throne of Egypt. He says that evil controls Egypt and that he has been sent by the gods to save us from it."

"Kamose is raising an army to crush this foreigner." Asaqra interrupted. "As loyal governors we owe it to the son of Seqenenra to support him. There is nothing to discuss."

"Let us speak openly," Haseth replied coolly, "Kamose is merely a child. Natash controls Memphis at the moment and it is he who is raising an army under Kamose's name. I can't help but wonder that maybe the hyksos is right; that we live in a dark time. Maybe Heaven is upset that Natash is ruling in practice."

"Whether or not Natash is ruling now, when the Hyksos people invaded we still had a legitimate king. They can't be sent by Heaven because Heaven would not divide against itself." Asaqra stated.

"I don't think you can dismiss Haseth so quickly, Asaqra." Musesis said. "We all know Natash was growing in influence under Seqenenra. He may have grown so strong as to control the king himself. If that is so then maybe Haseth is right to consider the hyksos' claim."

"Thank you, Musesis." Haseth said, "Now as I was saying, we need to decide what to do. Since it is possible that the gods no longer favour Seqenenra's line, we may not have to either."

"Blasphemy and treason!" Asaqra shouted.

"Since when was following the will of the gods blasphemy, Asaqra?" Musesis said calmly as he raised his head, firstly to stare at Asaqra and then at the rest of the governors. "It is not treason if we don't support Natash's rise in power. Indeed, some would say that to do so would be treason." He looked at Haseth and continued. "A good point has been made here tonight: we have to decide what to do. Egypt is in our hands so let us discuss what should be done."

"I would like to propose a solution—" Haseth said.

"Here we go," Asaqra muttered.

"I believe that we should support this Apepi—"

"See what I warned you about! Traitor!"

"We should support this Apepi," Haseth continued, "because Heaven has left Seqenenra. It has probably done so because he let Natash control him; his son will be no different. Heaven has sent us a new king, a strong king, and we should be grateful."

"Grateful to enslave Egypt to foreigners?! Can you hear what this man is spouting? He has sold out to the foreigner and now tries to trick us with his sweet words and unfounded rumours," Asaqra declared. Musesis coughed and started to speak but Asaqra cut him off. "Don't listen to either of them; they're in it together. They've already chosen to support the enemy." The silent governors stared at Musesis with a fierce gaze.

"I was going to say," Musesis began, "that I disagree with Haseth." He shot Asaqra a glance and continued. "If Heaven is behind this hyksos then he doesn't need our support. We should test Heaven: we should not support either of them. We should let the gods show whom they favour before deciding. All we can know at the moment is that it may not be Kamose and it may be Apepi." Many governors were nodding even before Musesis had finished speaking.

***

Ariadne waited patiently in line as people brought their issues to Apepios. *Do you know sir that there are three different kinds of barley grown in the southern outskirts of Avaris? Do you know that there are five in the northern but one of those is only suitable for cattle?* Ariadne wanted to inflict the boredom she was suffering onto the man who had set it on her. Instead she stood silently and waited to tell him her monthly storage report.

She saw Euouk walk to the centre of the room and stop, waiting to be the next to speak to Apepios. Ariadne thought to herself, *I wonder why he is here. He isn't scheduled to be. He must be asking a favour.* Unfazed by her hidden pondering, he began.

"O Great Apepios, you are truly blessed to have taken us this far. You have saved the people of Crete from death in this land. For that I thank you, we all thank you. You have done so largely by making use of the skills each of us possesses. For the young men you, have them fight; for those who know Egyptian, a thousand little jobs relating to them and for those knowledgeable with writing, you have us as your scribes. There is one thing you are missing though and that is a priest to use the beliefs of these people. They have accepted you as their king, yes, but without one of your own to guide them and their sacrifices, I fear they will never truly accept you. You need someone willing to learn their ways; someone willing to use them to strengthen your right to rule and our right to be here. I humbly ask you that I, as former chief priest of Malia, might fill this role for you."

Apepios didn't turn his head to look at Mepsiad standing nearby and neither did he turn it to look at the rest of the Cretans waiting for their chance to speak. He stared at Euouk for a while and then nodded.

"Yes, you make a good point, priest. We survive by having everyone fulfil their role as best as they can. You are a priest first and foremost so be a priest. You will need to learn their language and writing though if you are to be their priest. The same goes for every scribe here: if you want to serve in Avaris you must learn Egyptian. This is their land and we are here as their saviours. We should keep to their ways as much as possible."

Euouk bowed low then walked back towards the exit. He paused as he passed Ariadne and whispered to her while the rest of the court awaited the new speaker.

"Religion is where the power is, girl. You can count corn all you want but beware; your day will come." Ariadne looked up, past Euouk, towards Apepios and the court, trying to hide the fear in her eyes. "We lost Crete because of you. I will not let them forget it."

He slithered away through the crowd without another word. Ariadne fought giving way to the shiver creeping up her spine and listened in to the new man speaking to Apepios.

"—no sir, there was no consensus among the governors. Our man reports that most of them are planning to stay out of the conflict. They want to test your claim; they think that if you are sent by the gods then you will win whether they help you or not."

"Are there any who still support Kamose?"

"Yes sir, a few near Memphis have decided to throw their lot in with him. Not many though."

"And of the few who said they would support me, have they agreed to send troops as well?"

"Yes sir, three governors have said they would send men."

"Good. You may go." Apepios said and motioned for the man to leave.

As the messenger walked out of the centre, Ariadne stepped forward to take his place.

***

Apepios was reclining on a couch, a goblet of wine already in hand and a contented smile adorning his face as Mepsiad walked in. Mepsiad sat on the coach facing opposite Apepios, took the offered cup and spoke.

"Why do you look so bloody cheerful when these Egyptians still get your name wrong? Apepi, it sounds stupid!"

"Let them call me whatever they want. This is their land after all. They can call me 'goat's arse the many haired' so long as they call me king."

Mepsiad looked again at his friend, noticed the glimmer in his eyes, paused, and then replied. "You are cheerful. What's gotten you in this state? It's dangerous, you know, for leaders to be happy…"

"I haven't bedded an Egyptian whore and told her of all our plans. Don't worry. No, I saved them for you."

"I'm so grateful." Mepsiad said dryly.

"Do you remember that man who reported that most of the governors were going to stay neutral?" Apepios continued, now serious.

"Yes. I don't see how that helps us. You will be outnumbered again by a more determined and careful enemy. Our only real hope lay in these governors supporting your claim and bringing their men to your side."

"What ever happened to 'we can't trust Egyptians not to fight for anyone besides their pharaoh?'"

"You are their pharaoh now. Three governors are not enough and now we can't reconcile with the new pharaoh in Memphis."

"So, he will see our weak position, bring an army down and fight us in a pitched battle, no? It worked once before."

"They won't underestimate you a second time. He will bring a greater army than before and he will not be so easily tricked. He will simply stay in Memphis and wait for his army to become so large that you have no hope of defeating it. He will then come down and destroy you. So, I ask once again, why are you smiling?"

"Because he thinks as you do. What did the messenger say?" Apepios paused and looked up at a confused Mepsiad. Hearing nothing, he continued. "He said that the governors were abstaining from the fight. He said that they wouldn't support me and neither would they support the king of Memphis. Who needs their support more?"

"You do, obviously."

"What are the governors of Lower Egypt most useful for, hmm? It's not soldiers; it's grain. I have enough grain; my city lies on the Nile. He may have enough food to feed the mouths of Memphis but he can't support a large army without grain from Lower Egypt. The governors will not send it to him until he defeats me. See his problem?"

"I think I am beginning to understand."

"What is even better is that he will not see it until it is too late. He will think he has all the time in the world to raise a massive army and attack me at his leisure. He will have too many mouths to feed and then he will be driven by desperation to attack me to end the war as quickly as possible." Apepios looked up at Mepsiad who put the cup down and smiled. Apepios continued with grin of his own. "We will be able to pick the terrain against a desperate army. We will win because what looks like his greatest strength will be his greatest weakness, and all because the governors were indecisive."

"I hope you are right, Apepios."

"One more battle, Mepsiad. Then the Egyptians will come over to me. Then our people will be safe."

Fourteen

Dawn crept slowly through the window and onto the faces of the boys within.

"Daylight. Finally." Zedeck exclaimed.

"Do you think we'll die today?" Macanra's alert eyes darted to Adro.

"We might not even fight today. Scouts say their army is still a little while off." Adro replied.

"But they're coming. Today, tomorrow, what does it matter? We'll die someday soon." Macanra lamented.

"You never know, we survived one battle against them. Who knows? We might all survive another as well." Zedeck said.

"Survive…" Macanra mused.

"Yes, survive. It's always possible. If you were to survive the battle, Macanra, what would you do with your life?" Zedeck asked.

"I don't know. I'll probably stay in the army. At least that way we get fed. I don't understand this country—too much sand to graze sheep. Besides, if we win, being a soldier probably won't be that dangerous—there'll be no-one left to fight." Macanra said as he tried to force a grin.

"Well I have plans of my own. Something better to strive for than another day and another meal in my belly—"

"I could take up whoring," Macanra interrupted. "At least that would help pass the time and empty my purse. Can't think of what else I could spend it on." Zedeck started laughing. "What's so funny about that? Fine, tell me your big plan."

"I'm going to be a merchant. Papa always had this dream about sailing beyond the waters of Crete. I'd like to sail the world, cargo in tow, having adventures and getting rich along the way."

"Ha ha ha ha and you thought eating and whoring were stupid dreams. At least mine can come true."

"Not with your face—"

"Settle." Adro said sternly as Macanra held Zedeck in a neck-purpling headlock. Macanra grinned and let go.

"You've been quiet, Adro. What about you? What will you do if you survive this battle?"

Adro looked up at his friends and then spoke.

"I'm going to marry her. I don't care what I do. If we can be together, I'll be happy." Adro looked further, beyond his two friends, at the door of their little room in the tavern. He stared at the door waiting, hoping that she would come bounding up the stairs and into his arms. He kept staring as the seconds of silence grew upon each other.

***

"Before I begin, mighty Apepi, forgive me for talking in this dishonourable tongue. I hope that I may soon learn yours that we may talk in the speech of upright people." The dark-skinned man said in flawless Egyptian. "I come before you, mighty Apepi, to offer an alliance to you and the Cretan people whom you command. I offer you the friendship of the great kingdom of Cush. Together we will crush the hated Egyptians who do not wish to live at peace with the wider world of men. Together we will crush those who only look out for themselves and would see us all die lest we be a burden on them. Together we will make a new world; one of friendship and freedom from fear. What do you say, Apepi?"

Apepios looked at the man standing in the centre of the room. His face did not waver or display any sign of fear. If anything, he seemed relaxed, confident even, and sure of success.

"Cush honours me," Apepios began, "Cush honours the Cretans when we are still uncertain of victory. Cush trusts not in the force of arms but in the force of righteousness. You have sided with us because you know our cause is just. You know we will win because of this and even if we were not to, that it is better to side with the good who die rather than the bad who live and prosper. Gracious Cush, no man on earth could tempt me to refuse your offer; it is the offer of comradeship against a foe. It is the offer of freedom united together. It is harmony throughout the world, harmony which the false king of Memphis and his forefathers forsook for their own glory. Harmony which I, as the true king of Egypt, will restore as is my duty. Harmony which we will restore together. Go, tell your king that I accept his offer with thankfulness."

Ariadne stood there quietly wondering if she should vomit at all this talk of being the true Egyptian king. *Harmony, justice, freedom; they're just words. Still those words are keeping us alive. Guess it's better just to play along.* The Cush delegate bowed with the same expression on his face. Only the slight hint of a smile which emerged at the corners of his mouth seemed to imply that anything had changed. Once the Nubian had left the chamber, Apepios waved his hand slowly to silence the chattering and then spoke.

"My latest scout report says that the Egyptian army is three days away. They have been starving for over a week. Now is the time to strike. We will fight the Egyptians in the desert and take this land from them."

"Wouldn't it be best to wait here? If they are without food they could not besiege us in Avaris. Their army would break before we do." Euouk raised.

"My victory over them must be complete. It must be a battle to decide who deserves to rule Egypt. That cannot happen if they come roaring up and sulking back while we hide behind walls the whole time. If you are worried about their numbers though Euouk, do not worry for I have a solution. I have decided that all Cretan men must fight in this battle; all farmers and fishermen, all scribes and priests. It is only fitting for you all to take part in the battle where we win our safety."

Euouk stared back with a look somewhere between hatred, bewilderment and, needless to say, bladder releasing fear.

"But who will look after affairs back here in Avaris? The Egyptians may close their gates to you if you leave the city with no Cretans behind." Euouk asked.

"Oh that is settled easily enough. Ariadne, step forward." She promptly did so. "You will be in charge of Avaris while I am away. I am making you the chief scribe and vizier of Avaris for the next few days." He looked at Euouk and kept speaking, "She can keep the Egyptians busy for a few days counting grain and, besides, if we win then we have proved my claim as the rightful king of Egypt and they will surely open the gates with welcoming arms. If we fail, well, the dead don't need to worry about the affairs of this world, do they?"

Many pairs of frightened eyes stared back at him. Men confident that their jobs had secured them safety from having to risk their lives were now feeling the full horror of the war they had helped inflict.

"No questions then? Good, we start our march out to meet them today. Scribes, to the barracks!" he said the last bit with mirth as he winked at Ariadne.

***

"Zedeck, the breastplate goes the other way around. It's not meant to protect your arse as you run away from the enemy, quite the reverse." Adro joked as he put his greaves on. A few of the men, who were also putting their armour on, laughed to themselves. "This armour of ours is awesome. Egyptians can never get past it—this stuff makes us pretty much immortal. I'm going to stand in the front row. I'm going to win enough glory that I'll be promoted to guarding Avaris and then able to marry her."

"I thought you said you didn't care about what job you had?" Macanra asked.

"I don't. But I've been thinking it over and I reckon that after this battle we'll still get sent all over the place. He's still got to take Memphis and Upper Egypt even if this battle wins him the support of all the governors of Lower Egypt. I can't marry her if I'm never with her; what's the point in that?"

"You know what is pointless?" Zedeck asked. "Getting killed 'cause you can't wait a few more years. Take my advice and don't try for any of this glory stuff. If you've got a dream, live long enough to see it come true. There are other ways to get there besides risking your life unnecessarily."

"Ah piss off. I know what I'm doing." Adro grumbled before grabbing his own breastplate.

"I'd sincerely hope so," a voice said as its owner passed through the doorway. "See, there's a person with me who'd very much like you to come back alive." Adro looked past the friend he hadn't spoken to since that first day in Avaris. His mouth closed to a hair's breadth of actually being shut and his eyes narrowed, seeing only Ariadne as she walked into the barracks.

She walked up to him without saying a word. The well-bearded soldiers littering the barracks stopped their preparations to gape and grin at the pleasant distraction. As she reached Adro Ariadne put her arms around his chest, keeping his cold breastplate in his hands a little longer as she felt his warmth. Oblivious to the world around her, she nuzzled her neck next to his so her mouth was all but in his ear. There she whispered,

"Come back to me." He held her tight with his one free hand. "Don't get killed Adro. Come back to me." He turned his head and kissed her softly on the neck. Meanwhile she had taken one of her arms away from his chest and raised it. As he kissed her, Ariadne brought the hidden stone down three times on his head. He looked up at her, into her eyes filled with fear and a mirth she was trying to hide it behind. She smiled; she was able to hide it much better in the smile than in her eyes. Ariadne turned and walked away before her smile could waver. She walked carefully, deliberately—slowly, yet not too much so. She was trying to keep her composure, at least enough of it to look like she was in control; at least enough that Adro wouldn't think she was too afraid. Pity he could see her slight tremble with every step.

As Adro stared at her leaving, Emeko shifted impatiently from foot to foot. Before Adro could get back to strapping his breastplate on, Emeko stepped forward and spoke.

"I'm not sure this quite makes us even but it's a start, yeah?" Emeko held out his hand. "I'm sorry I told Apepios. Friends?"

"We've come too far by now," Emeko watched Adro uneasily as he said those words, "to let something like that stand between us." He grabbed Emeko's hand. "Friends." Zedeck and Macanra breathed a sigh of relieve and went on to punch and wrestle the other two as they had all done together countless times in the past. "You better keep our admiral alive out there

Emeko." Adro said once all four of them were in an entangled mess.

"King you mean. And yeah don't worry about that. Just stay alive yourselves, got it?"

***

The Egyptians came swarming towards them. If they were flies or locusts they would be enough to stir up their own winds. Adro stared back at them defiantly as did Zedeck and Macanra. They stared past his shoulders, one rank behind. They had a pretty clear view nonetheless; there was just one man between them and the charging enemy.

When it had been time to line up Adro had strolled to the front despite the silent protests from Zedeck and Macanra. They followed him with a reluctant sense of dread, knowing full well that with every rank forward they moved their chances of living rapidly decreased. Neither was game to match him though in the very front line. They stood right behind him in the second rank and then Macanra hissed over Adro's shoulder.

"You're an idiot. It's not too late come with us to the back of the phalanx."

Adro stared forward oblivious, determined, resolute.

"You're a bloody fool." Macanra continued. "Come on Adro, I for one would like to live long enough to see what's so great about women." Zedeck chuckled and Macanra raised his arms in frustration. They stood there silently for a minute. After a final gasp of frustration, Macanra spoke once more over Adro's shoulder. "You're a bloody fool but you're our bloody fool. We've got your back, Adro. Just don't do anything else that's stupid; standing there is enough for one battle."

They stood on the top of a long sand dune barring the way to Avaris, waiting for the Egyptians to come to them. The gritty sand bit into them as the wind blew around them while they waited. Still, they stood there waiting and eventually the Egyptians whom they had spotted in the distance were almost upon them. It may have been Adro's imagination but they seemed sluggish and tired. They didn't seem eager to race up at the bristled wall of Cretan spears staring down the dune at them. They didn't seem eager, but they came nonetheless.

Adro heard the cries of anguish as the first Egyptian impaled himself on Adro's spear in the momentum of the charge. He felt the sickening crunch as they pushed back with their shields, breaking countless bones of the Egyptians facing them. He continued for some time in an almost rhythmic trance. His pattern was only broken once one lucky Egyptian hooked onto his shield with an axe and tried to pull it back towards himself. Adro was caught off guard and teetered forward along with the shield. Before he could regain his balance, the Egyptian pushed forward and hit him in the helmet with the top of the axe. Sensing weakness the surrounding Egyptians converged on the dazed Adro. Many pairs of hands reached for anything they could, trying to drag him among them to finish him off. They succeeded in dragging him into their midst. In their excitement at capturing one of the vicious armoured wall they started to beat him with their hands and weapons. they were too compact for a clean cut but they seemed content enough to clobber him to death.

Upon seeing Adro dragged off by the Egyptians, Macanra and Zedeck charged forward. That they didn't spear Adro himself as they lunged at the frenzied mass of Egyptians was more a testament to the luck of a blind thrust than any exceptional skill on their part. They frightened off those

Egyptians nearest to Adro who promptly fell to the ground without their crushing weight keeping him standing. Macanra and Zedeck raced over to his body but, before they could even consider how to drag it back to their lines, more Egyptians came pouring towards them. And yet, the rest of the Cretans did not follow their brave charge but left the two to be swept aside in a sea of Egyptians.

When the sea had engulfed the boys and they could no longer be seen amidst the enemy, one of the Cretan captains raised a cry to the guilt-ridden men standing around him.

"Who are you men to be outshone by a few boys from Malia? Are we not as brave as them? Charge!"

The Cretan wave responded and crashed down upon the Egyptians below them.

***

"Sir, the centre is breaking!"

"They must hold! We are going well. All we need to do is hold our position and we will cut them down," Apepios replied tersely to the messenger. He glanced towards the centre then back at the scout and then nodded slowly. "The men won't break if I am there with them. Men of my personal guard, with me." Emeko started jogging off along with the rest, away from the highest crest on the dune and down into the chaos with Apepios.

Emeko was, naturally, somewhere closer to the back in Apepios' private ranks. He wasn't as tested as the hardened men who took the first few ranks. As the battle lingered on he was beginning to think that he would not actually fight at all, that was until Apepios saw the banner of the king of Memphis in the distance. Emeko saw Apepios' personal messenger run back through the ranks to the command tent, ready to have Apepios' fresh order blasted around them. Sure enough it was not long before he heard the notes start to sound, loud enough to pierce into even the thickest fighting. As the last note played Emeko's heart started beating faster and faster, as if by doing so it might escape the fate he was now condemned to. Six notes—centre to charge headlong into the enemy; to keep charging until further instructions. Apepios meant to reach his rival on the battlefield, no matter the cost of Cretan lives it might take to do so.

Emeko didn't feel it to be too bad at first. He was simply pushing hard at the men in front as they also pushed against the Egyptians. The deeper they got though, like an axe cutting into wood, the more exposed they were on the sides. As the line thinned out he saw men to his right having to fight Egyptians, men who, like him, had been in the relative safety of being at the back. He saw them get cut down one by one as the minutes slowly passed. Nevertheless, they were getting closer. They were almost upon the standard of Memphis. Emeko found himself scanning the men in the distance, eager for a glance at the Egyptian king. He was so preoccupied that he didn't realise the Cretans to his right were no longer there. He didn't realise the blood smeared Egyptian, triumphant over killing a Cretan just moments before, as he came towards him.

Fifteen

The stench made her eyes water. Ariadne couldn't tell if the rotting flesh the stench was coming from used to be a Cretan or an Egyptian. It mattered little as she walked through the battlefield, both sides littered the sand. No-one groaned or raised a half-dismembered arm asking for help. Those who could walk from this place had long done so and those who couldn't had already died or been carried away. There was just silence—well, silence except for the occasional cawing of crows.

A crow pecked at a corpse, the corpse of a boy. But it was not one of her boys, so that was alright. Her boys were lying inside one of the tents nearby for the sick and wounded. Their blood staining the sand beneath them as they groaned in sleep, an inch from death. Zedeck was the first to wake turning a furtive head and fitful eyes to see her smiling beside him.

It was he who told her of their charge into the Egyptian army trying to save Adro. It was he who saw her look of horror upon hearing how Adro had fought at the front in the first place. She who knew the outcome full well but had been oblivious to how it could have happened in the first place.

"But I told him to keep safe… to look after himself… to come back to me…"

"Technically you just told him to come back to you and I guess he has." She looked down at Zedeck, puzzled. "I have very good hearing. Anyway, he did it for you. He says he didn't want to wait; he wanted to marry you once the battle was over. He thought that he might get promoted and allowed to stay in Avaris."

Ariadne looked down again, this time not with a look of puzzlement but horror.

"Doesn't he know I would have waited? Doesn't he know I would wait till the end of time…?"

Zedeck coughed at that point, bringing up another round of blood-coated gunk. He timed it perfectly, as if he had planned it just to ruin her poignant moment.

"Oh yeah by the way the doctors say you guys are bleeding inside, not to mention being bruised from top to bottom—"

"Yeah I figured the second bit."

"Anyway, they don't think its fatal… they aren't sure though."

"That," Zedeck said before coughing once more, "is reassuring."

***

Adro awoke the day after. Ariadne had been sitting there in silence as Zedeck was sleeping. His eyelids were the first things to move. She noticed their flutter immediately since she had been staring absently down at him. It took him a few good blinks before his vision cleared and by that time she had risen from her seat and walked over to him. She sat down next to him and moved her face inches from his. Her eyes were the first things he saw clearly in the world. He didn't even try to speak. He just stared back at her, blinking every so often. After a while she bent down further to kiss him. When she tried though, as her lips brushed his, he groaned in pain—his first audible response to her. She realised that in trying to be tender she had inadvertently shifted her weight, and the knee she had rested beside his ribs was now pressing into them. She moved the knee away, finished the kiss then spoke softly.

"You deserved that."

He groaned again.

"Why couldn't you wait for me?" She switched her tone as suddenly as he had woken up. "You almost died." She leant over to grab a bowl of water for him to drink. "Zedeck says you came back to me so I should be grateful and not quibble." He groaned again as he gulped the water she was feeding into his mouth. "He's right. Still, you deserve all the pain you're in now, and then some." He groaned in the horror of expectation. "But you've come back. That's all that matters. We'll sort everything out."

***

Later that evening when Zedeck had awoken and Adro decided he could speak, Emeko rose from the brink of death.

"How's a man meant to die with you lot carrying on in the background?" he mumbled sleepily.

"Oh he's a man now is he?" Zedeck retorted.

"Don't make me come over there."

"You and what army?" Adro joined in.

"Argh, quiet will you? Hang on that's a point: the army. How did we go? Did we win? Did we kill the other pharaoh?" Emeko asked, his questions rousing himself from sleep to speak each successive word clearer and louder.

"Oh yeah, hadn't thought to ask about that." Zedeck said. All three of them looked at Ariadne who replied.

"Yes, we won the battle and, yes, it was because Apepios managed to kill their leader. He wasn't the king though, some official fighting for him. Apepios has taken the rest of the army south to Memphis to try and capture it. He thinks that will win him the war."

"Well at least we're here in the safety of the dead and dying." Adro said and then chuckled, "It just goes to prove that it's better to be among the dead today than join them tomorrow."

"That's not a saying." Emeko pointed out.

"It is now, and a pretty good one at that." Adro replied.

"Hey Ariadne, weren't you meant to be looking after things in Avaris?" Emeko asked.

"Yes, I was, and then the scribes who survived the battle came back. I asked Apepios and he said I could stay here with you guys till you're better. Once you are though he wants you all back to your places. None of you got any promotions for almost getting killed—he thinks he won the whole battle with that stupid charge so refuses to share much of the credit."

"Oh great," Adro moaned.

"Speaking of getting better, how's Macanra faring?" Emeko asked.

"He's no worse than Adro or Zedeck, it's just that he hasn't woken up."

But he didn't wake up. He continued to sleep the sleep before death. For three days the others slowly started to heal and he kept wasting away. On the forth morning his father entered the tent. He walked in slowly, fresh scars still gleaming with a red tinge, but nothing to match that in his eyes. It frightened Adro and Zedeck to see the man who not only Macanra but they had grown to fear, with eyes sore from tears. He turned to Ariadne and spoke,

"Word is my son still isn't better?" She nodded and replied,

"He sleeps."

"He's been sleeping for too long. It's unnatural. All the others are awake, why isn't he?" he asked her helplessly. "He's been bewitched by death I tell you. Death tried to catch all of you but caught him and now won't let him go." He paused and then spoke as if they weren't there, as if he hadn't just been speaking to them, "I wish I hadn't been so hard on the boy. I just didn't know any other way to be. Life's hard, no use hiding the fact. At least that's what I thought. I wish I had told him I loved him but I guess now it's too late." He turned around and looked at them all, as if it were the first time he had seen their faces. "It may be too late to tell him but maybe I can save him from this grip of death. Death wants a life, it isn't satisfied even after all this. Fine, I'll give Death a life."

Ariadne bristled, only too aware where this speech may lead. Adro saw her change immediately, from pity to distrust. He reached for her hand and squeezed it tight but it didn't help. *What can he do? What can any of us do against this man here? Three bedridden and all but dead boys and a girl… we can't stop him if he tries…* She started to shiver from fear, noticing the blade in Macanra's father's hand.

"Oh yeah by the way, Zedeck, your father's dead. He was a good sailor but he made a shit soldier." He said, once again the hard and blunt man they knew. "I'll tell him he should be mighty proud of you though when I see him."

Zedeck stared up at him in a mixture of shock from the news and fascination over what he was still planning to do. Macanra's father walked over to the sleeping body of his son and stood over him. He raised the hand holding the knife to his own throat and spoke calmly even though the blade rested so close.

"Any gods of Crete that haven't yet deserted us and any gods of this new land who will accept such an offering, I urge you to free my son from this embrace of death. I offer you my life in exchange for his. Let him live long in this world; give him a better life than I had. Death, if it's you that needs to be appeased, I ask you to take my life instead of my son's. Set him free; I offer myself to you."

With that he drew the blade across his throat, cutting it cleanly as he had done to countless sheep throughout his life. As his blood flowed down onto his son, as his knees buckled and as his eyelids started to flutter, he gazed down at his son hoping for a sign that his prayer was answered. His son's face was still unmoving, however, and just as pale as before. As the father's eyelids fluttered and closed, never to open again, so the son's stayed shut, oblivious to the offering of blood.

***

Macanra's eyes didn't open that day. They didn't open the day after either, nor did they open the day after that. A further week went by and he wasted away, some saying he was already dead. Eventually they did open though and his mouth shortly followed.

"Phew, I stink. Why didn't you wash my blood off me?"

Ariadne was there at the time. She smiled sadly as she looked at the dried blood caked all over him. She replied,

"We did…"

Sixteen

(Present)

The gust of wind died down as quickly as it had burst through the courtyard. It was gone. Once again the air was still, as if the wind had never come through to disturb it. But the grains of sand remained. If one had the eyes to see, they would notice that specks now littered the ground where before there had been none. Ariadne felt her skin, formerly soft and pleasant, now scratched and irritated by the sand blown onto her and staying, enjoying its new home.

As she resumed her walk, Ariadne thought of the last few months of their war. She remembered Adro complaining as he left that she would be speaking Egyptian by the time he returned, and that he wouldn't be able to understand her. He joked that she would forget their Cretan tongue and they'd have to communicate with hand gestures. *Funny, 'cause he came back speaking it better than I did.*

All four of her lads had left as soon as they were able to carry their shield and spear. They reached the army after it had already taken and sacked Memphis. The child pharaoh had not been there though. He had fled even further south, to Thebes. Meanwhile many of the Egyptian governors from Lower Egypt had already started pouring into Avaris offering their loyalty to the new king. *Apepios had won*, Ariadne thought, *he had saved us. We were accepted in this land. No wonder he took that deal from the emissaries of Thebes. They acknowledged Apepios as rightful king of the fertile Lower Egypt in return for allowing the child to rule Upper Egypt. No wonder they immediately asked for peace and trade; that rocky land could hardly support the men there without grain from the delta Apepios now controlled.*

Ariadne stopped her thoughts in mid-track, realising. She laughed quietly and bitterly to think of how hopeful she had been to hear that they had taken Memphis and made peace with the child king. Yes, the army returned to Avaris and, yes, Apepios took oaths of loyalty from the governors who had come to him, but as many governors stayed away as came. Ariadne saw Adro for a mere night before he was sent off out into the provinces to bring the governors who had not offered fealty to heel. And the bitterest thing, once the governors had given in, Apepios dispersed the army, sending garrisons to each and every governor to remind him which king he served. It had been a good ten years before she saw his face again.

As tears welled in her eyes at the memory, Ariadne wiped them away with a merciless efficiency. She was chief scribe to Apepios, king of Lower Egypt, she would be composed as she stood before him. Still, she had had Emeko for company those ten years. Apparently king's bodyguards stayed with their king, and Apepios quickly grew to enjoy the benefits of city living.

"—it is a disgrace, an abomination!" Ariadne heard faintly in the distance. She realised she had walked all the way from the courtyard through the maze of rooms to the grand hall without even realising she was moving the whole time. Now that she was within sight of the retainers and advisors, the elite who had a chance to influence the decisions of Apepios, she stiffened her walk, carefully placing each foot in front of the other for no other reason than to show that she was in complete control of herself. Suddenly she changed from a daydreaming woman strolling along in the ease of her youth to a deliberate and stern figure surging powerfully into the room, exuding confidence and authority. She walked through the standing crowd of thirty or so men and held back a smile as they knew to part before her. Having broken through she stood at the sideline, within sight of Apepios, waiting for him to call her. She stood and listened to the rant going on before her eyes.

"—it will not be endured I tell you! My people will not accept this injustice."

"Patience, dear friend," Apepios quietened the man before him. "When has Apepios not been good to Cush? I ask you to wait, to hold your accusations until the accused has a chance to hear your charges. I have sent for the ambassador from Lower Egypt and he will be arriving shortly."

The Cushite ambassador stood there all alone in the open, fuming at having to wait. He nodded slightly however and said no more. Apepios looked around while he was waiting and, seeing Ariadne, motioned for her to come forward and speak.

"O Great King of—"

"Skip the titles girl, we haven't got much time before the Kamose's ambassador arrives. Straight to the point."

"Well, in short, the Nile has barely flooded this season. There is little grain stored because we have been trading it away. Unless we do something, many people will starve." Apepios' eyes narrowed in concern as Ariadne continued. "But it appears that this is even more serious. An Egyptian scribe of mine told me that you are held personally responsible for the success of the Nile flooding. If it doesn't, then you are thought to have lost Heaven's authority as ruler of Lower Egypt."

"What is this nonsense?" Apepios asked with a rising irritation. "I gained Heaven's blessing on the field of battle, why should I lose it because some stream runs dry?"

"The girl is right." Euouk said loudly and slowly, as if he couldn't bear to utter the words but had no alternative. "The gods of Egypt control all things and you represent them in body. If the world is seen to be out of balance, such as the Nile not flooding, it is deemed your responsibility. In fact, it is even worse; you are seen to have lost contact with the gods, lost their support and their authority…"

Apepios looked sternly at Euouk, neither daring to say out loud how fragile their rule really was, how much was at stake and how serious this could be.

Quick footsteps could be heard approaching in the silence that now appeared. The ambassador from Upper Egypt did not hesitate upon reaching the crowd but drove through it with a haughty determination, retainers rushing to move from his path lest they be knocked down instead. As soon as he could see Apepios he began speaking.

"I couldn't help but overhear that you have a problem, Apepi—"

"What right do you have to speak to me as if I were your soon to be son-in-law?" The disgruntled retainers gave a dignified chuckle at the hidden joke and Apepios' disregard for the arrogant Egyptian. "You will address me with my proper titles or I will have you thrown to the crocodiles." Apepios said calmly and smiled.

The Egyptian looked at him with confidence, as if the threat had been nothing more than a request to dine with him later that day. He smiled in return and smoothly uttered the words,

"Great Hyksos King of Lower Egypt, the Mighty Bull, He who is strong of arm, the oppressor of the nine bows, Ra incarnate, son of Ra—Apepi." He paused and looked around the room before continuing, "I couldn't help but overhear that you have a problem."

"Flooding Niles and starving peasants are nothing compared to why you are here today, speck of grit." The Cushite ambassador interrupted, seething.

"He is right," Apepios said. "Cush has allegations, serious allegations against Kamose. I am here to judge whether I need to personally intervene in this dispute…"

"If that is your will, let us hear then what lies Cush dares to tell this time." The Egyptian said in a tone of rising irritation.

"O Great and Wise Apepi," the Cushite ambassador began, "Reports came to me not two days ago from my people. They say that Kamose's army has invaded our lands. They tell of crops burnt and the deaths of all who could not flee before them. This invasion force is stronger than anything we can muster. Cush, your dear friend, begs your assistance, Apepi. Fight with us, immediately, against Kamose's aggression."

"Where is the proof? Has this man seen such 'destruction' personally? No, he relies on the lies told to him by men sent by his deceitful king." The Egyptian immediately rebutted.

"Watch the slanders of your tongue, or lose it, arrogant one." Apepios said calmly.

"You call it slander to speak the truth, O Great and Wise King? These are lies and lies are told from liars so Cush's king is a liar."

"Pregnant women and children still sucking on their mother's breast! Monsters the lot of you!" the Cushite shouted back.

"Apepi, wisest of the Hyksos, I do not dispute that these claims are serious, merely the truth behind them. If it is found that my king has done such a thing then of course you are right to be angry. But, if I may make a suggestion?" He paused and, since Apepios did not say anything, he continued. "Send a delegation down to Cush to see for yourself whether or not this has taken place. The words of a Nubian are no greater than the empty wind which carries them, but no-one would dispute the integrity of your men, Apepi."

"My brothers and sisters will long be rotting in the ground by the time your delegation returns, Apepi. Strike now and we may yet survive Kamose's wrath." The Cushite pleaded. As Apepios looked from one to another, everyone could see his mind working away, coming to a conclusion. Before he could get there, however, the Egyptian spoke again.

"I fear you may be provoked by the cries of an angry man, Apepi, to take an unwise course without fully understanding all of the issues. Your problem, which I couldn't help overhearing about, is our problem as well. If the Nile does not flood, the people will lose faith in all of us. We must stand united in this troubled time. If we do, the people will have no choice but to accept us. If we bicker and fight, however, they will see that as further proof and tear us all down. Kamose merely seeks peace Apepi, so grant us peace that we may all live together. Do not do anything rash; test the words of this man before you put all of our lives in jeopardy."

Euouk motioned to speak and Apepios nodded his approval.

"I believe the Egyptian ambassador is right, Apepios. The Egyptians see anything which deviates in a bad way from normal life as a sign that the gods have left their rulers. You cannot afford to add the chaos of a war to a famine. He's right; if both kings of Egypt stand together in harmony and peace, the people will probably settle down but if you fight they will take that as a further sign that neither of you have the authority of Heaven."

"Well said, Hyksos priest." The Egyptian complemented.

"Well said my arse!" the enraged Cushite exploded. "Don't be led astray by their big fine words and talk of rebellion, Apepi! Gods reward justice and loyalty—regardless of what Egyptians think. You will keep Heaven's blessing if you help us in our distress, leave us and you will be forsaken. If the Nile's lack of flooding is a sign from Heaven then surely it is reflecting the evil of Kamose as he dares to invade our lands."

"What can this heathen Cushite know of Egypt's gods? Do not listen to him, Apepi." The Egyptian said.

"Damn Egypt's gods!"

There was a silence after Ariadne uttered that louder than she intended. All eyes on her now, she felt she might as well continue. "Who cares what gods think of us and what the peasants think of the gods? We rule by spear and shield and by the wisdom of our king. Surely, issues of gods aside, the decision is obvious? The Egyptians and Cushites have hated each other from long before we came and I dare say Kamose has no great love for us, having killed his father and taken the better half of his land. Kamose probably has invaded Cush and you owe him no love or loyalty—attack him now while his army is away and while it might still save our friends. We have precious few in this land."

"O Great and Wise Apepios," Euouk said as soon as she had finished, "this glorified scribe can be excused for intervening in such a heated debate; considering her womanly temperament she must have felt right at home." Some retainers could not help but burst out laughing, most, however, stayed silent. "But although we may excuse her little outburst, it should not be taken notice of." He turned to Ariadne and spoke to her, "It's your job to count the tallies for us and you've done that very well. Now leave the business of deciding what to do to those who understand how to run a kingdom."

Ariadne looked to Apepios for support but he said nothing. He looked around the room, from the ambassadors standing before him to Ariadne, Euouk and the retainers and advisors who filled the chamber. He sighed and spoke with resignation.

"Each of you tells me Heaven will support me if I support you. Upper Egypt tells me the gods will support peace and Cush tells me they will support war." Resignation shifted to confidence. "All this talk of gods is pointless. I am a god, so you have all said, so my decision has a god's wisdom and authority." He paused, daring either of them to disagree with him. Silence. "I will not go to war until I have proof." The Egyptian smiled and the Cushite grimaced in hatred. "I will send a delegation immediately and if they report that Cush has been attacked, I will kill Kamose and all of his men. If Cush has been hurt, for every injury tenfold will be given to Kamose and all who followed him. I want peace and I want my people to believe in my rule but if my friends have truly been hurt then I shall bring Heaven's vengeance on those who did it, regardless of who will oppose me."

Both ambassadors stared back at him dumbfounded.

"That is my word and it is final. The matter is finished."

The Cushite managed to nod his acceptance before storming out with a restrained poise. The Egyptian stayed behind however. Apepios started at him evidently waiting for him to similarly leave. Once it was apparent that he wasn't going anywhere, Apepios spoke to the Egyptian.

"All right, what else have you got to say?"

"I would like to offer a suggestion to help you keep the peace among your people, Apepi." The Egyptian replied warmly. "There is a ritual for kings whose connection with the gods has waned over time. It is meant to restore that connection and bring them once again into harmony with the gods. By doing so, it is meant to restore harmony in the land." The Egyptian looked at Euouk. "Do you know of this ritual, priest?"

"I am not sure. What is it called?" Euouk asked.

"A Sed festival." The Egyptian replied.

"Have you heard of it, Euouk?" Apepios asked.

"I seem to have forgotten that particular ritual, o Great Apepios, for I do not recall what it precisely entails."

"Tell us then, Egyptian, of this Sed festival."

"Gladly. You see one must understand that the relationship between the king and the gods is embodied not only in the world around but in his relationship with his people. A Sed festival rests on this principle..."

Ariadne was already walking out of there. She had had about enough of priests and their rituals for one day. She decided not to go back to work but to home instead. As she left the palace and was again confronted with the wind, she noticed the guard barracks in the distance. In the barracks' courtyard she saw wooden stakes covered with fading dried blood the odd tangle of rope lying on the ground. Even in peace soldiers still needed to practice their skills and prisoners and criminals weren't missed.

Hasn't been done in a while, such a shame really. It would be so great to see Euouk led towards there, realising there was no escape. Then where would his gods be? She smiled at the thought and felt her composure return of its own accord as she walked onward.

Seventeen

Ariadne shut the door with a firm hand which was already beginning to relax as she placed a beam across it. No-one would intrude on her now. She paused, taking a moment to savour the thick mud walls keeping the rest of the wind away. She felt it trapping warmth inside and saw the flickering shadow on the wall. Her husband must be at home, say one thing about him, he liked to cook.

Her husband was busily humming away around the corner, just out of sight, still oblivious to her entrance. She thought back to the position of the sun in the sky as she walked through the streets, *yes, he is between shifts, isn't he?* Well, even being chief scribe didn't pay so much that they didn't need a second job in the family, especially if she was to have little ones one of these days. Her throat tightened at the thought; in fear, in failure? *No*, she reminded herself, there was still plenty of time. They had only been married a few years, maybe they had just been unlucky, although she insisted the day that he made an offering to a fertility god, or any other for that matter, she would walk right out of there. Still, it was a comfortable life, one that suited her. Unlike for so long, she finally had someone to come home to. She hadn't realised it at the time but it meant a lot. She had had an ache in her heart which grew every day she came home exhausted from constantly reading records and organising people, she just didn't realise how much of it was pure loneliness.

Ariadne walked up past the corner to see her husband staring intently at the meal sizzling away before him. His eyes lifted at the sound of her footsteps so close and he smiled as they met her own. Without a word she strolled in an arch passing by his side to end up right behind him. She wrapped her arms around his chest and looked down contently at the food, still in silence. A silence which he broke barely after a few heartbeats passed between them.

"Ariadne,"

"Yes, husband?"

"What are you thinking?"

"Ten years," she murmured. "Do you reckon we can be forgiven for what we did? It was so hard waiting…"

He paused. She felt his muscles tighten slightly and knew he understood her question immediately. "Of course we can be forgiven for it," he said. "I felt a bit bad at first, don't you remember?" She looked at him and gave a painful smile. "But it worked out the best, eh?"

"The best for us you mean. I can't help but still feel sorry for him. Some days I wake up and feel like we've betrayed him. He'd been so good to me for so long…"

"Fate," He felt her eyes glaring into the back of his neck. "And by fate I mean circumstances, events and chance happenings." He added quickly.

"Better," she said warningly.

"Worked out for us in the end."

"But…"

"It was his own fault. He couldn't be here anyway, remember? It really was just you and me." Adro spun around then and kissed her tenderly on her lips. It lasted much longer than the few heartbeats of before. When he was done, he continued, "Not that you would have had it any other way than you and me?"

"Of course not. In those ten years I never touched another, never even thought of it." Ariadne said.

"Nor did I." Adro replied. "Though those camels were sorely tempting…" She raised a hand from being now on the lower part of his back, up to strike the back of his head. She hit with just enough force that he knew she was being playful.

"What can I say? A man has urges." She hit him again.

"Don't I know it…?" She lowered her hand from the air above his head, stroking his hair as it wound its way down, resting on his neck. "But if I ever see you looking at a camel the way you look at me I'll—"

"What? Marry me?"

"Hmmm, doesn't sound like a bad plan."

"Speaking of which," Adro said, "what was that 'husband' thing at the start? I have a name you know."

"I just like saying it that's all. Reminds me that this is actually happening."

"Well, *wife*, there's food to be cooked and it will burn if it's left alone, so how about you..." he shot her a cheeky grin, "let go so I can tend to it?"

"*Never...*" she said slowly, savouring his warmth. Adro smiled but continued regardless,

"But I bought this pigeon from a lovely old Egyptian woman in the market. It would be a crime not to cook it properly."

"Don't talk to me of Egyptians." Ariadne said and released her grip on him.

"Bad day with the underlings then?" Adro asked as he turned around to look after the dangerously abandoned food.

"No, scribes I could handle! It was this ambassador who turned up today in court."

"Mmhmm."

"Get this: The Egyptians invaded Cush and Cush asked for our aid. Apepios is doing nothing. He's not sending any men to help them out."

"He can't be doing nothing." Adro said somewhat unconvinced.

"He's sending ambassadors to check if it's happening—"

"See!"

"But it's the Egyptians! What more proof do we need?" she said and looked at him in all seriousness. "If you leave a baby by the Nile next to a crocodile and it cries out, you save it—you don't just leave it there to get eaten."

"So you would have us fight another war and risk your friend's lives, our lives, on a rumour?"

"Cush is our friend. I would trust our friend and come to their aid when they ask for it."

"They are our allies—there's a difference. I don't remember them loading us into boats when the seas withdrew and the heavens were alight." Adro said sternly. "I remember Zedeck's father risking his life waiting for us and who died afterwards fighting so his son might have a chance to live in peace. We have peace now. Allies are for war and we shouldn't start a war on a whim. I wouldn't send my mates off to fight on a whim for some poor man in the desert I've never met."

"You're so callous sometimes!"

"Callous?!" Adro lost it. "Callous? Forgive me for remembering standing in line shitting myself wondering if my friends and I would last the hour. Forgive me for wondering if I'd ever see your face again. When you say we should start a war and don't even think about the consequences—that's callous!" Adro paused after shouting the final word. He was panting. His fingers clenched the empty air and his heart couldn't stop pounding. They stood there for a few moments and then Adro's head dropped and he managed a thin semblance of a smile. "Sorry, my love. I'm sorry I shouted at you."

"It's ok," Ariadne said softly. She paused in thought for a little while before replying further.

"Whether we fight Kamose or not you've still got to admit the Egyptians are crazy."

"How so?"

"Well, all this stuff about the gods all the time. Everything always comes down to the gods. If we win, it's the gods; if we lose, it's the gods; if the Nile is dry then look out because the gods are mad with you again."

"It's harmless." Adro said light-heartedly before Ariadne looked at him with a face suddenly harder than the walls around them.

"Gods are never harmless. They make normal people do terrible things."

"True. True..." Adro said quickly. "But they're not always bad. When people have gods to believe in, it gives them purpose. They work hard and feel satisfied with life and their small part in it."

"None of these gods are real. If their gods were real they wouldn't want us in charge of their people. And if they are real and don't care so long as someone gives them sacrifices then they are weak and don't deserve worship in the first place so they might as well not exist. When people believe in gods they end up being controlled by fear. That's really what it's all about," Ariadne said bitterly. "All these gods are just made up so kings and priests can control people; so they can justify not having to work in the fields like everyone else."

"And when was the last time you held a sickle, my dear?" Adro said and smirked hoping to still deter her from another rant on the evils of gods and goddesses.

"Your father, Adro, he doesn't believe in it any more than I do. But he gets fed because, without someone to do the rituals, the stupid Egyptian peasants would rebel."

"Now, they're not all stupid peasants..."

"No?"

"No."

"Well then, remind me who had a country untroubled by fire from heaven but lost it anyway? It was these stupid Egyptians who bowed down to us and accepted it when we said we were their gods—all because we killed their king. They deserved to lose this land. They were born slaves."

"They did have fire from heaven." Adro muttered.

"What?" Ariadne asked partly annoyed at her flow being interrupted and partly intrigued.

"That old Egyptian lady who sold me the pigeon, she told me of when fire rained from heaven upon the land of Egypt. They've suffered hardship, same as us."

"What happened?" Ariadne had already forgotten her rant and was already enthralled. She'd never stopped enjoying a good story—a legacy of her mother she wasn't quite able to shake.

"Listen up then Ariadne, you might even feel sorry for them. This is the story she told me:

Back in the days long ago before any Egyptian had met men from beyond the seas, there lived a man of the desert tribes beyond the Nile. This man had been sold as a slave by his own brothers, so they say. He would have ended his days in obscurity if not for his powerful magic. For this man could read dreams.

Pharaoh had a disturbing dream which no priest or magician could decipher. He was told, however, of this slave and his power to read dreams. The slave told Pharaoh that Egypt would be filled with seven years of prosperity then seven years of drought. Woe to Pharaoh! Would that he had ignored the slave and suffered seven years of drought; it would have been better than what followed in the end.

Woe unto Pharaoh for he freed this slave and made him vizier over the whole of Egypt. He made him in charge of storing and dispersing the grain and so Egypt survived the drought. Alas, that he survived as well for his brothers came from across the desert sands in search of grain. Kind Pharaoh let the vizier's brothers and their families stay in Egypt for the vizier forgave them.

Years past and the vizier died. The drought left Egypt and the world beyond but these men did not leave. They stayed in Egypt and became many. They soon numbered more than locusts and no pharaoh knew what to do.

Then one day came a wise pharaoh. He knew that sometimes people must do difficult things to keep the world at peace. This pharaoh had all the sons of these foreigners killed so that they would not rise up against him. There was one son who was saved though, by the pharaoh's daughter. She had mercy on the foreign child and kept him as her own son. She named him Moses.

This Moses was no better than the rest of the foreigners, however. He grew angry one day and killed an Egyptian without cause. He showed Pharaoh that he had done the right thing in weakening these men. Moses ran away from Egypt and escaped justice. He escaped into the desert sands.

It is said that in the desert this Moses learned savage sorcery and powerful magic. It is said he wanted to make himself pharaoh of all Egypt but once he realised Egypt would not tolerate an imposter he decided to use his magic to become king of the foreigners instead. He promised them a kingdom far beyond Egypt if they would follow him. But they would not follow him—they did not trust him either so he put his dark magic to work.

He brought all manner of accursed plagues upon Egypt to show the foreigners of his might and convince them to follow him. He turned the Nile to blood and made the heavens rain fire and ice down upon Egypt. His last plague was the worst, the vilest of the dark arts. He killed off the firstborn sons of every Egyptian in the darkness of a single night.

By that point all of the foreigners had gone over to him. They wanted to follow the man with such power. And so Pharaoh let them leave into the desert but he did not forgive Moses for his sorcery. He sent an army after him to destroy him and his people so no-one with knowledge of such dark arts would be left alive to practice them. Moses still had his dark magic, however, and it was at its strongest in the desert. No-one knows how Pharaoh's army died but not a single man returned. It is said that afterward Egypt fought for a generation with the wild tribes of the desert who sensed weakness like wolves and closed in. Egypt suffered much because once a kind pharaoh helped a foreign slave and his brothers..."

Adro held his breath to end the tale with the ringing of utter silence. After a little while, he looked at a still entranced Ariadne and spoke, "So, what did you think? Feel sorry for them yet?"

"I feel sorry for the Moses people." Ariadne replied.

"What?"

"They had to put up with the Egyptians for centuries before they finally upped it and went. We've been here less than a generation and I'm already sick of them."

Adro sighed.

"Well, dinner's ready so you can at least thank that old Egyptian lady for the pigeon even if you don't sympathise with her. It will be delicious."

"Speaking of delicious..." Ariadne said, once again her playful self.

"Not tonight I've got guard duty." Adro said quickly carving the pigeon.

"Tomorrow then?"

"Zedeck's back in town. I bumped into him in the market earlier today and invited him to come by tomorrow for lunch." Ariadne frowned at him. "He says he's got lots of crazy adventures to tell us all about."

"I'd rather we had some crazy adventures of our own." Adro kept carving the pigeon. "It'll have to be tonight then. Last time he came over you started drinking before noon and both passed out before I got home from work. He'll be here *all day*."

"I told you I've got a night shift."

"When does it start?" Ariadne said, her eyes reflecting a mixture of hope and frustration.

"half an hour."

"Plenty of time!" Ariadne said triumphant.

"I have to be there in half an hour."

"Run then, I'll put a spring in your step..."

Eighteen

"49... 50. Here I come!" Multak spun around from the wall and started running even before he could see where he was going. Natir liked to hide in the nearby rubble while the others often scattered throughout the remains of the fort. *I'll get him this time. He won't sneak past me again.*

Multak's dark feet darted over the rocky remains strewn near the hole in the wall he had been counting at. Natir was somewhere under here. Waiting. Holding his breath. Listening for the right time to—

Movement. Not much but something. Multak saw feet being shuffled back into hiding. Multak raced towards Natir and, heedless of alerting him, shouted "I've got you!" sprinting all the harder.

Natir darted up from the rubble like a desert demon from the sand and bolted. He stopped after a short distance and pointed back towards the wall where Multak had been counting. Multak quickly glanced to see the others running from their hiding places at a chance to get there in safety.

"Do you really want to lose this round just because you tried to get me? The others are almost there."

"If I get you I won't lose this round."

"You have to catch me though."

Natir ran off again, deep into the fort, with Multak only a few footsteps behind. Natir darted in and out of the remains of the tents to the cries of "Made it!" at the wall. But Multak matched his every swerve—all the boys knew the fort like their mother's face and the sting of their father's hand. Natir pushed one of the decaying tent poles over as he raced around it. Multak was too close to stop and collided with it. While Multak was staggering Natir made use of the precious seconds he gained and raced towards another section of the fort's wall.

Natir was already halfway up the wall by the time Multak reached its base. Natir's hands and feet were quickly and confidently reaching for every jagged edge to propel him ever upward. Panting, he reached the top but didn't stop—he started running along the top of the wall towards his friends waiting on the other side of the fort.

Out of the corner of his eye Natir saw movement as he raced towards the counting spot. He quickly glanced back but Multak had not yet reached the top. As he turned his head back to the front he saw what it was. He saw and almost tripped as he stopped running mid-step.

Spears and shields. Men. Lots of men. Marching towards the ruined fort.

"Argh!" Natir heard a cry from where he had climbed and ran back toward it. He lent over the wall and looked down inside the fort to see Multak staring back at him in pain.

"You broke my leg, camel turd!"

Natir looked down at Multak's leg, saw the twisted angle and jutting out bone and grimaced.

"You broke your own leg. Shouldn't have climbed up after me if you couldn't do it." Natir looked back out towards the men quickly approaching from the distance and Multak noticed the look on his face change to immense fear.

"What is it?"

"I think they're Egyptians…"

Multak looked to Natir, his eyes pleading to not be left there alone.

"I'll get the others—we can carry you out together." Natir said determinedly.

Natir resumed his race along the wall and ran faster than before. *The counting spot is just up ahead. Not far. Not long now.* Natir stopped again in mid-step at what he saw. He crouched down low and his heart started pounding, filling his body with lighting. He saw three Egyptian scouts climb through the hole in the wall beside the counting spot. *They're here.* He saw the rest of the boys flee in terror before them. He saw one boy stumble and trip and one of the scouts stab him with a spear before he could rise again. And he saw the scout with the bloodied spear look up at him, stare him in the eyes and grin.

***

Chariot wheels thundered along through the dunes as salt-streaked and panting horses galloped forward. Kamose's eyes gazed ahead as if he were the great falcon itself, always alert and in search of his prey.

Over the next dune—a flicker in the distance—Kamose had but to point and his chariot driver whipped the reins mercilessly in pursuit. His prey would hear him coming but that was alright, he had finally found it and he would easily run it down. Kamose loved hunting.

His eyes narrowed as they passed over the next dune. He could see it now at the base of the next one. He was catching up. Kamose lifted his bow in anticipation and removed an arrow from his quiver.

Over the next dune and he was even closer: it was still at the base of the dune he was now riding down.

Kamose nocked the arrow. He could see the muscles in its legs surging as it desperately sprinted over the boiling sands.

Kamose pulled the string back. His prey tried dodging to one side, sensing the end and trying to salvage a few more moments in this world.

Kamose held his breath. The chariot wheeled around matching his prey.

And let go.

Silence.

For less than a heartbeat and then came the soft sound of an arrow piercing flesh.

Then came the almost human scream as pain rocketed through the body of his prey.

Kamose's chariot wheeled around again and he fired a second arrow, this time through the throat. His prey gurgled and blood spurted onto the sand beneath. Even before it collapsed onto the bloodied ground, never to rise again, Kamose's chariot driver said a light hearted, "Good kill."

Kamose nodded to the driver and then inclined his head back towards the body.

"Strap it behind the chariot." He said. His chariot driver did so unhurriedly and once the Nubian was firmly tethered, climbed back aboard and whipped the reins.

Those first few minutes passed in silence. He didn't need to ask Kamose why he didn't just kill the man in his sleep in the palace or some public execution square. No-one did. They all knew Kamose liked a good kill, especially when he was the one who delivered it.

After a while Kamose's chariot driver broke the silence.

"Have you heard back whether Apepi will declare war to support Cush?"

"News of my invasion would not have reached the north until a few days ago." Kamose calmly replied. "My ambassador to Apepi was instructed to get me more time. When they hear of my invasion he is to ask that Apepi sends ambassadors to check the claims for himself. If he succeeds then Apepi's ambassadors will have to cross the length of Egypt twice before he realises he made a mistake. My army will have long since destroyed Cush's cities, won back my mines and scattered the remnants to the hills."

"Shouldn't you kill his ambassadors like our dear friend from Cush here?" the chariot driver asked motioning to the corpse bouncing along behind them.

"I want war with Apepi. I just do not want it yet. If I kill his ambassadors word will reach him sooner than I like. If I let them inspect Cush's burning ashes and return I will have bought myself enough time for my army to have returned."

Kamose's chariot driver looked at the young pharaoh in admiration. *He is so young*, he thought, *but he will win us back our land.* He thought more for a second and then spoke again.

"But what if your ambassador to Apepi didn't manage to persuade him to wait? What if he rallies his army then and comes storming down to defend Cush?"

Kamose smiled and replied.

"It will take Apepi some time to gather his army. It is spread out all across the delta." He smiled again. "Even so, if he does not wait then he will still come in time. He will find Thebes undefended with my army still far away in the south. I will be caught between his army and the remaining Cushites who will rally to fight alongside their ally. I will be destroyed."

His chariot driver looked at him in horror.

"War is always a gamble my friend. Pray that the gods grant me victory as the true saviour of Egypt."

His chariot driver turned his head forward once more muttering, "I hope you know what you're doing."

"If this gamble pays off and Apepi does not rally immediately, I will win this war and free our people."

"How?"

Kamose winked and spoke softly,

"You'll see."

As they bounded over the last dune the sun blinded them for a moment, reflecting off Thebes' walls in the distance.

"You'll see."

***

This was the house, he was sure of it. *It'd better be*, Zedeck mused, *don't think I can survive another mistake.* As Zedeck stared at the wooden door glowing orange from the dawn he thought back to five minutes before.

It had been easily half an hour since he had left the tavern. Faltering steps or no he must be getting close. Wait he knew that corner—he had thrown up on it the last time he had been in Avaris. Zedeck walked confidently past the corner and saw a house. *This must be it. This must be their place.* Zedeck walked up to the front door and motioned to his two slaves, respectfully keeping their distance, to step up right behind him. Each carried an amphora of the best Bosporan wine—a perfect gift for his dear friend.

He banged his mug against the door. Wood met wood and the door rattled loudly in the morning calm. He looked down at the mug in his hand and took a gulp. The wine may be for Adro but surely he wouldn't mind if Zedeck had a drop or two along the way? No sounds of stirring inside. He banged again and raised his voice in an elegant melody,

"Come out you lazy guard! Co-ome out you lazy gua-ard!" Bang. "Co-ome out and seeeee, whether out of you or me, the better by far is meeee!" Bang.

Still nothing save for the chuckling of one of his slaves. Zedeck shrugged and started up once more.

"Come out you—" the door opened.

"What the fuck do you want, drunk?" an unfamiliar voice said from the darkness. The man stepped forward. Zedeck couldn't tell what glistened more in the morning light—that wholesome beard or muscular arms more toned than a bull's hind.

Zedeck just stood there—speechless.

"I'm only gonna ask you once more, drunk. What the—"

Zedeck held up his mug of wine to the man standing before him and said fearfully, "For you..."

The man looked down at Zedeck's mug. His favourite mug. He then looked back up at Zedeck. Zedeck nodded and filled his eyes with all the enthusiasm he could muster as he thrust the mug, half-full, into the hands of the man before him.

"Enjoy!" Zedeck shouted as he raced down the street, slaves barely a step behind. That was five minutes ago. This house had better be it.

Once more he raised a hand to motion his slaves forward. As they stood behind him nervously, he tapped politely on the door. He waited patiently and the door—

Stayed shut. He tapped again and still only mildly.

Within a minute he was banging on the door with both fists—the past nothing more than a wisp of wind among the gale of the moment.

"AAAADDDDRROOOO! AARRRIAAADNNEEE!" he shouted over the din of his banging.

The door opened.

"Zedeck! Come in before you bother the neighbours." Ariadne said sleepily.

"Too late..." Zedeck grumbled as he walked through the door, gesturing with one hand for his slaves to follow him.

As Ariadne closed the door behind them she muttered a quiet, "I don't want to know."

Zedeck kept walking onward towards the silhouette with his back turned lighting one of several candles littering the room. "Adro, how's the luckiest guard in Avaris going these days?"

"Sleep deprived, my old friend." Adro said as he turned with a grin.

"She's keeping you busy then?" Zedeck said returning it.

Ariadne whacked Zedeck across the back of his head and motioned to the smirking slaves to rest the amphorae down in the corner. Zedeck continued unfazed and laid down on one of the couches before turning to his hosts and saying, with the use of his hands as much as words, "Now due to an unforseen accident I might have somewhat mislaid my mug." Adro rolled his eyes and started for the kitchen. "Would it be too much trouble to ask for the use of," Adro returned with a mug in each hand—one extended towards Zedeck, "one of yours?"

Ariadne and Adro reclined on the couch opposite Zedeck and he motioned to one of his slaves. "Come boy, bring the wine." He turned to Adro, "This wine is from the Bosporus, no less." He said as the slave brought the amphora over. "One of my ships up there travelled beyond the Bosporus to see if there were any people to trade with. They came back with such outlandish stories that I'm not sure I believe them myself." He paused and glanced quickly at the pair opposite him to entrance them further. "Tales of tribes just of women baying for the blood of men—you'd go alright there Ariadne I reckon, though I'm not sure how well Adro would fair. The very same ship also landed in a land full of one-eyed giants! They say they only escaped by the skin of their teeth, literally—the giants weren't very hospitable; they ate half my crew."

"One-eyed giants my—"

"Language!" Ariadne said teasingly. "It's too early in the day to start invoking your own arse."

Adro smiled at her cheekily and continued, "What fool of a captain told you all this?"

"Now now Adro, Oulixeus is the best man I've got. He always comes back having gotten a better deal than anyone else could have managed. I've never known him to speak with falsehood." Zedeck took a long gulp of wine then smiled with his stained teeth. "Well, not to me anyway..."

"So how is business going then?" Adro asked.

"Great!" Zedeck said wiping his mouth. "I have six ships now and now that my Bosporan fleet has returned I will have enough money to finally repay the last of my loan to Mepsiad. I still need to give him a cut of course and pay a substantial tax to Avaris but I am making plenty of money. I am waiting for my fleet from the east to return so I can swap the cargoes and sell west to east and east to west." He paused to chuckle at his own wit, such as it was, before continuing. "I was surprised the last time it returned from the east. My sailors said there are some Cretans who have settled there. Trading with them is so much easier than trying to babble in local tongues."

"Trading all over the world, Zedeck, your father would be so proud of you. If only he could see you now." Ariadne said with a sombre smile. He returned one flattened slightly by bitterness.

"Yeah Papa would have loved it. Still..."

"We're proud of you too; you've come a long way."

Zedeck nodded at the both of them and replied, "We all have."

Ariadne turned to avoid the glare of the sun which had just risen to pierce through the window. "Speaking of long," she said, "I've got a long day's worth of tallies to be sorting through. I'll get ready to go to the palace. Reckon I can leave you two here alone and expect any wine to be here when I get back?"

"Don't worry Ariadne, my slaves will keep us in check." Zedeck said already chuckling with mirth. "You can trust them."

"Yeah, to refill your empty cups." She said chuckling herself, as she walked off.

Fifteen minutes later she was out the door and into the freezing street. *How did Zedeck walk all the way here in this cold? He must have drunk enough wine to warm a house.* She continued on as she did every winter morning—seething inside in an attempt to sooth her aching, frozen limbs but all the while walking with her calm poise.

Step after dignified step, after what seemed like an eternity she arrived at the palace. The guards looked just as blue as she did or even a little worse. She smiled as she walked past them and they responded with little more than a twitch on a face so frozen that any more of a smile would have shattered it. As she walked through the dim stone corridors she felt the cold radiating against her from all directions. It was even worse than outside, if that was possible. She continued on in her misery for some time before—

Bumping into a similarly shivering early riser as they both came around the same corner.

"Sorry!" Ariadne muttered before trying to dart past him.

"Hang on, Ariadne. It's been too long. How are you faring these days?" Ariadne looked at the man to see a slightly plumper and wrinklier Mepsiad than existed in her memory. "Are you with child yet?" He took one look at her and continued. "Not with a figure like that! Still, I guess you're just as useful to us in the meantime before you start popping out little soldiers here and there. It'll happen don't you worry."

She grimaced at the mention of her failure. It hurt just thinking about it in the quiet of night but to have some distant acquaintance talk of it so starkly made her shudder. And she was sick of all the reassuring voices. *What if it doesn't happen? What if I can never—*

"Ariadne?" Mepsiad broke her train of thought. "And how's Zedeck? Any word from him? If he's gone and marooned himself somewhere I'll have such a loss it will take years to recover. I've lent him quite a bit you know."

"He's back, he's back." She said quickly. "And with the craziest stories you ever heard."

"They're just that girl, crazy stories. Don't you worry—his drunken ramblings will be forgotten by the end of the week even by himself. But us, our work, we're laying the foundations for a great future. We're the ones who are going to be remembered." He smiled. "Still, there's work to be done. Neither of us can stay here chatting. With the country's coffers to look after, as well as my own, I'm kept pretty busy girl. You keep sorting through those grain tallies—it's important work you're doing make no mistake."

Ariadne gave a nod and kept walking. *Silly old man. What does the future matter if you'll be dead anyway. How about you go find yourself a nice wife and enjoy life while it's there. That is if you can find someone who'll have you. Rotten tactless old—*

"Good morning, Ariadne." Habshut said as Ariadne walked in a daze past her desk.

"Is it?" Ariadne grumbled.

"Well, apart from the agonizing cold, the imminent starvation of all of Egypt promises not to disappoint." Ariadne rolled her eyes. She hated chirpy early rises unless she was the one doing the chirping. Habshut went on, "Coupled with the loss of divine favour, the ongoing separation of the kingdoms and sour look on your face this morning—yes I can see today will be a great day."

"My king's going to get back the favour of your 'gods,' never fear." Ariadne replied sleepily. "As for the starving peasants, well that's what they do best. We can't feed them all."

"How is the Great King Apepi going to regain Heaven's favour?" Habshut asked.

"They mentioned something about a Sed festival. Do you know what that's about?"

"Of course! I had the honour to be present at one when I was very young. It is a great ceremony. The essence of it is—"

"I realised I don't care. It's too early in the morning for rituals and superstitions." Habshut turned away with indignation but Ariadne ignored her and continued. "Where are the latest tallies? I've got a job to do. Even if some peasants will starve, hopefully we can reduce the number who do."

Habshut fumbled around on her desk and handed the latest reports to Ariadne without a word. Ariadne rubbed her eyebrow and spoke in a softer tone. "Look, I'm sorry Habshut. Hey, if this festival whatsit does go ahead, would you like to spend it with me and my husband?"

"That depends. Is he as much of a self-righteous, god-snubbing, arrogant foreigner as you can be sometimes?"

Ariadne sighed. "Sorry. Nah he's not. He likes your people and your customs. He spends hours in the markets listening to old ladies tell him stories about Egypt before we came. He'd enjoy hearing you say what it all means."

"Are you saying I'm old?"

"No, I—" Ariadne sagged in defeat, composure utterly lost. Meanwhile Habshut grinned and chuckled.

"I would be happy to come and explain the Sed festival to your husband. Who knows, maybe you'll enjoy it as well."

Nineteen

"Put this on. We are about to leave."

"It's not fit for a king. Beggars wouldn't be caught dead wearing it."

"With respect, my king, they would." Euouk said.

"Surely the king of Egypt can wear more comfortable robes to a ceremony." Apepios grumbled.

"He can, my king, to any other ceremony he wishes. This one is different." Apepios ran his hand over the coarse stitching again and looked at Euouk with distaste. "The robe represents Osiris' mummification," Euouk explained. "You begin the ceremony as the dead Osiris and end it not only as the risen Osiris but as his son Horus ready to rule your kingdom anew."

"How can a king be two gods?"

"I think you're Ra as well. It's difficult to tell at times. Besides, a king can be whoever he wants whenever he wants."

"Can I just be Ra then and not bother with this scratchy peasant robe?"

"Well we could set you on fire I guess, but I'm not sure how well that would go down." Euouk muttered.

"What?"

"Nothing. Just thinking of the logistical difficulties of your suggestion. Let me put it this way. If you want a festival which reassures the people you have the gods' favour, you have to do this one."

Apepios grumbled in near silence as he removed his robe and held out his hand to Euouk for the ungainly one before him. "Fine."

"Very good, my king. It will be worth it—I assure you." Euouk said as Apepios draped himself in his processional robe. He shifted uncomfortably in it feeling the rough fibres against his skin.

"Back home we would have thought it a bad omen to dress up in the clothes of the dead." Apepios muttered.

"We aren't back home. We need these gods onside, or at the very least their people."

"True. Shall we?" Apepios asked as he motioned towards the door. He walked forwards into the adjacent room filled with the rest of the procession. They bowed their heads as he entered and he took his position at the back. Meanwhile Euouk moved to the front. He turned around and said to those standing there, "Let us begin." And the main doors of the palace were opened before him.

***

"I want to be at the front!"

"You hate religion why do you care?"

"What's the point in coming if we can't even see what's going on?"

"This is a sacred ceremony, stop your bickering!" Habshut hissed. Ariadne ignored her and continued.

"You've got muscles, *Mister Guard*, push!"

Adro shook his head in dismay. Meanwhile Zedeck downed his cup and tossed it onto the ground.

"Too right!" he said and then wiped his mouth with his sleeve. He raced passed Habshut, Ariadne and even Adro and plunged into the edge of the crowd with a cry of "Follow me!" Ariadne raced after him without a word and, after pausing to share a mutual eye roll, Habshut and Adro did likewise.

Their battering ram felt no pain as he surged through the mass of elbows and shoulders. Zedeck ignored the bruises already starting to form around his ribs and even his face and continued onward as if he were fighting in one of those battles he drank to forget. A black eye received and given in turn later and Zedeck emerged at the front. As he gazed ahead at the splendour, his knees started to buckle but Ariadne, having been right behind him, held his shoulders and stopped him falling. "We made it." She said, satisfied, and then looked out before her.

The first thing she saw was a wooden structure a few metres in front of her. Four steps led up to the dais where a man with a crocodile mask stood patiently.

"That's the priest of Sobek." Habshut explained. "See all those pavilions?" Ariadne looked around and saw more of the same buildings forming a chain far to the left and right.

"Yes."

"The king walks along to each of them and receives a blessing from each god." Ariadne peered to her right and saw the procession in the distance.

"I see."

"What about that one?" Adro asked as he pointed far to their left. Ariadne looked at it and saw an imposing pavilion twice as big as the others with steps leading up on all four sides. "What happens there?"

"There the king receives the blessing of Horus and his kingship over all the world is renewed."

"Pfft! All the world? The world's much bigger than Egypt, Habshut, I can tell you that." Ariadne once more returned to her mocking tone.

"Ignore her," Adro said grimly. "Is that the end of the ceremony?"

"No, not at all." Habshut replied unfazed—happy to have a change of audience from her mocking boss. "The king then goes into the main temple but no-one knows what rites he conducts. All we know is that once he returns he has shed death and been reborn."

Adro nodded solemnly but the silence was short lived.

"Like a snake, then?"

"Yes, Ariadne," Habshut sighed. "Like a snake."

Adro turned to Habshut and whispered, "Why did we bring her again?"

Whack.

Habshut smiled and whispered back, "I don't know she's yours not mine."

They stood there until their legs ached and yet the procession was only slowly drifting towards them.

"It's taking forever!" Zedeck complained and looked at Habshut.

"Shh! They're almost here now. Besides, in Egypt we take more time to do everything—"

"You're telling me." Zedeck grumbled.

"—we're more refined that way."

"I could have sailed around the world in the time its taking him to finish his little stroll." She glared at him. "Sorry, sorry, dignified march." She rolled her eyes. "Elegant parade."

They could hear the faint clapping and singing of the procession as it came towards them. Habshut ignored him and craned her neck to see. Zedeck kept staring calmly forward and continued.

"Glorious undertaking of the moving of the sacred foot." Ariadne chuckled.

"In front of the other sacred foot." Adro could make out the faces now. He grimaced to see his father leading the procession.

"And up the most holy of stairs—just like the other hundred most holy of stairs." Apepios had reached another shrine.

"Throwing incense at potbelly the cow-headed. Being nodded at by spindly arms Ibis-face."

"Hyksos heathen." Habshut muttered to herself.

"Bow down! Bow down before your king." Euouk shouted over the noise of the procession. The priests walking behind him echoed his words.

"Bow down before your king."

It looked as if the tide was receding before the procession as those closest bowed down followed quickly by those behind.

"Bow down. Bow down before your king."

Adro was the first of his friends to bow. After he did, he looked to his right to see a glimpse of Apepios. He was walking off the previous shrine now. In the corner of his eye Adro saw a glint. He blinked and saw an unsheathed knife quickly covered by an arm. *A knife!* Apepios had no guards around him. He was walking at the very rear of the procession out in the open, vulnerable.

The procession came closer.

"—down before your king."

Adro sprang up and raced forwards toward the procession.

Euouk looked at the man racing towards him and shouted, "You, bow down!"

Adro ignored his father and kept going. The priests gaped at him in horror. He was spoiling everything! The only man not only not bowing but running alongside the procession.

"He's got a knife!" Adro shouted but in the midst of all the noise no-one heard.

"He's got a knife!" He ran onward. He could see Apepios now who was looking at him with curiosity.

Adro sprinted all the harder.

Apepios tensed seeing the determination in Adro's face.

The glint shone again in the corner of Adro's eyes.

Suddenly another figure came racing out at Apepios.

The knife surged forward in an outstretched hand.

The man holding it a mere heartbeat away from—

Adro collided with the man. They fell to the ground together. First the man's head ricocheted off the stone beneath. Then his hand did after Adro raised it and smashed it down, releasing the knife from his grip.

Guards had come running by now and surrounded the pair. One of them picked up the knife, while two more lifted both Adro and the man to their feet. Adro saw his face. He was an Egyptian.

The guards looked at Apepios, wondering what to do. He eyed the man who had just tried to take his life. He looked at his dust-ridden feet up to his gaunt body and, finally, to his dazed face. "Kill him." Apepios said.

"Death to the imposter! Death to—" A guard had kicked the Egyptian, winding him. He raised his knife to strike.

"Slowly." Apepios said. He looked back at the procession which had stopped and waited in silence. He turned back to see his soldiers drag the Egyptian away from the edge of the crowd. With a vicious grin one of the guards methodically cut the main tendons in both of his arms and his legs. As the man lay there unable to even properly writhe in agony, the guard cut open his stomach and walked towards Apepios.

Apepios nodded and spoke. "Guards, form up. I want a real procession." They began lining up on either side of him, glaring at the crowd. Adro looked around awkwardly and started walking back to Ariadne.

"You." Apepios said. "You will guard my back." Adro turned and looked at Apepios. Apepios pointed to the knife on the stone ground. "Pick it up." Adro did so and stood behind Apepios. Protected from all directions now, Apepios shouted as he did in the midst of battle, "Forward!"

Musicians and priests froze in fear and were nearly knocked down by the soldiers walking towards them. They barely found their senses and scampered along in time. Along with the clapping of hands and songs rising from the throats of the singers, the distant cries of the dying Egyptian pierced the ears of those watching.

Apepios walked forward calmly to the next shrine. Adro and the other guards followed him but stayed at the base of the stairs. Adro ignored the words of the priest and kept darting furtive glances at the crowd, hoping to see Ariadne's face.

"Sobek grants you all life and dominion like Ra." He saw her! She looked at him with wide eyes and gestured with her hands, opening them upward and outward as if to say, *what??* He met her gaze and merely shrugged his shoulders slightly letting out a weak grin.

He walked onward following Apepios who had left that shrine to walk to the next. With Ariadne behind him, Adro's world became a blur of walking from shrine to shrine. Adro's mind cleared when they reached the last shrine—the one twice as big as all the others. Eight masked priests stood there—two each with their backs to one of the four stairways, all staring at the throne in the centre.

Apepios climbed the eight stairs at the front of the shrine while Euouk and the priestly procession stopped at its base. Meanwhile, his guards silently formed a perimeter around it. He walked between the two priests standing with their back to him and stopped when he stood before the throne. He looked at the pair of priests on the far side of the shrine staring back at him and nodded. They began speaking softly and clearly.

"Tjanen and Seth grant you all life and dominion like Ra." Apepios nodded again. He turned to his left.

"Khepri and Geb grant you all life and dominion like Ra." The priests to his left said in unison. He turned to his right.

"Isis and Nephthys grant you all life and dominion like Ra." He turned for the last time towards the steps he rose up, with his back to the throne.

"Atum and Horus grant you all life and dominion like Ra." He nodded again and sat on the cold stone throne beneath him. At this point Euouk started ascending the stairs facing the throne. He opened his mouth to speak and did so in a loud voice so even the crowds could hear.

"Horus appears resting on his southern throne and there occurs a uniting of the sky to the earth." The procession at the base of the shrine clapped, banged their instruments and shouted out for a heartbeat.

"Horus appears resting on his southern throne and there occurs a uniting of the sky to the earth." He said again and kept ascending the stairs as they shouted out once more.

"Horus appears resting on his southern throne and there occurs a uniting of the sky to the earth." Euouk was at the top of the stairs and stopped just a few feet in front of Apepios. He held his arms outstretched as the procession shouted once more.

"Horus appears resting on his southern throne and there occurs a uniting of the sky to the earth." This time the procession continued cheering for some time and the crowd joined them. In the noise all around them Apepios muttered quickly to Euouk.

"I want my soldiers to follow me into the temple."

"You can't do that!" Euouk replied, horrified. "They cannot profane its sacred presence."

"At the moment all I care about is my own 'sacred presence.' I'll not let another assassin get me in the shadows. They come with me or I'll end your festival right here and now."

"That man saved you from the wild Egyptian. I'm sure it was only a crazed lunatic."

"'That man' was your son, if I remember rightly. It seems you have forgotten about him. He has more wits about him than you do. Everything is connected Euouk. The 'wild Egyptian' was not working alone." The cheering had died down once more and Apepios rose to begin the next step of the procession. "May the gods of Knossos smite me if I don't uncover who is behind this." He hissed as they began walking off the shrine. He looked at Adro standing there among the guards with no armour and a single knife for protection. "And if I don't give the job of uncovering it to him."

"Adro..." Euouk murmured as he bothered to look for the first time at the face of the man who had saved his king. He was speechless as they made their way to the temple whose huge doors had been opened on their arrival. Apepios, however, had not lost his voice.

"Guards, secure the temple for me. I want no more knifed-fanatics. Got it?" Adro shivered as he began marching towards the dark entrance before him. but Apepios pointed to him and a few other guards.

"You, you and you. And you over there. You stand by me the whole time." Adro walked back to his king and waited patiently. After they finally started moving he couldn't help but look up at the roof as they entered the temple and feel the darkness enclosing over him.

***

Adro walked quickly through the darkness ushered in by hands without faces he would have recognised even if he could have seen them. His eyes were just starting to adjust to the dim light when he suddenly emerged into the glorious light of a room well-lit with candles and even a fireplace. Apepios was already seated near the fire as were Mepsiad and Euouk. There was a spare chair there, right next to his father. The servants motioned him inward and scampered away.

"Ah, the hero of the day has arrived at last." Apepios boomed as Adro sat down. "You did good, lad." He passed him a cup filled with Zedeck's imported wine. "Your father would be proud of you." He smiled. "Oh wait he is, isn't he?" Apepios looked cheerfully at Euouk.

"Of course I am. You have always been a courageous child, Adro." Euouk said without looking at his son. Adro merely nodded and sat there in silence.

"Well, we can't have this happy reunion go on forever, I'm sorry to say." Apepios went on with mirth. "But there's work to be done. You don't seem the sort of person who needs to be talked around to something, Adro. You're a soldier by now. A man and no longer the child I once knew. You will obey orders."

Adro couldn't tell if that last bit was a statement or question. After a brief silence he replied, "Of course."

"Good. Then don't look so grim. I'm promoting you. I'm making you the head of my Royal Guard." Adro opened his mouth to thank him but Apepios cut him off with a wave of his hand. "I do this because I have a job for you and one which needs such authority to complete it. Also because right now I think you're the most trustworthy man I've got. You're the only man in Egypt who stopped that blade reaching me; anyone else could have been behind it except you. Apart from your normal duty to protect me, I want you to find out if there is some plot to have me killed. The assassin was an Egyptian so start there. I have my suspicions Kamose is involved but my ambassadors have not returned yet from Cush so I am unsure. It may well be an Egyptian hired by Cush to spark the war they want me to join. I will be cautious in this before I lash out but, rest assured Adro, once I find who is behind it, I will make them suffer."

Adro bowed his head and the light of the flames swirled around his face. "Thank you, my king. I do not know what to say."

"Find me my enemy and I'll thank you, Adro. All Egypt will thank you." Apepios held his cup high then drained it in a single gulp. He refilled it and then did so to each of the other men there. Still standing, he said to Mepsiad, "We ought to leave these two to their reunion now business is over, eh? Come on off with you. Let's go run a kingdom, or get some sleep." Apepios chuckled as he started moving towards a room further into his quarters. "I'm thinking the later." He muttered as he walked off into the fading darkness.

Mepsiad rose with a nod and left from the door Adro had come from. Father and son sat there in a silence no fire could warm. Minutes came and went as each one sipped his drink to pass the time. After a while Adro put down his cup, still more than half full and got up. He walked towards the door and when could no longer feel the warmth of the fire at his back, his father spoke.

"Your beard's coming along nicely."

Adro stopped and stood still but didn't turn around. "Twelve, thirteen years, Papa? How long has it been since you said a word to me?"

"And you're as fit as ever."

"You didn't even recognise me when I ran straight past you!" he paused, panting as if he'd just run that stretch all over again. "And you never helped me. Not once. You had the ear of the king and you didn't even ask him to promote me beyond some menial guard. I could have been dead for all you cared."

Euouk didn't reply for a time. When he did his voice was harder than the stones around them.

"She's had no child. She's cursed. She's going down boy and she'll bring us all down with her."

"Will you give it a rest?!" Adro shouted as he turned around to face his father.

"We lost our home because of that girl, boy."

"Don't call me 'boy,' old man."

"I don't care what Apepios tells you to preen your ego when he wants you to do his dirty work. You're still a child."

"Was it worth it, Papa?"

Euouk stared back at Adro, his face as stern as ever.

"All those years you've wasted. All those years you haven't seen your boy grow older day by day." Adro laughed bitterly. "All because you couldn't let go of your hate."

"You want to talk hate, boy? You should look to your wife before you start accusing me. See her eyes when she looks at an Egyptian. She doesn't care about anyone but herself and those she likes. Barren or not, she's with you 'cause you warm her bed at night."

"Fuck off."

"She doesn't give two shits about anyone else." Adro stared, unaware his father even knew such a phrase. "She's cold boy. And I don't want to see you destroyed by her. She'd have us march off to war again. Untold thousands would die."

"We did it before—"

"To survive. Now we can rule to survive. I say let's do it. Join the system, control the system, rule the people and keep the peace."

"Sometimes many people have to die for what's right." Adro said darkly.

"Come back to me when you've grown up, boy. Make a start by getting rid of that witch. Don't come back to me till you do."

Adro turned in silence and stormed off into the dark corridor. Only then did Euouk allow the tears to start, and roll one by one down his wrinkled cheeks.

Twenty

Ariadne peered out into the corridor as she reached for the latest reports from Habshut. Her friend chuckled. She was too obvious, even now a month later. She still stood there—a calculated second longer. Waiting. Hoping he might just drift by. Another second or two had gone. She was about to turn her head and speak, any excuse to keep standing there with one eye on the hallway.

"So... how many scribes are getting so blind they can't find their way here on time?" Right on time.

"Two as far as I can tell."

"Uh-huh." Ariadne said absentmindedly, still peering into the hallway. "And are they old too?"

"Get back to work boss. He's busy just like the rest of us."

Ariadne's head snapped away from the hallway and glared at Habshut. After a brief, knowing smile from the face before her, Ariadne turned around and started walking back to her office. She passed by scribes busy at work, for all the good it would do. *It doesn't matter how many times we count the harvest. If there's not enough food, it won't feed everyone.* At last she reached her office. Ariadne dropped the new set of reports on her table and—

Turned around in the agony of being tickled just above her hips.

Slap! "That was for missing me in the corridor!"

Slap! "That was for tickling me!" Adro smiled. Not bothering to dodge the weak blows to his cheek.

She kissed him then on the cheek she had been hitting. "And that's for conspiring with my deputy to surprise me in my own office." His hand, still on her hips, held her tightly and drew her in close. He kissed her back, softly, sweetly; all the while holding the smile just in his eyes. When at last he stopped, he whispered to her.

"I had a spare hour, see." She kissed his neck.

"And wondered what to do with it." She left a mark.

"And thought to myself..." She started again.

"Ah... how about I see my beautiful girl?" She hugged him tightly and smiled. They stayed there for a time in silence. Eventually he spoke again. "But that hour was a long time in coming. I spent ages waiting in one of those scribe offices hunched over pretending to write. The Egyptian with me couldn't help but laugh from time to time. I thought he was going to give the game away!" Adro looked out her window up at the sun outside. "Yes, I'm sorry dear but I think I have to go."

She frowned at him. "But what about all these boring records I have to sort through?"

"I can't read, dear."

"You could chop them with your sword." Adro raised his eyebrows at her and shook his head slightly. "Do you even know how to use it?" she said cheekily.

Adro smiled. "Apepios said it's the Royal Guard's equipment. No matter that the Egyptians came up with it." He said as he glanced down at the glimmering half-crescent blade. "It will cut down anyone without armour, like that." He said clicking his fingers. "And Apepios expects attacks from angry Egyptian peasants."

"That's great, dear. But can you use it?"

"Not here. Not now." He said smiling. "I'd make a mess of your fancy table and official records."

"Then off with you." She said holding back the wickedest grin. "Go and make yourself useful."

Adro dipped his head down to one side and said in the thickest Egyptian accent, "With pleasure your royalness." He chuckled as he walked off down the corridor, saluting his accomplice scribe as he walked past. Habshut saw the two spots on his neck and nodded her head without a word as he walked past her and into the hallway.

Meanwhile Ariadne sat at her desk thinking fondly over the past month. It had come a long way from being woken in the early hours of the morning by a freezing hand or leg as he climbed into bed after a late shift. No more night vigils for Adro. Although some Royal Guards had night shifts guarding Apepios' chambers Adro was exempt because of his assignment. Ariadne could live with that. She could live with that very much. It also meant he had free reign to walk about the palace from dungeons to the main court and everywhere in between. She loved it when they "chance" met in the corridors. She licked her lips absentmindedly, and she loved him surprising her like he just did. *Ooooh, life is good.*

***

Aggelos tensed as people knocked him with their shoulders in an effort to get closer to the front. *He's on a podium anyway. We'll all get to hear him, you fools.* Looking up at the man about to speak he thought back to the night before.

"*We have to leave now. Tonight! Else Kamose will have our heads.*"

"*I want to stay and listen to his address.*" Aggelos said. "*It could be useful.*"

"*Are you mad? You'll be flayed then left in the desert to be eaten alive by scarab beetles.*"

"*If he wanted to kill us why did he give his general specific instructions to escort us back here safely?*"

"*I don't know! It doesn't make sense. It feels wrong. Everything feels wrong. Which is why I say we get back to Apepios right away.*"

"*A royal address from Kamose to his people. Do you really think Apepios is going to want to miss what he says in it?*"

"*We had our orders. See if the Egyptians invaded Cush. Well, three charred ruins and not a Nubian in sight later and I think we have our answer.*"

"*The general knew we were coming. He gave us escorts into the ruins to see for ourselves. He said he had been made personally responsible for our safety. And he brought us back to Thebes. Kamose is giving this address for us as much as the Egyptians today.*"

"*And you think we should play into his hand by listening to it?*"

Aggelos faltered. Suddenly unsure. "*I trust Apepios to see through any traps. I'm staying to hear the speech. I'll leave after that. Best of luck to you.*"

"*See you in Avaris then. If you make it that far.*"

Aggelos shuddered at the memory. What if he was wrong to stay? Too late now. He breathed in deeply and exhaled in a long slow breath. Kamose was about to begin.

"True men of Egypt. How many of you have suffered at the hands of the invaders? How many of you have lost brothers and fathers or had your wives and sisters raped by these vile men from the vile sea?" *We never raped anybody. Lying bastard.* Aggelos thought. "How many of you have given up the lands of your forefathers to come south with me to resist the invaders? All while I was only a boy." He paused. "But as you can see, my loyal subjects, I am a boy no longer. I am a man, a king and a god." He held up his hands to the sky, at once appealing to Heaven and showing the strong muscles of his arms to the crowd before him.

"Now this Apepi thinks of himself as a god too. And what if he is? Which god usurped the throne from the rightful king before being overthrown by that king's own son? As we all know, that god was Seth. This Seth-Apepi may have been destined to overthrow my father but I am equally destined to overthrow him. And I tell you, men of Egypt, that the time is ripe for such things to come to pass." Kamose looked around at the crowd before him, looking mere peasants in the eye. "The Nile runs *dry*. Not for hundreds of years has such a catastrophe befallen us. Such a thing never occurred under the reign of my father and, no wonder, because he was the true king. The gods waited until I, Horus the dispossessed, had come of age before wreaking havoc upon the land to show their displeasure at the usurper and usher in the time of change. They call to me, telling me to save the kingdom from this Seth king and his evil warriors." The crowd cheered.

"I will fight the Hyksos and litter their bones among the desert sands. I will cast them out of Egypt and restore order to my troubled land." They cheered again and Aggelos gulped in fear, covering his head with his hood. "Even the vile Hyksos testify to my success. For barely a month ago it has been reported that the chief priest of the Hyksos dared to defy their imposter king. He shouted something during a procession and do you know what he shouted to this imposter?" Kamose stared intently into the crowd, daring them to reply. "He shouted, 'Horus appears resting on his southern throne.' The chief priest of the Hyksos could not help but prophesy about me. The gods spoke through him whether he willed it or not. Take heed, men, of his words and tell them to all near and far. We go to war. A holy war to rid our land of this great evil."

As the crowds began to cheer in earnest then, Aggelos shuddered and tightly draped his cloak around him before rushing out and away from the crowd. *Apepios must hear of this.*

***

Macanra pried the last of the stones away before glancing up and down the quiet street one final time. It might have been dark but there was still a chance he could be caught. Nope. No-one there. He squirmed through the hole he had made and quickly filled it up again behind him. Good, the wardrobe was still there hiding him from view inside the room. He peeped out from behind his cover and saw no-one in the candlelight. Perfect.

Macanra snaked across the room like one of those cats the Egyptians choose to worship. He had to admire them—they were quick and stealthy even if they had the most selfish eyes out of any animal. He peered around the corner and saw one of her maids. He whistled a short and soft note and when the maid saw his face, she quickly ran up to him.

"The mistress is in her chamber." She said, pretending to look indifferent. He saw the gleam in her eye though. He knew they fought over spotting him and being the one to bring him to her. He jingled the slivers of bronze in his pocket and she couldn't help but grin. "The master shouldn't be back for hours. He's over at Katek's."

"That's what he told you this morning anyway. How about you go into her chambers just to make sure he hasn't come home early?" He held out one of the slivers and she nodded, her face determined.

While the girl walked off, he stretched his arms out and yawned as he leaned against the wall. Macanra knew he could get a whore at the local tavern but where was the sport in that?

Where was the challenge? The excitement? Much better use of his pay to fund for a real adventure. When he saw the girl returning at a rush he smiled to himself. He had chosen well, it was still too easy. Naasa spread her legs for anyone who was twenty years younger than her husband, and bold enough to risk offending the local governor in his own home. *He does catch some of us*, Macanra admitted, *still, no-one has my entrance. He ain't gonna catch me walking through the front door. Don't matter how many doormen he puts there.*

The maid motioned with her head for him to follow her. He got up and did so, strolling along the corridor casually. At last he reached her room and saw Naasa bent over the crib.

"How's my boy doing this chilly night?" he asked as he came up behind her.

"Hungry, like his father." She put the baby back down and turned around slowly re-covered her bare breast with her shawl. "Besides, you don't know he's yours. He could just as easily be my husband's."

"Nice one. If he ain't mine, my money's on the potter he caught you with the night after me. That would fit, you know time-wise, wouldn't it?"

"Shut up." She muttered, actually cross.

"Ha, you don't know any more than I do. Don't get all uptight about it. I didn't come here to make you all tight..." Macanra murmured as he put his arms over her shoulders. "I came here to help you relax..."

Twenty-One

Macanra slapped the soldier across his back and pointed forward at the gates now in view.

"Avaris!" he said.

"No shit." The man kept on walking.

"You know what that means?"

"I've got half a chance sleeping somewhere where I don't hear you snore all night?" the man responded. A few around them sniggered.

"Whores, my dear friend," Macanra put his arm around the man's shoulders. "A city filled with whores and taverns." The man shoved his arm away. "Whores in taverns, I suppose," Macanra said to himself as much as anyone.

"You won't have much time for your blessed whores, boy." The man said without looking back at him. "You know as well as I do, the entire army's been called in. We're here to prepare for war not fuck ourselves senseless."

"Can't see why we can't do both." Macanra countered. "What's gonna be our role in this war? Fuck some Egyptians. What will I be doing this evening...?" Macanra paused as if he actually expected them to reply. "Really it's like extra duties. Voluntary extra duties. I should be paid extra for my commitment to the war effort." Silence. "No?"

"If you don't shut up I'm gonna fuck you with your own spear, boy." The man had finally looked over his shoulder to face Macanra who simply smiled at him and walked on in silence.

For little more than a minute.

"Now I'm not saying that I can't score without paying for it, lads. Believe you me—I'm quite the charmer." They could see the faces of the archers on the walls by now. The gateway was rapidly closing in. "I enjoy the sport of it as much as the next man." He paused, gesturing forward at the sullen man walking in front. "Then again, perhaps even more." Macanra could see his shoulders tense. *Can't cause any trouble now not with them boys watching.* "But after so many weeks on the road I've developed an itch, my dear friends, one that needs scratching quickly without all the fuss of the chase." He paused as he walked through the gateway and then continued. "And besides, I'm not sure I'm in a fit state to bother those of high society tonight. If I smell anything like the rest of you do after our journey, I don't like my chances."

"That's a shame," a voice called out from a side street, "because I'd already arranged with your commander to have you over tonight."

"Adro!" Macanra called as Adro ran up to his side. "Looks like it's high society for me, lads."

***

"How's that one you were breaking through her wall to get to?"

"Oh, she whinges so much. 'Why are you leaving me? How can I survive with just my husband? I think I'm pregnant again.' I was glad to leave."

"You've become such a bastard, you know that?" Macanra shrugged. They rounded a corner and started walking past

Adro's home. Macanra glanced at the open window of a house next door where a young woman was staring out lost in thought.

"What have we here?" He smiled politely up at the woman.

"Don't even think about it. She's been a widow now for less than a month. She's a nice girl. She doesn't deserve the likes of you poking around in her affairs making a mess of things."

The woman was staring down at them. Macanra winked just before walking out of view.

"I don't know about that. So yeah, enough about me, what's up with you? Ariadne pregnant yet?"

Adro looked at him and grimaced. "Not yet."

"You can have my kid—I don't want it." Macanra said light-heartedly.

"You don't even know if it's yours. I think I'll pass." Adro tried to smile.

"What else then. You can't say nothing changes in the big city. What's new?"

"Actually, I've been promoted. Head of Apepios' Royal Guard."

"Ooh fanc', how'd you score that?" Macanra said, impressed. Adro replied in his sternest voice.

"I killed somebody." He looked at Macanra with a face tougher than his friend's cooking. Macanra held his gaze, gradually becoming uneasy until Adro burst out laughing. After a moment, Macanra did likewise. "Seriously though, an Egyptian tried to kill Apepios at the Sed festival. I saw what he was going to do and stopped him. Apepios thinks it might be part of some conspiracy to have him killed—what with Kamose's army encamped on our borders..."

"That's what I'm here for." Macanra butted in cheerfully. "He didn't think you were good enough, so he brought in the real soldiers who haven't gotten soft from city living." Macanra winked at Adro and laughed.

"Anyway, so he thinks Kamose might be trying to kill him off so we lose our best general plus our legitimacy or something. I don't fully understand it. Point is my job is to find any further threats and take care of them."

Macanra paused then replied. "Wow, lucky break. Wish I was there—would have beaten you to him. Then I could have your job. Nothing happens out in the provinces. It's so shit out there."

Adro laughed. "Well, tell you what. You can be part of my investigation. If you see any shady looking Egyptians, send them to me."

"Deal." Macanra looked around realising he didn't know where they were, having passed Adro's house some time ago. "Where we headed?"

"I've got to check out a possible suspect for Apepios' investigation." Macanra's eyes lit with excitement. "No, you can't come. Sorry. I'm dropping you off at Mepsiad's pub. Zedeck's there at the moment. Drop on by my house in the evening and we'll catch up properly."

"Will Emeko be there?" Macanra asked curiously.

"He'd better not." Macanra frowned at the tone of Adro's voice. "I can't risk him setting foot in my house after what he did."

"You mean after what you did?" Macanra replied coolly. Adro glared at him with a vague hint of guilt and kept walking.

"The pub's down that street and to the left. See you tonight."

***

A man sitting alone at a table in a low-lit bar motioned to the bartender to refill his mug. The bartender nodded from behind the counter. "Skypha, get this man another drink." He looked at the man sitting there. "Wine again?"

"Your finest." The man said miserably looking down into the empty mug before him.

"Coming up." These soldiers were a gods' send. The barmaid quickly emerged with a small amphora and darted across the busy room filled with tables of similarly pissed men. She stood over the lonesome man and started pouring his drink. "What's your name, stranger?"

"Emeko." The man said gruffly, not bothering to look her at all. He simply stared down at his mug being refilled.

The barman faintly heard the name from the bar and looked up.

"What was that?" he asked across the room with a stern voice.

"Name's Emeko."

"Emeko of Malia?" the bartender questioned further.

"Yeah, that's right."

"Get out." The crowd between them stopped chattering to listen in. "You ain't welcome here."

"This ain't Mepsiad's pub." Emeko retorted. "Can't see how our bad blood affects you."

"We look after our own in this city. Ever heard of a blacklist? 'Cause you're on it." Emeko ignored him and raised the mug to his mouth. The barmaid knocked it from his hand and it fell onto the table spilling wine over everything. He looked at her for the first time.

"Dumb bitch, you don't even know what it was about, do you? Still, you follow your master's orders like a dog." He stood up slowly from the chair. "You'll get what's coming to you one of these days whether you like it or not." Tension filled the room as quickly as all sound had left it. "Sadly."

"Get the fuck outta my pub right now 'fore I shout the rest of these men a round to do it for you." The bartender glared at Emeko. Emeko glared back and stared down each man nearby who was suddenly looking at him with interest. He raised both of his arms in the air and spoke calmly.

"I'm leaving. Don't want no trouble." He lowered his hands and started for the door.

"Get you to one of them Egyptian pubs down west-side." The bartender called out to him. "Scum there as ugly as fuck and only got beer but shits like you don't deserve no better." Emeko turned his back to the bartender and walked out without a word.

* * *

"Five talents—it's all I ask." Zedeck said confidently.

"Let me see if I understand you correctly." Mepsiad began. "You want me to cancel your debt so you can use your profit of five talents to hire my ships which would otherwise be making me money?" He turned his head to look at Zedeck sceptically.

"No, no. You don't seem to get it. I'll try again." Zedeck took a breath. "I repay my loan to you of five talents—"

"I like the sound of this so far."

"But," Zedeck continued, "in your generosity and wisdom you decide to reinvest the said five talents to me. I will use these to hire more of your ships and their crews so you will have the five talents anyway." Zedeck became more excited. "I will sail again to my trading partners up in the Bosporus who would be delighted to double my wine shipment. When I come back I will repay you and supply you with enough wine to fill your pub for a month for free. How's that sound?"

Mepsiad turned his head upon hearing a knock at the door. Raucous noise burst into the room as the door opened and a slave walked in.

"Master, a man called Macanra is here asking for your guest." He said, gesturing to Zedeck.

"Mustn't keep you two pisspots waiting now, should I?" Mepsiad said looking at Zedeck.

"He can wait." Zedeck replied. Mepsiad smiled.

"And so he shall. Pour our friend a mug of wine and tell him Zedeck is shouting his first drink while he finishes important business." Mepsiad said then motioned for the slave to leave. The slave scuttled out of the room with a nod and shut the door behind him. Mepsiad continued. "Determined, I like that."

"You know this is a good plan."

"What's to stop me from sailing there myself?" Mepsiad asked.

"I'm a better captain than any of your men," Zedeck said, smiling. "You know that. They couldn't find their way there and if they were lucky enough to get there they wouldn't make it back. Sea monsters by the dozen, more jagged reefs than you could count and a lack of respect for dear Poseidon. Nope they haven't got a chance."

"Who's this 'Poseidon'?"

"Sea god of the trading cities of the Bosporus. We're well acquainted. He keeps me safe, and my crew."

"Some new god of the seas? It'll never catch on. People won't start worshipping new gods from far away." Mepsiad said with a frown.

"For safe passage and all the wine you could drink I'm pretty sure men would worship death itself." Zedeck smiled.

Mepsiad laughed and poured more wine into each of their mugs. He raised his to his mouth, drank thoughtfully and then put it down.

"My ships don't get back for another month. Then it takes time to unload, eh you know the drill," Mepsiad said cautiously, "I'll tell you what. I know you have money stashed away. Eight talents now and two months' supply of wine with the prospect of renting my ships again in the future too. What do you say?"

"Deal," Zedeck said at once, triumphantly, "you won't regret it."

***

Emeko raised his hand glumly to knock once more on the door before him. Nothing.

"Adro!" he cried out in little more than a whimper, "Adro, surely it's been long enough." Silence.

Emeko looked up at the small window again to see a flickering shadow of a flame and closed his eyes to smell the meat sizzling. He sighed and slowly turned around. He glanced back one more time before starting his slow walk back through the gloomy street. *How could it end up like this?* he thought, looking up to the stars, *you have everything, my old friend, and I have nothing.* As he walked on, Emeko grudgingly picked a stick of silver out of his purse and flicked it into the air, catching it with as much misery as he tossed it. "Guess beer will have to do," he muttered.

***

"That's practically a fleet, Zedeck!" Macanra slurred as they walked on through the night. Zedeck turned, torch in hand, to grin with greater mania than his friend upon sighting a brothel.

"I know." Zedeck said waving the torch in emphasis. He drained the cup in his other hand and then, with the utmost euphoria, tossed it against a nearby stone wall. "You see," he said over the shattering of fine ceramics, "I've been thinking."

"Have you now?" Macanra said looking back at Zedeck with a similar glee before draining his own cup.

"How would you like a change in career?" Zedeck asked, trying to look serious. Macanra flung his cup as far into the air as it would go.

"Sure! Let's do it." Macanra replied. "I'll guard your pretty ships and you give me all the wine I can drink."

Macanra's cup shattered somewhere in the distance. Zedeck ignored it and looked at his friend from top to bottom before frowning. "We'll come to some agreement."

Macanra smiled and muttered to himself, "All the wine." They walked around a corner and Macanra turned to Zedeck with a serious expression of his own. "You know, though, that I couldn't do it until we're done with this pesky war."

"Of course, of course."

"And with any luck Apepios will ask all able-bodied men to fight." He looked at Zedeck from top to bottom. "Which I guess, if he's desperate, means he just might demand you fight too." Zedeck hit Macanra in the shoulder.

"I haven't lost my strength, Mac'." Zedeck smiled.

"Yeah, you always punched like a girl." Macanra smirked. "Speaking of girls, how far are we from Adro's place?"

"It's a few streets over. Almost there."

Macanra sighed loudly in relief.

"Better be. I'm so hunnngryy."

They turned around another corner and saw two men in the distance. One of the men was holding the other against a wall, pinning his arms and staring menacingly. They were talking in soft, hurried voices.

"Hey isn't that Emeko?" Zedeck said, pointing to the man grimacing at his victim. They stopped walking at stared at the men before them.

"Pub fight probably, let's move on. Adro don't want Emeko coming round." Macanra replied. Zedeck looked down at them once more and then looked back worried.

"The other guy's an Egyptian by the looks of him. No Egyptian pubs this side of Avaris. No pub fight." He looked at Macanra with confusion. Macanra thought for a second then his eyes lit up.

"You think we should tell Adro we saw Emeko being suspicious with an Egyptian?" Emeko kicked the Egyptian in the gut then brought his face close to his again. "Whatever it is, its harmless—you don't beat up your boss in the middle of the street if you're gonna do a hit for him."

"If I wanted an excuse to be with one of 'em, I'd make it look like I was in the middle of throttling him too." Zedeck counted.

"Look, we don't know shit. If you go telling Adro, he'll use it as an excuse to put Emeko away for good; trump it up even if it's nothing." Macanra's eyes looked at Zedeck pleadingly. "Let's think about this." Zedeck turned to look once more down the street at Emeko and the Egyptian he was occasionally hitting. Zedeck held his hand over his mouth, deep in thought.

∗∗∗

"—like this!" Macanra said as he drove his drumstick mercilessly down into Zedeck's neck. "He didn't know what hit him."

Zedeck reached for Macanra's hand but Macanra withdrew it too quickly and took a bite of the drumstick. Zedeck glared at Macanra and wiped his greasy neck on his cloak.

Adro poured more wine into Ariadne's cup as they shared a chuckle. "Sometimes," Macanra said solemnly, "I can still see his face, haunting me in the evenings." He paused. "Whenever I," he flicked his half-eaten drumstick across the table once more at Zedeck's face, startling him, "—retell the story." He burst out laughing. Adro did too, spurting wine all over Zedeck. Zedeck turned his head very slowly, first looking at Macanra and then at Adro. And then he kicked under the table.

"Uggh," Macanra groaned.

"You're still boys," said Ariadne, only half-thankfully.

All four of them continued eating in silence. Macanra and Adro shared the occasional smirk while Zedeck took to cutting his meat with more vigour than was strictly necessary.

"I've been wondering, Macanra," Ariadne began, "have the provinces started going hungry yet?"

Macanra swallowed. "No, not yet. But it's all those people have been complaining about for months. They've got a bit stored away but they know it's coming."

Ariadne frowned. "Do they blame Apepios?"

"Well if they did, they'd hardly tell a Cretan soldier, would they?" Macanra replied, ignorant of how rude he sounded. Ariadne curled her lip but said nothing.

"Tell you what they have been doing," Adro broke the silence, "they've been graffitiing that new temple we just finished building. Some kind of provocative thing written all over its walls."

"Really?" Zedeck asked.

"Yes, Apepios told me of it this afternoon. Wants to meet first thing in the morning to discuss it. Thinks it could be the same people who tried to have him killed."

Macanra had grabbed another drumstick and started biting away. "Better get on that," he said while still chewing.

"It definitely looks like something's being planned. If you guys see anything, *anything*, suspicious, please, let me know." Macanra and Zedeck exchanged a quick glance that ended as soon as it began.

"Will do," Zedeck said uneasily. They continued in silence as before.

"Isn't it nice all being back together again?" Macanra asked. He received nods of agreement from around the table. "I mean it feels just like old times." Adro smiled in agreement but Ariadne and Zedeck stopped nodding in anticipation of what was to come. Macanra raised his cup into the air. "It just seems like there's something missing." Adro frowned. "Someone... missing."

"I told you, he's not welcome." Adro said as forcefully as the glare he received in turn. Macanra drained his cup, still glaring at Adro.

"This bad blood's gotta be sorted 'fore it hurts you both. Just try talking to him," Macanra said.

"That would be a good plan if he hadn't sworn to kill Adro the next time he saw him," Ariadne said dryly.

"He wasn't himself. I'm sure he even forgot he said it by now," Macanra replied.

"I don't plan to ever see him again," Adro said, suddenly rather coldly. "Things change, guys, things change."

Twenty-Two

"I hired you to do one thing!" Apepios' voice boomed around his inner chambers.

"In my defence, I can't read." Apepios scowled at Adro standing before him.

"You should have been the first to bring this news to me." Adro shrugged softly. "Instead," Apepios continued, "that credit goes to your father." Euouk nodded, standing beside his son in front of Apepios. "Would you care to enlighten your son on the meaning of the graffiti?"

"Certainly, my king." Euouk began. "The graffiti was really a single phrase repeated over and over again. The phrase was, 'Horus appears resting on his southern throne.'"

"But that's what you said at the festival, where's the harm in that?" Adro asked his father.

"A few months ago, some of my spies in Egypt learned of the raid of Cush which is why the soldiers believe we are rallying to war—to defend our ally." Apepios said.

"We aren't?" Adro replied, still confused.

"On the way back, one of them was present at a speech by Kamose to a crowd of Egyptians. He told them he was foretold to regain his father's kingdom and kill me. He told them they were going to war. He mentioned a number of prophesies and omens and do you know what one of the prophesies was?"

"Horus appears resting on his southern throne," Adro said, suddenly realising. "So we're going to war not to save our ally but to save ourselves."

Apepios nodded. "Good, now you understand. Sit." Apepios motioned to a chair to his left. Adro walked over to it and sat down. "Watch."

Euouk still stood there before Apepios and motioned towards the door with his hands. "If I may be excused now, my king?"

Apepios shook his head.

"You told me you could be of use to me as a scribe and then later as a priest to use these peoples' beliefs against them." Apepios said rather calmly. "The Nile has not flooded and every Egyptian from the delta to the hills blames me." Apepios paused before continuing with some menace. "Your festival solution ended up with you quoting a line our enemies have twisted into a prophecy. The one temple we built for these people, the one now covered in graffiti, was dedicated to Seth, the very god destined to be overthrown by the son of the god he overthrew! How could you not have foreseen any of this?"

Euouk gulped. "The Seth temple was already under construction when we arrived..."

"You should have realised they would have associated me with him! I have news that in the South they say not only am I the Seth destined to be overthrown but that I commissioned the temple myself and, as it is the greatest temple in this city, I have honoured Seth above Ra, angering the gods and hastening my own demise!" Apepios roared.

Euouk stood there terrified as Apepios continued. "You have failed me in every way and been of more use to my enemy than me, especially in this hour of need. Kamose's army is now encamped at our very borders, poised to invade and besiege

Avaris unawares. Do you think a city half-full of Egyptians will sit back and starve for a king they think has lost the god's favour?"

Apepios clicked his fingers and suddenly two guards walked into the room. They walked up to Euouk and each took hold of one his arms. Apepios continued, "I have to fight this invader before he reaches our capital, largely because of *your* incompetence." Euouk was shaking his head fast, his eyes filled with pure terror. "And I have to defeat him. We can afford no more mistakes." He looked at the guards. "Guards, take this worthless man to the main square and execute him."

As they started to drag Euouk off, he looked at his son with pleading eyes.

"Stop!" Adro shouted. "Spare him, please!"

"He is worthless, worse, he is harmful. He needs to die," Apepios said, calm once more.

"You said you can't afford any more mistakes," Euouk said, his heart racing. "Killing their chief priest will anger the Egyptians even further—you can't do it."

"I can do whatever I like. I am their king and their god." Apepios nodded to the guards. "Go."

As they dragged Euouk out of the room, Apepios turned to Adro. "You are only still here because you have some use to me still and because despite your failings, I trust you. Do you understand?"

Adro nodded through clenched teeth.

"Good," Apepios said, "now listen here. Common peasants could not have made that graffiti; it must have been done by educated Egyptians."

"Yes, that would make sense." Adro replied.

"We can no longer trust the Egyptians within our government then. Any of them could have done it. You are going to issue an order, to your guards and to the various departments, to suspend all Egyptians from working at the palace until we have won this war."

"Everything will grind to a halt. We will lose any chance we had at feeding the starving peasants, let alone running the kingdom," Adro replied sceptically.

"Almost all our soldiers have already arrived. The rest will do so in the oncoming days. We leave Avaris in seven days. We will go south and fight Kamose. He has made it clear there can only be one king of Egypt." Apepios patted Adro on the back. "Just keep me alive until then."

**

The rat scuttled along in front of Emeko. He just sat there, in the dim alley, following its every movement with his eyes. He smiled, a sad, lonely smile, and pulled out some crusty bread from a pouch. Immediately the rat's nose twitched and it raced up towards him. It stayed just out of reach, its eyes transfixed on the crust.

"I'm not going to hurt you," Emeko said softly—one whiskered, dirt-covered creature to another. He held out his hand with the crust. The rat crept up close to his hand and sniffed. "Go on, take it," he gestured further. The rat snatched the crust and ran back out of reach. It sat there eating and occasionally looking back at Emeko in hope for more.

"You know, once I had better things to do than feed the likes of you," Emeko said to the rat. "Did you know that I was once in the king's private guard?" The rat continued to eat, unfazed. "Do you know how I lost it all?" The rat had finished eating and crawled within reach this time, sniffing for more bread. Emeko laughed and took out another crust. He held it out to the rat and this time it ate it from his hand. "I'll tell you."

It took years after those great battles to finally subdue every northern governor. Kamose's regent may have agreed we could have Lower Egypt but somehow the locals didn't just accept our rule. I was with Apepios most of the time. While Zedeck and Macanra, and yes even Adro, were sent to far off places for months on end, I stayed with the king in Avaris.

I'm told they were glorious days. But everything ends and never as expected. Eventually every northern governor had either pledged himself to Apepios or been defeated and replaced. Apepios reduced the time of mandatory armed service for us Cretans and for some lucky ones removed it all together. We hadn't seen each other for years so all agreed to meet up in the capital—for old times' sake.

Ah, to see the joy on that dear girl's face as Adro came back to Avaris. I'd tried to keep her company while he was away and I think she appreciated it, but we all knew there was only really one for her. It was so sad to see them come together again to know they'd have to part in a short while once more.

But where was I? I was telling you about how I lost it all. So, Zedeck had this plan, you see. He wanted to sail across the sea. He wanted to see far off lands and trade with them. He convinced Mepsiad to let him join one of his trade ships to learn the ropes and start his new career. Apepios had agreed to it since Mepsiad furnished his palace with some of the goods from each journey. It looked like two of us at least were finally getting somewhere in life.

Anyway, we all decided to celebrate in Mepsiad's pub, drink to new friendships and all that. I remember Zedeck asking us, "Come on, join me! We can all be together again and we'll get rich! What do you say?" But Adro would have none of it. He said, "Why trade one life away from Ariadne for another?" And he drank. Gods, how he used to drink in those days.

I wasn't going to trade my life in the Royal Guard to be some petty rower aboard a ship. And as for Macanra, well, he'd learned of the joys of women. He wasn't going to trade a nice pair of tits for smelly, hairy, burly men. Not his type.

Now, Mepsiad prided himself on having his bar run by only the prettiest of women. He reckoned that what he spent on them was more than recouped by the loosening effect they had on men's purses. So anyway, one of these women had happened to overhear Macanra's priorities and, before you could say "pouring," he was out helping her move some empty wine amphorae outside. They were gone for some time.

Meanwhile, the boss himself finally shows up. He comes through the door with an arrogance known only to men of money. He comes over to our table and doesn't even sit down. He just stands there and looks at Zedeck. He asks him if any of us are smart enough to join him as well but Zedeck just replies, somewhat embarrassed, that we aren't going to. He takes one look at us and do you know what he says? "Drunken fools. Dumb grunts, they're just going to die somewhere cold and alone if they don't take chances. You'll show them." Ha, the sad thing is he's right.

Anyway, Zedeck goes out at some point to take a piss and Mepsiad just gets up and leaves without so much as a word so it's just me and Adro reliving every memory from nicking one of Macanra's sheep he was meant to be watching to fighting side by side in those ghastly sand dunes. Then it happens. Mepsiad is over at the bar itself talking to one barmaid in particular. Now I've got to tell you, despite all his riches, he's more leathery than my Papa's old body-armour. This pretty young girl doesn't want him touching her, no matter how rich he is.

She tries to move away but he strokes her hair with the tips of his fingers. She whacks his arm with her hand, knocking his hand away from her face and then turns to flee. His face fills with rage and he grabs both of her shoulders, pulling her towards him. He *kicks her first, in the back of her knee. Then he starts laying into her with both fists.*

And everyone just watches. Worse, some turn straight back around—not their business, eh? Who'd dare to confront one of the richest men in Avaris in his own pub? I looked at Adro but he was so pissed he barely knew what was happening. Besides, wasn't his woman getting hit, was it? He looked away.

But I thought of my father, of all those years when he'd hit her, my own mother. I didn't care what she'd done. I just wanted it to stop. And suddenly I wasn't in a bar drinking with my friends. I was back home watching him pound her again and again. But this time I wasn't a child cowering in the corner begging him to stop. I was a man, and I could make him stop.

I got up. I was next to Mepsiad before anyone realised and, boy, did I let him have it. For every bruise that poor girl suffered, he copped three. He turned to face me but it was too late. I broke his jaw with two good hits and, before anyone could stop me, I'd kicked him so hard in the chest I broke some of his ribs.

But alas, as I said, all good things come to an end. Adro had come up behind me and grabbed my arms. Somehow, he pinned them behind my back and knocked me to the floor. I don't remember much after that. Adro saved that monster's life that day. Two more good hits and, well, doesn't matter now, does it?

Next thing I remember is us standing before the Great King Apepios himself. I'll never forget what he said to me. "I should have you killed. Pity, you showed such promise. You're lucky I have need of brutes like yourself. You will be sent to the harshest, most rebellious provinces where your skills will be of some use." He turned to Adro, who was also in the room. "I thought you were a child, boy. How would you like a chance to be a man?" Adro looked at him, confused. "Mepsiad has asked that, for saving his life, I give you Emeko's position in my Royal Guard." I could see in Adro's eyes that he understood before Apepios said it. "You would of course have to stay in Avaris with me, which may free you up for a more settled life..."

To his credit, Adro thought about it before answering. He just stood there, his mind racing. Apepios frowned in frustration at having to wait and then continued. "Or I could forgive your friend and send you off in his place. What will it be?"

"He didn't look at me that day, not even a single glance before he gave his answer. He hasn't looked me in the eyes, gods, he hasn't showed his face since." Emeko said to an empty alley, his only companion having long since scuttled away.

Twenty-Three

"Can you see him?" Zedeck asked in the darkness.

"I can't see shit," Macanra retorted.

"A shadow moved, I'm sure of it."

Macanra continued to peer around the corner doubtfully. "If it's a guard, you know he'll think we're the ones doing it."

Zedeck saw the faintest flicker in the distant darkness and smiled. "It was your plan to interrogate one of 'em before telling Adro about Emeko. Want to back out?"

Even Macanra saw the next movement. The shadow was creeping closer. "We owe it to him. I'm not handing my friend over unless I know he deserves it."

"Stay here then. I'll creep around behind him. Wait for my signal."

Macanra watched patiently as the shadow crept closer and closer. Soon he was in view and Macanra could see him painting the same scribble again and again as he went. Macanra tensed, knowing it mustn't be long before Zedeck was in place.

Suddenly, out of the dead of night came the call of a sea bird—a trick Zedeck had only perfected with age. Macanra sprang around the corner and started racing at the Egyptian standing all alone before him. The man saw him almost immediately, dropped his gear and bolted.

Macanra chased him through the darkness but he already knew where they were going. He and Zedeck had scouted out the alleys and roads around the new temple earlier that day. That's why they picked this spot. There was one small road that lead straight back to the Egyptian side of town. And, sure enough, that was the route the Egyptian took.

Macanra saw him race around a corner just ahead and then heard the loudest whack. Macanra was there in moments to see Zedeck standing with a bloodied block of wood above a body not doing much better. Macanra bent down and put a hand on the man's wrist.

"Good job. Let's get him out of here," he said.

Without a further word, Zedeck grabbed the Egyptian's feet while Macanra grabbed his shoulders and they slowly started carrying him back the way they came.

***

Misakh felt the warmth trickle over his face on that freezing night and smiled for an instant before opening his eyes. His shoulders ached from the cold and his wrists were sore from the ropes which bound him but to see two grinning men pissing onto his face was enough to make him long for a dip into the Nile in the middle of winter. He blinked and spat but that only made things worse. Fortunately, they quickly ran out of ammunition. As they were re-covering themselves, one spoke to the other.

"I think he's awake."

His friend laughed. "I think you're right." The friend had finer clothes on. Not just the coarse cloaks of soldiers. He had a nicely woven robe. Someone important?

"We have a few questions for you…" the first man said.

Misakh looked around the room quickly to see knives on a table and little chance of escape.

"Hyksos scum!" Misakh shouted before spitting at the first man.

The man wiped it off and grinned. "It begins," he replied, reaching for one of the knives.

"You can kill me today but you can't stop our people taking back what is theirs," Misakh said with hopefully more bravery than fear in his voice.

"That's a good start. At least we know we have the right person," the finely dressed man said. "How do you plan to do that?"

Misakh thought over what he had been told to say if caught. Hopefully it would be enough. "Your Great King will die, Hyksos. Horus' time has come. Horus appears resting on his southern throne and he will take back the land of his father."

The first man laughed. "I'd wager our king against yours on any battlefield, anywhere. Your king is little more than a boy."

Now it was Misakh's turn to smile. "We shall see."

The finely dressed man looked seriously at Misakh and spoke. "How will your king kill ours?"

Misakh shrugged. "Who can say?"

The knife tip slammed into his hand before he saw it move. Misakh screamed in agony as he realised the first man had stabbed his hand. The first man wasn't laughing anymore.

"You can say." He paused. "Will our king die before they meet in battle?"

"I hope so." Misakh grunted.

"Will he be killed by a Cretan?" The first man was straining, very tense.

"You ask very specific questions. You must know more than I—" The knife twisted around in his hand causing Misakh to almost faint with pain. The first man stopped twisting it and looked Misakh in the eyes, waiting. Misakh thought through the pain on what he was and wasn't meant to say.

"Yes! Yes, one of your own will kill the king."

"Is it Emeko?" the first man asked, anger filling his eyes.

"I don't know his name!" The knife twisted again. "I don't!" It was too much to bear. "Go to the third street in from the west wall." The knife stopped twisting. "There's a pub with no name hidden down a back alley." Both men were watching him now, hanging off his every word. "They plan it from there. They will know the name of the man who will kill your king."

The eyes of the finely dressed man filled with sorrow. "That part of town is the only spot that Mepsiad hasn't been able to get to blacklist Emeko. It's got to be where he drinks these days." Strength flowed out of the first man as he all but withered at the news.

"Why would he do it to us?" the first man all but whispered.

Misakh saw his chance to hurt his captors and he took it. "Money and power. What else guides people? I know whoever he is, he will be paid a fortune for killing your king." Misakh looked both of his captors up and down before continuing. "A soldier and a merchant, you'd be the first to sell yourselves at the sight of true wealth. Go to the pub and say I sent you. With any luck they will give you a cut and, who knows, they may even let you live once the old order has been restored."

The finely dressed man grimaced and looked to his friend. His friend nodded. The last thing Misakh saw was a block of wood coming towards him that seemed somehow familiar.

Whack!

"What do we do?" Macanra asked Zedeck. Zedeck was already packing the knives away.

"We do as he says. Leave him here and go to this pub during daylight. "If we find Emeko, we bring him to Adro and maybe, just maybe, save our king."

***

Adro's footsteps echoed loudly as he entered the room. Habshut looked up from her desk and smiled wearily.

"How's the boss?" Adro asked.

"If you've got any sense in that caring head of yours, you'll leave her be," Habshut replied to a now frowning Adro. She motioned with her arm up the corridor. The long silence was only interrupted by the odd scribe, lucky enough to have been born elsewhere from this accursed place, scratching away with a quill, now and then.

Adro nodded after a time and spoke. "So, you two are holding the fort then?"

"More or less," Habshut replied. "We never had many Hyksos scribes. Now the king has seen fit to fire basically every Egyptian in the palace, our work has become nigh impossible."

Adro held his hand to Habshut's shoulder and squeezed it for a moment. "Yeah," he sighed. "Still, we'll pull through." Habshut smiled again wearily and Adro turned and walked out.

"We'll see," Habshut muttered to herself.

***

"You have to fire her." Adro said calmly as he dipped a chunk of bread into the bowl of stew before him.

"I'm not firing my best friend!" Ariadne said before doing the same.

"You drive each other crazy. You always end up arguing, about everything." Adro countered.

"Not firing her." Ariadne said forcefully then continued eating in silence.

"Look, I like her too. But we have orders from Apepios himself—no Egyptians in the palace until we win the war. Don't think of it as 'firing,' just 'temporarily suspending her duties.'"

Ariadne laughed. "'Temporarily suspending'—you're starting to get your father's smooth tongue."

"Listen," Adro said forcefully, "we need to be above reproach. Apepios—"

"Apepios can go—" Adro glared at her and she stopped herself.

"Apepios can go wherever, and do whatever, he likes. He can *fire* me. He can fire *you*. He could put me on the front line or he could make me his vizier when this is all over. Don't you get that?"

"So you want to be his vizier?"

"No!" Adro cried out as one begging to be understood. "I just don't want to leave you again. He holds the power of life and death." Adro held back tears as he got up and walked over to Ariadne. "I saw him order my father to death. He did it right before my eyes, and you know why? To show me he could do the same to me... or even to you." Ariadne had risen too and they held each other tightly, all thoughts of fighting were gone.

"What am I going to do?" Ariadne asked after a time, still holding him.

"Explain it to Habshut, she'll understand. Tell her it won't last long and she's always welcome at our place." Adro half-explained, half-pleaded.

Ariadne held his head in both her hands and then kissed him softly on his forehead. She nodded and they just stood there for a time, holding each other.

Twenty-Four

Macanra and Zedeck turned up yet another street. They started scanning the houses methodically, just like the last eleven streets. About half-way along, Zedeck saw one which caught his attention.

The clay bricks forming the walls of the building were cracked and worn like every other house in the street. The two men who walked out of it seemed little better. But that was the point. No-one had bothered to shut the front door which had been open before the men left. Zedeck watched as one man stumbled up the street into the distance and the other stumbled towards them and kept going.

Zedeck nudged Macanra and craned his neck in the direction of the building. There was a third man lying sprawled on the ground in an alley next to the building. Macanra took it all in and then nodded. They walked over to the building, peered up and down the street and then walked inside.

The place was just as grotty on the inside. It reeked of all kinds of spills. Besides the lone barman at his post, very few men were there at all, even less that could stand up and intervene if things went awry. Macanra started walking around the pub, eying every drunken sot as he went. Zedeck stayed by the bar and smiled at the barman.

"Forgive me, Hyksos, but I do not think you are here for my beer." The man said cautiously.

"We're searching for a friend." Zedeck replied, his smile obviously strained. The barman looked at him and at Macanra walking menacingly up to every table, peering at the faces sitting there. He saw the tense muscles on both of them and the casual way their hands rested on the knives hanging on their belts.

"You do not look like a friend to whomever you seek."

Zedeck snarled at the barman. "His name's Emeko, a Hyksos. Does he drink here?"

"I do not know the man but, if I did, I would not tell you. I would be a better friend to him than you."

Zedeck looked at Macanra, who had searched the place twice. Macanra shrugged. Zedeck turned to the barman once more.

"I guess we'll be staying for your fine beer after all." Zedeck walked over to a table and Macanra followed him. Zedeck whispered to Macanra once they sat down, "Let us wait and see."

***

"We don't have enough food, my king." Ariadne said before a room of well-fed, rich men. Some looked away in scorn, as if such a thing could affect them again. Apepios looked stern but gestured for her to continue. "As it stands, the provinces are already starving. Every day you march south, the worse it will get. If you don't defeat Kamose and return immediately, not only will Avaris start to starve, but even your army too."

The empty chamber resounded with the din of every voice erupting at once, trying to be heard.

"Enough!" Apepios roared. "How many days do we have, precisely?" he said more calmly.

"I cannot say..."

"Then how do we know we don't have more time?" another voice called out from the crowd around their king. Ariadne ignored them and looked at Adro, who was standing near Apepios. Adro looked away. She looked at Apepios himself.

"My staff have been reduced to nearly nothing because of your fear." The surrounding faces looked on in horror at how she spoke to the king. "Even if you win this war, there won't be enough time for us to organise to redistribute the grain back to the provinces. Many will die because we are so behind with our records. I can't tell you how much time you have left; it's already too late."

Apepios stared back at her, giving nothing away.

"With permission, I'd like to return to my work, my king." Ariadne said coolly.

Apepios nodded and there was a fearful low chatter as Ariadne walked out of the hall. Mepsiad turned to Apepios and muttered softly to him.

"She's right. Four provinces are already in open rebellion against us. More will follow if we don't return their stores of grain."

Apepios held up his hand and, this time, everyone in the room went silent. He began to speak.

"I know the dangers we face, from within and without. But the plan stays the same. Kamose will be suffering from the same supply problems that we are. He needs this fight as much as we do. Everything comes down to the battle to come. For, make no mistake," he looked at each man there, slowly, his gaze piercing into them, "this is not a fight for two kingdoms, but for two peoples. If we lose, my friends, we lose everything." Apepios stood up and started walking out of the room himself. "And so," his voice boomed around the room as he walked away from them, "we will not lose."

***

Macanra drained the dregs of his mug while Zedeck sat back still watching the door. Macanra looked around the room, now completely empty except for the barman and themselves. Macanra sighed and then smiled slowly.

"He's not here," he said, but Zedeck kept staring out at the door. "Cheer up. Next time we find him in a pub, we'll buy him a drink." Macanra paused. "See that star?" He pointed out the door. "Do you remember when that was a sunset or when the sun was at its height?" Zedeck looked at him and he continued. "He'd have come by now." Macanra edged closer to Zedeck and whispered in his ear, "We'll tell Adro of this place first thing and he can send the guards in. It has to be where that Egyptian said." Zedeck nodded, finally, and rose.

Macanra walked out with a cheerful grin but Zedeck followed him with a grim face only rivalled by the bartender as he watched them go.

As they walked out into the open air of the evening, Zedeck finally let the beginnings of a smile emerge. "I guess you're right," he said and turned to look at Macanra. He glimpsed past him, however, and saw the passed-out man from before still lying in the alley. The hint of his smile vanished, and his heart missed a beat, as Zedeck walked back slowly towards the alley and the man lying there. Macanra followed behind, his cheerful demeanour fading too. For, the closer they got, the more they recognised their old friend.

Zedeck felt a rising fury with every step. Beneath the greasy, stubble beard and stench of rat shit and spilled beer lay the man they had been looking for all day. Emeko was fast asleep, oblivious to their presence.

Zedeck kicked him hard, right between his legs. Emeko woke with a groan.

Zedeck kicked him again as Macanra walked up behind them. Emeko recognised his attacker immediately and then looked at Macanra muttering a weak cry, "Help!"

Macanra lowered down and grabbed Emeko by the shoulders. He picked him up and slammed him against the wall of the alley.

"Dirty, fucking traitor!"

"Please!" Emeko cried as Macanra kneed him in the gut.

"Please..." he said, winded. "Let me explain." Macanra and Zedeck both glared at him with the look only a betrayed friend could give. "Just hear me out. Then feel free to kill me here and now or take me wherever you wish."

Macanra looked at Zedeck who seethed as much as he did. Zedeck nodded and they turned once more to look at their old friend.

Twenty-Five

Macanra and Zedeck walked down the street with determined steps. Emeko followed along behind them, his hands chafing from the rope which bound his hands, itself held in front by Macanra. Emeko still hurt from his beating but they carried on regardless, forcing him to hobble at a run, though such a thing was as pitiful as it sounds.

After what seemed like an endless march of half-tripping over the loose stones on the road, Emeko and his captors arrived at Adro's house. Macanra pulled the rope, bringing Emeko closer. He held it tightly but Emeko just sagged, grateful for the rest. Zedeck banged on the door.

They heard Adro's muffled shout from the other side of the door. "Who's there?"

"Your favourite drinking companions." Zedeck shouted back.

The door opened and Adro smiled as he spoke to them. "Come in." Zedeck started walking inside but Adro spotted Emeko and put his arm across the doorway, blocking Zedeck. "What's he doing here?"

Macanra held up the rope, bringing Emeko's bound hands high into the air and into view.

"Do you remember asking us to tell you if we found out anything about any further plots to kill the king?" Zedeck said.

Adro nodded.

"We know who's going to kill the king." Zedeck continued. Adro looked first at Zedeck and then at Macanra, both of whom stared back with a deadly seriousness.

Adro paused, looking at Emeko and the rope wound around his hands. He brought his arm down from the doorway warily and said, "Come in then."

***

The sentry bowed down before him as he approached. Kamose didn't know whether to laugh or cry; the man was lying face-down towards the camp with the darkness and the desert to his back. But Kamose did neither of these things, for he was a king.

Kamose walked right past the sentry and kept on his path of the outskirts of the camp. No sooner had that sentry risen at the departure of his king and returned to his duties, then the next sentry in the distance noticed him and bowed down.

Kamose walked slowly and carefully, balancing the double crowns of Upper and Lower Egypt on his head. The small procession of trusted friends and servants which followed behind him matched his careful pace. As he passed by the next sentry, Kamose saw the wonder in the man's eyes as they darted up to the double crown and the man who wore it.

Kamose continued like this for some time before finally turning into camp and meandering back to his tent. Everywhere he turned, his people bowed down before him with a sense of awe and reverence. Finally, he reached his grand tent and entered inside, his entourage following in behind him.

Not one complained as he sat in the only chair at the far end of the room. They all just stood there before him, weary from the night's cold and longing for bed but willing to wait till they were dismissed, come dawn or beyond. Now, in the private company of his most trusted friends, Kamose smiled.

"I told you the double crown was a good idea." He said, pointing to one of the courtiers before him. "The men see our victory already at hand and it gives them courage."

The man addressed nodded quickly. "As always, your ways are right and wiser than our own, O Great King."

"Tell me," Kamose said, this time addressing the two aged generals among the courtiers, "how many men are still to arrive?"

"None, Great King," one of them replied. "The last contingent arrived from Thebes this evening. We are at our full strength." He said proudly. "Our spies say Apepi will soon head out to meet us here but I say let us march to him. We are less than a day's march from the border. Let us fight the imposter in the lands he so foolishly calls his own. Let us show him who they really belong to." He said, gesturing to Kamose. Many men around him nodded, eager and full of excitement. They all looked at Kamose, waiting on his answer.

Kamose paused, smiled again and then began. "What if I told you that we could take back our kingdom without needing a pitched battle? What If I told you we could walk through Lower Egypt with our enemies being handed over to us in chains? Would you wait another few days for that, my friends?"

The courtiers looked at each other, confused and yet no less excited. However, none dared to reply to their king.

"Sleep well, my friends." Kamose said with the glint of excitement even in his own eyes. "It won't be long now."

***

Ariadne walked along through the cold, trying her best to calm her tired mind. She couldn't help but see figures and tallies before her eyes even now.

"—it's not too late, Adro." Ariadne heard faintly from her house in the distance. She hurried along. Something didn't feel right.

"This is madness! How do you three think you could even get to him?" Adro replied. Ariadne quickened her step.

There was a pause before Zedeck replied. "We'll find a way."

Ariadne tripped and stumbled as she approached her house.

"I'm pleading with you. You're all going to die."

She was on her feet, *almost there.*

"No, Adro," said a vaguely familiar voice, "if anyone—"

The door slammed open and Ariadne burst into her house.

"What's happening?" she asked as she quickly took in the room before her. Zedeck, Macanra and a third man stood there with their backs to her, facing Adro across the room. A piece of rope lay on the ground slightly behind the third man. At her intrusion, all three turned around.

"Ari—" Zedeck began.

"You brought *him* here?" she said, pointing at Emeko whom she now recognised. "Get out of my house!"

Without waiting for anyone to comply, she raced up to Emeko, grabbed him by the arms and started pushing him back out the door.

"You threaten my husband in our own home?" she accused.

Emeko turned and held her arm with his hand. "Ari—"

She kicked him between the legs, unaware that she had inadvertently fulfilled a favourite proverb of her Egyptian scribes about camels and straw. Emeko dropped to the ground and she turned and looked fiercely at both Macanra and Zedeck.

Zedeck took the cue and started walking out but Macanra turned to Adro.

"This isn't over." He said before following Zedeck's lead. As they picked up Emeko and carried him out into the darkness, Adro muttered in response.

"No, it isn't."

Ariadne immediately shut the door and locked it again. She turned around to Adro who was visibly shaking. He stumbled over to a chair and collapsed in it.

"What happened?!" she roared with almost as much anger at him as she had given to their friends. Adro didn't speak but held his head in his hands, still shaking.

Ariadne sighed and walked slowly over to him. She put her arms around him and kissed him softly on his head. They stood there for a while, neither saying anything.

"They're going to die." Adro said eventually, almost a whisper.

"Why was Emeko here?" Ariadne asked.

"I've been very busy trying to uncover any further plots against Apepios." Adro began. "I learned that their next attack was actually going to come from a Cretan they had convinced to switch sides. I didn't know who it was though." Adro sighed. "Apparently Macanra and Zedeck went searching too." He laughed bitterly. "While we were searching for a Cretan, they started from nothing and kidnapped a suspicious Egyptian who led them to a hideout with the very Cretan we were trying to find."

"Emeko?"

"Yes—"

"Then why wasn't he tied up? Why were they arguing with you?"

"There's more to it." Adro replied sadly. "Emeko was a wreck after he was banished. No prospects for promotion, ever, and he started drinking more than the rest of us put together. He had no chance with us so he switched sides."

"What does that have to do with Macanra and Zedeck?"

"Kamose's men promised him boundless riches. When Macanra and Zedeck found him, he promised the same to them in turn to be his accomplices. And they agreed. They came here in disguise." He pointed to the rope on the floor. "Emeko was bound with that and they led me to believe they were handing over a prisoner; a traitor and the last threat to Apepios." Adro was no longer shaking now. He rose from the chair and walked across their house, still speaking as he went. "But no sooner had I let them in than they loosened his ropes and gave me a choice—either join them and help them kill our king, or die here and now for him."

Adro returned with a coat and stared at Ariadne with utter seriousness. "They'd just finished hearing me tell them I would never betray our king when you arrived." He held her cheek with the palm of his hand and kissed her forehead softly, gratefully. "I think the only thing that stopped their greed for killing me was the shame of doing it in front of you."

Ariadne held his hand by her cheek, as much, for once, out of fear as out of love. "What are we going to do?"

"They'll be desperate now they're exposed. I'll think they'll try something as soon as possible. I've got to alert the Royal Guard immediately." He held her arms with his hands, rubbing them to comfort himself as much as her. "I know you don't always like our king, and, truth be told, sometimes neither do I. But he's our only chance to win this war. Without him we're finished."

Ariadne nodded and hugged him back.

"Bar the door once I'm gone and don't open it for anybody." Adro opened the door to their house, put the coat he was holding around himself and walked out into the night.

Twenty-Six

Emeko was alone in the darkness with nothing but pain for company. If only that were true; for it was not completely dark, and he was not entirely alone.

They had beaten him with rods—he remembered that much. When he awoke it was to a headache worse than a hangover at sea and a body that ached down to his very fingertips and toes. He lay there on a table, completely naked and unbound, but he was as helpless as he was free. It was more than simply pain, he couldn't raise an arm let alone lift himself off and leave.

But awaking to pain and a body which couldn't move had only been the start. Once they knew he was awake they started working away with their knives by candlelight. He had been cut and stabbed; slashed and poked, until the table dripped with his blood. Always, the question was the same. Always, he gave the same answer.

They had let him be for some time now. He didn't understand at first but eventually realised they'd changed tact. When he had been surrounded by pain constantly he pushed back and defied them but as he lay there by himself in the cold somehow every bruise and every cut, every broken bone felt more painful with each passing minute.

Footsteps. Someone new had entered the room. They shut the door behind them but came no closer. They remained in the shadows. One of Emeko's torturers tried whispering to the newcomer but in a room that silent for that long, Emeko heard every word.

"He has not been broken. He maintains his innocence." Silence. "Watch."

Emeko started panting as his torturer began walking towards him. His whole body tensed and he started to sweat.

"I need to speak to Apepios!" Emeko shouted as the torturer took a torch from the wall. "He is in danger!"

No-one responded. The torturer was upon him.

"You have to warn—" Emeko gasped for breath as the torturer held the naked flame to his hand.

"AAARRRRGGGHHHH!" he cried out in agony, too feeble to move his hand out of the way.

"AAARRRRGGGHHHH!" his screams continued as his hand started to sizzle.

Slowly, the newcomer walked out from the shadows and stood above the table holding his friend. Adro looked down before him and waved an arm to signal the torturer. The torch left Emeko's hand but the agony remained.

Emeko looked up to see Adro staring back down at him, saw that perfectly calm face in the flickering light and quivered.

"We have Macanra." Adro said and took the torch from the torturer. "We have Zedeck." He held the torch to Emeko's foot and waited as he cried out once more. He took it away. "You have lost, Emeko." He stared at his friend with the uttermost hatred in his eyes, or was there a faint hint of fear too? "You will not kill our king."

Emeko winced and shut his eyes tight.

"You are going to die. They are going to die. It's your choice. You could die slowly…" He put the torch just near enough to Emeko's toes to warm them slightly. "Or you could just let it all go." He took the torch away, walked over to the wall and replaced it once more.

All was quiet save for Emeko gasping in pain. Eventually he spoke. "I, Emeko of Malia," he grunted through pain, "admit that I was part of an attempt on the life of Apepios, king of the Cretans..."

***

Ariadne took her normal route through the windy streets leading to the palace. Adro had joked when he first saw her house about its location; it was a maze between there and the palace, why did she pick such a spot? She had only laughed and told him it made her feel at home.

Except she didn't feel at home this morning. For the first time since living here, Ariadne carried a knife, hidden away in her clothing. Every corner she turned she expected to see Macanra and Zedeck or Emeko and a gang of Egyptian peasants. Every corner she gripped the knife for comfort.

But no-one came. She kept walking unharmed as she passed each street. The barracks were just up ahead. She would be safe now. They wouldn't dare attack so close to so many guards.

Ariadne relaxed her hand on the knife and walked with more confidence. As she reached the edge of it she saw a guard standing on duty who smiled at her and raised a hand in greeting. He couldn't possibly know how relieved she was to see him. She smiled for the first time that morning and waved a hand with enthusiasm.

As she walked further on, Ariadne peered into the barracks' courtyard searching for a sight that helped her get up every morning. Sure enough, it was still there: Euouk's body rotting on the stake he had been impaled on. Ariadne only wished it was her on father on it instead.

This morning she saw another stake plunged into the ground and another body on top of it. Gazing at it to see who it was, she realised, like an insect squashed but not yet dead, it was still moving. As she peered closer she realised, with as much revulsion as relief, that it was Macanra.

Pausing for a mere instant, Ariadne changed her course and walked into the barracks' courtyard. As she walked up to Macanra, she could hear his low groaning and another, faint sound from within the barracks. She heard the sound of hard things colliding against each other amidst muffled cries of pain.

"Apepios will die." Macanra said faintly at hearing someone approach.

She turned to him. "You deserve this." She said more forcefully than she believed. "You were going to kill our king."

"Is that what he told you, Ari?" Macanra said, opening his eyes.

Ariadne didn't reply. She heard another muffled crack come from the barracks.

"Is that Zedeck in there?"

Macanra nodded. "One hundred strikes with the rod, then..." He gestured feebly to the stake running through his gut and out his back. "He hasn't got long now."

Ariadne winced as she faintly heard Zedeck receive another blow.

"Neither does Apepios." Macanra said again.

"Where's Emeko?" Ariadne said, worried.

"Adro had him killed earlier this morning."

Ariadne sighed with relief. "Then Apepios is safe. None of you can get to him."

"No, Ari," Macanra said through pain, "we were never a threat to the king. The threat is Adro."

***

"The other two are being executed as we speak." Adro said to Apepios and Mepsiad. All three were walking down a corridor in the palace.

"You said Zedeck was one of them?" Mepsiad asked.

"Yes." Adro replied. They turned a corner to see another pair of guards nod as they walked passed.

"That is... regrettable."

"Regrettable?" Apepios asked, in no mood for sympathy.

"He was a fine captain and he always turned a profit. From what I knew of the man he was too cool-headed for something like this."

Apepios scowled but Adro replied. "He was one of my dearest friends, they both were. I never would have expected either of them capable of such treachery."

"The third?" Apepios asked.

Adro looked at Mepsiad, who knew full well who the third was. "Unfortunately," Adro said, "we know Emeko was capable of many things. Even before I heard it from his own mouth I had little reason to doubt his guilt."

They turned another corner, this time to a crossroads. Apepios stopped and spoke. "Mepsiad, I want you to represent me at the council this morning. I'll be in my inner quarters planning the upcoming battle." Mepsiad started walking off to the right. "Adro, you did well. Now come with me. I would feel safer with you there beside me."

Apepios walked off to the left and Adro, with a soft smile, followed dutifully behind.

***

"It started that night we came to your place for dinner." Macanra shifted a bit around the stake and groaned as splinters dug into him. "We saw Emeko in the street along the way. He was with an Egyptian. There was something suspicious about it."

"Why didn't you tell Adro?" Ariadne asked.

"He'd have used any excuse to put him away. We had to be sure." The sound of wood crashing against bone echoed in the barracks and filtered into the courtyard as Zedeck was stuck again. The face of the graffitier flashed before Macanra's mind.

"We caught one of 'em. He told us the next attack would come from a Cretan and he told us where they planned everything." Macanra looked at Ariadne earnestly. "Plan seemed simple enough: if Emeko was there, he was the one."

"And did you find him there?"

"We did." Macanra replied warily.

"Then why are you here?!" she said, striking the stake that held him.

"Place was a pub. He was pissed, lying in his own filth in an alley beside it." He looked her in the eye. "If you were gonna get paid to kill a king, don't you think they'd at least give you a room to stay?"

Ariadne didn't respond. Another whack from the barracks helped fill the silence.

"Eh," he said then groaned once more as he raised himself slightly on the stake, "we thought same as you at first too. Gave him a right beating. But then we listened."

Ariadne felt a rising fear, unsure whether she wanted to hear anymore.

"That night Emeko was with that Egyptian—we'll he'd been coming back from your place, wanted to make amends. He saw Adro talking with the Egyptian in an alley. He crept closer and overheard them. He just caught the end of it—some order from Kamose. Why was a foreign king giving the orders to the newly appointed chief guard?"

Ariadne frowned. "He made it up. He lied to you."

"It fits, Ari." Macanra kept going, determined. "After Adro left the alley Emeko caught the Egyptian and tried to beat an explanation out of him. That's what we saw walking on by."

"Then why didn't he tell anyone?"

"The Egyptian tried to escape but it got out of hand. Emeko stabbed him; killed him."

"How convenient."

"These things happen."

Ariadne eyed the stake puncturing her friend's body. "You don't say."

"The Egyptian didn't tell him anything. He had nothing to go on and he'd killed his only source. Who would have listened to him?"

"You'll have to do better than that." Ariadne started walking away amidst the sound of Zedeck receiving another blow.

"We heard that a Cretan will try to kill Apepios and Emeko overheard Adro receiving orders from our greatest enemy. Who else could it be?"

Ariadne stopped and turned around to face Macanra once more.

The guards inside the barracks had started dragging a half-limp Zedeck out towards them.

"If we really wanted to kill Apepios, then why did we go to Adro first? What would it serve?"

Ariadne was worried now. Macanra was right. Something didn't fit.

"To persuade him to do it for you?" she said, searching for something, anything but the alternative...

"Then why did we bring Emeko? Do you think Adro would ever risk everything he has to help the man he hates most?" He looked at her sternly. "You know he wouldn't." She looked back unable to disagree but desperately wanting to. "If we were trying to kill the king, he wouldn't have been there. It would have ruined any chance we had. Tell me I'm wrong."

Macanra looked over to Zedeck being propped up by two guards. Others were digging a small hole for the stake to rest in.

"Tell me I'm wrong or stop them killing Zedeck." Macanra pleaded, looking at her once more.

It couldn't be. Ariadne stood there, motionless. Then she walked up to the guards holding Zedeck.

"Do you both know who I am?" They nodded.

"My husband wants to speak more with this one," she said, gesturing to Zedeck. "Tie him up by all means but he's not to be killed yet." The men holding Zedeck hesitated while the men digging the hole ignored her completely. "This comes direct from Apepios through my husband, head of the Royal Guard. Understood?" All men were looking at her now, even a dazed Zedeck. "I'll be returning with my husband shortly."

Reluctantly, they started filling in the hole. The two men holding Zedeck began dragging him back inside. Satisfied, Ariadne turned to walk out of the barracks. She looked over at Macanra who nodded with determination despite grimacing from the pain.

Ariadne nodded softly in return and continued on her way. Once more she was on her usual path up towards the palace. She gripped the knife even tighter than before.

***

It couldn't be. A thousand possibilities flooded Ariadne's mind as she raced through the corridors of the palace. *Somehow it will all make sense.* She had reached the entrance to the main chamber and peered inside. She saw Mepsiad addressing a crowd of the most powerful men north of Thebes. Only two were missing: her husband and her king.

Ariadne turned and walked back the way she came. *That doesn't mean—*Ariadne rid her mind of all such thoughts and quickened her pace. If Apepios was still in the palace, there was only place he'd be. His own personal quarters may take up a fifth of the entire palace and be guarded at each entrance but the king had to be in them somewhere.

As each passing minute went by, Ariadne couldn't help but imagine Apepios' blood draining more and more from his body. *He is in a dark room, helplessly looking at the door, hoping for someone to come in and save him in his final moments.* Ariadne saw a door in the distance guarded by two guards. *No, he is alive, he's having a bath and Adro is in some training field practicing for the battle ahead.* She took a breath and walked towards the two guards.

"This leads to Apepios' quarters, right?" she asked politely and walked forwards.

"We have strict orders to let no-one in." One of them replied.

"What if I told you the king was in danger, now more than ever?"

"The chief is with him. He's as safe as can be." The other one replied.

"Urrghh!" Ariadne raised her hands in frustration. "No, that's the point!"

"What do you mean?"

The door behind them opened. Adro walked out calmly and shut it once more. He saw Ariadne standing there and his eyes lit up in surprise.

"What have you done?" she said, horrified. Adro nodded to the guards and stepped forward towards her.

"I've had a long, hard night, Ariadne. I need to sleep."

"Where is Apepios?" she asked.

"Resting in his inner quarters. He doesn't want to be disturbed. He'll come out when he's ready."

"You didn't...?"

"Come on, Ari, let's go." He reached for her arm but she drew it away in horror.

"I need to speak to Apepios!" she shouted. Adro frowned.

"I need to speak to the—"

Whack! Adro's arm move faster than an arrow from a bow. His elbow collided with her temple and she collapsed, unconscious.

Adro turned to the two guards standing there staring with a mixture of amusement and mild worry. "Sorry about that. She gets... emotional sometimes."

They nodded. Adro picked up Ariadne's body and draped it over his shoulder before slowly walking away.

Twenty-Seven

Ariadne awoke slowly. She felt warm. As she rolled over she could feel the blanket not only draped over her but tucked under her back and legs as well. She opened her eyes and looked around.

Ariadne was on the couch in their living room. The front door was shut but didn't seem barred or locked in any way. Adro was off to the side sitting down with his back to her, literally—his tunic was lying on the ground beside him. She moved her hands instinctively to the edges of the couch to push herself up and realised that they hadn't been tied.

She continued. As quietly as any cat, she untucked the blanket and lifted herself from the couch. She started creeping towards the door when Adro spoke.

"Ah, you're up." He hadn't even turned around. She stopped. "I'm really, truly sorry I had to do that." Ariadne vaguely remembered the last few moments in the palace. "I just couldn't have a scene there."

She looked at him, confused. "Why haven't you...?" She held her hands out, the blanket falling off her shoulders.

Adro didn't respond. He hadn't even turned around. His right arm was moving in deliberate arcs. His hand must be on his chest and moving too. Despite everything, curiosity got the better of her and Ariadne walked over to Adro. He still didn't turn around so she walk around and in front of him.

Adro was painting something onto himself. It took her a moment to realise. He was half-way through painting the Eye of

Horus on his chest. He looked up at her, stopped and put the brush down.

"You're free to leave. I won't stop you. You're too late though, it's already been done."

"What?!"

"Ask me anything. The time for secrets is over." Adro said calmly, looking earnestly up at her.

"Did you kill our king?" Each word was said with deliberate slowness, as if he might misunderstand if spoken otherwise.

"Yes, earlier today. Right before I saw you."

"What have you done?!" Ariadne looked around for something to hit him with. Although she was unbound and the door unlocked, it seemed he had hidden all the knives just to be safe.

"Let me tell you. You won't help anyone by running off to the guards now."

Ariadne fumed and paced before him. While he was waiting, Adro picked up the brush and started painting once more.

"For starters, what's with that?" she said, pointing at his chest.

"The true king fancies himself a new Horus." Adro replied and put the brush down once more.

"The *true* king?"

Adro smiled and pointed to his chest. "This is the sign that I work for him. Tonight we are going to leave this city and head to Kamose's camp as quickly as possible."

Adro waited in the ensuing silence, hoping it was starting to sink in.

"You treacherous, dishonourable, pathetic excuse of a man!" Apparently so.

"You know what your problem is, Ariadne?" Adro said, matching her frustration. "You've become the very thing you hate most."

She glared back at him, furious despite not having any idea what he meant.

"You've said it yourself before: we're ruling these people through their beliefs about their gods. They're slaving away, like animals in the fields, gathering food for the very people that killed their fathers, their brothers and husbands. Their sons."

She looked back at him, unfazed.

"If they're stupid enough to believe it why shouldn't we rule them?" she retorted.

Adro fumed. "And the worst part is, you don't care! You're letting terrible things be done to these people and using 'the gods' as an excuse. You're as bad as my father."

"What about *our* people—"

"Our people?! You mean the people that tried to sacrifice you? The people who marched beside me, happy for me or my friends to die so they could rule this land. What do we owe them?"

"You're one to talk. What sort of a man orders his friends to die so he can kill his king?"

Adro stopped. "I pleaded with them. I had made arrangements for all of them, even Emeko." He looked her in the eyes and betrayed at once both the earnest heart she had known, and a calculating mind she hadn't thought him capable of.

"They wouldn't listen to me; couldn't see past Cretan and Egyptian. They couldn't see that what we are doing is wrong. In the end I had to decide, and I chose to free a nation."

They paused for a while, Adro with nothing left to say and Ariadne appalled beyond words.

"I couldn't save them from themselves, Ariadne," his face hardened in determination, "but I can save you."

Ariadne scowled and paced in front of him once more. A thousand questions filled her mind. So much still didn't add up. After a while she spoke.

"Why did you stop that man at the Sed festival?"

Adro smiled. "Kamose is a wiser man than Apepios. He is far more patient. Kamose knew our rule rested on two things: the Egyptians accepting our right to rule them, and that we won that right through our victorious king. When the Nile didn't flood he saw it as his opportunity to break both of those."

"I've heard this all before—the Nile doesn't flood so the gods don't like the king."

"No," Adro replied with patience, "that was only the start. Such a thing could blow over if Apepios could last until another season of good harvests. Kamose's real plan was to get Apepios to oppress the Egyptians further. Apepios' response to the attempt on his life set in motion both the demise of Apepios and Cretan rule itself."

"What do you mean?"

"Apepios started distrusting Egyptians and he hired me. If he'd been killed then and there, many in the provinces would have just accepted a new Hyksos ruler. By waiting, Kamose set me up to take Apepios down whenever he liked and he drove Apepios to set the Egyptian people against himself." Adro paused and then continued. "You take away all positions of authority in the capital, and take all the food from starving provinces to feed a fully Cretan army and how do you think the Egyptian people will respond? Half of the kingdom is already in open rebellion! The other half will follow once they hear, now, of Apepios' death. It was all a matter of timing. And Kamose's timing has been to perfection." Adro stopped once more and waited, thinking this time she might finally understand.

"These people will never be free, Adro." Ariadne replied. "You can stay here and watch this new king you trust treat them just as badly as we have," she started walking over towards the door, "but I'm not."

Adro got up and followed her. Ariadne stopped at the door and turned around. "They haven't killed Zedeck yet. I got them to stop until I spoke with you first. And now," she said with an icy coldness, "if you love me, if you ever loved me, you are going to set Zedeck free and he and I are going to sail far away from this mess you've created."

Adro stepped forward, mouth half-open in shock.

"But we...?"

"There is no we!" Ariadne finally burst. "Not anymore! The Adro I loved died with Macanra and Emeko."

Ariadne opened the door to their house and stormed out into the yet peaceful neighbourhood. Adro stood there for a time, his face torn by pain. He turned around and grabbed his tunic. He placed it over himself, hiding the still unfinished Eye of Horus, and followed her out into the street.

***

Zedeck limped along towards the dock. Ariadne tried again to hold his arm as he fumbled along but he shooed her away with it. As the sun was setting behind them, Ariadne and Zedeck walked ever closer to a ship docked at the pier. Another solitary figure walked behind them at a distance.

In front, the crew seemed to be packing up for the night. Most seemed to be carrying something to or from the boat. One of the men saw the two approaching and, not stopping to put down the bundle of rope he was holding, shouted out,

"Hey there, Zedeck!"

"Peteos, good to see you!" Zedeck replied.

"What are you here for, man? Come to join our voyage after all?"

"Yes, as it turns out. She is too." He said and gestured to Ariadne.

Peteos raised an eyebrow. "Something I should know?"

"Yeah, we gotta be out of here tonight or we won't see another."

"Listen, I don't know what you've gotten yourself into..."

"Not just me, Peteos, you, everyone. We need to leave, tonight."

"You know we don't sail at night."

"Row slowly if that's all you can do, but we need to leave Avaris."

"Why? What's so urgent that we can't get a decent night's rest?"

Ariadne turned away as Zedeck began explaining the situation. She saw Adro silhouetted in the sunset, watching them. Just making sure. *No!* she thought. She couldn't bear to think that there was still something worthwhile in those eyes looking sadly back at her. She couldn't bear to think of the life she was giving up to sail once more into the unknown. She couldn't bear to look back and think, what might have been. Worse, what could still be. All it would take was a few footsteps and she knew he'd come running for her.

"Ariadne." Zedeck said softly.

She didn't respond but continued to look out at Adro in the distance.

"Peteos says they'll leave tonight and that there's a spot for each of us."

"Where are we headed?" Ariadne asked absentmindedly.

"East," Zedeck replied.

Ariadne looked away and then turned around to face Zedeck. She nodded and started walking off towards the ship. All the while, a lonely pair of eyes stared at her back as it slowly drifted off into the distance, eyes that held out hope despite her every fateful step.

PART THREE

Twenty-Eight

Ariadne squinted as she gazed out at the sea before her. It wasn't just the sea that was glittering. The morning sun shone straight into her eyes but as she peered through the glare she could see something else shining in the distance. As the minutes slowly rolled by, the stone walls of a city came more and more into view.

"What did you say it was called?" Ariadne asked a startled Zedeck. She didn't blame him for jolting with surprise; despite his near constant companionship it was the most she had said to him in days.

"Ashdod." Zedeck replied. He looked at her and saw, for the first time since they left, a hint of the old Ariadne, of her curiosity. "Do you remember I told you that on my last voyage to the east we met some Cretans?"

"Vaguely," Ariadne said, still staring out to the horizon.

"It seems we weren't the only ones to flee Crete after what happened. We had most of the fleet but other stragglers and survivors apparently banded together and set off on their own. They came here."

"What happened once they arrived?" Ariadne asked.

"I don't quite know." Zedeck answered with a shrug. "But I know they didn't have to fight as we did. And I know they now rule five cities in this new land." He rubbed her shoulder with his hand, tenderly, as if all her pain were concentrated in that one spot. "There'll be somewhere here we can start again."

Ariadne finally turned around. Zedeck felt sick upon peering into her eyes ablaze with a rage that had been festering ever since they had left. Zedeck was entranced by the hate; it seemed he was peering through her eyes and into her very mind. He saw desperate men fighting for their very lives in the streets of an Avaris rife with flame. He saw thousands starving in fields by the banks of the Nile and he saw the rotting corpse of his best friend atop a wicked spike, alone in the emptiness of a deserted city.

Zedeck blinked and once more saw nothing but those hate-filled eyes. He opened his mouth to speak then thought better of it and stared out past her to the city in the distance.

***

"She's not your wife, is she?" Zedeck frowned in response to the barmaid who just placed a bowl of soup before each of them. "You sit with a whole foot between you and you've barely spoken since you got here." She gestured to the smoky interior of the pub they now found themselves in. "And," she continued, bending in close and whispering to his ear, "I heard you booked two rooms to stay in." She bit his ear slightly before withdrawing once more, smiling coquettishly before turning to walk off. "Either she's not," she said over her shoulder, "or you've had such a falling out..." She bit her lip and then turned her head forward and kept walking.

"What a piece of work," Zedeck mused.

"She's clever and she's direct," Ariadne replied, smiling for once. Ariadne saw her in the distance bending over to pour a drink as much for their benefit as the man she was now serving. "She's cute too—you could do much worse." Zedeck started laughing as well and quickly looked back to the soup he had been pretending to focus on all along.

"What are we going to do here, Zedeck?" Ariadne asked, suddenly serious. "Are you going to join that captain when he sails out again?"

Zedeck, mouth half-full of soup, swallowed quickly and replied. "I'm not going to leave you to the likes of this," he said, gesturing around the pub. "You deserve a better life than pouring drinks for sailors and letting them pour into you in turn." Ariadne nodded, not shocked at all by his bluntness. "We'll get you sorted out as a scribe to one of lords of these five cities, then I'll think about myself. Half a day, tops, at a port and I'd find someone willing to take me on."

"Let's see if the lord of Ashdod will see us tomorrow then," Ariadne said, satisfied with his plan.

They began to eat, once more in the comfortable silence that had become their life. Ariadne noticed Zedeck's eyes following the barmaid as she walked from table to table, despite his best efforts to appear indifferent. She seemed to wipe down the empty tables out of habit as much as anything, though most were already clean. There weren't that many people in the tavern and those that were there were busy eating or drinking the afternoon away. It didn't take her long to come back to them. She sat down on the bench opposite and started again.

"So, my ox-eyed lovers, what brings you to Ashdod?"

Zedeck started laughing, just a little bit, and then spoke. "Her husband," he said pointing to Ariadne, "killed my two closest friends in the pursuit of making us all fabulously wealthy for the rest of our days." He paused, as if it had only just sunk in for the first time. "Being the great wife that she is, Ariadne here stopped him killing me and then ran off with me, willing to face a life of utter poverty, anything to avoid staying with the man who will become the richest and most powerful Cretan in the whole of Egypt."

"Sorry I asked." She started to get up again. Zedeck chuckled once more and looked at Ariadne who smiled in turn without looking up from her soup.

"She doesn't believe us." Zedeck said dryly.

"Is any of that actually true?" The barmaid stood, hovering over the chair, wary but wanting to sit and listen further.

"He left out the bit where he was vomiting blood for two days after we left. Check his ribs and you'll still see the bruises." Ariadne said. "Is there anyone here who can tell me about how our people got here, what happened in those early days?" Though curious, Ariadne looked oddly serious.

"Yes," the barmaid replied, suddenly short of words, "over there." She pointed to a man sitting over in a corner, eating by himself.

"Thank you." Ariadne replied. She smiled and motioned to Zedeck, "Hear him out, he won't disappoint." She got up and winked at Zedeck as she turned to walk away. Zedeck smiled and looked down at the table, lost for a moment in thought. He looked up at the barmaid.

"There were four of us to begin with: the son of a shepherd, a sailor, a soldier and a priest. We were fine until she showed up." He said in a playful tone, inclining his head towards Ariadne. The barmaid chuckled and Ariadne smiled as well, walking closer to the man in the corner.

Her first thought was that he looked so very plain. Easily forty or fifty, the heavily tanned and wrinkled skin didn't do anything for his looks and neither did the spiky beard more grey now than the traces of black which clung on. He had the odd scar up and down his arms from where someone had gotten the better of him with knife or spear. He seemed engrossed in his meal yet wasn't rushing it. He had the slow, plodding pace of someone who appreciated every bite and every second he had to do so. By now Ariadne was at his table, almost hovering over him.

"I'll let you know if I want another drink. Go pester someone else," he said between bites, eyes still down at the food-covered board. Ariadne sat down opposite him, waiting patiently. He looked up at her and, after taking another bite, spoke again. "What's your name?"

"Ariadne of Knossos." She replied.

The man's eyebrows raised in interest. "You're a long way from home." He looked around the tavern, seemingly for the first time, noticing the barmaid sitting near Zedeck. "You're not a barmaid, are you?"

"No, I'm not." Ariadne said with an air of loftiness. "Tell me about our people. What happened when they first came here?"

The man looked at her carefully, as if he was searching for something. He pushed the board to the side and out of his reach, keeping his eyes on her the whole time.

"You're speaking with Alkaios of Gournia." The man began. "I was the first man to speak with these Canaanai; the man who called out across the crashing waves to those standing on the shore."

Despite everything that had happened, Ariadne relaxed and sat onto the bench beside him. She felt the magic of a new and exciting story about to be told.

Fire. Fire and water. There seemed to be no end to the destruction. The bodies of the unfortunates floated amongst the debris. Many died inside their own homes. Walls caved in at the force of the waves tearing through our village, crushing those inside. Those with sturdier houses fared no better, drowning inside them all the same.

It didn't stop when the seas withdrew and the sky stopped raining fire. Those that tried to drink from streams or wells around grew sick and died. Most of the crops had been washed away or spoiled as well. The whole land was cursed and we knew, either the gods had abandoned us, or they were behind such a cruel change of fate. Either way we knew we were doomed.

Those of us who survived had fled the village to the high points but that was almost as bad as being there. You saw the home of your childhood and your parents' childhoods being torn apart and scattered across the land. You saw the bodies, so many bodies.

As we searched the high hills for clean water and whatever food we could find, our numbers slowly built up. We found more survivors each day, each one heartbroken but determined to survive. Then one day a ship sailed into our harbour. Our few fishing boats had been dashed against the houses but this ship had come from another place. The men of Zakros were not affected by the waves that came ashore. Those waves passed them by. But the men of Zakros saw the darkness in the skies and they saw the sea churning in the distance. Once the waves died down they sailed up the coast, searching for survivors.

I had eaten nothing but berries for days and the water they collected from a spring high in the mountains was never enough to go around. These men came and offered us the chance to start again. They were gathering up all who would come with them and were going to sail off and leave our desolate land. They believed more havoc was yet to come and they would be next. Maybe they were right. I wouldn't know. I haven't been back since.

Five ships sailed out from Zakros searching for survivors and any trace of the main fleet. They never found the fleet. It didn't take long before the ships were packed. Children slept on the deck and people learned to walk around them, over them if need be. Everyone pitched in. Men and women, young and old, everyone rowed or helped in some small way. I guess I'm saying, we became family in those few days, grew stronger bonds than father and son, brother and sister, we knew what we had suffered and that we were all each other had left.

Days passed on the sea. It was a form of death to be surrounded by so much water and have so little to drink between us. My belly raged like a fire to see fish and dolphins swimming around our ship, just out of reach. And the land. We constantly passed land; rocky, desolate land, inhospitable. Besides, we had little grain to plant and no time to wait, we needed help to start again, not just some dirt.

Was it the fourth or the fifth day we saw them? It might have been longer. Time passed differently under the scorching sun out at sea. At first it was just a few fishermen, looking at us from the shore. We decided to send a single ship forward to try and talk with them. By the time we were within earshot there were hundreds of people on the shore including what looked like some kind of royal procession.

I was on that ship. We had all but landed on their beach and no-one was saying anything to each other. We just stared at them and they stared at us. I realised someone needed to say something so I moved to the prow of the ship, waved my arms and shouted out as loudly as I could,

"I am a friend. We are some friends from the sea."

Those on the shore became excited and started shouting things back at us in their own tongue. They waved us in with their hands and gestured for us to beach the ship, so we did. When we landed they kept repeating one thing again and again, "Philos tines! Philos tines!"

They pointed at me as I jumped off the ship and said it again and then they pointed to themselves and said "Cananim." They thought "Philos tines" was our name for ourselves.

"Why?" Ariadne interrupted.

"You weren't listening to the sounds of our words. Listen again, but as one who hears for the first time."

Ego eimi philos tines philoi esmen ek tes thalattes. Those were the first words they heard. And they have never forgotten them. Philos tines, it's what they call us even now.

"So what happened next?" Ariadne asked.

We did meet the leaders of their city that day. They didn't know what we were saying for those first few days but they gave us shelter and food and waited patiently. When they learned what happened and that we wanted land to start again, they offered to help us build a city and gave us land on which to do so. We started off with one and now we rule five cities here. Our people prosper.

"And you would have known all that if you weren't new to this place. So, tell me, please, why are you here?" Alkaios concluded his tale.

"I am as you were all those years ago, fleeing a home in search of a new life."

"Fleeing Crete?" Alkaios asked, musing.

"Fleeing a land I can no longer live in." She said guardedly then softened. "I am a scribe and I will find a king in this new land to take me into his palace. I will start here, in Ashdod."

"You don't want to work for the king of Ashdod." Alkaios said as if it were common knowledge. "He is miserly and cares little for scribes. No," he started eating once more, "you want my lord, the king of Gath. He would take you in a heartbeat." Ariadne looked at Alkaios who kept stuffing his face as she made her decision. He seemed earnest enough.

"Gath it is."

***

"I'd hoped never to have to trudge through another desert as long as I lived," Zedeck complained.

"May your days be long and those of your people too," Ariadne rehearsed for the fortieth time in the language of the Canaanai.

"Very good." Alkaios said. "You learn fast."

"Sand," Zedeck said, ignoring them and pointing all around him. "Heat. More sand. The only things alive want to kill you."

"Do you remember what else I taught you?" Alkaios asked.

"I want that one. I don't want that one. I am a Philostines. My name is Ariadne—"

"How do you say, 'I hate the desert?'" Zedeck interrupted.

"These people have a saying," Alkaios said and said it in their tongue. "It means, 'The desert has no friends, those alone in the desert have no friends either.'"

"Ha, something useful at last." Zedeck said. He and Ariadne tried to repeat it a few times. After hearing their garbled attempts, Alkaios chuckled and muttered, "You'll get there."

They kept walking along for some time, Zedeck every now and then repeating, "The desert has no friends..." As they reached the top of another hill Alkaios pointed into the distance.

"See, my friends, you won't be saying that too much longer." In the distance lay the walls of Gath.

***

"Just this way, not much further." Alkaios said, eagerly leading them onwards. Despite herself Ariadne was eager too, almost nervous with excitement. *I need to get this right.* "May your days be long..." she murmured under her breath as she walked up the final couple of stairs leading to the throne room.

As she took those first few steps into the throne room, the king of Gath rose from his throne and stood with outstretched arms. Ariadne was still looking at the ground in front of her feet but, as her head rose to look at him, she stopped—first uncertain, and then very afraid.

"*You!*" she spat loudly, to Zedeck's confusion.

"The desert has no friends," she cursed in her newfound tongue, "those alone in the desert have no friends either."

The king of Gath frowned and his outstretched arms fell to his side once more. Ariadne turned around immediately and stormed back the way she came.

Twenty-Nine

"Murderous, good for nothing fanatic!" she mumbled under her breath as she stormed back down the stairs. She had barely taken a few steps before a guard stepped out from the corner before her and stood there silently blocking her way.

"Thirteen years, Ariadne." Spirysidos' voice rang across the room behind her.

"Let me pass!" she shouted at the guard. He didn't move so she hit him on the shoulder. He didn't flinch. She struck again, this time at his face but he blocked her arm with his hand then grabbed it and pinned it behind her back. He pushed her, step by step, back up the way she had come.

Zedeck was just standing there, aware of what was happening but unsure of what to do. Ariadne turned to look at Alkaios standing beside him with a calm, almost cheerful face.

"You knew!" she yelled accusingly.

"Of course I knew." Alkaios replied. "We all did."

"Ever since I became the king of Gath I have had men out looking for you." Spirysidos said and started walking towards her. "And every guard of this city, every merchant who has passed through, I gave the same offer: untold wealth to whoever finds me my lost daughter."

"I haven't been your 'daughter' for a long time." Ariadne seethed.

"Look around you, Ariadne." Spirysidos said, gesturing with his arms to the walls of the room and the palace beyond. "Alkaios says you came here to beg for work but, dear, you don't have to work another day in your life."

He was inches away from her now. She looked back at him, yes with a raging anger in her eyes, but a hint of weariness too.

"Let me feed you at least," Spirysidos continued. "One meal together," despite sounding like he had rehearsed himself a thousand times, Spirysidos choked up and, for a moment, couldn't speak, "that's all I ask. Just let me hear about where you've been, what you've done for the past thirteen years. After that, if you don't want to stay, I swear, you can go and I'll send you with as much food and gold as you can carry. I'll give you guards to take you anywhere you want to go in this land and protect you along the way." He looked into her eyes, eyes he hadn't seen for years but dreamt about every night. He searched for some way back into her life, pleading.

Ariadne looked away and turned to face Zedeck. Zedeck dipped his head briefly, the slightest nod to accompany the pleading look in his own eyes. She knew that look, she had seen it plenty of times in Adro's, Emeko's and Macanra's eyes as well. *Men!* Ariadne thought. *It always comes down to food, doesn't it?*

***

"—and so Kamose is probably sacking Avaris as we speak, if he hasn't already done so." Ariadne concluded. Spirysidos was sitting there mesmerised while Zedeck stuffed another handful of grapes into his mouth.

Ariadne reached for her cup of wine and drank from it, deep in thought though no longer sharing. "So I'm guessing he's not Adro," Spirysidos said after a little while, pointing at Zedeck.

"No," she said, smiling despite herself. She stopped, realising once again who she was talking to. "No, this is Zedeck, the friend I saved from being killed."

Zedeck had just stuffed more food into his mouth; figs it looked like, though he was snatching his next bite before he'd finished the last one so it was hard to keep track. He waved his spare hand at Spirysidos in acknowledgment.

"You left your husband?" Spirysidos asked with the faintest hint of accusation.

"I left my husband." Ariadne replied sternly.

You always leave people, always run away rather than face your problems, rather than fix them, Spirysidos thought but didn't dare say. Instead he nodded, and raised his cup. "To my daughter, the most determined girl," he stopped himself and then continued, "the most determined woman, always sure of her path."

Zedeck raised his cup also while Ariadne stared at her father, searching for any hint of malice in those words. She frowned, unsure for the merest instant then let it go and inclined her head with an accepting smile instead.

Spirysidos put his cup back down and spoke once more. "I guess it's my turn, Ariadne. Do you want to know where I've been, how I became king here? Ask me anything."

Ariadne paused in thought. Seizing the opportunity, Zedeck asked, seemingly in all seriousness, "So if you buy ten amphorae of wine in Gortyn, and thirty in Pylos, including the costs of food and wages for your crew, how much would you need to sell the wine for in Avaris to make a profit of twice what you set out with?"

Spirysidos blinked.

Zedeck pushed his shoulder hard then, trying to be friendly but pushed a little too hard and Spirysidos had to grab the side of his couch to stop himself falling off it.

"Where's Mama?" Ariadne asked rather softly as Spirysidos steadied himself once more. Spirysidos' shoulders sagged a bit at that, *Thirteen years and that's your first question?* Still, it was understandable.

"When I returned from that beach, your mother made it very clear we were finished. That next week was hard. Not only were we fighting to stay alive after the waves crashed into our home and every morsel of food was a tiny prize, but she would take nothing I found, nothing I offered her."

Spirysidos had waited a long time to see his daughter again and Ariadne could feel the weaving of another story coming along.

A simple question. Ariadne sighed. She could feel the beginning of a tale being woven before her. *He's going to tell me everything that's happened since he saw me, isn't he?* She saw the eagerness in his eyes; the hope, and softened just a little. Ariadne reached for her cup and sipped it, listening intently.

By the time the ships came searching for survivors, I was on the brink of wandering off from our little camp up on the hilltop and just disappearing. One more dead man in the wake of such a calamity, what did it matter when I'd already lost everything that mattered? But when I saw those ships sail in, I knew I had a chance to find you again. I didn't know where you had gone but I knew I would find you, if I had to search for the rest of my life.

You've probably already heard by now how we met the Canaanai and they gave us a city to live in. We were all grateful and many stayed there and began to start again. I was restless though. I travelled to every city in their land, asked in every king's court and every grotty pub if they had heard of you. In the end I became a bit of a legend myself. Cities I approached for the first time would open their gates to me and take me to their king straight away, even if only to tell me, "No."

Then one day, I came to Gath. I was in one of the pubs, asking every traveller the same questions, when a group of rough men walked in. They weren't soldiers but they immediately started giving everyone orders. Two men blocked the front door and another two searched for the back. The rest told everyone to stay seated as they scanned the room. It wasn't long before they found him.

A lone man sat in the corner, minding his own business as he had done since I arrived. Three of them walked over to him while the rest mingled around the rest of the pub, making sure none of us interfered.

"You really thought you could come back to Gath and we wouldn't find you?" one of them asked with a wicked smile. "We have guards at every gate who take our silver, men on every street. How many steps do you think you'd taken inside these walls before we knew you were here?" The man swallowed nervously.

"My king?" a guard interrupted. No-one had even realised he'd entered the room.

"Yes!" Spirysidos said with frustration.

"The men of Gezer are here to see you. They have word of the invaders..." The guard began.

"Not today." Spirysidos said firmly and glanced at his daughter.

"They have marched hard to reach you so quickly..." the guard continued.

"Then they will be grateful for some rest. Tell them I will see them first thing tomorrow." The guard hesitated, taking in the scene around him. He'd heard the tales just like the rest of them. He wouldn't change his king's mind tonight, nothing would, not even if the invaders were at their very walls. "Go." Spirysidos said shortly, impatient at the guard just standing there. The guard turned and left and Spirysidos continued.

The man who had been talking suddenly he stabbed forward with a knife, punching deep into the seated man's belly. He could have cut him anywhere, made it quick, but he didn't. He withdrew the knife amidst the man's groaning which grew more feeble with every breath. Those men didn't race out of there but stood, watching him die in agony and occasionally glancing around at the rest of us.

Everyone else in the pub looked away, appalled or afraid, probably both. But all I could think of was the net. Whoever these men served, he had enough power to find those he was searching for. In that moment I saw my answer. I could search this world for ten lifetimes and not find you but if men searched for me, if they kept a spare ear, listening for your name, I might just have a chance.

I stood up and spoke to the one who had stabbed that poor man, still bleeding to death where he sat.

"I want to join you."

I wasn't sure who was more surprised, the thugs standing there or the people sitting around me. The man I addressed simply nodded, looked back at the seated man whose eyes were fluttering as he took his last few breaths, and then turned to walk out. I followed them.

The gang took me in and made me one of their own. I did bad things, Ariadne, terrible things I hope never to do again, but I grew in power among them, and we grew more powerful in Gath. I knew I needed to be at the top to have as many men as I could searching for you. One night, after months of careful planning, I killed our leader and took control of the gang. By then we practically ran the city, even the king paid us heed. But it was not enough.

As it stood, living in the shadows I controlled one king, one city. I knew, though, if I came out into the light, if I became the king, my influence would spread across Canaan and beyond. I walked into this palace one night, each guard nodding to me as I passed. Almost every one had been bought off or threatened into accepting a new master. I strode down these corridors knife in hand—my own men wouldn't follow me any other way. I took the life of the king while he slept and by dawn was sitting on his throne. I've been here ever since, waiting for the day when I would find you.

"You killed so many people..." Ariadne said, unsure of what to feel.

"Criminals like me for the most part," Spirysidos replied. "And a weak king. But, yes," he said, fear tightening his throat at the thought she might leave him again, "I have killed many people in the hope I might see you again. Now that I see you here before me, I know it was all worth it."

Ariadne tried to think, it was too much to take in. She was fighting her eyelids to stay open and couldn't help but yawn from exhaustion.

"I'm sorry, I've been rambling on." Spirysidos said. "I have a room prepared for you, it's been ready ever since I became king. You have the softest bed in Gath and the floor is sprinkled with fresh petals every day." He said, excited, forgetting for an instant his daughter wasn't twelve anymore and wouldn't have cared for a floor of flower petals even then.

Ariadne yawned again. *I can decide in the morning,* she thought. Spirysidos led her away while Zedeck sat there eyeing the wine, trying to decide if he should refill his cup or not.

After a maze of corridors Ariadne would normally have been delighted to work her way through, they finally arrived at her room. As she entered she almost cringed at the luxury she saw around her; Purple blankets, a cedar frame, and petals of more flowers than she could name littering the floor beneath her feet.

Too tired to argue or judge him further for one night, Ariadne climbed into the bed and rolled over, facing away from Spirysidos and the door.

"But what about Mama?" she asked sleepily, still facing away.

"She talked of going back to Knossos, Ariadne, to wait for you there if you ever returned to Crete. I don't think she would have told me but when I left for that ship I saw the first spark of hope in her eyes as well. She couldn't bring herself to ask and she didn't have to, when she said she'd be in Knossos I knew what she meant."

Ariadne yawned once more. "Was that so hard?" she asked absentmindedly.

Spirysidos watched her in the darkness as she drifted off to sleep. Memories came and went as he stood there. It hadn't just been criminals, and it wasn't always quick. He saw the faces of innocent men he had beaten or killed and rival gang members he had tortured for information. He saw the face of the king he had murdered, sleeping as peacefully as his daughter before him now.

Spirysidos stroked her soft hair with the back of his hand and then bent down and gently kissed the back of her head. As he rose, his face relaxed and lines, seemingly wrinkles of old age, faded. He walked casually out of the room, shutting the door softly as he went, and meandered down the hallway, each breath a long, slow sigh of relief.

✢✢✢

Asaiah climbed the last few rungs of the ladder and jumped onto the walls of Makkedah. Sword in hand, he turned, flinching, expecting a blow but none came. All he saw on the walls were a few dead bodies and his cousins standing proudly around him.

While Asaiah waited for the rest of the men to reach the top of the wall, he peered out into the city. No fires had started yet, though with every third man carrying a freshly lit torch, he knew it wouldn't be long. He could vaguely make out bands of people in the city blocking alleyways or waiting on rooftops with stones to throw. Asaiah turned to see the men around him forming into ranks along the walls, the sun reflecting off bronze swords and helmets. He looked back at those people cowering in the alleys, he didn't like their chances.

It wasn't long before he was no longer staring down at them but marching towards them on the streets of their city. He saw a door slam in the distance and a frightened face peer out from a window. Asaiah felt a knot in his stomach. It wasn't fear; fear he had felt on the battlefield around Gibeon as they fought men who outnumbered them. No, what he felt looking at that frightened face was something worse than fear.

Asaiah shook his head, hoping the feeling would go away. As he got closer to those blocking the road, however, it only increased. He saw cripples and wounded men standing side by side with women and children big enough to hold a knife. There was no thirst for glory in their eyes, only fear and a hope they might somehow live.

Asaiah turned and looked at the men marching beside him. *Surely we aren't going to do this?* He saw eager faces around him, not a hint of the guilt he felt welling up inside. His steps slowed but only for an instant as men behind pressed up against him, pushing him forward.

The Most High has given us this land, Asaiah tried to reminded himself. *We are doing his will.* He looked ahead once more, into the eyes of people so very much afraid but standing their ground nonetheless. He was only a few steps away now, no more time to think.

Thirty

"Are you gonna stay?"

Ariadne looked at Zedeck. The same question had been rattling around in her mind all morning, without an answer in sight.

"I don't know." She said. Ariadne turned around briefly to make sure no-one else was nearby. Her father, his guards, they were nowhere to be seen. She looked down to the food laid out before them. There was enough here to keep her going for days and yet, when they were done, she knew servants would come and take what was left over and she wouldn't see it again, each meal would be brought to her fresh and new.

"I hate the man I left behind but..." she stopped, struggling to find the right words, "a part of me can't just ignore all he's done to find me, even if he did appalling things along the way." She looked at Zedeck and saw him frowning at that.

"I know you think that makes him like Adro, but Adro killed his own people, his own..." Ariadne couldn't bear to say it. "At least my father killed foreigners and criminals who probably deserved it anyway."

Zedeck shrugged. Not convinced. Ariadne saw it and continued, quickly, "But then I remember what he did, all over again. Can I ever forgive him for that?"

"If you left here, where would you go?" Zedeck asked. "Could you live with a man you hate if you knew he'd never hurt you and you'd have anything you wished? You left Adro when he offered the same thing."

"I know!" she said, suddenly angry. Her anger left almost as soon as it came. A thought occurred to her. "Last night just before I fell asleep, he mentioned Mama was at Knossos. I think I'll hold him to his offer to take me anywhere I want to go. I'll go back to Crete, back to Knossos and find Mama again."

Zedeck had just reached for a date but stopped to nod slowly. "Yeah, that's a good plan. It gives you time to decide along the way." He munched on the date, almost nervously before asking, "Will you need me as well?"

Ariadne paused for a moment. "I hadn't thought about it to be honest," she said. "I doubt I'd be in any danger. And besides," she started chuckling, "you're the one who always seems to need rescuing."

Zedeck took her barb in good humour before continuing. "It's just that I might end up taking him up on his offer of gold and an escort too." Ariadne smirked. "What? I ate with him. I listened to him too, didn't I?"

"I don't think the offer was for you." She said dryly.

"I'm sure he's got enough to share, especially with one of your oldest friends who's dutifully looked after you these past thirteen years." Zedeck said with a light-hearted confidence. He suddenly stopped in thought then spoke with as much seriousness as he could muster. "On that, if you do decide to leave him, please wait a day. I don't want to be asking an angry king for money."

Ariadne shook her head half in disbelief though she knew he was serious. "What's the new plan then? Buy a ship? Start sailing once more?"

"No, not quite straight away." Zedeck said, somewhat embarrassed. "Do you remember that woman at the pub in Ashdod?"

"Yes..." Ariadne said, a smile beginning to broaden on her face.

"Well, her name's Einela. Turns out she's got a great—" Zedeck started excitedly.

"I know what she's got a great—"

"Business mind." Zedeck interrupted in turn. "Nice personality too, once you get to know her."

"Mhmm." Ariadne replied, utterly convinced.

"Turns out she's been saving to start her own dye shop by the port. She offered to let me help her set it up but with a bit of backing from your father we could expand to a warehouse." Zedeck had that gleam in his eye, of one who saw untold riches ahead. "With a bit of underhand dealing and a touch of luck we could have a monopoly in say five, ten years."

Ariadne rose from her couch, suddenly intent on finding her father. Zedeck was oblivious.

"Of course, I will need a ship at some point, but I can probably get one cheap from a rival merchant we'll send broke along the way."

"Sounds like a real partnership." Ariadne said as she left the room. The hallway she walked down echoed with Zedeck's voice, as he continued to talk on despite the lack of audience.

Ariadne had no idea where her father might be but that suited her fine. She needed time to think. Time to be alone. *After all these years, some part of me misses him. Why do I miss him?* Ariadne cringed at her own weakness but kept walking. *If I leave for Knossos without him, I'll never see him again. Why does that matter? Why do I care?!* she screamed aloud in her own mind.

He grew wealthy and powerful to try and find me, or so he says. What if he's prepared to give it all up; this city, his kingship, all of it? Is that enough—enough to deserve a second chance? Ariadne noticed a guard in the distance ducking his head into every room. He looked down the hallway and saw her wandering, nodded to himself and motioned with his fingers for her to follow him. She gazed around her, taking the palace in with all its beauty and grandeur. *Surely it's enough.* She started following the guard as he walked back down the hallway. *But what if it's not?*

***

"Utterly routed." Tola said with dismay. Seeing Spirysidos grimace in anger, he quickly continued. "Not many survivors made it to our gates but those that did vowed never to fight again. They think this Joshua and his tribes are unstoppable."

"And what do you think?" Spirysidos asked.

"It is not for me to say." Tola replied cautiously. "My lord Horam, king of Gezer, asks that you let his army stay for a night in your city. He wants his men fresh to march to Lachish. Horam says he is bringing silver with him and will pay you in full for the supplies he needs."

"These wanderers are on my very doorstep. Do you think I would give them any excuse to attack my city?" Spirysidos asked with disbelief.

"Do you think they will attack a city full of men standing bravely on its walls?" Tola retorted. "Save Jericho, they have only attacked empty cities after defeating their armies in the field first. Keep your men safe behind your walls and they will pass you over, I assure you."

"Then why does your king march south to fight them? If five kings together could not beat these people, what gives Horam hope he can?" Spirysidos pressed.

"He has no choice." Tola hissed. "Would that he hadn't married his daughter to Japhia of Lachish, but he did. Now with Japhia and his army defeated and these wanderers marching south, who else will save his daughter in Lachish? This Joshua is sure to sack the cities of the kings who opposed him and Lachish, like Makkedah and Libnah are all unprotected and on his path."

Spirysidos looked at Tola intently. "Horam has already started marching, hasn't he?" he asked.

"He will be here in just over a week." Tola confirmed. Spirysidos' shoulders sagged. "We knew you could not refuse a king's desperate attempt to save his daughter." Tola said, smiling. "We won't forget your help in this, king of Gath." Tola rose and finished his cup. "I trust I have the honour of staying in your palace until my king arrives?"

Spirysidos nodded, bitter at having been played but it was true, he would not withhold his aid. Tola bowed low and walked off without another word.

Spirysidos watched him go. *You had better be right, Tola.* For a moment Spirysidos saw hordes of desert tribesmen climbing ropes and ladders, trying to scale his walls. Spirysidos shook his head to clear his mind of such thoughts. *Give him his chance, I know I would ask for no less.*

Spirysidos raised his head and saw Ariadne standing in front of him. He didn't say anything for a heartbeat, thinking she was another vision too. When he blinked and she was still there, he rose from his own seat and moved towards her. Ariadne turned to the guard who had led her and thanked him. When she turned back around, her father was right in front of her, arms outstretched for the second time in as many days.

Ariadne scuffled past him uncomfortably and sat down. Not yet. She wasn't ready. She wasn't sure if she'd ever be ready. Spirysidos turned with sadness in his eyes, lowered his arms and sat opposite her.

"I saw a man walk past me in the hallway. He seemed relieved." Ariadne said trying to break the awkward silence before it grew too big. "What did he want?"

Spirysidos sighed. "There are men who have been wandering the deserts for years but wander them no longer. Tales of their atrocities east of Canaan have spread far and wide. They leave none alive of those they defeat; women, children, some say even the animals. All perish."

"Where are they now?" Ariadne asked.

"They crossed into Canaan earlier this year. Since then they have destroyed two cities." He paused, wondering how much she actually cared. Still, she did ask. "It's complicated. Many kings talked of joining together as one army to resist them, myself included, but some promised themselves as slaves to the invaders, trying to be spared. We split over what to do with these traitors. Most of us wanted to save our men to fight the invaders themselves, but five kings banded together to try and make an example of the traitors. They thought if they took the most powerful traitor city, Gibeon, no-one else would think of changing sides."

"Did it work?" Ariadne asked, genuinely interested.

"Not exactly. That's what the man you saw in the hallway came to tell me. They were defeated on the plains outside Gibeon. Completely destroyed. Now their cities lie open with no warriors left to defend them." Spirysidos cursed softly to himself. "This Joshua and his wandering tribesmen will waste no time. They will try to destroy these empty cities as soon as possible."

"What are you going to do then?" Ariadne asked. "Seems like it was their own fault. They should have taken their chances at home or together with the rest of you, not gone off by themselves."

"Yes..." Spirysidos said, surprised at his daughter's quick grasp of politics. "I think you're right. For myself, I'm going to keep my soldiers well-fed and my stores well-stocked, ready to repel or outlast any attack. Unfortunately, one king Horam of Gezer thinks otherwise."

He quickly told her of Horam's plan to rescue his daughter from Lachish. Her reply was not entirely comforting.

"You said *yes*?"

"I could hardly say no." Spirysidos replied, reaching out his hand to hold hers. He looked into her eyes and, uncomfortable as she was, knew she understood.

Ariadne pulled her hand away instinctively. She realised that was probably the worst thing she could do before making her request but began, even so.

"I've been thinking a lot about you, Father," she started, still unable to call him Papa—it just didn't feel right, "about what you've said. I want to take you up on your offer—to help me travel anywhere I wish."

Spirysidos' heart sank to hear it. *She wants to leave, even now, after everything I've done?*

"But I have one further condition," Ariadne continued. "I want you to come with me. I want you to leave this city you've come to rule, leave its riches and the power you've spent so long building up. Give all this up and come home with me," Ariadne paused, and her mood darkened for an instant, "or you will never see my face again."

Spirysidos didn't know whether to cry in joy for the opportunity or sorrow for the darkness he saw in her. It took him a moment to gather his words to reply.

"Follow me." He said, rising. He walked over to a series of small windows at the far side of the room. Spirysidos peered down for a moment, and then inclined his head for her to do the same. Ariadne looked out to see the city of Gath teeming with life. She saw people arguing in a marketplace and others strolling along in streets. In the distance she could see men patrolling the wall around the city and others guarding the gates.

"I rose to power to find you, it's true." Spirysidos said slowly. "But I am responsible for all these people. At another time, perhaps I could just step down and not many people would die but at the moment," he looked at her, eyes ablaze, begging her to understand, "one mistake and all their lives could be taken away. These invaders will not give them a second chance. No-one else is strong enough to guide this city while *they* pass by its walls."

"So you're not coming with me?" Ariadne asked, more hurt than she thought she'd be.

"I will!" His temper raged for the first time in her presence since he had seen her. "Just give me some time. Let me save these people, then I will leave them, this city and this land behind." Spirysidos held her shoulders softly with both hands and, for once, she didn't flinch. Was that a look of—it couldn't be? Was it pride in her eyes as she looked back at him? He smiled at her and, for the first time since arriving, she smiled back. "I will take you to Knossos, I promise."

***

Zedeck couldn't believe his luck as he plodded along, his back already aching from the pack he carried. Spirysidos told him he had to carry his food in there as well but that still left more than enough gold and silver to buy up a sizeable portion of the port. He thought of Einela, slogging away in that pub night after night. He couldn't wait to see her face.

Meanwhile, Spirysidos and Ariadne watched from the gate as Zedeck slowly grew smaller in the distance.

"Are you sure you can spare the guards?" Ariadne asked her father looking out at the other specks around Zedeck. "Can you trust them?"

"I have picked every man in my guard myself. They are good, loyal men; don't worry about your friend." Spirysidos replied. "But those ten men? They are more afraid of heights than anyone I have ever met. I don't need fainting men manning my walls no matter how good they are with a spear."

Ariadne chuckled then turned to her father, suddenly sombre. "Thanks though, for helping him start again."

Spirysidos saw the sincerity in her eyes and replied warmly. "I'm happy to help someone you care about. And," he paused to wrap an arm around her, to keep her warm against the chilling night air, "what's a bit of gold if we're not going to stay here long enough to enjoy it?"

Ariadne turned to him, excited at the thought of seeing her mother once again. "You mean it, don't you?"

"Of course I do, Ariadne." He relished in saying her name to her and not to just another stranger in hope. "As soon as we're done here, we will go home."

Thirty-One

Ariadne woke up to the sun shining through her window. She blinked a few times then rolled over, covering her head with the blanket. Adro used to joke that it was the one thing she'd never grown out of and, despite managing to get up early sometimes, she agreed.

Today was meant to be some great ceremony in honour of the king of Gezer before his men left the city. Ariadne tucked her arms under the vast swathe of purple and vanished beneath. She couldn't care less. If it was still going by the time she arrived, sure, she'd have a look. It wasn't worth an extra hour or two of sleep though.

Her mind drifted as she dozed there. She was back at Knossos, watching her mother pick saffron from the fields. She was in the palace, discovering another hidden room. She was fighting with the other kids in the streets and running from her father, his eyes filled with murderous discipline. When she awoke again it took her a few moments to realise that Gath was real; that she hadn't simply been living a dream these many years and her mother wasn't in the next room.

Ariadne didn't roll over this time. Slowly, one sleepy foot at a time, she rose from her bed. She found that new dress, the one with swirling with patterns of red, purple and blue. When Spirysidos first bought it for her she had shuddered at the expense but now she put it on without a second thought. It was a nice dress, after all, and someone had to wear it.

She walked out of her room lazily and into the corridors of yet another palace she had come to master. The servants had stopped bringing food to her rooms in the morning once they realised she enjoyed walking past the kitchens in her daily explorations.

She drifted past them today, as every day, just long enough to take a freshly baked roll and the odd bit of fruit. They smiled at her as she did so, too busy for her to stay and chat but happy to feed the king's daughter. She started to pick the bread apart as she walked—an old habit from her years in Avaris—half of her meals had been on the go.

In no time at all, Ariadne was out of the palace and winding her way through the busy streets. He had said something about a podium near the palace? Ariadne shrugged, she'd find it. As she searched from street to street her mind wandered once more.

How long will it take to sail to Crete? Will we land in Malia just in case? Is Malia even around anymore? Does Papa even have a ship or will he have to hire one? What will Mama say when she sees me? What will she look like? What will she do when she sees Papa— Ariadne stopped in mid-thought. Anger raging across her mother's face, disappointment as she saw Ariadne with *him*. She felt a twinge of guilt. *I can still decide, I don't have to take him with me. I can still make up my mind.* She noticed the colours of her dress in the corner of her eye and felt that twinge again.

Ariadne shook such thoughts from her mind and kept walking. She saw the smoke before anything else, rising faintly in the distance. As she pricked her ears Ariadne could hear the faint murmurings of people somewhere in the distance too. Ariadne quickened her pace, excited.

It wasn't long before she found the edge of the crowd. People hustled together, craning their necks to see. Ariadne started pushing her way through them, a skill she had honed since childhood. She could vaguely hear crackling and wondered what kind of ceremony required a fire. She was getting there, almost close enough to see, when she heard the faint screams.

Ariadne pushed people hard then as she raced forward, all tact forgotten. She saw the flicker of flames rising above the mass of crowd still in front of her. At last she was through, enough to see the podium clearly, bile rising in her throat.

She saw the small boy burning alive, his arms tied as he lay atop the stone alter. Crackling wood underneath him was already beginning to blacken. She didn't know if the poor boy was curled into a ball from a hope the pain would stop or his muscles had tightened cruelly in shock, but, as she stood there helpless, Ariadne seethed with an anger rising higher than the smoke.

Ariadne scanned the podium and, to her horror, saw her father standing calmly, if somewhat grimly, next to a stone-faced man staring deeply into the flames. Ariadne surged forward in fury, pushing two grown men aside with the force of her arms to charge onwards into the gap she had made. Spirysidos was looking out at the crowd with a weary boredom, oblivious to his daughter coming closer with murder in her eyes and hands twitching in expectation.

It had only been moments since she began her frenzied charge but Ariadne noticed the boy once more and stopped. He wasn't moving any longer. He wasn't crying out or struggling; one moment he was there and the next he wasn't, only his still burning body remained.

Ariadne's thoughts flashed quickly through her mind as she stared up at the podium. Slowly, her savage faced calmed once more. Bit by bit, Ariadne forced composure through her body until she was in control again. With a cold determination,

Ariadne turned around and started sliding in between people, going back the way she came.

***

"You burned a child alive!"

Spirysidos had just entered the room, a look of surprise spreading across his face.

"I—"

"That innocent boy died today and you stood by and did *nothing*." Ariadne hissed with raged. She stopped then and looked at him, her face contorted with fury, silently daring him to speak.

"King Horam of Gezer," Spirysidos began slowly, aware she waited to snap at any misplaced word, "follows the ways of his people. The gods of this land only bless those who sacrifice something they cherish. To be sure of a great blessing they say you need to give a great sacrifice..."

"Have you learned nothing of the thirteen years we spent apart?" Ariadne shouted, her finger pointing accusingly at his face. "Or do you need a reminder?"

"What would you have me do? *Hmm*?" Spirysidos replied with a rising anger. "I rule a city of men who all believe the same things. Do you really think the mob who gathered to watch would let a foreigner interfere?"

"He was just a boy—"

"Children die every day." Spirysidos countered forcefully. "Horam has dozens of wives and scores of sons. This daughter he is trying to save, she was his first child. No father loves anything more than his first child."

She looked back at him and seethed but had no words for him. Spirysidos continued.

"He has sons already married with children of their own, what was this boy going to become?"

"He could have been anything." She raged, finding her voice once more, "But he had no chance, it was taken from him, *by his own father.*"

"You say what you like, you think what you like," Spirysidos roared in anger. "One, I wasn't going to bar my gates to a man bringing an army to save his daughter. And two, once he was here do you really think I could have stopped him doing what he did?" Spirysidos slumped slightly, still standing opposite his daughter, his face still held high in defiance but he slumped nonetheless. "I don't like this land any more than you do. I've lived here too long," he said with weariness. "You're right, of course. Let's leave this place before it destroys us. Let's go back home and start again."

Ariadne felt it, this was her chance. She felt the weight of her decision, the consequences, and gritted her teeth.

"I want to go home..." she began, noticing the triumph in her father's eyes. She held up a fist instinctively but relaxed it into an outstretched hand, to her father's surprise. He took it and they both stepped forward, embracing one another.

"But if you *ever* let another child die while you just stand there," she said, holding him tightly, "I'll find my own way and you'll never see me again."

After a moment, Ariadne released her arms and Spirysidos did too, and they stood apart once more. Each one stared at the other awkwardly for a few seconds and then Ariadne turned around and rushed into the room behind her. She returned with a bowl of food in each hand, extended almost as a peace offering.

"I went to the markets earlier today," she said, changing the subject completely. "I thought we should have a taste of travel food to practice us for our journey."

Spirysidos took the bowls offered to him and peered into them. What sort of a daughter buys mouldy food for her father? Still, he didn't argue. He placed the bowls down on the table in the corner of the room while Ariadne went back to get the rest of it.

As she returned with cups and stale bread in one hand and a small amphora of wine in the other, Ariadne saw servants peering through the doorway, checking nervously on the two of them. Half the palace had probably heard.

Spirysidos smiled at them for their concern then shooed them away with a flick of his wrist. He sat down at the table as Ariadne placed the cups down and poured wine into both of them. She sat down herself as her father raised his cup to his lips and drank thoughtfully.

Ariadne took an olive from one of the bowls and started to eat it. There was an art to eating olives, shredding the flesh off with precise, methodical bites, all the while keeping the pip gripped between teeth. Once she was done, she spat the pip into her hand and placed it back into the bowl.

Meanwhile, Spirysidos had eyed the food distastefully, preferring instead to sip more of the wine in his cup. Ariadne broke some of the bread off and then broke it again, in two, offering him a piece. Spirysidos took it and after chewing the crusty mass a bit, drank more wine to soften it. His cup was already half-empty.

Ariadne chewed her bread in silence, not once raising a hand to her cup. Spirysidos coughed, feeling his throat scratchy and he downed the rest of his cup. Ariadne swallowed the last piece she had been working away at and smiled at her father who was coughing louder, now visibly in pain.

Spirysidos looked at his daughter as his heart thumped quicker and quicker. In between coughs he found he was wheezing just to breath. He grabbed the table and tried to lift himself out of his chair but stumbled and fell onto the floor.

Ariadne stood carefully, grabbing her cup as she did so. While her father lay there sprawled on the ground, Ariadne slowly tipped her cup over and poured it on him. She started with his face but moved her hand deliberately so the wine spattered all over him, staining him from head to toe.

When it was empty, Ariadne placed it back on the table, staring down at him the whole time.

"Do you honestly think I could forgive you for what you did today?" Ariadne let her rage out again. It had been unbearable to lock it away even for those short minutes but somehow she had borne it.

"He was a boy, not a girl..." Spirysidos said weakly, understanding at last.

"*Do you think that matters?*" she replied.

Spirysidos tried to push himself up off the floor but his arms gave way again and he fell back down once more.

"I guess not." He said through clenched teeth.

"I gave you a second chance, Father."

She kicked him hard in his still gasping mouth, knocking his head backwards. "And you failed me." She said with deep bitterness. Spirysidos curled up, holding his face like a child, like the boy in the flames would have done if his arms had not been tied. Ariadne stepped over him and walked into the next room.

Quickly, methodically, she packed proper food she had bought at the markets as well. She took a long, plain robe and wrapped it around herself, covering all traces of wealth. Lastly, she took a knife with her right hand and, after taking a deep breath, pulled the forearm of her robe down to cover both her hand and the knife.

Ariadne walked back into the room where her father still lay on the ground. He was breathing still, though barely. She could see tears in his eyes, by now mingling with blood from his mouth and dripping onto the floor beneath. He didn't even try to escape, he just lay there broken, waiting to die.

She looked down at him in scorn and then walked out into the hallway, but that was only the beginning.

***

Ariadne's pulse quickened as she tried not to run, walking as fast as she dared. As she worked her way through the palace, her grip on the knife tightened every time she saw a guard or servant in the distance. All the while her ears were pricked for the sound of footsteps running up behind her.

Ariadne thought of the embrace she had given him, and shuddered. *It was the only way,* she told herself. *He thought I'd forgive anything.* She smiled for a second, despite everything. *He wouldn't have believed me if I hadn't been a bit angry before relenting.* Ariadne passed another guard, nodding her head politely. The tired man simply nodded in return, stifling a yawn. As she passed, the smile returned to her face, *I played him well, and I needed to. I needed him to trust me, one last time.*

Servants came and went, sometimes pushing past her, other times stepping out of her way. It didn't matter to Ariadne, what did was that they all left her alone. After what felt like a lifetime, her heart still racing, Ariadne walked out into the moonlit sky.

She breathed in the cool night air and sighed with relief. Ariadne kept walking and, once she was out of sight of those last few palace guards, turned a corner and began to tuck her knife away in the folds in her robe. Adro had taught her how to conceal a knife in the most unlikely places and, as much as she still hated him, she was grateful. Her knife sat comfortably resting just above her hip but not pressing into her. She knew she could get to it in moments if she needed.

Ariadne walked the last few minutes towards the gate in an odd feeling of peace. She would make her way back to Ashdod and find a ship and, somehow, she would get home. Who knows, maybe Zedeck would already have one she could borrow? He never missed the opportunity for a good bargain.

The last two guards of Gath stood in the gateway before her, chatting the night away. The gate was firmly shut, as it was every night, but she was the daughter of the king. They would let her pass. In the end it had been easier than she expected. One of them had looked at her plain clothes and frowned, not convinced, but she had responded in turn with confidence,

"If you do not open this gate, I will return with my father and you will wish you had." The irony was not lost on her, but she maintained her stern face nonetheless.

She saw all sorts of questions across their faces. Why are you leaving at night? Where is your escort? Why are you dressed so plainly? But, in the end, it was not worth the risk, they knew it, she knew it and the gate opened before her.

Ariadne heard the gate closing behind her as she kept walking out onto the pebbly road which lay ahead. She was safe, and she was free. Ariadne trekked along at a good pace, wanting to be far away from that place by morning.

Thoughts wandered in and out of her mind as she walked. Ariadne imagined servants coming into her rooms, aghast to see her father dead at their feet. Or maybe they wouldn't be appalled. Maybe they secretly hated him as much as she did. She would never know.

Ariadne heard the rustle of sand and thought nothing of it, *must be the wind.* Then came the unmistakable sound of pebbles turning underfoot. She spun around trying to see. Then nothing.

Thirty-Two

Nausea came and went but was never more than a low threat. Her head and neck ached, and there was nothing but darkness and pain. For a time, Ariadne continued in misery, floating in the void. Then, slowly, she realised she wasn't floating. The void was moving and she moved with the void, bobbing to its rise and fall, following its currents along. But it wasn't a void; Ariadne felt her head lolling with every step, and her legs and, the more she felt, the more she realised her whole body was bouncing to the steps.

Whose step? Ariadne opened her eyes and the void left her. She felt the skin of a stranger and cringed. Ariadne blinked in the sunlight, blinded once more but for a moment and then she saw. Men marched behind her, men marched in front of her, and the man carrying her over his shoulders marched as well.

Ariadne threw herself to the ground with all her weight, overbalancing the man and toppling him over. Soldiers around her chuckled and helped them both back to their feet. Ariadne recoiled at their touch and moved to leave the line of men but another elbowed her roughly and blocked her path.

Ariadne walked onward looking down for the first time. Her arms were bound tightly with rope and tied off with as good a knot as Zedeck or Macanra could have done. Ariadne swivelled her hips instinctively, feeling the knife still safely hidden away. That was something. She realised they hadn't even taken her outer robe off her. They must have knocked her out, tied her and then started carrying her through the night, just one more unlucky woman at the wrong place, at the wrong time.

Ariadne glanced over her shoulder and saw men staring at her unashamedly from behind. She shuddered. She hoped the day would last and night would stay forever far off. Smothering her fear, Ariadne stepped forwards more quickly, catching up to one of the men in front. She wouldn't talk to those who stayed behind and stared, though they were probably all just as bad.

"Where are we headed?" she asked and the man looked at her puzzled. She realised she was speaking Cretan and repeated once more in the tongue of this new land.

"Lachish," the man replied.

Ariadne waited for him to expand upon it but he just kept walking.

"Is this Horam's army then?" she continued.

"Sure is." *Great conversation this one.*

Ariadne slowed her step and was once again trudging along by herself amidst the mass of Horam's men. She thought back to the boy, burning in the flames and of his father standing there. Yes, she could find that face again. Once more she felt the knife hilt by her hip and drew comfort from it. Let night come, she would be ready.

***

Ariadne peered into the flames, wondering how much longer she had. All around her men were shouting and drinking, some were even wrestling after the long march. She smiled bravely to herself. They would come for her soon, she knew it.

All day she had tried to undo the knots that bound her hands but still she was tied. They would not unravel for her and without her hands Ariadne knew she was doomed. Even if she ran off, how long would she last? They had taken her food, they had taken her freedom and soon they would take her dignity itself. It seemed hopeless. Indeed, the men who grinned foully at her from time to time evidently thought so too. But she had been given plenty of time to think, time to plan, and she was not afraid.

Or so she told herself. Until now she had been around men who cared for her, however awful they ended up being to everyone else. Ariadne may have left in utter disgust but she had still felt safe while she was with them. Now, as she looked at those savage faces, she knew she was very much alone. And very, very afraid.

She didn't know the oaf's name, only that he had come up behind her and pulled her up, his hands under her armpits, lifting her away from the peaceful flame and her dour thoughts. She kicked at the ground, trying to turn and face him all while men in front of her watched, and laughed.

After dragging Ariadne back a few steps, the man suddenly let go with both hands and she fell to the ground, stunned. In moments, he had circled around and planted himself on top of her. He reached for her arms, expecting them to flail and hit him but she pushed up with her hips instead, knocking him off balance. In one fluid motion she dodged his grasping hands, elbowed him in the face and used the force of her hips to knock him sideways. They rolled together for a half-turn but instead of staying on top to try and wrestle him, Ariadne slid her legs together and rolled off the top of him. As she kept rolling, she used the momentum to push against the ground; first from her tied arms, then from her back as she sprang up and onto her feet.

All eyes around looked at her in interest, and desire. Ariadne turned quickly as the dazed man beside her stumbled to his feet. She looked out into the crowd of men and, seeing one probably no older than herself, pointed to him and spoke loudly, though breathless.

"You, you first." As the oaf beside her reached for her once more, the men around them shook their heads and gestured to the chosen youth. They had expected her to fight all the way; she could see they were amused she had found one of them to her liking, amused enough to grant her her wish.

Slowly, almost coyly, Ariadne walked up to the young man who stared back at her in amazement, unable to conceal his eagerness. Ariadne stepped right up to him, brushing up against him as her mouth reached to his ear. "Away?" she asked innocently, inclining her head away from the main campfires. The young man grabbed her hands and led onwards, not glancing back even once.

He led her into the darkness, or as dark as that night could be. The moon shone bright and they could still see each other clearly, could still be seen by the men of the camp, but at least they felt alone. The young man spun her towards him so their bodies touched once more, desire filling his eyes. Ariadne tried to touch him with her hands but fumbled awkwardly. She lifted her bound arms, keeping her hands tantalisingly low, and spoke softly.

"Could you untie the rope?" She paused. "You won't regret it." Ariadne turned them both so the young man was between her and the camp, blocking most of their view. He began unwrapping the knots without a second thought. *The fool.*

Ariadne smiled at the young man with mischief in her eyes, which he took for a good sign and smiled deviously in reply. A short time later the rope was undone. Ariadne dipped her arms downward, letting the rope slide off the end of them. As the young man watched, enthralled, Ariadne grabbed the edges of her robe and dress in each hand and slowly started lifting.

The young man pressed himself up against her as she did so. Ariadne's hands jostled around, grabbing more of the robe as she pulled upwards but more of it seemed to spill over her hands. The young man was busy with his own attire, lifting his tunic in readiness.

Her hands were dangerously high for her tastes but she found it. At once the young man stabbed forth to be met with a blade in turn. Both blades clashed, and the stronger one prevailed.

Ariadne thrust deeper into him, up to the hilt. His mouth opened wide to scream but with her free hand she pushed his face into her shoulder, holding him tight. In the distance men watched without shame and chuckled to one another.

"She doesn't muck around," one said to another, watching the young man slump and half-stumble onto Ariadne.

"She'll get through the whole army by dawn at this rate," his friend agreed.

"Ha, look," a third said, pointing to the blood spreading on her gown in the distance. "Guess he caught her at a bad time..."

The young man groaned against her but she held him tightly and he grew weaker by the second. It was horrific to hold him there, Ariadne wanted to push him away and keep stabbing at his face for good measure but she held him close. For as long as he was up against her, she was safe from the next man.

Ariadne felt his blood spurting against her, staining her pale robe and spreading quickly. It thickened in some places and started dripping to the ground beneath. Ariadne saw eyes upon her from the camp growing more curious by the second, no girl bled that much. As one man started walking towards her, his curious smile quickly vanishing into a deepening frown of concern, Ariadne knew her ruse was finished.

Changing tact, Ariadne withdrew her bloodied knife and pushed the body of the dying man forward. As he fell back-first onto the ground, still spurting from his wound, the men of the camp saw and realised what had happened.

The first man raced forwards at her but Ariadne snarled at him, baring her teeth with her mouth wide open, like a vicious hound after it had tasted blood. Ariadne knew she was bound to die, but she was free and she had a knife. She would take some of them with her.

The man racing towards her stopped in mid-step, frozen for an instant in fear. Once the fear subsided he still did not lunge but started to circle her while more men raced towards her from the camp. Some of these new men carried knives and one or two even brought a sword. Each one looked at her through eyes half-filled with anger and fear.

Ariadne stepped back and back, further into the darkness but she was quickly becoming surrounded even so. To her surprise Ariadne heard footsteps, far behind her, softly at first, then racing forward over the ground.

The men in front of her were still a few feet away. Ariadne risked a glance backwards and then turned completely to see hundreds of men running in the moonlight. These men were not half-awake, carrying knives and circling a lone woman; they wore helmets, carried shields, swords and spears, and charged forward eager for a fight.

As Ariadne turned back once more to the men facing her, she saw them already running back in fear. Ariadne stopped for a heartbeat, and then charged forward ahead of the unknown soldiers behind her. All thoughts were gone. Only rage remained.

***

Asaiah sat down between two bodies, watching in curiosity and mild concern at the woman before him. She crouched over a big man, long-dead but Asaiah had seen her seek him out among the corpses. She stabbed and cut again and again into the body beneath her. Arms, chest, face; she seemed not to mind where she struck so long as she kept going, tearing him apart.

Asaiah had been one of the men who came up behind her, walking softly, waiting for the signal to charge. He had seen her toss that first body onto the ground and, as the men of Gezer came for her, couldn't help but feel proud of this woman who stared back at them defiantly.

When it had been time to run, he knew he ran that little bit faster, hoping to catch them before they reached her. As those men turned and fled, Asaiah sped forward with the rest of the army, hoping to catch some of the slower ones before they could arm and regroup. But when that woman turned and chased them first, he thought she must have been an angel of the Most High, leading them to victory.

Now, as he saw her channelling her fury into that one dead man, Asaiah thought to himself, *No, she must be real. Angels don't stab dead bodies in anger.* Asaiah looked around him, watching his brother Israelites finish off the wounded men of their camp and begin tending to their own. He sighed. No-one knew what to do with her. It had been plain she didn't like Horam's men so the Israelites had fought around her in the massacre that followed their charge into the camp. Now, as the first few rays of dawn began to creep over the hills in the distance, he knew someone would have to decide.

Slowly he rose and searched for the leader of his band, Ahiram. Ahiram never tired, or at least that's what everyone believed. He was still standing, shouting orders to anyone within earshot and, as Asaiah approached him, he couldn't help but smile.

"Asaiah, you're alive. Good. Take three men and—"

"Ahiram," Asaiah didn't often interrupt him, but this was a special case, "what are we going to do about that woman?" he said, pointing to Ariadne a short distance away, still stabbing.

Ahiram had seen her too, they all had. Truth be told he was as awed by her as the rest of them. But he didn't want a crazy woman in his tent, eating his food one minute and slitting his throat the next. Ahiram shrugged.

"Leave her."

"In the wilderness?" Asaiah asked, gesturing to the rocky land around them. He knew as well as Ahiram that they would take every scrap of food from their enemies before they marched off.

"Let me take her and look after her."

Asaiah looked over at Ariadne once more, her anger not close to subsiding.

"She's all yours." Ahiram said then turned to fresh faces coming to him for orders. Asaiah walked back, satisfied. Meanwhile, Ariadne had finally revenged herself enough on the man who had grabbed her from behind the previous night. She threw her now quite blunted knife down on the ground and, seeing someone approaching, wearily rose to her feet.

"You are the wanderers of the desert, come here for land?" she asked awkwardly, hoping he spoke the tongue of the Canaanai.

"We are. And who are you?" He sounded strange; his words were not quite the same as she had been taught but Ariadne understood him all the same. She looked down at the man she had disfigured, now beyond all recognition, and spat at what remained of his face.

"You can have it." She replied, turning around, ignoring him. Ariadne staggered along, looking for any kind of bladder or flask which might have held water. Asaiah realised and unbuckled one from around his waist, offering it to her. With not a drop in sight anywhere else, Ariadne begrudgingly took his and gulped the water down.

"Where do you come from?" Asaiah asked.

"Knossos... Malia... Avaris... Gath..." Ariadne said between swallowing and drinking more. Asaiah stared back at her, confused. She looked at him and tried to think of something he would understand. "I am a Philostines. Have you heard of them?"

"Yes." He replied. Ariadne kept drinking his water until it was all empty, not bothering to speak further. "What is your name?" he asked again.

"Ariadne." She tossed him back the bladder.

"Come with me, Ariadne the Philostines."

Ariadne looked at him, looked at those around him. *Men, all men.* She scowled. "Why should I come with you?" *Where was that knife?*

"Because we have food, and shelter and..." Asaiah thought of words to convince her, a woman that brave shouldn't die alone in the scorching sun. He thought back to when he first saw her, at what he had witnessed. And, finally, he thought he understood.

"I won't touch you." He saw her shudder and lean away from him. Asaiah unbuckled his scabbard and held it forward to her. "You can carry my sword as long as I don't need it. I won't trouble you and neither will anyone else."

Ariadne stood for a while, staring into his eyes, wondering whether to believe him. Asaiah felt her gaze boring into him, as if she were the Great One peering into his soul. Some of the Israelites had already loaded their arms with anything worth carrying and were already walking out from the camp. Ariadne snatched the sword, still looking at him and strapped it around herself before walking off. Asaiah bent down and quickly took her knife from the ground where she had left it. At a light run, he started off after her. She hadn't even asked him his name.

Thirty-Three

The Israelites arrived at their own camp that afternoon. Utterly exhausted, many just climbed into their tents and fell asleep, dropping whatever they carried at the entrance. Some others sought food to bring them back their strength, starting fires and leading frightened goats or sheep away from the main flock.

Asaiah walked through the camp weaving in and around tents, over sleeping men who hadn't quite made it to their own and around the fires being started. Ariadne followed behind, eyes always glancing to her scabbard every few steps just to make sure it was still there. Neither had spoken a word the whole time.

Eventually, they arrived. Asaiah pointed to a tent clustered among all the others but, to him, it was home. He lifted the tent flap and held it open as Ariadne walked in beneath it. There was not much there. A couple of blankets covered the ground and there were a few bowls to eat out of but Ariadne saw no glint of gold or silver, and the blankets themselves were plain and bare. Ariadne felt the central beam holding the tent up, it felt smooth beneath her hand and she realised it must have been raised and packed away almost daily. This was a tent for fast travelling, a tent for war.

Asaiah rushed past her and started unravelling the blankets, tossing some aside in his search. He found a long robe, less dirty than the one he was wearing, shook it and started folding it neatly. Ariadne was frightened he was going to take his clothes off then and there, but he placed it back down on top of the blankets. As she watched curiously, Asaiah searched around till he found a spare knife and placed it beside the robe. Lastly, he found another bladder of water and filled up a bowl with it before placing the bowl on the blankets as well.

As Asaiah rose and started to leave the tent, Ariadne reached out and took hold of his arm.

"What is that?" she asked, pointing down at the robe, the knife and the bowl.

"Our custom," Asaiah began, confused that she did not already know; that such a thing was not done everywhere by everybody, "when we kill our enemies, we may rescue any of the women who survived and bring them to our home. We must let them mourn for a month and not touch them." *A month of peace and quiet doesn't sound too bad.* "They are to wear new clothes, not the ones they came in with, and must shave their head as a sign of their mourning."

"And after the month?" Ariadne pressed, sensing there was more to it.

"After the month we take them to be our wives." Asaiah said, his cheeks beginning to blush.

Whack! Ariadne hit him with the butt of the scabbard and began drawing his sword.

"Peace! I brought you here to feed you and keep you alive, that is all." Asaiah said, arms raised palm outward to show he meant no harm. "You are free to go wherever you like. I will not stop you."

Ariadne held the sword half-unsheathed, glaring at him, expecting treachery. Asaiah sighed and, hoping that breath wouldn't be his last, turned his back to her as a sign of trust and started walking out of the tent once more.

"Take your robe!" she called out to him.

Asaiah stood at the entrance to his tent and shook his head. "For your mourning."

Ariadne slid the blade into its sheath and stepped towards him.

"What is your name, wanderer?" she asked.

"Asaiah." He said proudly, happy she had finally asked.

"My husband's was Adro. Adro caused many of my people to die and, though I will never see him again, I will not mourn for him." Ariadne paused but, since Asaiah kept standing there, she continued. "What is your father's name?"

"Gaddi." He replied, confused as to where this was all heading.

"My father's name was Spirysidos. He was the king of Gath and I killed him not two nights ago. I will not mourn him either."

Ariadne let the silence drift between them, thinking she had made her point but Asaiah, though horrified, was not satisfied.

"What of your mother?" he asked.

"I will see her again. Soon I will make a voyage across the great sea and be with her once more. So, tell me, Asaiah son of Gaddi, why should I mourn?"

Asaiah opened his mouth to speak but had no more words for her. He turned and left the tent, letting the entrance flap down after him. Ariadne looked down at the robe distastefully and started pacing around the tent. She thought of her situation, alone among a new band of foreigners and no closer to the sea where ships could take her away from this land and back to Crete. For all she said to Asaiah, she hadn't the least clue how she was going to get back.

As she kept pacing, Ariadne's thoughts untangled for the first time in days. She thought of her mother and Knossos, of Adro in Egypt and Zedeck in Ashdod. Her mind wandered to Gath and the chaos they must have been facing now she had killed her father. One thing was for sure, she didn't regret doing that.

Who are they, she thought, *to tell me to cut my hair?* Ariadne had never paid too much attention to it until now, brushing it occasionally and giving it the odd trim, but she would rather cut them in their sleep than touch one hair on her head on their say so.

And cry? She wouldn't cry. She would laugh and sing and tell them stories her mother had told her when she was very young. She would show them she was very much alive, and not to be ordered about.

Ariadne looked down at the robe on the blankets a final time. No, she wouldn't wear that boring thing. It probably smelled of old sweat and man. She undid the scabbard belt and took off her outer robe. It was still covered with dried blood, and she tossed it to the floor with disdain. Her colourful dress beneath was fairly clean though, and she wasn't taking it off for anyone.

Ariadne bent over the bowl of water and splashed some onto her face. She did that a few times, rubbing the dirt and dried blood away and, as the water stilled, smiled at her own reflection. After a quick thought, Ariadne lowered her hair into the bowl bit by bit until she had soaked it. Then, she began teasing the knots out with her fingers and ringing it out bit by bit, the dust of the journey leaving her with every squeeze. *Shaved,* she thought, *I'll give them shaved...*

***

Ariadne lifted the tent flap and walked out into the fading sun of the early evening. She smelled roasting meat, goat if she wasn't mistaken. And she was starving. Ariadne peered around the nearby campfires until she found one with Asaiah at it and started walking over to it, his sword re-strapped over her dress.

And every man stared at her, for her hair cascaded down her shoulders, washed and clean and with all number of plaits through it. The men were taken back, they had plainly never seen a woman emerge from one of those war tents with her hair still intact. Not only that but many tried to look away uncomfortably as their eyes disobeyed and travelled up and down her dress. Let them look. She had a sword and Asaiah had promised her safety and, besides, they couldn't touch her for a month. She planned to be long gone by then.

As she got closer to Asaiah's fire, he turned around with a defeated but not altogether unhappy smile.

"No mourning then?" he asked, already knowing the answer.

"No mourning." Ariadne replied, sitting down beside him. She saw the small nod on his face as he turned back to the fire and realised he accepted her decision. *Good. Just as well.*

Asaiah had been chewing away at a leg of goat but he stopped and offered it to Ariadne. It looked good. She took it and thanked him but he was already rising, going back to the spit to get some more. When he returned, Ariadne asked him the question that had been floating around in her head for hours.

"Why are you doing this?" She looked up at the man who helped keep her alive. It was the first time she had properly looked at him. He was a rugged man, hardened by constant travelling and war but he had no blemishes on him. His face was clean though he had a full beard, which Ariadne always hated. He had hair of his own, also dark, which fell to his shoulders though, she thought with irony, it was so scrappy that he was the one who needed it cut. Overall, he didn't look too bad—there were uglier men in the camp she could have been helped by.

"I have seen enough women and children die since we came to this land." Asaiah said, pushing aside the thoughts which came back to him, thoughts of Makkedah's streets. He still stared into the fire. "I didn't want to see one more."

Ariadne sensed his pain and decided to leave that one there. But she had many questions for him, which she asked between bites.

"How much land do you need, Asaiah?"

"It's not about land." He said. Ariadne frowned sceptically. "The Most High promised this land to our forefather and now evil men litter it instead." He continued quickly, seeing her disbelief. "They honour false gods and sacrifice their children. They commune with spirits and fallen angels. Surely, you've seen some of it?"

Ariadne paused. "Are you any different?"

Asaiah recoiled, appalled. "We are not to do any of those things. The Most High has forbidden it."

The Most High? Ariadne thought to ask about him but then realised she couldn't care less. *What was one more desert god?*

"So your god loves women and children and that's why he's helping you go from city to city killing them?" she asked instead, not passing up a chance to bate him.

Asaiah tossed his half-eaten bone into the fire and stood up without a word. Ariadne saw him shaking as he walked, though maybe that was just the flickering light of the flames glowing all around him.

As Asaiah walked along to another fire, Ariadne thought to herself. *What strange people. Who takes land not to keep themselves alive but to kill off another's gods?* She watched him find a spot with his back to her and sit down. Mildly worried she had just lost her chance of finding somewhere safe to sleep that night, Ariadne rose and started walking over to the second campfire.

Thoughts came and went from her mind as Ariadne searched for something to say. In the meantime, her feet kept moving and she found herself standing beside Asaiah in moments. He looked up at her and said nothing, merely turning back to stare into the fire.

"My mother's name is Mariaten." She began almost pathetically. She didn't know what else to say. "When I was little she was always telling me stories." Asaiah didn't turn around but some of the other men there did, listening with interest.

So she told them of Rinatair and Glanaron, of Birchidar and all the rest. She told them of gods and goddesses, and of wars, of brave men and their deeds. And, slowly, even Asaiah turned to listen, for all men like a good story.

Many men around other campfires had long since gone to their tents by the time she had finished, but the men around hers' sat entranced. When she finally stopped, she saw excitement in their eyes and she realised, they might speak with a different tongue and have different gods but all men wanted to be remembered for glorious deeds. Ariadne watched them walk off in the silence one by one and knew they would dream of the battles ahead.

All men left, except Asaiah, who still sat there by the fire. Ariadne sat down, as there was finally room to sit. All through her tales he had been silent, they all had. Now he turned to her with a curious smile, past anger forgotten, and spoke.

"You tell of the lives of others, Ariadne. You tell stories of people long dead and of gods who never existed. What's your story?"

And so she told him. It was as simple as that. She didn't know why she did. Maybe it was just because someone had asked. Whatever the reason, Ariadne began right at the beginning, back in Knossos. As the stars came out and the moon shone once more, Ariadne told of the bull-leap and of Malia, she told of the earth shaking and her father's friends coming to take her to the cave.

"They're as bad as the men of Canaan!" Asaiah said sternly. "Once we're done here we should cross the sea and free your land."

"You mean kill my people?" Ariadne said and laughed sceptically. In truth, she didn't know who her people were anymore. So many were either dead or had betrayed her. But she let that one go and kept talking. She told Asaiah of her friends who rescued her and of the raging sea which destroyed their home. But, when she started to talk of Egypt, Asaiah interrupted.

"My people lived in Egypt for many years. It is a bad place. We were weak there, slaves of the pharaoh. Thanks to Moses, we escaped and now we are here, warriors and strong." *You couldn't spin a tale well enough to earn a crust of bread*, Ariadne thought with disdain. *But that name*, she remembered that name.

Asaiah yawned and started to stand up but Ariadne kept talking. "My husband once told me a story of a Moses who used dark magic on the Egyptians and took their slaves away. Was that your Moses?"

Asaiah started shuffling off towards his tent but he replied as he went. "Dark magic? They would call it that. But yes, that was us." He kept walking until he reached the tent and, since Ariadne had also risen, held the tent flap for her to enter. Once inside, he continued. "And now we're here. And the Most High will go before us and give us victory just as he did when we left Egypt."

Ariadne rolled her eyes but said nothing. Plainly, Asaiah believed every word. *Not another one.*

As Ariadne watched with fascination, Asaiah moved the robe, bowl and knife from where he had had left them and took a blanket from the rest of the them. He walked back to her and pointed to the many blankets at the far end of the tent.

"You can sleep there." He said.

"And you?" She hadn't expected that.

Asaiah shrugged and lay down by the entrance to the tent. Wrapping himself in his one blanket. "It's not a bad night." He was lying. It was freezing. But Ariadne was not going to argue. She went over to the other blankets and pulled them all around herself, even rolling one half up as a pillow.

Ariadne could hear him shivering though he tried his best to hide it. "Is this another of your customs?" she asked softly.

"No," Asaiah replied, rolling over, "it's 'cause I like you."

Thirty-Four

Ariadne awoke to the sound of a sword scraping against a whetstone. She sprang up, eyes half-closed, her heart already racing.

"Calm down." Asaiah said. He sat there carefully scraping his sword again and again. "We're going to take Lachish today. I need my sword."

Ariadne said nothing, her mind still adjusting. "There is a woman in Lachish..." she began.

"There are plenty of women in Lachish." Asaiah replied tersely.

"The daughter of Horam, it's why he sent his army down from Gezer." She said, sitting up.

"What of her?" he asked, eyes never leaving the blade.

"Could you save her?"

Asaiah's forehead creased. "I'll see what I can do." He stopped, holding the sword up to the light coming through the crack between tent flaps. He put it back in its scabbard, satisfied. "You ran towards our enemies, knife in hand; some of these women will stand against us. I can't promise anything."

Ariadne nodded. It was enough. "When will you be back?" she asked, curious, nothing more.

Asaiah shrugged. "Tonight. Tomorrow. The day after. I don't know." As he rose, strapping the scabbard to himself, he continued. "If I don't came back," he said somewhat lightly, "find a man called Ahiram. He saw you fight. He'll look after you."

Ariadne glared at Asaiah as he finished the last of his preparations, not convinced. As he lifted the tent flap, she spoke and he turned his head to listen.

"And what if he's dead too?" she asked.

Asaiah grinned. "Then shave your head." He left, letting the tent flap fall. Ariadne laid back down and rolled over, eyes closed once more, and stifled a chuckle. She lay there for a while, tossing and turning but sleep would not come.

Ariadne got up and walked across the tent but that just made the feeling worse. As Ariadne started to peel the tent flap back to peer outside, she heard voices in the distance and a great fear came over her. Her hand raced back as quickly as if it had touched a boiling cooking pot, and the flap fell down, fluttering in the breeze.

Ariadne panted though she didn't know why. She stumbled across the room, searching for anything that might give her peace. Ariadne saw her knife, the one she had left Gath with, and fell on her knees, clutching it to her breast. Still stained with blood and about as dull as her new companion's mind, it was hers nonetheless and it had kept her safe.

She washed it first, washed away the blood of those men she had killed the night before. She felt a little bit better, so washed it again. Next, she found Asaiah's whetstone and began scraping her knife along it on an angle, as she had seen him do.

Hours past and still she had not left the tent. She found some mouldy bread hidden away in a pouch but ate it all the same. Once she was done with her knife, she rested it by her side and picked up his which he had left behind. It was the same one he had laid out previously for her to cut her hair. It wasn't blunt at all but Ariadne sharpened it all the same.

She sat there, just staring at the entrance, a knife in each hand. After a while, Ariadne could feel the sun going down and wondered where the day went. And still Asaiah did not return. As night came and the cold drew forth, Ariadne wrapped the blankets around herself but still sat there, facing the entrance. It wasn't until long into the night when sleep finally overcame her and, when it did, Ariadne slumped to her side, still holding the knives.

And that was how Asaiah found her the next morning as he entered his tent. He saw the knives in her hand and, though didn't quite understand, knew better than to take them from her. He filled his bowl with water and started washing his body and the odd cuts he had received.

Ariadne's eyes flittered open after a while as the almost rhythmic splashing of water droned on in the tent. She groggily sat back up, grasping the knives instinctively, though they had never left her hands. Asaiah flinched as Ariadne tensed up, taking the scene in before her. After a few moments, Ariadne carefully put the knives down and only then did Asaiah speak.

"We took Lachish."

"Did you find Horam's daughter?" Ariadne asked.

"We might have. What was her name?"

"I don't know," Ariadne confessed. Asaiah shrugged.

"Some women survived. I'm sure you can ask them."

Ariadne nodded. "What are you doing today?" she asked.

"I don't know." Asaiah replied. "We'll rest up for a few days before heading south. There are a few more cities we need to take before we can go north again."

"What's up north?"

"The women and children are camped around Gibeon. You'll get to meet my family." Asaiah said casually.

"Do you have a wife, children?" Ariadne asked.

"Not yet." Asaiah smiled cheekily and she thought to hit him but refrained. "But I have a younger brother who'd love to hear all your stories." Ariadne smiled at that.

"I don't want to stay in this camp." She said suddenly. "Can we go outside? Hunting, scouting, I don't care what. I just..." she looked at him almost pleading, "I just need to get away from here."

Asaiah nodded, too confused to understand but smart enough not to ask why. "Of course."

***

"Find my sheep!" and so there they were, scrambling up a hill where Asaiah thought he had spotted it an hour ago. They stood on the top of the hill, no sheep in sight.

Asaiah had looked like he was keen to go hunting. Ariadne saw him pack a sling and some smoothed stones before leaving the tent. They hadn't gone ten steps beyond the camp before someone had called out to him about their sheep and Asaiah had simply nodded and agreed to find it.

Ariadne saw frustration spread across his face now as he scoured the horizon all around. She didn't mind though. She had his sword once again and she was outside and away from that camp full of men. She had seen women younger than her being led around the camp, tears still filling their eyes. *It seemed they mostly save the pretty ones,* she thought then shrugged it off. Right now, she was alive and free and no-one else was her concern.

Then Ariadne saw it. Her thoughts gone in an instant. The sheep had inadvertently doubled back on them and was at the bottom of the hill. Ariadne whistled and Asaiah turned. She pointed and he followed the line of her finger, seeing the sheep. They were off once more.

Neither spoke as they raced down the side of the hill, partly to not alert the sheep but they had also come into a comfortable silence for the most part. He didn't talk too much and Ariadne liked that. It was just the two of them, scrambling over rocks with a single goal in mind.

They heard the sheep before they could see it. It was bleating nervously as it sensed it was no longer alone. Asaiah motioned with his fingers for Ariadne to start circling around it as he crept forward. Suddenly, the sheep bolted, racing straight towards him.

In the mere seconds Asaiah had before being trampled, he did the only thing his inner warrior could think of. He dodged to the side, half-falling, in a desperate attempt not to be run over. Asaiah half-turned as he fell, trying to grab the sheep's back leg as it bolted up the hill. He missed. And landed face-first into the dirt. Ariadne was laughing so hard her whole body shook. But, within moments, they were both racing back up the hill they had just come from.

As Ariadne and Asaiah crawled, ran and slipped their way back up the hill, they slowly gained on the sheep. It was slipping as well in its hurry to escape them. When it was almost to the top, and only a few feet away, Asaiah leaped at it, catching its fleece and tackling it to the ground.

The sheep kicked for a time but Asaiah would not let go. He turned it on its back and carefully swapped his grip so he now held its front two legs. To Ariadne's fascination, the sheep could do nothing in such a grip, and Asaiah was able to drag it back down the hill.

Once there, Asaiah flipped the sheep around, picked it up and hoisted it onto his shoulders. He grinned at Ariadne in triumph who grinned back as well, though for a different reason. Ariadne couldn't stop thinking about how funny he had looked when the sheep almost bowled him over. She glanced at the sheep and, for a mere instant, it looked like it was grinning too.

***

By the time they returned to the camp Ariadne could see Asaiah's arms dripping with sweat. They had stopped a few times on the way back and each time he put the sheep on its back and held it there while he recovered his strength. The man who had lost the sheep had tussled Asaiah's hair and thanked him mightily and then had just walked off with it. No reward was paid, no favours offered and, as Ariadne and Asaiah walked away themselves, she turned to him, puzzled.

"He's not your father or brother is he?"

"No." He replied.

"Uncle? Cousin? Family friend?" She kept going, determined to find a connection.

"No," Asaiah said. "I can't even remember his name. But we he help our own out here. It's the one only way you survive."

Ariadne thought to push more but then noticed the women walking about the camp. To a head, they were all shaven, and some didn't seem to have stopped crying since she left. Ariadne felt oddly repulsed but kept walking.

"Who's that?" she asked. Until now every Israelite she had seen walked around by themselves. This man was followed by two men a step behind, ever eying those around.

"That's Joshua." Asaiah said almost reverently. "He's a very holy man. The Most High speaks to him and he leads us now Moses is gone."

Ariadne stared at the holy man walking away from her. He had slightly longer hair than the rest of them and it looked like he washed his beard every day but, apart from that, he didn't seem too special.

"So your god talks to him?" she asked, interested.

"Yes." He replied.

"What does he say?" Ariadne continued, curious but thought she already knew the answer.

"He tells us we will win so long as we do not fear our enemies and so long as we keep his rules." Asaiah said.

"Has your god ever talked to you?" Ariadne asked.

Asaiah bit his lip and then started walking away from her, something she was beginning to find annoying. She started following him then stopped. *Fine.* She walked back the way she had come, searching for that man and his sheep.

It didn't take long before she found him. He was milking a ewe into a bowl, humming along to the thudding of teats. The man looked up at her and smiled and Ariadne sat down next to him.

"Thanks again for finding her." He said. Ariadne nodded and then reclined, stretching her arms out to support herself. It was the first time she could remember feeling the breeze and hearing the songs of birds in the distance. Ariadne felt the warmth of the sun on her skin and the gritty dirt under her palms, and she smiled. Not because she had heard something funny or recalled a fond memory, she just smiled. Happy. At peace.

"And this one, she's Bilhah, she's very shy." He had a name for each of them. They were his girls, every one. Ariadne wondered what the ram thought of that but decided not to ask. Ariadne decided she liked this man, content with his simple life. He hadn't asked her for any help or put a bowl in her hand, he was content to let her sit by him as the sun rose in the sky.

He even let her have some of the milk. It was warm but Ariadne decided she liked it. It helped that she hadn't eaten anything all day but, even so, it was creamy and fresh and she knew she'd gladly have it again.

Eventually, the sun started on its homeward journey and Ariadne did too. She meandered back through the tents of the camp searching for Asaiah's. She wasn't quite sure how she recognised it in the end, she just knew. And, sure enough, her bloodied robe was still there as were the blankets as well, but Asaiah was nowhere to be seen.

Ariadne went back outside. *Where is he?* She scanned the faces of men walking around, but Asaiah's was not among them. She saw one though, who had been there on the night she first arrived and ate by their campfires.

"Have you seen Asaiah?" she asked him.

"He didn't stay long. He got something from his tent then went back out into the hills." The man said, shrugging. *Why did he go back?* Ariadne wondered.

With the light beginning to fade and a warm set of blankets on offer, Ariadne didn't quite know why she left the camp. She just knew she had to find him.

***

"And look after her, Ariadne." She had crouched and listened patiently for a while as he spoke. As he uttered those words, though, she knew she would not forget them as long as she lived.

"Keep her safe from harm and bring her back to her mother, across the great sea. Give her many years in her land and many children when she is ready for them. Look after her, lord, and give her all she requires."

Ariadne peered at him, watching in fascination as Asaiah kept speaking to a small tree burning up in front of him. She saw the flint at his feet as he knelt there and she wondered how much longer that glorified shrub was going to last.

"And keep my father safe, lord, for I hope he is well. Keep my mother alive to see grandchildren and keep Elah out of trouble in the meantime."

In the end there was only one place she knew she might find him. That hill. The hill they had seen the sheep on. The hill they had run up and down and up again to catch it. And there he was. Kneeling at the top talking to a bush he had set on fire.

Something in her knew she couldn't interrupt him so she waited, and watched, and listened. He had been going since before she arrived and he didn't sound like he was stopping anytime soon. Safety from his enemies and strength to smite them, beauty and glory and never-ending youth, yet somehow humility and wisdom as well. It would have been funny to hear if it hadn't been his heart pouring out as he thought no-one but his god could hear him. So, Ariadne stayed there, crouching silently.

Eventually he stopped though, oddly, the tree had not burned up completely. Only then did Ariadne rise and walk up to him. Maybe he thought she was his god coming up from behind, or maybe his knees were sore from all the kneeling. Either way, Asaiah paused briefly before rising and turning around.

When he saw her he did not jump in surprise, turn in fright or slump from disappointment. Asaiah calmly picked up his flint and walked towards her as well.

"How long were you there for?" he asked. He appeared calm and Ariadne couldn't tell if he was embarrassed, offended or genuinely at peace.

"A while," she admitted. "Is that how your people talk to your god?" she asked. It seemed a stupid question, but she had never seen anything like it.

"Not really, though I did hear him speaking to me once." Asaiah said, staring out into the evening sky. "Long ago, when I was very young, just wandering about, I heard him call my name and I knew it was him." Ariadne made an effort not to ruin the mood as they started walking back down the hill. "But I haven't heard him since and when you asked me earlier today, I remembered about the fire."

"What about the fire?" Ariadne asked, still confused.

"I remembered that Moses heard the Most High through a fiery bush in the wilderness and I thought to myself, 'If it worked for him, maybe it will work for me?'"

"Did it?"

"I don't know," Asaiah admitted. "I didn't hear him speak but that doesn't mean he wasn't listening."

Ariadne said nothing as they walked back, leaving Asaiah to his thoughts. It didn't feel right, telling him it was all a lie. That's what it was though, wasn't it? For the first time in a long time Ariadne wasn't so sure. *That's silly. Nothing happened on that mountain, not even a wind stirred.* Ariadne shrugged it off. *Nothing in it.*

It took a long time before they made it back to camp. It had long gone dark but they knew the way and as they walked along they had seen campfires in the distance. When they actually arrived though, Ariadne rubbed her hands together in expectation of the warmth that awaited her.

Asaiah had barely eaten anything all day but he walked past the men sitting by the fires and kept going till he found his tent. His feet ached with every step as the tiredness which had seemed so far away had come upon him all at once, as soon as he had reached the camp.

Ignoring niceties, Asaiah strode into his tent, knocking the flap aside but not staying to hold it. Ariadne followed happily enough behind. She had gotten sick of him holding it back anyway. In truth, she had expected to hear women crying out that night. For all Asaiah made of his god and his ways, she doubted the women she saw earlier would be left alone. But if any woman did scream or cry out that night, she did not hear them.

Ariadne lay down in the mass of blankets at the far end of the tent while Asaiah wrapped himself in the one at the entrance yet again. She knew he shivered. He had shivered that first night and it kept her awake, for a time. She knew she could sleep through it this time though, just one more sound of the night.

But as she rolled over, Ariadne realised her fear had gone, or at least in part. Instead, she felt a rising guilt in its place. The guilt filled her, spreading to the edges of every limb. It spread from the tips of her toes to the top of her head and then formed words of its own.

"You can sleep here, if you like." She didn't even realise she had said it but once she had, Ariadne realised she meant it.

"You sure?" Asaiah asked, not believing her but desperately wanting to.

Ariadne paused, but she already knew her answer. "Yes, come on, before I change my mind." And one minute they lay apart, at opposite ends of the tent, and the next they lay back to back, keeping the cold at bay.

Thirty-Five

Ariadne saw the sprawling mass of tents and carts in the distance and her eyes opened wide in excitement. It was hard not to be awed. The main Israelite camp just off from Gibeon looked like a second town, a second city almost.

She could see the change in Asaiah, though he tried best to hide it. He walked faster, carried more and complained less that last day of their journey. It wasn't just him. The whole Israelite army seemed to surge forward as one and Ariadne found herself getting caught up in the excitement too.

Children ran out to greet them, racing along the edges of the army, searching for a familiar face. Uncles would clap them on the shoulder and point them onward to where their fathers walked.

"Did you have any children?" Asaiah had asked one night.

"No, we... "Ariadne didn't quite know how to say it. "We were unable."

Asaiah had left it there and asked no more about it. They had walked for a long time each day, rising with the dawn and going long into the evening before setting up camp, getting a few hours of sleep and doing it all again. The Israelites had sacked the last few cities and towns who opposed them and they were coming home.

And most nights, when they were alone together, Ariadne and Asaiah would ask each other some new question they had thought of throughout the day. It had become their rhythm, their life and Ariadne was sorry to see it go.

"So how do you talk to your gods?" Asaiah had asked.

"I don't. They're not real. They're just stories. Or if they are, they're so weak they're not worth worrying about."

Asaiah had nodded at that approvingly. Only his god held power, all the others were weak or made up. He liked that. And she liked him. For his simplicity, his earnestness and, by and large, for their hatred of the same things.

Ariadne realised she was getting used to his god who wanted children to live and women to be safe from harm. His god probably wasn't real, just like all the rest, but she could put up with it. It was better than most of them.

She knew not all the taken women saw it her way. Many, maybe even most of them, still clung to their old gods. One or two even had a small statue. When one particular woman had shown her statue to Ariadne, she had just laughed and thought to tell one of the Israelites about it. Those women worshipped the same gods who took that boy in the fire and, as far as she was concerned, the Israelites were right to rid the world of them. Nevertheless, whatever she thought of their gods, Ariadne liked the other women well enough.

She didn't understand them though. They had all seemed to succumb to this 'one month' rule and the sound of men humping away could be heard most nights now. None of the women seemed to protest. Indeed, some seemed to welcome it. Ariadne shuddered at the memory. They'd lost their homes and their loved ones, Ariadne didn't know how they could bear it. Those were the times she shifted uncomfortably; not the thudding away of men in the distance, but the lone piercing groan of a woman at the end of it.

Oddly enough, Asaiah was her greatest comfort at that time. Her month had well and truly passed and still he didn't touch her. Night after night he'd climb in beside her and turn his back, just like she did, not once asking or pressuring her. For that she was grateful.

Her thoughts were interrupted as a boy, no more than ten, ran up beside her.

"Asaiah! Asaiah!" The boy grinned uncontrollably and Asaiah smiled down at him. He was carrying a few tent poles with another man and had no spare hands but that didn't stop his brother.

"Elah!" Asaiah whined. Elah had latched onto his leg and now Asaiah carried weight above and below with every step. Elah grinned all the more and Asaiah had to shake his leg hard to loosen his brother's grip. Elah fell and tumbled along in the dirt, laughing the whole way. Ariadne reached down and picked him up, holding him into the air.

"Who are you?" Elah stared back at her, unafraid, bobbing along with her every step.

"Ariadne." She replied.

"That's a funny name. Are you his wife now?" Elah asked, gesturing to Asaiah.

"No, she laughed and glanced briefly at Asaiah. *Hope? Regret?* She couldn't tell what she saw so continued. "We're just good friends."

"Mum'll be so happy you finally found a woman!" Elah said to his brother.

"Better go on and tell her then, eh?" Ariadne said chuckling and put the boy down once more. After a brief glance at his brother, Elah scampered off as quickly as he had come, kicking up dust as he went.

***

Ariadne raced around the tent to her right, three pairs of little feet not far behind. She dodged past a confused man staring at her as she went. She ignored him and kept going. Behind her, Elah and his friends shouted incoherently as they passed the tent. They saw her in the distance. The chase continued.

Completely lost and thoroughly enjoying herself, Ariadne ran harder. Five kids had started the chase, and another two had joined in as she rushed past them, but her legs were long and they hadn't caught her yet. She was constantly ducking and swerving in and out of tents, confusing herself as much as them but that didn't matter, she had nowhere else to be.

It had started well enough. Ariadne had been welcomed warmly by Asaiah's family who asked him all manner of questions as he set his tent up beside theirs.

"How many did you kill?"

"What's the land like down there?"

"When are you going to marry her?" his mother had cheekily asked, gesturing to Ariadne.

And the questions kept coming. Ariadne had quickly grown bored as few of them were directed to her. She held things when instructed and stood there the rest of the time, staring out into the rest of the camp. And what she saw did not please her.

Everywhere she looked she saw wives, eager to greet their husband's return, change in an instant upon seeing the women walking beside them. Tears of relief turned to anger and betrayal and more than one started beating either her husband or the woman he had brought back. Ariadne flinched as she saw the blows landing on unsuspecting women, wearied by the day's walk. With Asaiah's family mainly just ignoring her, glad to have him back, she knew she was one of the lucky ones.

At last the tent was raised and still they kept talking. A stew had been boiling and now everyone ate, sitting around Asaiah and asking even more questions. But all that did not last.

The men were being gathered. All the men who had gone south with Joshua and had brought a woman back with them, they were to meet altogether just outside the camp. And so Asaiah had risen and left shortly after the summons, as puzzled as the rest of them.

And that was how Ariadne found herself running from seven children, only three of whom still gave chase. She should have known then, for she had been a child once. She should have known they had not given up.

They didn't stand before her and block her path, she would have just run a different way and escaped. Instead, they hid, and they waited while the three pursuers led her towards them. And Ariadne ran on, oblivious, until four bodies crashed into her, two from each side, jumping out from tents seemingly empty.

Ariadne laughed as she rolled around on the ground, children grabbing at her hair and dress triumphantly. Elah and the two with him slowed down as they approached, shouting victory cheers as if they had defeated all the armies of Canaan.

But young children are ever fit and never content so no sooner had they captured Ariadne then it was her turn to chase them. They scattered in all directions and Ariadne, puffed and aching, nevertheless gave chase.

She caught a few of them but it was hard going. Most of the time they stayed together in groups of two or three, always ready to bolt in a different direction as soon as she came upon them. It was after finding one such group at the edge of the camp that she saw the Israelite men coming back from their private meeting. She let the boys run off as she watched the men, seeing Asaiah stumbling moodily along with the rest of them. His face was grim. Whatever they had discussed, it didn't look good.

***

"What do you mean I have to leave?"

"I thought you would be happy. You can go back to Crete." They were in Asaiah's tent, just the two of them, though, all around, many were having a similar conversation.

"I thought you said your custom was you could take any women you liked to be your wives?" Ariadne half-stated, half-asked.

"Apparently that doesn't go for Canaanite women. Joshua says all women who came back with us have to go. He says you all worship the gods of this land and will lead us astray." Asaiah said, trying to convince himself as much as her.

"I'm not a Canaanite—I hate their gods. Tell him that. Tell him to let me stay." Ariadne didn't know why she was arguing. Yes, she wanted to go back to Crete, but she liked it here and she wasn't quite ready to leave.

"I tried. I told him about you but he didn't care. The rest of them were grumbling enough as it was and, if they had to lose their new women, there was no way they would let you stay." Ariadne listened, thinking of the beatings she'd seen earlier. *This Joshua isn't listening to his god. He's just trying to keep all the Israelite women from killing his soldiers in the middle of the night. He makes his rules up as he goes.*

She spat, and he thought she was angry at the other men. She let him think that. No use telling him his leader was as pious as she was and as controlling as an Egyptian priest.

"Tomorrow, you will all gather together outside the camp. We will give you enough food and water to reach Gezer and, after that, you'll be on your own." Asaiah told her, less stoic than he tried to appear.

"Come with me." The words were barely formed in her mind before they had left her mouth. Ariadne found they had a way of doing that when Asaiah was around. "Leave your family, leave your people and come with me." There, she had said it—realising what she truly wanted for the first time.

Asaiah was as shocked as she was and took a few moments to speak.

"I can't leave my family. You can't ask that of me." She took his hand then, softly, for the first time. She looked into his eyes and pleaded silently, no more words mattered. She had none left to give.

But she gave him what she did have left, for, if she wasn't going to see him again; if that was to be their last night together, she wanted it to be one they'd both remember and never forget.

***

Ariadne felt the ebb of the tide as it tugged against the boat being rowed slowly out from the shore. She opened her eyes and looked back at the beach they were leaving. The skies had darkened and the water reflected the almost black clouds above. Waves crashed against rocks in the distance and also against the beach itself, riding it all the way up till they could go no more.

Standing there, all alone, was a single man. He was up to his knees in the water and was showered with spray as waves crashed in front of him. Ariadne peered out in the distance, trying to make out his face, while the boat rowed, stroke by stroke, taking her further away.

Ariadne raced to the front of the boat and clung on, hanging just over the prow. She could just make out those features and, suddenly, she had a name for the face. Asaiah.

Asaiah stood there not moving, his eyes betraying nothing more than the misery of the wind whipping at his face and the salt stinging his eyes. His mouth was closed tight against the spray and it stayed shut as he watched her boat become smaller in the distance.

"Asaiah!" Ariadne screamed over the roar of all that was between them. "Asaiah!"

But he didn't hear. He just stood there, watching. And that's when the rain began. Droplets at first, the tiniest specks of heaven falling from the sky. Ariadne watched in horror as droplets of fire rained down from above on the coast she knew only too well. For she recognised those buildings and she recognised that beach. It was Malia. And the sky was raining fire.

The oarsmen rowed on regardless and it was only then that Ariadne turned to see them. There were only two, and each had a cold face; nothing but a blank look as they stared past her at Malia going up in flames.

Ariadne recoiled as she saw them, looked away then turned back to make sure she hadn't mistaken them. To her left, Spirysidos, her father, rowed one oar and, sure enough, to her right rowed Adro. Both men kept staring ahead, neither acknowledging she was even there. And the rain thickened and the wind roared and the boat rowed ever onward.

Turning back to the beach, Ariadne cried out to see fire had spread across the landscape. Everything besides the sand and the rocks was burning. Everything, except for Asaiah.

He stood there, ever unchanging, undisturbed by the fire, just like her boat—it seemed to pass them both by. Ariadne turned once more, one final glance at those who rowed, before diving into the sea.

Down she went, ever so quick, and she swam beneath the waves. Ariadne kicked her legs and pushed with her arms, struggling forward towards the beach. And, as she rose for air, Ariadne looked ahead to see a great shadow looming from behind. She turned to see a wave that reached up to the heavens. And, as it crashed, she turned her last, not fearing to finally die.

And slowly her eyes opened to the coming of the dawn. Ariadne saw the ground light up, inches from her face. The light shone under the gaps between the tent and the ground and through the flapping, open entrance.

She rolled over just to check, though she already knew he wasn't there. His side of the blankets was still warm from when he'd left. So, as the sun rose that morning, Ariadne rose with it. She washed herself and brushed her hair, plaiting it just like that first day she came to them. She packed the remainder of her things and, after a long, drawn-out breath, walked out into the morning sun.

Some women, little more than girls, were snivelling in the morning cold, huddling together like lambs against the frost. Others saw her as she walked towards them, saw her stern face and confident walk, and they nodded.

Ariadne walked to the centre where supplies had already been piled up. She grabbed a bag as eyes stared at her from all around. She wasn't going to wait till she was told to leave. She wasn't going to spend her days comforting blubbering fools too weak to start again. Ariadne was going to survive. She had a long trek ahead of her. *First Gezer, then Ashdod, then,* Ariadne thought with a smile, *then Knossos.*

Historical Note

When I read Historical Fiction, I often find I'm even more excited by the Historical Note at the end than the book itself. How much of that actually happened? How much of it was true? I can't help but wonder. I'm sure some of you at least are wondering the same about this book. But, before we begin, I feel we need to have a bit of a discussion on the nature of truth itself and its relationship to history.

When you ask, how much was true, my answer can't help but be, well, what do you mean by true? If you mean every character existed, every event happened and every minute detail of the book perfectly aligns with the historical record, then sorry but this book falls short of that goal. But I was never looking to write a book obsessing on the microcosm, I wanted to present the Bronze Age world through a bigger lens, and subordinate individual facts to the bigger picture. So my answer is, anyone well-acquainted with the Bronze Age world will be able to pick apart the facts that I've left out, misused or flied directly in the face of, but I hope they will also be able to appreciate what I'm doing on a deeper level, and why.

What I've tried to do is give you an authentic experience of living life in the Bronze Age, as best as we can understand it, and walk you through three key moments I find deeply fascinating from the time period. The first of these is the catastrophic volcanic eruption on Thera (Santorini) and its cataclysmic effect on the Minoan civilisation. I wanted to imagine how people with no understanding of modern science would have reacted to something so terrible, let alone try to make sense of it. The second is the Hyksos invasion of Egypt, seen from both the perspectives of the Egyptians themselves as well as those who invaded them, whoever they might have been… And the third is the Philistine settlement in southern Canaan. I'm trying to bring to the public consciousness the knowledge that the people known to most of us as the Philistines were almost certainly proto-Greek peoples who settled the southern shores of Canaan around this time. And, given that all these moments occurred roughly at the same time, from a broad historical perspective, I lost little sleep in merging them together into a single lifetime to be experienced by my protagonist.

Speaking of, let's start with Ariadne herself. Did she exist? No. Not in the way I've presented her. Her life is entirely my own creation. And yet, we know from the archaeology that the myth of Theseus and the Minotaur (for it's always framed in that way—never Ariadne and the bastard who left her hanging), is largely, dare I say it, bullshit. Why call it Ariadne then? I wanted to bring to your mind this time period and the assumptions you have about it, grounded in a mis-remembered mythology, before dashing them with a more authentic take on the period. I wanted you to think, this doesn't match the story I've been told so far. That's my point. The myths we have are more likely to lead us astray if we take them as bare-faced history. What's more, that story has been retold a thousand times. By freeing myself from it, I'm not only able to present the time period in a more authentic way, but I'm also able to give you a fresh story too, one you hopefully won't be able to predict quite so easily.

That sounds great but, still, can you tell me which bits are based off facts then and which bits you made up, besides the main character? Fine, caveats aside, let's get into it. Starting with the Minoan world, I'm someone who's convinced that, despite the revisionist literature, bull-leaping did occur there and must have been an important part of palace life. Also, it was fun to write about—and that's another overriding factor for what to keep and what to leave out. What about the Tree Dance and the myth of Birchidar and Rinatair? They're my creation again but done so to try to explore some of the most iconic aspects of Minoan culture—the figurines of women holding snakes up in the air, and the motif seen again and again we like to call "The Mistress of the Animals." With these, and many other aspects of the culture, I've tried to weave together the insights we got from archaeology and present them in an entertaining way. And there are multiple layers of interpretation to most things. Those objects are part of the body of evidence for Minoan Crete being a matriarchal society, but I think they, along with many others, help give us an insight into Minoan attitudes towards spirituality as well. I've tried to capture in my myth what I think must have been some form of contention within the Minoan religion; the balance between nature at its purest and man-made civilisation. I'm convinced the earliest societies must have wrestled with this on a fundamental level, perhaps even more than we do today. If I've been able to share these deeper historical perspectives with you along the way, then I'll consider myself to have succeeded after all.

Did they have human sacrifice though? Ignore the underlying historical trends for a second, I want to know if it actually happened. In short, yes, we have a strong and unpleasant tradition of human sacrifice in early Greek culture, though the Ancient Greeks were quick to talk up the practice among their enemies and forget it amongst themselves. Interestingly, it seems to be a practice among some modern historians, regardless of what culture they're studying, to admit the possibility of human sacrifice as a phenomenon but argue against it vehemently in the case of their particular culture. For all the interesting research done more recently on Phoenician tophets, I'm not convinced the peoples of Canaan, and their descendants across the Mediterranean, didn't practice child-sacrifice. On the contrary, I would argue historians who claim this are arguing in the face of the evidence itself, no matter how many times they want to re-look at it. And I would say the same goes for Minoan Crete. I'm convinced the finds at Anemospilia indicate human sacrifice was practiced, though perhaps not within the palaces themselves at the height of Minoan culture. I've tried to portray my best interpretation of how the practice may have fitted into Minoan culture, namely, as a tradition of an earlier time period, the memory of which may have carried on and been tapped into in times of great distress, and quite possibly conducted out of sight of the great palaces. While I took my general inspiration for the cave in the book from Minoan peak sanctuaries, I kept Anemospilia in mind for the attempted sacrifice itself.

As for the eruption at Thera, well, what can I say? One of the worst volcanic eruptions in human history occurred on an island not far from Crete at the height of Minoan flourishing. It blew out a sizable chunk of the island and covered what was left in ash and pyroclastic flows. If the earthquakes leading up to it didn't cause enough harm, then the tsunamis which followed and volcanic debris raining down from the sky must have been enough to halt the Minoans in their tracts. Whether many of the palaces which were destroyed around this time were done so directly due the effects of the eruption, the chaos that must have ensued afterwards, or the Mycenaeans who came in not long after and established their control, ultimately matters little. Regardless, for the Minoans, their civilisation very quickly came to an end. It is no wonder the man who excavated the pre-eruption settlement on Thera, Spyridon Marinatos, concluded this event must be what inspired the myth of Atlantis—a glorious civilisation cut short in an instant, at its height. One can't help but wonder what happened to them.

And around this time, we have two very interesting events occurring: the Hyksos invasion of Egypt and the Philistine settlement of Canaan. I'm not ultimately arguing the people who did these things were the Minoans, I want to make that very clear, though the bow could be drawn… Regardless, I chose to use the Minoans as a cultural amalgam to be able to link the events in an entertaining way.

Starting with the Hyksos invasion of Egypt, what was it? The time period is generally known as the Second Intermediate Period and a few things occurred there. Partly, there was a breakdown in the Great King's (Pharaoh's) ability to maintain his authority over Egypt, but a bigger problem was that a foreign invader came in and took control of much of the land in Lower Egypt. These Hyksos invaders controlled much of the good land for a few generations before finally being cast out. Interesting situation, but who were they? Our best guess from the archaeological record is that they were Semitic peoples of a similar culture to those in southern Palestine. Now, you can draw your own conclusions as to what that might mean, but I actually chose to base them off a less well-supported theory instead—that they might have been the nebulous Sea Peoples.

The Sea Peoples are an interesting feature of Bronze Age archaeology. We have Egyptian and Ugaritic texts mentioning them but we don't ultimately know who they were. I find the arguments that they were some kind of proto-Greek, Aegean people to be fairly persuasive, and I would actually side probably with Mycenaean—but that's a story for another time. In a nutshell, they were raiders and invaders who attacked people all up and down the eastern Mediterranean. The only catch is that this was hundreds of years after the end of the Second Intermediate Period, and the Theran eruption. It's possible they were active earlier and we just haven't found much evidence for them though, given our stronger evidence for the Semitic culture of the Hyksos, it's not so likely.

And yet, we have Minoan frescoes at Tell el-Dab'a—the site of Avaris, the ancient capital of the Hyksos kingdom. And so sometimes one wonders. My understanding of the dating of the palace and the frescoes is that it is slightly problematic and that, though many people come down now on a late dating, i.e. post-Hyksos rule, it's still possible they were painted earlier, during the Hyksos rule of Avaris. For the purposes of writing fiction, however, the possibility of a Minoan influence on the Hyksos, who may themselves have come from the Aegean, was too good to pass up.

I didn't make it all up, however. I tried my best to be as authentic to Ancient Egyptian culture as I could. The whole relationship between the Great King and the stability and order of the universe, Ma'at, is strikingly similar to the Mandate of Heaven in China, and deeply fascinating in its own right. The concept itself was certainly a double-edged sword, able to justify one's conquest of a failing regime then also justify your own overthrow in a bad year. The Sed festival was indeed used to renew the king's life-force and connection with the gods, symbolically being reborn as a rejuvenated Horus. I couldn't help but keep the phrase as I first read it for the ritual, "Horus appears resting on his southern throne and there occurs a uniting of the sky to the earth."—as soon as I read it, I knew it was perfect. See, the Hyksos did build a temple to Seth, or possibly Baal-zephon, being Semitic Syro-Palestinians, whom the Egyptians interpreted as Seth. Regardless, the Egyptians were able to use their Osiris myth (Seth overthrowing Osiris and his son Horus overthrowing Seth in turn) as propaganda for their war of liberation. Dodgy Minoan origins aside, I was able to keep fairly closely to what happened with the political history of the Second Intermediate Period. The propaganda and political motives were all largely there already, as was the tension between Egypt and Cush. As for the leaders of the Egyptians and the Hyksos, Apepi was actually the name of the last Hyksos king, and it was Kamose, son of Seqenenra who largely defeated the Hyksos and was probably the one who sacked Avaris, though his successor cast them out for good.

I want to say one quick thing about the battles before I move on from Egypt. The Minoans didn't fight head to toe in bronze armour or have bronze on their shields. The depictions we have of Minoan soldiers is almost always of them being unarmoured and having large, rectangular shields covered in some kind of hide. As for them fighting in a phalanx, well, studying the phalanx is complicated. A lecturer once told me, if you look at your sources searching for a phalanx you can find it, but that doesn't mean it was there. And I think he was right. From the few depictions we have of Minoan soldiers together, it's just possible they fought in some kind of close, cohesive group, but more likely than not they didn't in the structured way we understand the phalanx of Classical Greece. And yet, it was fun to write. So much fun to pit Greek phalanxes full of bronze-covered soldiers against people with inferior weapons and organisation. Besides, I needed a plot device to help them overcome being outnumbered. I'm ok with it, though happy to confess here what I did and why. A final point to make, however, is that given I merged them with the Sea Peoples, themselves possibly being Mycenaean, it's just possible my depiction isn't as inaccurate as it seems. The Mycenaeans definitely start to resemble the hoplites of later periods in armour, shields, and potentially even formations, so, as with many things in the Bronze Age, the verdict is arguably still out.

As for Canaan, well, let's start with the elephant in the room before getting on to the origins of the Philistines themselves, namely, the Israelite invasion of Canaan. While I hope most of you have found my exploration of the event entertaining and thought-provoking, I recognise there are probably two groups of people who may be annoyed I chose to include it. Most academics would tell you the Exodus and the Israelite invasion of Canaan never happened and so to depict it as a true element of history, alongside the Theran eruption and Second Intermediate Period, is probably anathema to them. Likewise, I expect there are some people deeply versed in the traditions which have come down to us who will find any depiction deviating from their traditions anathema as well. To both such groups, I do not apologise. I consider the event too interesting not to include in the plot. I tried to approach the Ancient Israelites fairly but historically as I have every other group, exploring their culture and the social and political motivations that influenced them at the time. One thing I will say for a potential Exodus though is that, if it did occur, it was almost certainly the Israelites' version of the Hyksos phenomenon, or it occurred hundreds of years after the Second Intermediate Period. To have depicted it occurring before the Theran eruption is almost certainly incorrect and, yet, suited my purposes just fine. Again, happy to tell you here where I have flown in the face of the past.

And so, we come to the Philistines themselves. The archaeological evidence is quite clear that they were Mycenaean in culture though how politically connected they were to Mycenae is unknown. We first have evidence of their arrival a bit after the end of the Second Intermediate Period, and not too long after the Theran eruption, though they appear to not have become a dominant political force for a few centuries. As far as we know, the Philistines settlement in Canaan was largely peaceful, in contrast with however the Ancient Israelites rose to prominence there. Whether both events occurred concurrently or not, they were definitely within a relatively short time of each other, historically speaking, bearing in mind the ancient state of Israel did form in the region, Exodus and Israelite invasion or no.

But see, to me, the very fact that these people were Mycenaean, were proto-Greek, has huge ramifications for how we perceive the early Greek world. We get the impression that the Phoenicians (Canaanites) brought a written script and knowledge of seafaring to the Greek world. And they did, but only after the original native script was lost in the Greek Dark Ages. Same for seafaring. Once we realise we have Minoan frescoes in Egypt, Mycenaean settlements in southern Palestine and both Minoan and Mycenaean pottery in Sicily, all before the end of the Greek Bronze Age, it seems only fair to say there was an early Magna Grecia most of us are unaware of. Perhaps I took some liberties with Zedeck's adventures and the places he travelled to, but I used them to demonstrate the interconnectedness I believe was there, and the spirit of exploration, long before we normally consider it to have been so. I used and reworked a few of those myths because I firmly believe not all of them necessarily date from the end of the Greek Dark Ages as is normally assumed. The myth of Icarus and Daedalus fleeing to Sicily corresponds too well with the archaeological remains not to be some kind of cultural memory of the unknown Magna Grecia. As for the rest of the myths, well, we will probably never know for sure but I would be surprised if none of them had an older origin as well.

I would like to end by discussing how I've approached different names and phrases. Let's start with Philos tines for Philistines. The link I drew between the words was completely made up, as was the phrase I used to connect them, Ego eimi philos tines philoi esmen ek tes thalattes (I am a friend. We are some friends from the sea). As someone quite rightly pointed out to me, it's not even good Greek. But it gives you a good sense of the etymological games historical linguists play sometimes in trying to find explanations for the names of different groups. And, while we might not know if there was a proto-Greek word or phrase which led the Philistines to be called Peleset or Plistim, from the land of Keftiu or Caphtor (in Ancient Egyptian and Hebrew respectively), we do know there are a variety of ways people name themselves and those they interact with. I'm not convinced by most of the current etymological explanations for these words and chose instead to provide a possible solution myself. I believe a misunderstanding of speech on first contact, itself lost to history, is ultimately just as plausible as most of the other explanations we currently have. And, as in all things, it was fun to write.

As for the names of people themselves, I have not taken a uniform approach but, rather, tried to tailor each name to the needs of each individual character. Ariadne's name has the most significance, as I discussed above. Some have special significance, either historically or in their meaning, while most are simply plausible constructions within a proto-Greek set of phonemes. I tried to keep a Greek flavour of spelling to them as much as possible though at times I opted for a more familiar Latinised spelling such as Bosporus rather than Bosporos, and Zedeck rather than Zedek to better convey the eta sound I envisaged to English readers. Where I didn't have historical figures to draw upon for Egyptian and Hebrew names, I did my best to also be authentic to their languages but kept more closely to Latinised spellings nonetheless. I did so especially for well-known figures such as Moses and Joshua—considering it was more important that people were clear which historical figures I was referring to.

I do apologise for the length of this Historical Note. In fairness, it is my first and I felt there was a lot I needed to cover for those who were interested in how the book matched up to history. I plan to be more succinct in the future. Nevertheless, I hope you have enjoyed both the story itself and this note as well. I look forward to sharing more of Ariadne's journey with you in the future.

About the Author

Daniel Agnew doesn't live in the English countryside with his wife and three kids, he lives in Australia, surfing and swordfighting when he's not writing or trying to pay the rent. He graduated from the Australian National University with a Bachelor of Classical Studies, postponing further study to work on his writing. *Ariadne* is his first novel.

Acknowledgements

I'd like to thank the following people for helping me in one way or another. Without you this book would not have been possible:

Michael, Graham, Julie and Peter Agnew, Catriona Thompson, Jennifer Griffin, Stewart Harrison, Kylie Hetherington, Peter Londey, Paul Burton, Chris Bishop, Elizabeth Minchin, Ioannis Ziogas, Erica Bexley, Alexander Cook, Eleanor Carter, Robert Somerville, Jesse Pratt, Rhys Smith, Chris Andrews, Jennifer S. Lange, Larry Rostant, Kristian Bonitz and Nathan Sheppard.

If you've come this far, I reckon I could be forgiven for thinking you've enjoyed *Ariadne*. Why not leave me a review online? You'll make my day.

Feel free to get in touch via Facebook @danielagnewauthor or Twitter @danagnewauthor. And, if you still haven't had enough of me, feel free to check out my blog at

www.danielagnewauthor.com

Mar sin leibh